Beggars Would Ride

MARY MINTON

CENTURY PUBLISHING
LONDON

First published in Great Britain in 1985 by
Century Publishing Co. Ltd,
Portland House, 12–13 Greek Street,
London W1V 5LE

ISBN 0 7126 0863 X

Photoset and printed in Great Britain by
Photobooks (Bristol) Ltd.

TO ALEXANDER CORDELL
who encouraged me to write this book

Prologue

'Home Ma'am?' the chauffeur said.

Rose Kimberley stepped into the limousine. 'Yes, Davies, home.' She sank back into the seat and closed her eyes, drained as always after every Spring and Autumn Collection, yet pleased at another success. The car nosed its way into the early evening traffic.

Normally Rose was able to begin unwinding once she had settled down for the drive from London to Surrey, but this evening, after about fifteen minutes, she found herself still tense.

Was it her age catching up on her? In two days she would be sixty. Rose dismissed this immediately. Her age had never bothered her. She felt youthful, was energetic. She enjoyed her birthdays. It was the one time of the year when those of her family who could manage it, came for her party. It was a joy to her.

So why this tenseness, this depressive mood?

Something began teasing at the back of her mind. Something to do with her sister Elizabeth. But what? Whatever it was Rose found it impossible to bring to the surface. There had been all sorts of minor crises, always were at every show, one expected it, but none had been insurmountable. In fact, most were dealt with in seconds. Well, whatever it was would no doubt surface later, once her mind was free from all the impressions of the day.

But the tension remained within Rose until they reached the country roads, where the comfort of the car and the soporific, gentle swish of tyres on the tarmaced surface lulled her into a semi-doze.

She roused when the car slowed to take the sharp right-hand turn through the stone-pillared entrance to the drive. Then accelerating, they drove through the sweep of parkland towards the house, a house she had thought so ugly on first viewing it and which she now loved as though it were a person.

In the autumn dusk thin wraiths of mist rose from the still water of the lake and hovered in the hollows. Rose gave a sudden shiver, the atmosphere seeming to reflect her mood. If only she knew what was troubling her.

When the car drew up at the foot of the wide stone steps Rose gathered up her sable stole and briefcase. The chauffeur came hurrying round to open the door and help her out. Rose thanked him then said, 'Davies, you will remember to collect Mr De Veer and Mr Eagan from Gatwick airport in the morning? Both men are expected to arrive but my husband could return alone.'

'I shall be there in good time, Ma'am. The master would never forgive me if he was not back in time for your party.'

'We do have a day spare to allow for any hold up.' Rose smiled. 'This year is very special, my whole family should be here.' She went up the steps.

Her maid met her in the hall and took her stole and briefcase from her. 'How did the day go, Ma'am?'

'Excellently, Kate, a great success. What I need now more than anything is a cup of tea.'

Kate said she had already taken a tray up. She had made the tea when she saw the car approaching. Rose started up the wide staircase with its gracious curve and delicately-wrought ironwork, then paused as the elusive teasing began again. This time she was convinced it was to do with something unpleasant, but it still eluded her.

Always, no matter how busy Rose had been, she felt a sense of peace when she entered the sanctuary of her own special room. It was not only that the décor was in restful colours of dove grey and soft blues but that so many pieces in it had been given with love from family and friends. Paintings, ornaments, rugs . . .

Rose said, 'My sister Elizabeth will be calling this evening Kate, but I don't want any other visitors.' Kate promised she would not be disturbed and after pouring the tea, withdrew.

With a small sigh, Rose sank into the depths of a chintz-covered armchair. She closed her eyes. And immediately the events of the day sprang to life: the feverish activity, the near hysteria – assistants rushing about with arms full of dresses, their brows glistening with sweat, dressers cajoling, soothing, bullying mannequins, tempers flaring on the least provocation.

'My shoes!' shrieked one doe-eyed mannequin. 'Someone has taken my red shoes!'

'They are on your feet, Chérie,' soothed Bertha, her French dresser.

'Bitch!' hissed another girl, swearing undying hatred of her companion, who had trod accidentally on her foot. Yet the same evening when they left they were arm in arm together, laughing.

There was too small a space for so many people, for such constant activity, dresses and ensembles having to be changed in a matter of seconds. The heat was trying too, the bright lights, so necessary, turned everywhere into a hothouse.

A tall blonde, naked apart from the hat perched on her head, snatched at the skin-tight dress she was to wear, and swore roundly in Swedish as her nail caught on a gossamer thread, snagging it. Mannequins with heightened colour and murder in their eyes pushed and jostled, yet when they went out on to the podium they looked as serene as if they had spent the whole morning dressing.

Rose could see all the colours, a kaleidoscope of colours and the richness of satins, silks, velvets and delicate chiffons of clothes she had designed herself. She could hear the applause, and the tumultuous acclaim for her *pièce de résistance* – 'Illusion', created in a gossamer material of gunmetal shade, with all the iridescent colours of a raven's wing, a material that changed shades with every movement of the wearer. On the excessively wide sleeves were stitched at random elliptical pieces of the material, so that when the arms were lifted one saw a flock of tiny birds in flight, or petals floating gently on a thermal wind. A cowled hood closely framed the sculpturesque face of Clothiloe, the most photographed girl in the world. Her expression, the clarity of the large, widely-spaced grey eyes, made one think of cloisters.

Then there were the people crowding round Rose after the show, showering congratulations on her. 'The best ever . . .' And she protesting she was only a small part of it, so many people involved, so much work, the girls who had been subjected for the past six weeks to numerous fittings for each garment, perhaps as many as forty, and a Collection could contain over a hundred garments for show by a handful of mannequins. And not least of all were the seamstresses, the tailors, the furriers, all having worked overtime to be ready, some even working through the night.

One of Rose's wealthiest customers had come waddling up to her and said, 'Oh, my dear, it was magnificent, but why do I not have your slender figure and bearing? I come from a long line of dukes and earls and look like an overblown barmaid, while you, who work for your living with your art, look as if you might have descended from a royal house. You have such class.'

Class? Rose wondered what her customer would have said had she told her that she had been born in a slum tenement, was the second eldest girl in a family of eleven, and had grown up in the nineteen twenties, when unemployment was rife and when Saturday night brawls and wife beating were the regular things. Had it not been for Charles and her sister Elizabeth –

Elizabeth? Yes, of course, Rose found a reason at last for her unease.

When her sister had arrived that morning saying she *must* speak to her, it was important, Rose had told her – later, there was so much to do. To which Elizabeth replied in a tight voice, 'Enjoy your glory, what I have to tell you won't get any worse for waiting.'

There was another incident too, when, at the height of the show and feeling the glow of success Rose had said, 'Well, we've come a long way since the days when we sold secondhand clothes from a market stall.' To this her sister had answered with a scathing look, 'Have we?' and walked away.

Rose wished now she had followed up these strange remarks. What was it that could not get any worse for waiting to hear? Something to do with their husbands? No, they would have said something when she phoned them early that morning.

Vivid images of both men came into Rose's mind. Charles, stocky, curly-haired, some grey in it now, blue eyes fringed with thick dark lashes, giving them a smoky look, lovable, full of good humour. And Alex, tall and very attractive, always meticulously groomed, seemingly aloof on first meeting, but with a sense of humour too, although he would always be the more serious one.

Both men were in America at the moment and had, for the first time, missed the Collection. But it was important they go, there was industrial strife in the sister company of one of their biggest concerns in England.

Rose had an odd feeling that these incidents were going to change her life in some way. She had experienced such things before. She moved round the room, needing to find assurance in all the pieces given with so much love over the years. The Le Blonde prints from Charles, with their gentle village scenes, the madly expensive Tiffany lamp Alex had bought her. Rose went over and switched on the lamp, and felt warmed by the glowing colours of the wisteria-shaped glass shade. Such a beautiful piece. There was the pole screen with its tapestry hunting scene, that Elizabeth had given her. And the fine Kasham silk rug, presented to her, with great ceremony, by her four sisters on her fiftieth birthday. Then there were all the lovely Dresden pieces given to her by friends and various members of the family over the years, and the dreadful bright blue china boot, a seaside memento, with letters in gilt that said, 'A Present from Brighton'. But oh, so precious. Rose picked it up and held it to her, seeing again the faces of her small daughter and son willing her to like it, when they brought it back from their first holiday away from her. David, solemn, watching her from brown eyes flecked with gold, and Caroline, her big grey eyes pleading with her for approval, as she shifted from one foot to the other in her impatience.

'Mummy, you *do* like it?'

'I adore it, my darlings, you could not have bought me a more beautiful gift. A boot! It will bring me luck.' She had hugged them both, David drawing quickly away, unwilling to be thought a mother's boy, but Caroline hugging her, throwing her arms around her, hot sticky fingers on the back of her neck.

There was a knock on the door. It was Kate. 'Your sister is here, Ma'am.'

'Oh, come in, Elizabeth. Shall I get Kate to bring you some tea, or would you like a drink?'

'I shall have a drink later.'

Elizabeth sank into an armchair, closed her eyes momentarily, then gave a deep sigh.

'What a day – is it all worth it?' She got up and moved round the room. Elizabeth could never sit still for long, but usually she would be talking all the time. Now she was thoughtful as she picked up ornaments and set them down.

Elizabeth, who had the darkest hair in the family, was still beautiful, although the tightness round her mouth at the moment marred it. She was wearing a simple black suit and a white pure silk blouse and looked as elegant as any mannequin.

'How did the buying go?' Rose asked, unwilling to broach the problem troubling her.

'Couldn't have been better. It still never ceases to amaze me that a woman will pay a thousand pounds for two pieces of material stitched together, with a hole for the neck and two for the arms and a girdle slung round the middle.'

'Oh, Elizabeth, you have no soul! You mean the Peking silk, it's exquisite. And the intricate work that went into it! Who bought it?'

'Mrs Hunter Edison.'

'Not for herself?'

'Oh, yes.'

'She couldn't, she's –'

'Yes, I know, like an elephant. It's ludicrous, but there she was, as excited as a kid going to her first party, sweat pouring off her. Oh, she said it was for a niece but I know she wanted it. It was so funny, I know I shouldn't laugh but –' Elizabeth's mouth began to twitch. Rose began to giggle then they were laughing helplessly together, as they had done when they were young.

Rose reached for a tissue and wiped the corners of her eyes. 'Oh, dear, you know what Gran Eagan used to say, "so much laughter is bound to end in tears".'

Gran Eagan? Rose felt a wave of nostalgia as she thought of her pint-sized grandmother, who had scolded her and clouted her, moulded her, and who had also been instrumental in helping her further her career . . .

Elizabeth had suddenly sobered and Rose knew then their laughter had held a touch of hysteria, a release of tension, knew that it could easily have ended up, as it usually did when they were small, with tears.

'Yes,' Elizabeth said quietly. 'Gran was right in so many things.'

Rose, knowing they were both avoiding more important

issues decided to broach them, but dealt with the second incident first.

'Elizabeth, why did you say, "Have we?" in a scathing way when I mentioned during the show our progress from our market days? You made it sound as though we had achieved nothing.'

Elizabeth walked over to the window and stood with her back to Rose. 'What have we achieved?'

'You yourself have talked about our meteoric rise to power.'

Elizabeth turned swiftly. 'We've achieved wealth, and fame, oh yes, we have stores all over the place, we export to many countries, we have factories, boutiques, but what about our personal lives? My daughter is a whore – and –'

'Elizabeth!' Rose stared at her sister, shocked. 'That is a dreadful thing to say.'

'It's true, nevertheless. Marianne will pop into bed with any man who wants her, who even *hints* at wanting her.'

'No, no, you're wrong,' Rose protested, distressed. 'Marianne is a lovely person, she wouldn't do such a thing.'

'She *does* it, Rose, she's admitted it.'

'I thought she had such a happy marriage.'

'Who has?' There was a sudden despair in her sister's voice that brought Rose's head up. 'I've asked myself many times, Rose, if *I* married the right man.'

'Elizabeth – ?'

Her sister met her gaze squarely. 'I'm being honest. What about you, Rose? Have you never asked yourself the same question?'

'No, never,' she said, but her voice lacked conviction. She began shredding the tissue in her agitation. What had made her sister ask such a question, and at this stage in their lives? Did Alex and Charles have any doubts about their respective marriages? Neither man had shown any inclination to stray. Not in England anyway.

'And you had better hear the rest,' Elizabeth said. 'Our

"Chicane" number has been on the rails in two stores in town for two days, and selling like mad.'

Rose blanched. 'You can't mean it, we would have known.'

'You know now. I have also been told it's on sale in America – and not in one of our stores.'

Rose sank on to the edge of a chair. 'A spy. *Who?*'

A sudden bleakness came into Elizabeth's eyes. 'I'm sorry to say that one of our children is the guilty party.'

Rose felt for a moment that her life's blood was draining away. 'Which one?'

'David or Jonathan, I presume. Marianne wouldn't be bothered to go to so much trouble and Caroline has no meanness in her at all. I only know it's happened. I had it on good authority. We'll have to find out.' Elizabeth picked up her handbag and gloves. 'Rose I must go. Like you, I need a sanctuary. I've kept this bottled-up inside me since last night. I feel my head will burst.'

'Oh, Elizabeth, I stopped you from telling me this morning, stopped you from sharing the load . . . I'm sorry.'

'I had no intention of telling you before I arrived. I spoke on impulse. It was a good job there was no time for the sharing of confidences. It would have served no purpose.' Elizabeth paused. 'The men could know already and with a day before the party to thrash it out we might be able to greet the family without appearing as though the world were about to come to an end.'

'It feels as though it already has come to an end.' Rose looked at her sister with stricken eyes. 'We've weathered many storms over the years, but this – this is different . . .'

'Rose, no matter which of our children it is nothing will change between the four of us, we're too close for that. I'm sorry to leave you on your own but I have to go, I need to be alone.' Elizabeth brushed Rose's cheeks with her lips. 'Try and get some rest.' With that she left.

Rose put her hand to her cheek, touched by the gesture. Elizabeth was not a demonstrative person, but Rose knew, that in spite of the veneer of hardness her sister showed to the world, she was capable of deep feeling. It would hit her hard if Jonathan were the culprit. He was her favourite and because she loved him so much she was more critical of his behaviour than of anyone else's. But Jonathan, an extrovert, who brought a gaiety to any social gathering, took it all in his stride. Once he said to Rose, lifting her off her feet and swinging her round, 'Why can't Mum be more like you, Auntie Rose?' Then he added as he set her down, 'No, I like her the way she is, she wouldn't be Mother if she were to change, would she? You always know where you are with her.'

Rose realised with a feeling of guilt she was thinking of Jonathan as being the culprit. If she were honest, David would more likely be the one responsible. But a criminal didn't have to be quiet, withdrawn. Many a crime had been committed by a happy-go-lucky person.

Crime? What an ugly sound it had. And yet industrial spying was a crime, and made more despicable if someone in the family were responsible.

How upset Charles and Alex would be. She could feel the pain of their hurt. They would not believe it, not believe that either Jonathan or David was capable of such an action, of stooping so low.

Had their children been too indulged? They had never known what it was to struggle, or to have known the wonderful feeling of achieving something after having struggled. And yet, when they were children they had not been given too much pocket money. None of the four had.

Rose went over to where the miniatures of the four children hung by the side of the marble fireplace. Marianne, lovely, pensive, Caroline beaming, Jonathan roguish, and David – secretive? No, there was an innocence in all of them, just as there had been an innocence in her younger brothers and sisters in those far-off days, when to have a whole penny to spend on sweets was the ultimate in luxury. How far away that seemed . . . another world.

Chapter 1

1926

Birthdays were not something people in Hackett Street celebrated, but to Rose Kimberley, who was sixteen that day it was, she felt, an occasion for some jubilation.

Apart from the fact that her mother had been safely delivered of her eleventh child, cousin Charlie had offered Rose the chance to help him with his secondhand clothes stall.

Rose seated herself in the old rocking chair in front of the fire and rocked gently to and fro. Just think, no more getting up at six o'clock every morning to go to the laundry. And perhaps no more attacks of bronchitis.

An attack had kept her at home this week, and in spite of the agony of coughing she had enjoyed it. She was enjoying the unusual peace of the kitchen now.

The younger children were with neighbours for the day and the rest were at school, or at work.

From the bedroom behind her came the clear voice of her sister Lizzie, the more gentle tones of her mother and the sharper voice of Gran Eagan. Soon either Lizzie or Gran would erupt into the kitchen and demand that tea be made.

Rose stopped rocking and burrowed lower in the chair, wanting to savour these precious moments of peace. It was one of those days in November that never came to full light. In the morning the smoke from the factory chimneys had hung low over the rooftops, by midday a fine drizzle wet the pavements and now in the afternoon rain pattered gently on the window panes.

In the quickly darkening room, with the firelight reflected in the bright polish of the steel fender, and dancing flames prettying the lines of shabby washing stretched across the room, the whole took on a deceptive air of comfort.

Suddenly the rain became a deluge. It lashed against the panes and cascaded down the gutters. People could be heard scattering for shelter, and it seemed to Rose that most had sought it in Bennett Buildings. Footsteps clattered on the wooden stairs, raucous, complaining voices echoed from various landings, doors slammed and now the only sound was Nellie Borthwick's gramophone churning out once more, *Keep the Home Fires Burning*.

Nellie's boyfriend had been killed at the end of 1918 but although the war had been over for years she still played it. Sometimes one of the women would yell, 'Nellie, get shut of that bloody record or I'll break it over your head.'

The outer door opened and Rose looked up to see her grandfather come shuffling in, shoulders hunched. He sat on the stool near the fire, and turned down his coat collar.

'Enough to drown a body. Couldn't work in this weather.'

Sam Eagan was a billposter by trade. He was good at his work but drink kept losing him his job. He took out a clay pipe, filled it from an oilskin pouch then jerked the pipe stem over his shoulder towards the bedroom door.

'Has the babby come yet?'

Rose sat up. 'Yes, it's a girl, but I haven't seen it yet.'

'So Edie's not gone yet. Oh, Gawd, if she sees me sitting here – she'd have me sticking bills if there was a hurricane going on.'

As he finished speaking the bedroom door opened and his wife was framed in the doorway for several seconds before going back into the room for something. With a whispered, 'I'll be back,' Sam got up and slunk out.

Edie, a bowl in one hand and a towel over her arm, came

across the kitchen, her tiny feet tip-tapping on the lino, her stiffly starched white apron crackling as it brushed the table edge.

'Rose, is that kettle boiling?' she demanded. 'Your Ma's dying for a cuppa.'

'It will be in a minute.' Rose pushed the kettle from the bar on to the fire with her foot, which brought an angry snort from her grandmother.

'That's right, scald your blooming foot and we'll be having you laid up again.'

'Then I'd get a bit more rest,' Rose replied amiably.

'Don't you speak to me like that, you saucy madam, or I'll give you a clip across your earhole.'

Edie advanced with hand upraised. Rose laughed and ducked.

Gran might be pint-sized but she packed a punch like a sledgehammer. And it was not only the young who came in for the brunt of her wrath. Some men, bullies for the most part, had been soundly belaboured with a broom by Edie, when they refused to get out of bed while their wives were being confined.

And many a surprised child had found itself being scrubbed by Edie before being put to bed.

In spite of her hardness, however, Rose loved her grandmother. If ever she needed advice it was to her she went. The advice might be harsh but Rose knew it would be sound, and right.

She said now, 'Can I see the baby, Gran?'

'When you bring the tea in, and hurry it up.' Edie went back into the room. As the door closed the outer one opened and Sam peeped in. Rose beckoned to him that all was clear. He grinned and came back to his stool.

The next moment he was sitting like a statue as the bedroom door opened again. Then he relaxed. It was Lizzie.

All the Kimberley children but Lizzie were fair and blue-eyed like their mother. But although Lizzie had her father's dark curly hair and brown eyes she did not have his quiet, gentle temperament. She was only a year older than her sister, but acted more like an aunt.

She rounded on Rose now. 'Get out of that chair, our Rose, and roll this mattress up and put it away. You're better now.'

Rose, who shared the mattress at night with three of her sisters, had enjoyed the comfort of lying on it on her own during the daytime this past week. Reluctantly, she got up to do the task and was told by Lizzie to 'hurry it up'.

'Hark at her,' said Sam, 'getting bossy just like Edie. You're a bonny lass, Lizzie, but you watch it, or you'll turn just like your grandmother. *She* was bonny when I married her.'

'Someone's got to do some bossing around here,' Lizzie snapped, 'or nothing would get done. You know what Ma's like.'

Rose nodded. They all knew what her mother was like, big and warm and generous and lovable, but all she wanted to do was to sit nursing her offspring in the old rocking chair. Ashes could be piled high in the grate, a mountain of dishes in the sink, but she would never see them.

Rose, wanting to change the subject and unable to keep her secret any longer said, 'Lizzie, when Charlie came in this morning he told me I can help him with his clothes stall.'

Lizzie stared at her for a moment then she exploded.

'Oh, that's good, isn't it? You get the chance of *two* jobs and I don't even get one. I wanted to go out to work when I left school three years ago, but I couldn't because Ma kept on having a kid every year and I had to stay at home and help.'

Lizzie dropped into the rocking chair and rocked vigorously, sending the springs wheezing and groaning.

Sam took the pipe from his mouth and spat into the fire. 'If you break them bloody springs, Lizzie, your Ma'll have something to say to you about it.'

'And Gran'll have something to say to you if she sees you spitting into the fire,' Lizzie retorted.

'What's wrong, love?' Sam's voice had softened. 'Tell your old Granda.'

'I've told you. I want to go out to work. I'm stuck here day after day looking after kids, wiping their snotty noses, washing dirty nappies, cooking, cleaning. I hate living here, hate the people –'

'Lizzie Kimberley, that's a dreadful thing to say,' remonstrated the old man. 'There's a lot of good people in the Buildings, people willing to help –'

'Gossiping women that's all you ever see,' Lizzie went on, ignoring him. 'Go to the yard for a bucket of water and they're there pulling someone to bits. There's no privacy. Go to the WC and you have someone banging on the door and telling you to hurry up. I hate the life I tell you, hate it!'

Rose and her grandfather exchanged disconcerted glances as though both were unable to cope with such a situation. Lizzie had never even hinted at how much she disliked her life.

The rocking chair gave a deep grouch as Lizzie brought it to an abrupt halt. 'You don't know how I feel, do you? You don't understand.'

Rose nodded quickly. 'I do, I really do.' She stood hesitant, reluctant to make her sacrifice, yet knowing it would be only fair to her sister. 'If *you* would like to help Charlie on his stall, Lizzie, I'll stay at home.'

'I don't want to sell secondhand clothes.' There was distaste in Lizzie's voice.

'Then what do you want to do?' Sam asked. 'Go into Meggeson's?'

Lizzie glared at him. 'And be one of Maggie's fairies? Is that how you see me? My God, I want something better than that out of life.'

Meggeson's was a rope factory and the women and girls working in it were considered to be rough.

'I've got brains,' Lizzie said. 'All the teachers at school told me so. I want to use them, perhaps work in an office.'

'Our Alice will be fourteen at Christmas,' Rose pointed out. 'She could take over from you.'

'Our Alice?' Lizzie gave a derisive laugh. 'She's worse than Ma. I could just see the two of them at home all day, reading twopenny novelettes. Oh, forget it.' She got up. 'Make the tea, our Rose, the kettle's boiling.'

Lizzie went to the cupboard at the side of the fireplace and brought out a roll of pink-sprigged wallpaper – the remains of a job lot bought by Charlie – and handed it, with a pair of scissors, to Sam.

'Make a traycloth, will you, Granda, please.'

Their mother, who had been a lady's maid before she married, liked pretty things and the family, whenever possible, did their best to supply them.

Sam was good at making things with paper, and Rose watched him cut a piece from the roll, fold it into an oblong and start tearing out fragments. His fingers were short and blunt-tipped but he worked at lightning speed.

This gift of his was partly responsible for Sam losing so many jobs. He would go round the pubs in a dinner hour armed with a bundle of newspapers and do his 'tearing act'. It was all right if just the regulars were in, then he would perhaps be treated to a half-pint of beer, or two halves, but if a ship was in port, the sailors, to egg him on to make strings of dancing dolls, would stand him to pints – and Sam would go rolling back to his job and either upset a can of paste on a passer-by or fall off the ladder.

Rose, never failing to be fascinated at this gift, watched the last scraps of paper float down to join the pile on the floor. With a 'Hey presto!' Sam shook it out with a flourish and there Rose saw a traycloth so fine and lacy she likened it to a cobweb moving gently in a breeze.

'It's lovely, Granda,' she enthused. 'It's one of the best you've ever made. Ma'll be delighted.'

Lizzie brought the dustpan and brush and swept up the pieces.

Before Rose could pour the tea Edie came out to say it had taken them so blessed long to make it her mother had fallen asleep. 'And leave her to sleep,' she said. 'This little 'un's taken more out of her than the others. Time she stopped having bairns.'

'And so say all of us,' declared Lizzie.

Edie put on her coat. 'I'm going home now to see to Charlie's tea, but I'll be back.' To her husband she added, 'And you can get off your backside and fetch me some potatoes. I've run out of them.' She marched out.

'And you can get off your backside,' the old man mimicked. 'Don't get much chance to sit on it when she's around.' He made no move to follow her.

Lizzie spooned condensed milk into three enamel mugs.

'We may as well drink the tea now it's made and have it in peace. In another half hour the kids will be in, and they'll be ravenous. Can you put the stew on the fire, Rose?'

Rose lifted the big iron pan from the hearth and hefted it on to the glowing coals. 'I'm ravenous too,' she said.

Normally the children came home at midday to a hot meal and had bread and marge or bread and jam when they came in from school. But when a baby was due the practice was reversed.

Rose always thought that Lizzie managed to make tasty meals out of the little money she had to spend on food. Today the sixpennyworth of mince in the pan had the addition of a couple of leeks, some carrots, a swede, potatoes and dumplings. Already the meal was beginning to smell appetising. Lizzie went to get the big spoon to stir it.

Rose's gaze kept going to the paper traycloth and at last she said, 'Do you know, Granda, I bet if you made some of these you could sell them in the market for a penny each.'

Sam knocked the dottle out of his pipe against the grate, then drew the back of his hand across his nicotined moustache. 'A penny each, eh? Worth thinking about it.'

'Just think, if you made two hundred and forty you'd have a whole pound.'

The old man's head jerked up. 'Two hundred and forty? You had me bamboozled for a minute, Rosie. I was just beginning to see the pennies and silver joeys dropping into me cap. Two hundred and forty? Not bloody likely. That's work, me fingers would be wore down to the bone.'

Lizzie laughed, and it transformed her, took away the tightness around her mouth. Rose, taking a sip of tea, eyed her over the rim of her cup. What a strange mixture this sister was. She had Gran's wiry figure and her obsession for cleanliness and tidiness, but where brains were concerned Lizzie was out on her own. She could tell you where any place in the world was, and could add up a string of figures in her head so fast you could imagine she was guessing the answer. But the answers were always right. Dave and Frank had tested her. They had written the figures down to add up.

Lizzie also had a way with words. It was she who had taught them all to spell by holding spelling bees in the evenings. It was fun.

Rose decided she must give her sister a second chance of going out to work.

'Look, Lizzie, I meant it when I said I would stay at home if you want to get out of the house.'

'I've told you, I'd be no good at selling secondhand clothes.'

'I wasn't meaning for you to –'

'I think you would do well at it, Rose, you're good at titivating things up.'

'Who wants to titivate secondhand clothes?' Sam demanded. 'You go round the houses buying them, flog 'em in the market and that's it.'

'That's Charlie's way,' Lizzie said, 'but it wouldn't be Rose's. You've seen what she can do with a twopenny dye and a few scraps of lace with the clothes he brings for the kids, and us.'

Rose, astonished and delighted at such praise from her sister confided her secret dream.

'Shall I tell you something? I hope to have a dress shop one day and do my own designs.'

'Oh Gawd,' said Sam. 'Now she owns a dress shop and she hasn't even stood in the market yet.' He wagged a finger at Lizzie. 'Don't you go encouraging her, gal. Rosie's a dreamer, she gets carried away. Look what she was going to make me do with those traycloths.'

'If Rose wants a dress shop,' Lizzie said quietly, 'I'd do everything I could to encourage her. I'd encourage anyone who wanted to better themselves, who wanted to get out of the Buildings. Folks stagnate here. In the meantime . . .' She stirred the stew.

When the whole kitchen was filled with the appetising smell of the meal simmering on the bar there came a hiccuping cry. 'The baby's awake,' Rose said, 'I'm going to see it.' As she went into the bedroom her mother leaned over in the bed to lift the baby from the cot.

'There, there,' Sally soothed her new offspring. 'Did your Gran leave you all on your own in the nasty old cot.'

Rose said softly, 'Hello, Ma. So it's another girl.'

Sally Kimberley pushed the tendrils of hair away from her brow and gave her daughter a beaming smile. 'And the image of her Dad.' There was pride in her voice. 'Isn't she a little beauty?'

Rose had never found newly-born babies beautiful but she always thought them heart-catching and this one was no exception.

The dark hair, as soft as thistledown was damp and showing signs of curling. The baby's clenched fist was against its mouth and was sucking vigorously. Rose laughed. 'Poor little thing, she's hungry. I'll get you a cup of tea, Ma, then you can have something to eat when you've finished feeding the baby. Are you still going to call her Lilian now she's dark? You know the saying, "as fair as a lily".'

'Yes, I know, but it's a nice name and it was your father's choice. He'll be in soon, see the fire's built up, love. It's been a terrible day, he'll be soaked to the skin.'

Rose had often thought that only her mother understood their father. He was a big man, brawny-looking and with very little to say in the house.

Alice once said, 'And wouldn't you be quiet if you were digging graves and burying people all day?'

He never made a fuss of any of the children and Rose had put it down to lack of feeling until the evening she overheard him talking to her mother in the bedroom. Her father had been speaking about a baby that had been buried that day.

'Twelve years they waited for a child,' he said, 'and it seemed all right when it was born, but two days later it suddenly died.' After a pause her father had added, 'When I saw that tiny white coffin and the faces of the parents I had to ask myself if there could be a God.'

Rose had wondered then if her father gave her mother all the babies to make up for the ones who died. There were many in their district who did die. She also decided it was shyness that kept her father aloof from his children, but there was so little opportunity to get to know him. After he had his meal he went to the pub and stayed there till bedtime. Not that he drank much, he had never, ever come home the worse for drink.

Seconds later the children came charging up the stairs. It was as though a horde of Red Indians had invaded the Buildings. There were blood-curdling yells before the door burst open and four figures hurtled in.

'Has the baby come yet?' This from seven-year-old Judith as she dragged off her coat and scarf. Rose told her yes, they would see it later.

Alice started complaining to Lizzie about Tommy. 'He threw my hat over the Gissons' wall and the door was locked and I couldn't get it, and he's going to get wrong from the teacher for pinching Minnie Weldon.'

'Quiet,' Lizzie yelled. 'Now pick up those wet things and put them over the clothes horse to dry, and get your boots off, *and* your stockings if they're wet.' Then as Tommy took off his cap and shook off the drops she gave him a push. 'Not on my steel fender!'

The fender was Lizzie's pride and joy. She cleaned it every morning with emery paper until it gleamed.

To Alice she said, 'You go and get the little ones from Mrs Jones. She'll have had enough of them by now.'

'Let our Nancy go,' declared Alice. 'She never does anything, it's always me.'

'Nancy's going to get the water.'

'It's not my turn,' wailed Nancy, 'I fetched it last night.'

'That was the night before.' Lizzie picked up the zinc bucket and thrust it at her. 'Now get out, at once, both of you, or else –'

They both knew better than to go on defying Lizzie. A clout from her hand could be as punishing as Gran's. Nancy went out, slamming the door behind her. Alice followed and they could be heard squabbling as they ran downstairs.

All the water used had to be drawn from taps in the yard. Taps that served all the families in the Buildings. And all the Kimberley children, apart from the tots, had to take turns in fetching it.

Nancy came back with the water, slopping it all over the floor and Alice followed to say that Mrs Jones would keep the children until their bedtime. Lizzie began to serve up the meal.

The squabbling broke out when the children started to check with each other how many grains of mince they had. Tommy, poking about his plate declared it wasn't fair, he had only eight pieces of mince and Alice eleven. Nancy said glee-fully she had fourteen and when Alice leaned over and tried to scoop some up with her spoon Lizzie not only clouted her, but the other three. Which, as Rose pointed out was hardly fair, seeing that Judith had not raised a word of complaint.

'Well that's in lieu of,' Lizzie retorted. 'She'll be up to some mischief sooner or later.'

The two eldest boys went to night school on a Friday evening and when they came out they went straight to a widowed aunt where they and Tommy slept every night. Lizzie had been on to her parents for months to try and find somewhere else to live with an extra room, or rooms, and had even found a house to rent, but nothing came of it. It all added up to money, the shortage of it. Perhaps, Rose thought, they might be able to move if she did well with the secondhand clothes.

When Charlie came that evening Rose was lucky enough to have him to herself for a while.

Charlie never walked into a room, he breezed in. 'Hi there, kiddo, how you doing? Feeling better? You look better. Happy birthday. Got something for you.' He drew a small silver locket on a chain from his pocket. 'Saw this the other day, thought you'd like it.'

'Oh, Charlie, it's lovely, what a surprise, a present. Fancy you remembering this was the day.'

He gave her a broad grin. 'Couldn't forget the date of me favourite cousin's birthday, now could I. And I'll have no trouble in remembering this little un's birthday either. Another girl, I hear. Could have done with an extra lad in the family.'

'Ma is satisfied, in fact she's delighted because the baby takes after Dad.'

'After your Dad? Hope she won't have to shave.' Charlie's eyes were twinkling.

Rose laughed. 'Oh, go on with you, you and your cracks. Do you want a cup of tea, Charlie, there's one in the pot?'

'No, ta – just downed three.' Charlie sat on the edge of the table and eyed Rose in what she thought was a rather odd way.

From as far back as she could remember her cousin had been someone special to her. She loved him, not in the way sweethearts did, more the way of loving an older brother. Charlie was not good-looking but he had a lively face, laughing blue eyes fringed with thick dark lashes, and a smile that had girls running after him.

Charlie took girls out from time to time but never became serious with any of them. He was unusually serious now. Rose said, 'What's the matter? You're looking at me as though seeing me for the first time and didn't quite know what to make of me.'

'And do you know, Rosie girl, that's exactly it.' He slapped the flat of his hand on his thigh. 'Hit the nail right on the head. One minute you seemed just a kid and now you're sixteen and grown up, and a damned pretty girl you are too.'

'Do you really think I'm pretty, Charlie?'

He slid off the table edge and gripped her arms. 'You're lovely, kiddo, and there'll soon come a time when you'll turn fellas' heads, and their hearts. And that's the time to watch out, do you hear?'

'Yes, Charlie,' she said, acting demure, and wondering at the same time why his words should have set her heart racing so.

'Right, Rosie. Now, how about this job? Do you still want to help me on the rag stall?'

'Oh, yes, yes of course. I told Meg Ferrer to tell them at the laundry I wouldn't be coming back. It was being in the steam all the time that kept giving me bronchitis. I never had it before I went to work at the laundry.'

Charlie said, 'Well, then, Rosie, if it's fine in the morning come around about eleven o'clock or half past and we'll go through the last lot of clothes I bought. Then, if it's fine on Monday I'll take you with me buying round the Lismond area.'

Lismond Park district was talked about as the posh area, where the 'toffs' lived. Charlie said, toffs nothing, half of them were on the verge of bankruptcy. The women were all top show – fur coats and holes in their bloomers, or wearing none

at all. It was a well-known fact. Rose asked why, if they were
so badly off, they sold their dresses, and Charlie explained it.

'You see, Rosie, the women have to appear with their
husbands at social functions and need to have changes, they
can't go in the same dress all the time. They'll get a sewing
woman in for a few coppers a day and her meals, and she'll
alter the dresses, and when they can't be transformed any
more they flog 'em to me.'

'But what you pay them won't buy them new clothes.'

'No, but it will pay off some of the acount at the shop where
they are used to buying and then they can order some more.
It's a hand-to-mouth existence. No different to the women in
the Buildings here, only they're usually struggling to get
money to keep body and soul together.'

'I don't understand it,' Rose said, shaking her head. 'The
husbands must earn good money to live in such big houses.'

'They do, but they have to keep up appearances. They
send their children to private schools, they have to have
servants, they entertain so they have need of a good cook to
serve decent meals. They have to put on a show and
appear affluent, even if they don't know how they're going to
pay the next bill that comes in.

'Mind you,' Charlie added, 'all the Lismond lot aren't the
same. There's Mrs Chalmers, whose husband has a hundred
pots of gold at the end of every rainbow, who buys and
discards stuff after one wearing. I pay her a good price for
them and they never see the market stall. I flog 'em to Mr
Rosenberg who has a clientèle for them in London.'

Charlie grinned. 'You've seen a bit of life here in the
Buildings, but you'll see life of a different sort when you come
out with me. And some characters – the bad, the rotten and
the nice, the kind, gentle ones like Mrs Patterson . . .'

'I'm looking forward to it,' Rose said, 'and I'll be round to
Gran's first thing in the morning whether it's hail blow or
snow to help you sort out your stuff.'

Chapter 2

When Rose walked round to her grandparents' house the next morning she had the excited feeling of a new life opening up for her. The house, one room up and one down was in the next street. There was a tiny garden at the back, and a shed where Charlie kept the clothes he bought. Gran insisted he kept them there because, she said, they smelled.

The dampness of the shed added a fusty smell to the clothes, mingling with stale body odours and cheap scent. At first Rose used to be repelled by it but now she was used to it and found that after the clothes were out in the air the smell disappeared.

The front door led straight into the living room and when Rose knocked and went in, Charlie called, 'Hello there, Rosie. I've got everything ready for you to look through. I've brought them in here, don't want you standng in the shed getting cold. I'll get them cleared away before Edie's back.'

The room, simply furnished, included a double brass bedstead. Edie had a brass fender and she polished this and blackleaded the grate every morning to a mirror brightness, and was as fiercely protective over both as Lizzie was over the steel fender.

'Well now,' Charlie said. 'Where do we start – these dresses – ?' He placed various items in different heaps, pricing them as he sorted through them. 'We might get a shilling for this if we're lucky, or ninepence for this –'

Rose picked up a pale pink blouse that was faded. 'This is

pure silk, Charlie. If I was to buy a twopenny dye I could make it look like new.'

He shook his head. 'No, my love, this is what the customers want to do. They want to buy something for sixpence and then say to their family, see what I've made of this, bought a twopenny dye and – they get a kick out of it, they've achieved something.'

'But surely all the women won't want to do this?'

'No, and the majority don't want to do such ordinary things as repairing. Now this is where you'll score, Rosie. There's a lining in this coat here that's come undone, a dress split under the arms, they'll beat you down if there's any repairs to be done, and it's the extra coppers you get if the stuff's decent that add up to make your day.'

Rose did not want to do repairs, she wanted to pretty things up, but she said, 'All right, I'll do them.' She picked up a blue dress. 'You ought to get quite a bit for this, it's in good condition. How much, five shillings?'

'No, no, nothing like. A couple of bob perhaps, or one and six. I'm going to pass on a piece of advice that Mr Rosenberg gave me when I first started and that is, small profits and quick returns. That's how he made his money. Now remember that, Rosie.'

'Yes, I will.'

Charlie leaned over and began to sort through a sack. A separate pile needing repairs was eventually set aside and was so large Rose was beginning to wonder if she would not be better off staying at the laundry. Then Charlie went upstairs and came back with a bulging linen bag.

'Now these are special,' he said. 'These are what go to Mr Rosenberg.' He cleared the table of the rest of the clothes then tipped the bag out. 'How's that then?'

Rose caught her breath. It was like taking a peep into Aladdin's cave. A flimsy chiffon dress patterned in jewel colours lay tumbled against a delicate blue satin nightdress with hand-stitched appliquéd lace. 'Oh, Charlie . . .' Rose fingered the dress. 'How beautiful. And this,' – she picked up a negligée in cream silk, edged with swansdown. 'And this' – a celanese accordion-pleated skirt in olive green with matching jumper. 'What I would give to be able to wear clothes like these.'

'You will, Rosie, you will, you've got it in you. I've seen the dresses you've made for the kids, at times.'

'Oh, come on, Charlie, muslin at a penny a yard –'

'I know, that's why you'll succeed. It's the extras you put on the dresses, you're creative. That smocking you did on the little 'uns' dresses, it was professional. Look, Rosie, have a sort through this stuff and pick yourself a dress.'

Rose liked the soft green celanese jumper suit with the pleated skirt and although she could think of no occasion when she could wear it, she asked if she might have it.

'Here, with my love, me old sweetheart. I'll have to go, promised to meet a pal in the Jolly Miller. I'll bring all the clothes that need repairing to you later. Take your dress with you, I'll find you a piece of paper.'

With the rest of the clothes in the shed and the better ones back upstairs Charlie knotted a spotless white muffler at his throat, tucked the ends into his jacket and pulled on his cap. And a few minutes later Rose was watching him going down the street, his cap pushed to the back of his head, his walk jaunty. People in doorways hailed him. 'Hello, there, Charlie . . . are you all right, Charlie . . . how you doing, lad? . . .'

Rose smiled to herself as she turned to go in the opposite direction. Everyone loved Charlie, it would be good to work with him.

Normally she worked at the laundry on a Saturday so it would be a special treat to be at home. Lizzie and Alice and Nancy always went to the market on a Saturday afternoon to do the shopping, taking the youngest children with them. And as Tommy would be out and the two older boys working she could read some stories to her mother. Ma loved romances. Rose had to admit that she did too, but although her mother's heroes were always based on film characters, like Rudolph Valentino, the man Rose dreamed about was a rather nebulous figure, based on a composite picture of men she had had a crush on in the past, a teacher, an under-manager at the laundry, the son of the people in the big house opposite the Park.

The crushes had ended when each man married.

Situations where Rose and her hero met were always a little vague too, and so was the type of dress she wore. But now, with the green celanese jumper suit in its wrapping of newspaper clutched to her Rose saw herself pirouetting for her lover's approval, the pleats of the skirt flaring out around her.

When she came to a stop her hero was looking deeply into her eyes and saying softly, 'You are so beautiful, my lovely Rose.'

The voice which penetrated the dream was the raucous one of Mrs O'Halloran yelling to her youngest from the window of the Buildings, to get off his backside and go a message for her.

Which strengthened Rose's determination to get her dress shop and seek a more gracious way of living, where women did not hang out of windows yelling to their offspring, nor use the word 'backside'.

When Lizzie saw the jumper suit she gave a sniff. 'Going up in the world, aren't you? Still it might come in useful some-time. Put it aside. As Gran would say, "it'll eat no bread".'

Lizzie and Rose were in the bedroom when the outer door opened, and seconds later their Aunt Maude drifted in. Maude was their father's sister and as far back as they could remember she had worn the same pudding-basin hat and black coat. And as far back as they could remember she had spoken in the same monotonous, recitation voice.

'Would have come yesterday,' she said, 'but couldn't manage it.' Her melancholy gaze went from the baby in the cot to her sister-in-law.

'How are you, Sal? So it's another girl. Looks puny, hope you rear her. I mustn't stay long, last time I was here Bert chopped down the bloody mantelpiece for firewood. And grumbled ever since 'cos he's nowhere to put his feet. The fire was low when I came out, so if I don't get back he'll have the bloody banisters next. I'll call again tomorrow. Ta-ra for now.'

And she drifted out without the girls or their mother having had a chance to say a word.

'Honestly,' Lizzie said, 'Aunt Maude gets worse. And Bert – Fancy chopping down the mantelpiece. How on earth did he find the energy?'

Bert, at five foot nothing and as skinny as a twig had never done a full day's work in his life, and the idea of him wielding an axe was just too much. The three of them dissolved into helpless laughter, and as Rose dried her eyes she thought how lovely it was to hear Lizzie laughing. She had the carefree look that had not been there since her schooldays.

Perhaps it would come again if their circumstances changed.

Charlie arrived with the clothes to be repaired while Lizzie was dishing up the midday meal. She invited him to stay for a bite but he said he had already eaten, a sixpenny steak and kidney pudding, sold by the café next to the pub.

Saturdays were what Charlie called his free days. He would perhaps go out early morning to the quayside and talk to the men on the ships, and not come home until late. Or he would get on a tram and spend the day at the coast, or just 'mooch around', have a few drinks with his pals, have a sleep in the afternoon and go to the music hall in the evening.

'But I'll sit down and have a cup of tea, Liz,' he said now.

Lizzie snapped at him for putting his elbows on the table. 'What's the good of trying to teach the kids manners,' she said, 'if people like you show them a bad example.'

Charlie winked at Rose. 'I can't escape it, can't go anywhere without being nagged.' To Lizzie he added, 'But you're right, kiddo, I'll try not to do it again.' He punched first his right elbow then his left. 'Now you remember that, you two.'

The children roared their delight at this.

Charlie, like his grandfather, was an entertainer, but always for the children. He would draw a face on his clenched fist, tie a handkerchief round the 'face' and move his fingers, making different expressions. In the firelight he would throw shadow figures on to the walls with his hands, of dogs, cats, rabbits and men with caps on, or top hats.

For variety he would get down on his knees, tie an apron round his neck, then putting his hands in a pair of boots make the boots do a dance. There were always cries of, 'More, Charlie, more!'

Rose said, 'You really should be married and have children, Charlie, you'd make a lovely dad.'

Charlie grinned. 'I'm waiting for the right girl to come along.' He got up. 'I must go. I'll pop in and say ta-ta to Sal.'

When he had gone into the bedroom Lizzie said, in an urgent whisper, 'Don't talk marriage to Charlie. He was married during the war. Doreen walked out on him.'

'Married?' Rose felt a sense of shock. 'Why didn't you tell me?'

'Because Charlie hates anyone knowing, so don't say another word about it. Get the kids ready, I'm going shopping in a few minutes.'

Rose was still thinking about Charlie's marriage when she took them into her mother to give them a hug and a kiss.

When this was done, Alice came in for them. She said, looking wistfully at her mother, 'I wish I could stay and hear Rose read the stories.'

'Well you can't,' called Lizzie. 'I need all the help I can get with shopping to do and kids to look after.'

Alice lingered. 'What story are you going to have first, Ma?'

Sally fingered the few magazines on the bed. Every story in

them had been read so many times she knew them all by
heart.

'I think we'll have the one about the sheikh who carries the
rich spoilt heiress to his tent in the desert.'

'And tattoos the name Ahmed on the girl's back to show
her she now belongs to him,' said Alice, an ecstatic note in her
voice.

Charlie looked from one to the other. 'Tattoos his name
Ahmed on her back? It's a blooming good job it wasn't
Abdullah or he'd never have got it all on.'

'Oh, Charlie, stop scoffing,' said Sally. 'They're good
stories.'

'You know what Freddie Martin has to say about sheikhs,
Sal. They're mucky, they never wash and they stink to high
heaven.'

Alice was indignant. 'They do not! Anyway, not this one.
He has a bath every day in the oasis and his servant dresses
him in the most lovely white silk shirts – and –'

'Oh Lord,' said Lizzie, coming in, 'they're off again. Come
on, our Alice, and you, Rose, have the tea ready for when we
get back, do you hear?'

Rose promised, and when the girls and Charlie had gone
her mother said, beaming, 'Now love, let's get started. After
we've had the one about the sheikh we'll have the story about
the poor girl who goes into service and marries her master.'
She raised the bedcover and added, 'Get your boots off and
come in beside me.' Rose nestled close to her mother's big and
lovely warm body.

An hour later, after all the favourite stories had been read
and her mother had dozed off she began to think of Charlie
again and his marriage. And she knew she just had to find out
more about it.

But Lizzie had no more information to offer and warned
Rose she would cause trouble if she probed any further. It was
a taboo subject. So with that Rose had to be satisfied – at least
for the time being.

Chapter 3

When Charlie left the Buildings he made for Freeman's Road where the trams left to go to the coast. The sea was the one place where he could always find a sense of peace. And peace was something he needed right now, with his mind in such a turmoil.

Here he was, tied to a wife he hadn't seen for years and not only in love with his sixteen-year-old cousin Rose, but hankering after Lizzie, who at times he felt he could hit. He tried to be nice to her but she was always stabbing at him with that sharp tongue of hers. It would serve her right if he roughed her up sometime.

Roughed her up? Charlie was appalled at this unexpected savagery in him. He had never hit a woman in his life, nor did he want to. Was it because Lizzie reminded him of Dorrie and Dorrie had made such an utter fool of him? Told him he had made her pregnant and demanded he marry her. And he, poor sucker had, only to find out on their wedding night the kid she was carrying was not his. Dorrie had wanted to give the child a name, she said. The father of it, another soldier, was married.

Because of his own childhood he had told Dorrie he would accept the baby as his own and try to love it, and felt he might have done when he came back wounded from the Somme and saw the boy, a little ginger-haired mite, but a week after he was home Dorrie up and left, taking her son with her. And he had not seen her since. According to what he had been told she had had a few men while he was away.

The solicitor told him he could presume her dead after seven years, but warned him if his wife did turn up he was still considered legally married to her. So, marriage was out until he could find her and try and get a divorce. He had hired one of these private detectives to trace her but so far there had been no result.

After the war, with few jobs for the 'heroes', he had patched up a broken-down barrow and set up a fruit stall at the kerb, buying the poorer fruit at first. Even that had been hard to sell with so many men out of work, and every penny he saved had been a small triumph.

He had had a stall in the market before the war. Charlie gave a mirthless smile. Shouting his wares had given a hoarseness to his voice. Dorrie had told him it was attractive when they first met. When he came home from France she called him a 'coarse-voiced sod'.

Freeman's Road was on the edge of town, with the trams going through fields on a single track to the coast. A new housing estate was springing up. Soon there would be shops and schools and later, no doubt, factories would encroach on the countryside.

Not many people travelled on the coast route during the week but on Saturdays there were usually a few families, the children with buckets and spades, even in cold weather, as it was today.

There was a tram waiting and Charlie climbed to the upper deck, which was open. The fresh air might clear away some cobwebs.

A few riotous children came clambering up the stairs and immediately began to undo the leather aprons on the backs of the seats. The conductor followed, gave them all a clip on the ear and ordered them back downstairs to their parents.

'Kids,' he said feelingly to Charlie, as he began to re-roll the aprons. These pieces of leather were useful to spread over the knees if it suddenly rained. The conductor went back downstairs and Charlie was alone.

A few moments later the tram set off on its journey, and as it trundled along a few sheep and cows raised their heads from grazing and watched the tram's progress with curious eyes, even though they must have seen the contraptions numerous times.

Charlie might have thought it a good life to live on a farm had he not experienced it as a child. He had not allowed himself to think of his childhood for years, and now as he began to peel away the layers it hurt.

He had been in the same position as Dorrie's child, only in his case his father had been a sailor with a roving eye. His mother, ashamed and determined not to let her parents know, ran away, leaving a note to say she was getting married and would be in touch. By devious means she found her way to Dorset where she became a drudge with a tight-fisted couple on a farm. And there he and his mother lived a life of hell.

Pride kept her from letting her family know, and it was only when she knew she was dying she wrote to Gran and Gran came and took him back to live with them, first burying his mother.

His grandmother at first had seemed so hard it was Sally he had turned to, but now he loved her and was grateful for the way she had brought him up, teaching him to be honest and to make his word his bond. It had stood him in good stead with both the traders and his customers.

Two stops further on a young man came sprinting up the stairs. 'Morning,' he said to Charlie, 'a bit fresh, isn't it?'

'Yes, it is.'

The man made his way to the front, touching the backs of the seats on either side as he passed. This action brought vividly to Charlie's mind a picture of a bloke named Lecky, with whom he had palled up during the war. Lecky always touched chairs, bar counters, empty glasses, tables; said he didn't know why.

When Charlie was first demobbed, war to him was the

carnage of the Somme where nearly half a million Britishers alone were slaughtered. Later, when the nightmare faded it was Lecky who stayed in his mind. Charlie smiled to himself remembering the wiry little figure, the cheeky face, the man a born mimic and a comic. There were many different accents in the regiment, Scottish, Irish, Welsh, there were men from Lancashire and Yorkshire, and the Cockneys – Lecky could take them all off. He also took off the young captains with their la-di-da voices, who talked about their parents as mater and pater.

Lecky once said, 'I can tell you plenty of tales about the gentry. I had a friend who was a butler. Some of the stories would make your hair curl.'

Charlie felt he had learnt so much about life since joining the army nothing would shock him. And Lecky's stories didn't, but the droll way he had of telling them made him laugh, so that sometimes he felt drunk with laughter.

Now sitting on top of the tram, going through the peaceful countryside, he wondered how he had ever laughed during the war.

There must have been a time when the earth of the battlefield was hardbaked but he had no memory of it. All he remembered was mud, inches deep, standing in it in the trenches, trying to sleep in it, squelching in it over No Man's Land, and the constant bombardment of guns, blasting the ears drums, shells exploding, and the carnage, men minus an arm, a leg, a head, men who had had bayonets twisted in their guts . . . and the rats – oh yes, the rats . . .

Then he and Lecky had caught a packet together, Lecky shot in the head, he in the side and thigh, and they had lain in the mud while it rained and rained, and men screamed in agony around them.

Lecky started rambling. He couldn't die, he mustn't die, he said, he had to live, it was important, would someone save him?

Charlie, in agony himself, had tried to calm him but when

Lecky went on rambling, imploring to be saved so he would not 'let the side down', Charlie grabbed him by the collar and with a superhuman effort dragged him to the comparative safety of a shell hole. Then he passed out.

He woke up in a field hospital and was so ill himself he was not sure whether Lecky was there, too. When he did enquire he was told he had been shipped home, and Charlie did not see his friend again.

Not in person, that is. What he did see, after he was demobbed was Lecky's photograph in a national newspaper, with a paragraph underneath announcing the forthcoming marriage of Mr Leckworth Malgliesh to the Honourable Dorothea Cortlon. Charlie had sat, staring at the rest of the words . . . Lecky, the only surviving son of a Lord! And Leckworth Malgliesh – what a blooming moniker! No wonder Lecky had wanted it shortened.

Where was he now – living in some mansion? And had he changed since the day he enlisted as a private? Charlie wondered if the Honourable Dorothea had a sense of humour and if she would appreciate her husband's jokes and gift of mimicry. He hoped so. It was Lecky who had kept him and a lot of other blokes sane, during the war.

The fields gave way to clusters of cottages then rows of houses, and before long he caught a glimpse of the sea. The air was different here, tangy with the smell of seaweed and on his lips was the taste of salt.

Always before he went along the sands he walked the length of the pier and back. Here he caught the full force of the wind, which he found exhilarating. There were twin piers, granite built, each nearly a mile long, with a lighthouse at the end. Inside the piers the water was calm, but beyond the harbour mouth two small ships kept disappearing into deep troughs then appearing again. In the distance an ocean-going liner looked stationary against the skyline.

Although the sea attracted Charlie, which he could have inherited from his father, he had no particular wish to be a sailor. He liked the buying and selling, the bargaining, being with people. He would like to branch out, go to London, start up in the East End. The odd times he had been to see Mr Rosenberg he had been taken with the flow of money that changed hands. He needed money, this business of tracing Dorrie was draining him at the moment. Perhaps with Rose helping he could handle more goods.

Normally Charlie would go as far as the lighthouse, stand looking out to sea for a while then walk back. But today the waves licking along by the side of the pier gathered momentum then crashed over the bulwarks, falling with a spray-drenching cascade. Two boys were playing a dodging game and not succeeding. Many a time when he was a boy he had had a good hiding from Gran for coming away from the pier drenched to the skin.

Charlie retraced his steps, climbed the slope at the end then went down the steps to the rocks, eventually making his way to the water's edge. Although the sea was choppy there was something leisurely in the way the cream-frothed waves rolled close to his feet then receded. And it was then Charlie felt the peace seeping into him.

Perhaps things would work out all right. The private 'tec might find Dorrie and he could start divorce proceedings. It would take time, but then it would give Rose a few more years to grow up. He could wait. She might not, of course, want to marry him. There were things against it, like the twelve-year difference in their ages, and the fact that they were cousins. But then there were successful marriages where the man was older, a *lot* older, and he knew of two couples who were full cousins and their children were all right.

It was the way Rose was with him that gave Charlie hope, she was so warm, so affectionate. If he brought anything for the family she would throw her arms around him and kiss him. 'Oh, Charlie, you're so kind, so good, I love you.'

He felt a great tenderness for her deep inside him. There was such an innocence about Rose. Not an innocence regarding the facts of life. No girl could live in the Buildings, especially in two rooms with a family the size of the Kimberleys and not know that twice two made four. It was more a simplicity, a trusting of people, her wide-eyed wonder at a gift, at things she had never seen before, like the time he had first taken them to a fair.

Charlie had a feeling that even if Rose were in the midst of sin and vice she would still retain her innocence.

He clambered over the rocks at the end, crossed the road and walked to the fishermen's cottages where the women sat at their doors, all with crabs and lobsters for sale, all the pieces of cardboard proclaiming the same price, sixpence for a crab, a shilling for a lobster. Charlie stopped at the first cottage which he always did.

'Hello, Annie, got a nice big one for me today?'

'I have that, Charlie. Caught specially for you. Your Gran and Granda'll have a feast of this one.'

'I'll have another, as well, Annie. Aunt Sal has had her baby girl. It'll be a treat for her and the family. And how is your youngest getting on, had trouble with his walking, didn't he?'

The two of them talked, exchanging items of news and when Charlie left with the two lobsters in a big string bag he felt purged of all the problems that had beset him.

Chapter 4

It was a morning of high winds when Rose set out with Charlie on the Monday to buy the secondhand clothes. But the sun was bright and the sky a clear blue.

'Grand morning for washing,' Charlie remarked cheerfully as he pushed the empty barrow. 'The womenfolk will be pleased.'

Although it was still early lines of washing were already flapping in a number of backyards, and as usual there were the groups of gossiping women round the wash-houses.

There were lines of washing out too in the back gardens of the houses in the Lismond area, but here no garments with holes in them were displayed, nor sheets with patches. In one garden there was a line of large white fleecy-looking towels, and another of smaller striped ones. The striped ones bobbed and danced in the wind then all were blown high in unison, reminding Rose of gaily-skirted, high-kicking dancers she had seen in last year's pantomime at the Palace.

Charlie opened a gate further along. 'We go in here, Rosie. This is the Palmers. Never get any further than the kitchen, but I take some good stuff and we'll be given a cuppa.'

Rose, following Charlie up the path passed two sheets on the line which had fine crocheted lace edges. The pillow cases further along were also lace-edged. One of the pillow cases billowed out and caught Rose's cheek. It had a lovely, fresh, clean smell. She decided when she was rich she would have sheets and pillow cases like these.

The kitchen door was open and as they reached it they were greeted by an enormously fat woman. 'Hello there,

Charlie, and is this the cousin you were telling me about? Rose, isn't it? A right pretty lass. Come in the pair of you, I'll mash you a cup of tea.'

They were sat down to mugs of tea, and shortbread that melted in the mouth. Charlie chatted brightly to Mrs Cobb, who was the cook, telling her funny little incidents that had happened in the market.

And Mrs Cobb, whose eyes were like currants in a puff-pastry face said, 'Aye, it's good to see you, lad. Brightens up my day.' She wheezed a little. 'Getting old, I'm beginning to wonder what's going to happen to me when I can no longer work.'

'You old, Mrs Cobb? Go on with you, you're like my gran, always busy, always on the go. You'll never be out of a job, not while you can cook like this.' He held up a piece of shortbread. 'You could make a fortune starting a bakery and selling this alone.'

'Hark at him,' Mrs Cobb said to Rose. 'Me in a bakery. Takes me all my time to get out of a chair these days.'

'Bet you'd jump out of it quick if there was a fire under it,' Charlie teased.

Mrs Cobb began to laugh, her eyes disappearing into the folds of flesh, her chins wobbling. 'Aye and I bet I would 'an all, lad. Needs must when the devil drives, as they say.' She nodded towards a bag beside the dresser. 'The mistress left you that, said she knows you'll treat her fair. You're to put the money in the envelope.'

Charlie sorted through the goods, put some money in the envelope, then pressed some coins into Mrs Cobb's hand. 'That's for being a good girl,' he said, with a grin.

'Ta, Charlie, you're a good lad.' To Rose she added, 'You look after him, love, he's worth 'is weight in gold is Charlie. Hope I'll be here next month to see you.'

'Of course you will,' Charlie declared. 'You'd better be, I want some more of that shortbread!' He squeezed her shoulder. 'Now you take care of yourself, do you hear?'

Outside he said to Rose, 'Poor soul, she gets fatter every time I see her. She must be filling with water. I hope I'm wrong.'

With the bag on the barrow he trundled off along the lane.

During their visits to the next three houses Rose had a glimpse of an opulence she had seen only in films, and discovered that Charlie could be different people with the various types he met.

With a tall, rather austere lady he became a man of the world, discussing politics in what seemed to Rose to be a very knowledgeable way, and disagreeing with the lady at times without giving offence. Rose felt quite proud of him.

At the next house when the small, plump, pleasant-faced woman began determinedly to bargain with him over the clothes, Charlie became the market trader, willing to play ball with her, but having already named a fair price and sticking to it. Yet at the same time, letting the woman think she had won the contest. They parted amicably.

In the house further along the furnishings and the woman were an eye-opener to Rose. Here they were invited to Madeline Chalmers' boudoir, a room made luxurious with deeply-piled carpet, silk hangings and drapes and a bedcover of pale green satin. The chiffon negligée Mrs Chalmers wore was also in pale green. She reclined on a sofa, the negligée draped round her, a blonde, shapely woman with dark slumbering eyes.

She addressed Charlie as Charles, and completely ignored Rose.

Then followed a scene that was pure cinema. Rose watched fascinated. She had seen too many films not to know what Madeline Chalmers was up to. She was the vamp trying to win over the hero. And Charlie was magnificent, acting cool and detached, letting this vamp know he would not be won over.

Madeline, true to form, rose gracefully from the sofa, and walked across to the dressing table, the negligée a foam of chiffon on the carpet. All her movements were voluptuous.

When she turned she was smiling, at least her lips were, but there was now a hardness in her eyes. She glanced at Rose then said to Charlie, 'Did you say she was your cousin?'

'That's right, my cousin Rose,' Charlie said.

'So you felt you needed a bodyguard?'

'A lot of folks round here keep big, barking dogs,' Charlie said. 'Rose has a way with animals.'

Madeline Chalmers permitted herself a small smile. 'I would have preferred that you had braved the barking dogs yourself, Charles. And, I might add, I do not conduct business with a child present.'

'Rose is no child, Mrs Chalmers. She's sixteen and all woman.'

Rose felt like applauding. Charlie's slightly hoarse voice had never sounded so attractive, so masterful. And yet at the same time she knew he could lose one of his best customers. She waited now, with a breathless feeling, expecting any minute being asked to leave with Charlie.

But no, Mrs Chalmers pointed to a wardrobe and told Charlie to take the parcels from the bottom. Then she said, 'You can settle up with me the next time you come. I have an appointment,' and she swept out of the room.

Rose whispered, 'Oh, Charlie, you'll never get any more stuff from her. I shouldn't have come.'

'I'll get it.' Charlie spoke with confidence. 'I'm a challenge to her. If ever I was to give in that would be the end of my visits.'

Rose could not resist asking him, with a teasing smile, if he would like to give in to Mrs Chalmers. Charlie slung the bags on to the barrow, stood a moment, thoughtful, then said, 'Yes, I would, but I'd never do so, because I wouldn't want to be chucked aside when she wanted to move to other pastures. And believe me, kiddo, our Madeline has fed in many pastures.' He gripped the handles of the barrow and raised them. 'Come on.'

Rose knew of the tenderness in her cousin, but it was never more apparent than when they called on Mrs Patterson, an elderly, rather frail-looking woman with a gentle expression. When she came limping into the room Charlie exclaimed, 'Why Mrs Patterson, what have *you* been doing? Jumping off the garden wall?'

In spite of the jocularity in his voice there was a genuine concern in his eyes.

'Nothing so wildly exciting as that, Charlie. I tripped over a rug and hurt my hip.' The old lady's eyes held an impish glint. 'Doctor Hurst had to carry me upstairs, and it's a long time since a man did that.'

She turned to Rose, smiling, 'And you must be Charlie's cousin. Sit down, my dear, it's very nice to meet you.'

By the time they had finished the round Rose was so full of impressions she could hardly wait to tell her mother and Lizzie.

Charlie left her with the promise to call for her at seven o'clock the next morning.

Most of what Rose had seen of furniture and furnishings were glimpses through partly-opened doors, but this was enough to have her go into realms of ecstasy.

'There was this beautiful crystal chandelier in the hall and suits of armour and spears and shields, and in this other house this blue carpet. Oh, Ma, you could tell your feet would sink in it right up to your ankles, and you should have seen Mrs Chalmers' boudoir – yes, *bou – doir*, just like you see on the films, all satin, pale green and her negligée – well!'

Her mother's eyes became dreamy. 'I know just what you mean, Rosie,' she said, and began to reminisce about the houses where she had been lady's maid, and about the people, and their finery.

Lizzie said, 'It's time you two came down to earth, you're *here* in Bennet Buildings, in Hackett Street, not some fancy mansion.'

Rose laughed. 'I'll be down to earth all right later. I have to start on the repairs of the clothes ready to go to market in the morning.'

'I'll give you a hand. Alice and Judith will help too. We can have a spelling bee, then it won't make the repairs seem so much like work.'

They found out how to spell a number of new words and most of the repairs got done, but not because of Alice's help. Her hands got sweaty, she said, the needle stuck and the thread got twisted. Rose teased her saying that she would not be much use in her dress shop when she had one and Alice looked up, excited.

'A dress shop? Do you mean it, Rose, are you really going to have one?'

'I hope to, eventually.'

'Oh, I would love to serve in a dress shop. There's nothing I'd like better. Will you have it by the time I leave school? I'll work hard, I'll sew properly, I won't let my hands get sweaty or my thread twisted. I promise, I promise!'

'I don't know when I'll get my shop, Alice. Not for some time, I expect, but if you do learn to sew carefully and help me with the things Uncle Charlie gets for the market there might be a job for you.' Alice could not do enough after this.

The next morning at ten to seven Rose carried the sack downstairs and stood in the doorway to wait for Charlie. Although she was used to leaving the house early, and in the dark in winter, she had a trembling feeling in the pit of her stomach. Would she be any good at selling? Would she be able to chat up the customers as Charlie did? Would they expect it of her?

Sounds, which had merged into the background on other mornings seemed to have acquired a new clarity, as though all her senses had come alive with this new venture. The clip-clop of the heavy shire horses pulling a dray had a ringing sound, the milkman calling, 'Milko!' was more musical, the clatter of his cart over the cobbled street louder, the voices of the women coming with their jugs and tin cans to get them filled sounded louder too. Then Rose heard whistling and knew it was Charlie approaching with the barrow.

She went to the kerb. 'Hello there, kiddo,' he greeted her. 'You're prompt. Feeling all right, not nervous?' She said, no, no, she felt fine.

As usual Charlie was greeted on all sides as he went back along the street and as Rose walked by the barrow she felt self-conscious. There was no reason for it – circumstances had not changed in any way.

Yes, they had. Yesterday she had been a free agent. Now she was on her way to become a secondhand clothes dealer, a trade which would be despised by the better-class people.

Rose tried to think of Charlie's words about some of the women wearing fur coats and having holes in their bloomers, but all she could see was a crystal chandelier, a deep pile blue carpet and Madeline Chalmers' boudoir.

An image, however, that quickly disappeared when they reached the market. The noise was deafening, the market men and women calling to one another, making quips, barrows being trundled, hampers on wheels pushed along. The flames of the naptha flares wavered in the morning wind and the paraffin smell of the flares mingled with the tangy smell of oranges. They were smells Rose was used to, and liked. This was living, no matter what the better-class people thought.

'This way, Rosie girl.' Charlie stopped to introduce her and Rose was flattered at the whistles she got. One big man put an arm around her and Charlie growled for him to get his big paws off her. The man said amiably, 'No offence meant, Charlie,' and Charlie replied, 'And none taken, Fred.'

And Rose discovered this was the way of the market people, brash, kind, fighting with words one minute, all forgotten the next.

Charlie stretched some thin rope from pole to pole and on this he hung coats and better dresses. The rest was tumbled in a heap. Rose began to sort them into piles, underwear and blouses and dresses, but Charlie jumbled them all up again. 'They like to poke through them,' he said, 'seems more like a penny dip. They don't know what they're going to find.'

Rose had thought they were much too early but by the time everything was on the stall there were quite a number of women milling around.

A girl came rushing up. 'Charlie, I want a blouse, I'm going to the Palais tonight. Cora Letts tore me only good one off me back last night 'cos she thought I was making eyes at her old man. Making eyes at 'im! Cor, I'd want me brains examined, wouldn't I?'

Rose pulled out a white silk one with lace trimming. 'How about this?'

The girl gave her a scathing look. 'Wi' my skin? I'd look like a bloomin' corpse. I want a bobby dazzler one, sommat that 'ud make Bobbie Bunker sit up and take notice. Get me?'

'What about this one?' Charlie held up a blouse patterned in bright colours, puce, a vivid green, royal blue.

'Just the ticket. I'll give ya threepence for it.'

'No, you won't, it's a tanner.' Charlie grinned. 'It belonged to the Queen of Sheba.'

'Oh, yeah, and who else? Hi, it's got a button missing.'

'It's in the British Museum, one of the relics.'

The girl laughed. 'You're a relic, chuck, but I love you.' She handed over the sixpence for the blouse. 'If Bobbie Bunker doesn't take me home tonight I want me money back.'

'That's a promise, Daisy. Just don't do anything I wouldn't do.'

'Chance is a great thing. Ta-ra, be seeing you.' She hurried to a vegetable stall, where customers were waiting for her.

Charlie shook his head, smiling. 'She's one on her own is Daisy. She has a different feller every night, most of them married. I'm surprised she doesn't have more black eyes than she does. Hello there, Mrs Higgs, what can I sell you this morning?'

A few more women came up and clawed among the

garments. Charlie began his spiel and soon he had a sizeable crowd.

'Here you are, girls, dresses straight from Paris. Here, Maggie, this one'd fit you. Give me a couple of bob for it.'

'A couple of bob? I use better stuff than that for floorcloths.'

'All right then, I'll give you something that'll make your old man sit up and take notice.' Charlie held up a huge pair of pink flannelette bloomers. 'There, Maggie!'

'I'd get me old man in them an' all, keep the both of us warm in bed!' There was a burst of laughter. 'If they're cheap enough I'll have 'em, Charlie, make the little 'uns some knickers.' Charlie told her threepence and she took them.

'And now this is very special, a Sunday best go-to-Church dress, belonged to one of the crowned heads of Europe.'

'My old man crowned me last night,' a woman quipped. 'With the chamber pot!' This brought another burst of laughter.

The patter went on between Charlie and the women, and Rose, who had thought there was more talk than selling going on was surprised, when the crowd drifted away, to find out just how many of the garments had been sold, and although Charlie had insisted that the women liked to titivate blouses and dresses themselves Rose noticed it was the things that could have done with a bit of renovating that were the ones left. There were blouses that were faded, a pink one and a blue one and a pale green that was almost white in parts, there were dresses that were frayed at the neck, which Rose felt could have been made saleable with perhaps a velvet binding and the addition of a lace-edged jabot.

Charlie had once given her a large bag of bits – pieces of lace, of ribbon and some scraps of velvet, cut on the cross, and some squares of white chiffon, which he said might come in for trimming up the dresses of the girls. Rose decided if these faded blouses and tatty-edged necked dresses were not sold by the end of the day she would ask to take them home and see what she could do in the way of renovation.

When they were not sold Charlie agreed to her suggestion and said he would bring them round to her home. Then he pressed three shillings into her hand. 'We've had a fairly good day, Rosie, you've brought me luck. If I get more I'll give you more.'

'But, Charlie, three shillings is half of what I would get at the laundry for a whole *week*. And I really haven't done very much.'

'You've done a lot,' he said softly. 'It was good to have you here.' Then he added briskly, 'Now come on, let's get cleared up, there'll be no more done today.'

Rose was full of her day in the market, just as she had been when they went round the houses.

'They're such marvellous people, Ma, both the customers and the market people. Gran had given Charlie some bread and cheese for us and people from the fruit stalls brought me oranges and apples and pears and bananas. Here, I've brought them home. Mind you, they won't do it every day. Charlie said it was sort of for my christening. Oh, I love it, love it, I can't wait for tomorrow. Tonight I'm going to renovate some of the dresses and try and dye one blouse. I did have some of that pink dye left. If it's all right I'll get some dyes for the other blouses.'

'You're not doing any renovating or dyeing tonight,' Lizzie said. 'It's the concert. You'll have to go to look after our Alice and Judith and especially our Tommy. He's got some mischief in his mind, I can tell by his face.'

It was the Girl Guides' concert and families were expected to give their support. This year it was 'Ali Baba and the Forty Thieves'. Alice was furious because their cousin Effie, Aunt Maude's daughter, had been chosen to be one of the forty thieves. 'She's so cocky about it,' she said, 'you'd think she was a blooming film star!'

None of the children liked Effie. She was sneaky and all had suffered at one time or another through her tale-telling. Tommy had never forgiven her for snitching to the park-keeper about him and his friend climbing trees, nor for lying and saying he had stolen three birds' eggs.

In spite of denying it vehemently to the park-keeper he had had the man's stick across his back. Tommy ever since had been awaiting an opportunity to get even with Effie.

He had said darkly he hoped she would develop mumps or measles or something before the concert, but Effie remained her usual fat, stolid self and had come around the night before to let them see her costume. The baggy trousers were made from old flour bags, dyed red, her sash was a red and white knitted scarf and her turban a piece of old sheeting. Alice had said cattily, 'It's a good job they're not all as fat as you or the stage would collapse.'

Lizzie had asked how they were going to pack forty thieves on to the little stage and received a scathing look from Effie.

'Of course there won't be forty, silly.' She eased the scratchy flour bags from her plump thighs. 'We could only get four earthenware pots so the four of us will run across the stage, round the back of the curtains and on to the stage again. We do this ten times so it makes it *seem* there's forty.'

'Well, and who taught you that four times ten makes forty?' Tommy asked nastily, and got a push from Lizzie.

In spite of the ill-feeling there was always something exciting about going to a concert and they were all ready to leave an hour before it was due to start so they could get in the front row.

They were at the door when Lizzie said, 'Just a minute, our Tommy,' and held out her hand. 'I'll have what you've got stuffed up your jersey.'

Tommy swore he had nothing and looked as innocent as the new baby.

Lizzie reached over and pulled out a pea-shooter. '*And* the peas,' she said.

'Aw, Lizzie,' wailed Tommy, 'I wanted to take a pot-shot at Effie.'

'I know you did, and I'm telling you now, and this goes for

you too, our Alice and you, Nancy *and* Judith, if I hear of any trouble from you I'll knock your heads together. Rose, I expect you to see they behave themselves.'

'Yes, Lizzie,' she said, but knew there would be no tale-bearing from her.

They managed to get in the front row, and so did Aunt Maude. The noise inside the hall was deafening. Kids galloped up and down the gangways while their mothers screamed at them to come and sit down. Rose could see her aunt's mouth moving but could not hear a word she was saying. And Miss Potter, who was playing the piano, might just as well have been playing a dummy keyboard for all the impression she was making. But when a man appeared and asked for silence, saying the show was about to begin, the only sounds were the cracking of monkey nuts and some of the children sucking oranges.

Tommy gave Rose a nudge and when she looked he was grinning broadly and indicating a pea-shooter in his right hand. She mouthed 'no' and he mouthed 'yes' . . . and the concert began.

After the show had been on some time there was a rattle of chords on the piano by Miss Potter, and the thieves appeared, dedicated looks on their faces as they strained to clutch the pot-bellied jars to them.

At first the four panting girls were so spaced there was always one going behind the curtain as the next one appeared on the stage. But gradually, the ranks closed up so that at times the stage would be empty, and the audience, who had been counting the thieves, would hold their breath until the next one appeared.

The girls had gone round five times and breaths suspended waiting to chant 'twenty-one', when suddenly there was a great crash behind the curtains and voices wailing, 'Oh, me arm, oh me leg, get off me hand . . .'

Three anxious mothers jumped up and thrusting their way along the rows, their feet crunching on a carpet of monkey nut shells made their way to the stage and disappeared behind the curtains.

Aunt Maude said, in her expressionless voice, 'If them vases have broken they could all be lying there with their bloody throats cut.'

'I hope Effie's has,' Alice said with feeling.

But Effie was the only one to emerge from the disaster. She came tottering on, her turban awry and her short wiry hair sticking out from underneath it like sore fingers. Her striped sash had slipped up under her armpits and she clutched at the waist of her flour-bag pants with one hand, while the other frantically held onto the vase, that was now minus a lip.

Effie plodded on, her breath rasping in her throat, sweat dripping from her chin. By the time the audience reached 'thirty' she was steaming, her eyes had a glazed look and she was definitely beginning to flag.

Young Judith whispered, 'Poor Effie.'

Tommy said, 'Poor Effie nothing,' and aimed the pea-shooter. The pea caught his cousin on the cheek and, with a feeble cry she clapped a hand to it. The pants, without support, began to slip, then the vase slipped. It fell with a thud and rolled towards the back curtain. As Effie bent to retrieve it the flour-bag pants slid to her ankles, displaying a plump pink bottom.

The target, for Tommy, was too good to resist, but as he raised the pea-shooter once more Judith said, 'Poor, poor Effie,' and with a shamefaced grin at Rose he lowered it.

Aunt Maude just sat there impassive, as though a display of her daughter's pink bottom was an everyday occurrence.

After the show Tommy and Alice solemnly shook hands, no doubt feeling that justice had been well and truly done. But when they went galloping on ahead Judith, clutching Rose's hand said, 'I would have cried if I'd been Effie,' and Rose, hearing the tears in her young sister's voice felt ashamed that she had found a satisfaction at Effie's come-uppance.

Chapter 5

The following evening Rose worked on the unsold garments she had brought home from the market, dyeing two faded blouses to a soft pink and putting trimmings on the rest. To her delight they sold quickly the next day.

She loved the market, liked the stallholders and the customers, but after a while she began to feel restless. The customers were inclined to treat her as a kid sister of Charlie: it was him they wanted to serve them. She needed something to handle that was her own. If only she had sufficient money to buy material she would make garments, but every penny she took home was needed.

When there was a lull at the stall she would scribble dress designs on pieces of scrap paper. One day Charlie picked one up and said, 'Hey, what's all this then?'

When she told him he put an arm across her shoulders. 'Poor old Rosie, you've really got it bad, haven't you? We'll have to see what we can do about getting you some material.'

'Oh, Charlie, do you think you could? Something cheap?'

He wagged a finger at her. 'I'm making no promises mind, so don't get all excited. And it could be weeks before I pick up something.'

Three days later Charlie turned up at the Buildings with some rolls of material. 'Salvage stuff,' he said. Although all were singed at the edges and had watermarks the middle parts were untouched. One roll of white muslin was patterned with sprigs of forget-me-nots, another had lavender stripes with polka dots between the stripes. The other rolls consisted of a deep pink marocain, one in saxe blue and a serge in chocolate brown.

'So there you are, Rosie girl, you can get your teeth into that lot. It was cheap, works out about threepence a yard so you should get a good profit from whatever you make up.'

Rose fingered first one and then another of the materials. Easter was ahead. The majority of women made an effort to get new dresses for their children, even if it meant them getting into debt. Not that she wanted them to get into debt, it would save them that if she could sell the garments at a price they could afford.

'I'll need to make a lot,' she said, 'so I can sell them at rock-bottom prices.'

'That's daft,' Lizzie exclaimed. 'You don't build up a business that way. It doesn't say because you got the material cheaply that you have to sell the made-up garments for next to nothing. Treat your material as though you'd paid full price for it. You make your profits from getting your stuff at bargain prices.'

Gran Eagan, who had come in unnoticed, bustled forward. 'I've been listening to the lot of you and you're all behaving as if you had a factory. You can't even think in terms of making up a lot of garments. There's the cutting out, the stitching, the finishing off, the pressing –'

'But don't you see, Gran, I have to make a quantity if I'm to make any profit at all,' Rose persisted. 'Oh, I wish I *did* have a factory . . .'

'If wishes were horses beggars would ride,' retorted Edie. 'That's the trouble with young folk, they want to run before they can walk. Start by making a few garments and see how you get on. That's *my* advice.'

'And it's sound advice, Rosie,' said Charlie. 'Alice and Nancy and even young Judy can help with the finishing off.'

Although her mother's treadle machine was old and used mainly for patching, it stitched well if looked after. Both Alice and Nancy could use it, so that was one big problem settled.

Rose worked at an astonishing speed and with the help of the girls – and even Gran who did some buttonholes, she had completed, at the end of two days and working late at night, ten dresses for small children, ten for older girls and six blouses for women. When it came to pricing she reckoned one and elevenpence for the small sizes, two and eleven for the larger ones and three and eleven for the blouses. Which had Lizzie almost shouting her head off.

'You're not fit to go into business, our Rose. You're giving the stuff away. I'll price them.'

Rose insisted that *Lizzie's* prices were too high, and in the end a compromise was reached with Charlie coming into the argument.

'I always think of Mr Rosenberg's maxim of small profits and quick returns, but even he would point out that you have to take into account the cost of your thread, your lace, and ribbons and buttons, plus the coppers you've given the kids for their help. And *you*, Rose, have to be paid for your labour, as well as Lizzie.'

In the end the prices were fixed at two and eleven, and three and eleven, and six and eleven for the blouses. Rose wanted to round the figures off but Charlie said that two shillings and elevenpence sounded much cheaper than three shillings.

Rose had reason afterwards to be glad about these prices because within half an hour of putting them on the stall every garment was sold. 'We're in business,' she said, hugging Charlie. 'I'll start making some more.'

To Rose's surprise the first opposition to her garment-making came from her mother. Rose had been in the habit of washing the lino in a morning, rubbing it dry and doing the cutting out on the floor, which gave her more room. This had worked all right while Sally was in bed, but on the second morning she was up and nursing the baby she complained about the mess.

'Well you'll have to put up with it, Ma,' Lizzie snapped, 'and that's it. No one's disturbing you.'

'Rose keeps asking me if I'll get up while she moves my chair.'

Lizzie and Rose exchanged helpless glances and Rose said gently, 'I must do this cutting out, Ma, but I'll be as quick as I can.'

That afternoon when Sally had gone into the bedroom to lie down Lizzie said to Rose, 'I hadn't realised just how spoiled Ma is, and we're the ones responsible. She's going to get a rude awakening one of these days because I'm going to rebel. She's going to have to get off her backside and do some washing-up and cleaning.'

Rose shook her head. 'It's too late for her to change. If only we had an extra room, or a small shed where I could cut out.'

'Well, we haven't,' Lizzie snapped. 'So get on with it.'

The next lot of garments sold just as quickly as the first. Charlie started teasing Rose, saying she would soon need to have a stall of her own. She said she hoped that after Easter she would be able to start paying him for the material and the money he'd put out for buttons and threads.

'Leave it for the time being, Rosie. I could say I'll stand you the material but that would give a false impression. You've got to learn about costs. You know what they say about business, you should expect to make a loss the first year, hold your own the next and start making a profit the third, that is, if you're any good.'

'Oh, I'm sure we've made a big profit with what we've already sold.'

'I hope so, kiddo, I hope so.' Charlie gave her an affectionate grin. 'If confidence will get you anywhere you'll go right to the top.'

Rose and the girls stitched frantically every minute they could find and on the Thursday before Good Friday the last batch of garments were on the market stall by eight o'clock in the morning.

At half past they were sold out. 'Astonishing,' Charlie said. 'Seems to me I'm wasting my time selling secondhand clothes when the new stuff vanishes as quick as a conjurer can wave his wand.'

Lizzie, who had come with them to the market to do some shopping retorted, 'Yes, but you don't have sunken eyes or bleeding finger ends, all you have to do is to pick your goods up, put them on the barrow and be ready for selling the next day.'

'All right, I take back all I said. Anyway you can give your eyes and your fingers a rest tomorrow.'

Rose, with a feeling of being unable to unwind knew if the next day had not been Good Friday she would have started cutting out more garments. But Good Friday was a Holy day and no one was allowed to stitch on even a button.

On the Saturday morning Rose had her first lesson in finance, and was astonished when Lizzie, after totting up all the figures said they would need to make up all the rest of the material before showing a profit.

'That can't be,' Rose declared. 'Look at all the money I took in the market, for the dresses *and* the blouses –'

'Yes, but look what's had to be paid out. There's the rolls of material and all the extra trimmings Charlie bought – I've put his money on the dresser for when he comes. Then there's wages I've set aside for both of us and pocket money for the girls. And they've earned it, they've worked damned hard.'

'I know but I feel I haven't made very much, not for all the work that's been done.'

'You've gained one very important thing, Rose – experience. You'll know in future how to price your goods. And don't forget, when you make up the rest of the material you'll have money in hand. Cheer up!'

Rose decided to use the brown serge first to make up some of the new coat-dresses. Once started she got excited about it. She made one to button up the side and stitched cream braid in a zig-zag pattern around the neck and cuffs. On another she put cream lapels and cuffs. She made several more using different coloured braids, fine ones and heavy ones, and varying the patterns. The one she liked best had great detail at the waist and up the sleeves in a fine silk coffee coloured braid. It took her a long time to do and she had Lizzie scolding her.

'You're mad, our Rose. Not only are you spending too much time on them but they won't sell in the market. You need a shop in a better class district for that type of stuff.'

'Better class people come into the market,' Rose insisted. 'And they, like other women, are looking for bargains.'

'But you can't sell those as cheaply as the other dresses you made. Now you *can't*, Rose. Be sensible. You'd far better start making up the marocains for the girls who go to the Palais on a Saturday and want to be dressed up a bit.'

Rose started on the marocains.

Unhappily Lizzie was right. Although the majority of the marocain dresses sold not one of the coat-dresses found a buyer. Women fingered them and admired them but asked when they would have a chance to wear classy stuff like that. Why didn't Rose make them something more 'everyday like', but a *little* bit dressy. She promised she would, in time. But she still kept putting the coat-dresses hopefully on the stall.

They still remained unsold and Rose was beginning to feel despairing about them when a dapper, elderly man came up to the stall and swept off his black homburg hat. The top of his head was bald but he had a thick fringe of silvery hair that curled up at the ends, reminding Rose of a professor in a film she had once seen.

He greeted Charlie. 'How are you, my boy?'

Charlie's whole face lighted up. 'Why, Mr Rosenberg! What are *you* doing here?'

'I knew I would give you a surprise. I've been further North to do some business and broke my journey to see you. I called at your home and your mother told me it was here you would be.' Mr Rosenberg spread his hands and beamed. 'And so, here I am.'

Rose was fascinated by the man's strong foreign accent.

Charlie said, laughing, 'It's the best surprise I've had for some time. Oh, meet my cousin, Rose Kimberley. Rose helps me on the stall.'

'Delighted to meet you, Miss Kimberley. Charlie is a very fortunate man to have such an attractive helper.' This coming from any other man might have sounded like flattery, but Mr Rosenberg said it with an olde worlde courtesy.

He began to examine the coat-dresses, remarking they were different from Charlie's usual run of goods. Charlie explained they had been made by Rose and at this Mr Rosenberg showed a great deal of interest. He asked the price and when told gave a nod, said Rose had talent and he would like to buy them all. Lizzie, who had come up at that moment protested. She said to Rose, 'I think he's trying to pinch your ideas.'

Rose stared at her in astonishment. 'But Lizzie, this is Mr Rosenberg, he buys from Charlie.' To Mr Rosenberg she added, 'This is my sister, Lizzie.' He raised his hat and acknowledged Lizzie quite unperturbed.

'No, Miss Kimberley,' Mr Rosenberg spoke gently, 'I have no wish to steal your sister's ideas. She has a talent which I feel is being wasted here. I wanted the garments to show a colleague who, I feel sure, would be interested in employing your sister as a designer in his factory in London.'

'Rose is too young to leave home,' Lizzie snapped. Charlie said he felt inclined to agree.

Rose, angry, looked from one to another. 'Anyone would think I was a five-year-old. I'm old enough to speak for myself.' She turned to Mr Rosenberg. 'And I should like to discuss the matter with you, if we could find some other place.'

Charlie, looking a little shamefaced, said, 'Perhaps you could come home with me after the market's over, Mr

Rosenberg. It's something that Rose would have to discuss with her parents.'

As it happened Mr Rosenberg was unable to stay. He had to get back to London, but he told Rose if she needed any advice concerning her work to come to London and he would be pleased to discuss it. To Charlie and Lizzie he added, 'And the invitation of course includes you too.'

Lizzie left in a huff, Charlie said he would walk with Mr Rosenberg to the top of the market, and Rose was left fuming.

When Charlie came back she rounded on him. 'I thought you at least would have been on my side. Lizzie has no right to try and take over my life. I've lost a sale of all those dresses through her.'

Charlie soothed her. 'I'm sure she thought she was doing it for the best, Rosie. After all, you can't chuck everything up and go haring off to London at the drop of a hat. You must know in your own mind that your Ma and Dad wouldn't let you.'

Rose, talking to them of Mr Rosenberg's proposals, caused the flare up of a family row. After all, she was no more than a child. Another ten years would be soon enough – if she was in the same mind then.

'You're ruining my life,' Rose declared. 'It's a chance in a million.'

'Rubbish,' Lizzie said. 'All Rosenberg wants is your ideas, but you're either too stupid to realise it or you won't let yourself accept it.'

'Please, please,' their mother said, all tearful, 'don't quarrel, I can't bear it. Life is too short for quarrelling.'

Gran Eagan said, her expression softer, 'Be patient, Rose, stop wanting to live before you know anything of life.'

And her usually quiet and gentle father said firmly, 'The matter is settled. Rose is not going to London and that is that.'

Although Rose was forced to give in she knew there would come a time when she would go to London, even if it meant heartache. But as that was for the future she would build up the business here and save every penny she possibly could.

Rose had never been one to sulk but that evening she found it impossible to overcome her feeling of animosity towards Lizzie, whom she blamed wholly for spoiling her chances of going to London. But the following evening when they went out for what they called their 'Saturday shopping spree' they were easy and friendly, giggling at silly little things like two kids.

There was something special about mingling with the people thronging the High Street, where most of the shops kept open until midnight. There were few people who had money to spend on anything but necessities, yet on this one night there was an impression of prosperity with the brightly lit shop windows. Women, many of whom wore black shawls and possibly their husbands' cloth caps during the week, sported a coat and hat on Saturday night. Many of the men too discarded their mufflers and wore a shirt with a tie. People who had worked a sixty-hour week, or more, emitted an air of freedom. Flagg Market held a special attraction. This was a street market, different from the one where Charlie had his stall. The stalls in Flagg Market and the shops surrounding them could provide Saturday night 'treats'. Delicious aromas drew the crowd. There was the roast potato man where jacketed potatoes roasted in the glowing charcoal stove. Customers stood around, blowing on their fingers, in between trying to peel back the top of skin so they could take a bite of the hot morsel. And if you happened to burn your mouth you could cool it from the stall next to it with a penny icecream cornet.

Opposite the icecream stall was Mr Heuser's pork shop. This was always packed on Saturday nights and it took Mr and Mrs Heuser and their six children to keep the customers moving. Links of plump pork sausages were festooned on gleaming steel rods, there were red-skinned polonies, black puddings and white puddings, chitterlings, pies, faggots and golden pease pudding bubbling in a pot. People brought their basins to put it in.

But the main attraction for the Saturday night pleasure-seekers was the pork sandwiches. These cost sixpence and were, of course, an extra special luxury.

When Rose and Lizzie were small they would stand with their noses pressed to the window, saliva running down the side of their mouths, as they watched Mr Heuser, in his spotless white coat, slicing pork from a huge joint. Beside him was a bowl full of crispy pieces of skin and next to it a dish of steaming gravy. Mrs Heuser's task was to cut through a bread bun, dip the lower half in the gravy, put on it a piece of pork, a portion of crispy skin and a touch of sage and onion stuffing. After the top half was replaced a piece of greaseproof paper was wrapped round it, and before the customer was outside the door a bite would have been taken out of it.

Rose, who was trying to save every penny she could to further her business said to Lizzie, 'I've decided we're both going to have a treat tonight. Would you like a pork sandwich or a fish and chip supper?'

Both girls looked towards the fish and chip shop a few doors away, where for sixpence too, one could get a whole haddock, fried golden in batter, chips and mushy peas, the peas cooked with a ham bone for flavour. Alternatively you could have, instead of chips, potato fritters. These had a crisp batter, and always seemed to taste of roast beef dripping.

'Oh, isn't it awful,' Lizzie said, 'having to make a choice.'

Rose nodded and the gaze of both returned to the pork shop window.

Mr Heuser, happening to glance up and see them, waved his fork and smiled.

Many people had benefited from the Heusers' generosity. A few sausages wrapped up for a family where the man was in prison, or out of work, through no fault of his own. And yet some of these same people had been part of a howling mob wanting their blood during the war.

It was when news came of the sinking of the *Lusitania*. It needed only one man to throw a brick through the Heuser shop window and shout, 'German bastard' to incite a few people who had gathered. Within seconds a crowd were yelling, 'Let's get him, string him up, string the lot up.'

It was only the arrival of the police that had stopped the mob, but the business was finished. Two years ago they had started up again.

'I'll have a pork sandwich,' Lizzie said, with a decisive nod. They went into the shop. 'Give me the money,' she said, 'I'll get them.' Lizzie was a 'pusher'. The customers were standing four deep. Within a couple of minutes she was in the front line. A boy shouted, 'Hey, Lizzie Kimberley, you were behind me.'

She grinned. 'I'm not now, am I?'

'Cheek!' There was no malice in the word. 'You haven't changed since we were at school.'

'I have you know.' The boy and the one next to him laughed.

Rose liked her sister in this pert, happy, mood, and she always looked so much more attractive. Many a boy had angled after her but she was choosey.

When Lizzie eventually reached Rose, the two pork sandwiches held above her head, she said, 'It's as big a fight to get away from the counter as it is to get to it. Here . . .'

They had both bitten into their 'treat' before they got outside and Rose looking at Lizzie saw a beatific smile on her face. Life seemed very good at that moment.

Rose was just wiping away a dribble of gravy from her chin when someone called their names. They both turned and Lizzie said, 'It's Charlie.' He was pushing his way towards them.

'Well,' he said, looking from one to the other. 'You're enjoying yourselves aren't you? Jimmy should be here somewhere, I lost him in the crowd. Oh, well, we'll come across him. Where do you want to go?'

'We want to stay here for a while,' Rose said. 'We like it here.'

'Right, come on then.'

Although Rose thought electric light was a wonderful invention she hoped the stalls would never use it. There was something eerie and exciting about naptha flares, the flames wavering in the breeze, the smell, the smoke drifting upwards.

They walked in the direction of the statue of William Flagg from whence the street got its name. He had been a benefactor to the town many years before. Rose felt sorry for the statue. The pigeons made it their resting place and the bronze figure was always dirty. When it rained there were rivulets among the droppings on his cheeks, as though William Flagg wept at the indignity of it. There was always talk of cleaning him up, but there never seemed to be any money for it.

Charlie steered them towards a stall where no item cost more than a penny. 'See if we can get something for the kids,' he said.

As well as novelties, such as a monkey on a stick and a dancing paper bear between two sticks, and balloons and toy trumpets, there were household goods like clothes pegs, starch, tins of toothpowder and emery paper. Charlie bought a number of balloons at three for a penny, making all the children alike with their gifts so there would be no fighting.

A short distance away a man began banging a drum and another to play a trumpet. Charlie laughed. 'Old Bill Skillet is back, haven't seen him for months.'

A person could have an aching tooth drawn for a shilling. The music was not only to attract the crowds but to drown the shouts of the person having the tooth extracted. It was something Rose would never watch. When any of the children had a loose tooth to come out Gran would attach a strong piece of thread around it, fasten the thread on the handle of a partly-opened door, and when you were least expecting it she would bang the door shut and out the tooth would come. She hoped she never had a tooth out by Mr Skillet's methods. The pincers he used were enough to make you feel faint!

They stopped to listen to a bearded man in a top hat selling a 'miracle' elixir, but Rose left them to look at ribbons and laces. When she was about to return she stopped in her stride. Charlie had his arm across Lizzie's shoulders and Lizzie was smiling up at him. She looked radiant and Rose, to her surprise, felt a twinge of jealousy. She tried to dismiss it, but it remained, taking some of the shine from the evening. And yet, Charlie in no way resembled the man of her dreams. She would not want to marry him. It was just that – well, he fussed her a little, made her feel she was someone special, and it was good to have someone who cared.

The people from the second house of the music hall had spilled into Flagg Market. A man with a barrel organ came on the scene and as he turned the handle, churning out the tune of *Lily of Laguna*, three couples, the worse for drink, began teasing the red-jacketed monkey. Then one of the women began to dance, picking up her skirts and trying to kick her height. She fell on her back and there were roars of laughter and ribald remarks.

Charlie said, 'Come on, time to leave, they'll start fighting any minute. Let's get you two out of here.'

Chapter 6

Normally, Rose and Lizzie would go before midnight to the meat market, where the remaining meat was auctioned off, the butchers having no means of storing it. This week Charlie had managed to get them two rabbits, so they were fixed up for their Sunday dinner.

Charlie walked home with them. In spite of the lateness of the hour there were plenty of people about. There always were on a Saturday night, and always plenty of noise. Further along the street a drunken man lay in the gutter, laughing uproariously as a companion tried to get him to his feet. Raucous voices came from alleyways. Shawled women stood in doorways, no doubt waiting for their husbands to return. In some homes the wife and children would be without food but the husband would still have his beer on a Saturday night.

A window in the Buildings suddenly shot up and a head appeared. It was Mrs Beeby. She began shouting abuse to Milly Munroe who was standing below talking to two men.

'You there, Milly Munroe, you filthy whore! You leave my old man alone or you'll feel the weight of my foot up your backside.'

Milly, in a scarlet dress, the neck low-cut, laughed up at her. 'Who'll help you, Beeby me darlin'? I could black both your eyes in the time it'd take you to raise your blooming foot, you big fat bag!'

'Just you watch out, that's all.' The head was withdrawn and the window slammed shut.

Charlie grinned. 'Heaven help Willie Beeby with a woman like that. Nag, nag, nag!'

'She nags because of having a husband like Willie,' Lizzie retorted.

Charlie knuckled her under the chin. 'But you wouldn't nag, would you, love? You'd be sweet and loving to your husband.' Then he added in more serious vein, 'I think you only pretend to be tough, Liz.'

Lizzie's expression softened momentarily then she punched him on the arm. 'Oh, go on with you, Charlie Eagan. I'll tell you something, you must have some Irish blood in you, you've got all the blarney, and those smoky blue eyes of yours could only have come out of Ireland.'

'Smoked by the peat from the bog. Begorrah you could be right at that, Mavourneen.' Charlie's face was one broad grin. 'I'll be away now to see if I can find me bosom friend James McRory. So I'll be bidding goodnight to the both of you.'

Lizzie laughed and went into the Buildings. Rose lingered to watch Charlie walk along the street with his jaunty air. Every now and again he swept off his cap and called cheery greetings to the people he passed.

Lizzie shouted, 'Come on, our Rose, what are you gaping at?' Rose went in and followed her up the stairs. Judging by the raised voices coming from various landings there were more than the usual quota of Saturday night rows in full swing.

In contrast everything was quiet when they reached their own door. Their father was always late coming in on a Saturday evening and when their mother was up she would be chatting to Alice and Nancy, who were allowed to wait for bed until Lizzie and Rose were in. This was only on a Saturday.

When they went in both girls were in their nightdresses sitting by the fire. The mattress and bedclothes were already on the floor. Alice put a finger to her lips and nodded towards the bedroom door.

'Dad came home early, Ma had a headache. He's gone to bed. They said to say goodnight to you and not to make a noise.'

'We're not thinking of dancing a fandango,' Lizzie said drily.

'What's a fandango?' Nancy asked.

'Never mind, make some cocoa then we'll get settled for the night.'

Alice went to get the enamel mugs. 'Did you bring us anything?'

'Charlie sent some balloons, but you'll get them in the morning. And think yourself lucky to get anything. Now – shut up, I'm tired.'

'I'm not saying anything,' Alice protested, her voice rising.

'Shut up, will you? You'll have your father out.'

They drank the cocoa with Alice and Nancy asking questions in whispers, as to where they had been and what they had seen.

But all Lizzie would say was to wait until morning.

Alice and Nancy slept at one end of the mattress and Lizzie and Rose at the other. The two younger girls always lay whispering for a while as though they shared great secrets. Most times Lizzie would give them a kick after a while and tell them to shut up, but tonight she said nothing. Rose wondered if she was thinking of Charlie.

The possibility that her sister might be a contender for his affections distressed Rose, yet Lizzie was the last person she would want to begrudge having happiness. She was the one who had done all the caring for the family, who had sacrificed her longing to take a job. Rose decided if Lizzie loved Charlie and he loved her then she must stifle any feelings she had for her cousin.

Alice and Nancy stopped whispering and for seconds there was silence. It was as though everyone in the neighbourhood had settled in their beds. Then suddenly the night erupted into sounds from all over, dogs barking, a tom caterwauling, bawdy singing, some people shouting, a woman screaming. The screaming came from along the landing.

Lizzie sighed. 'The Hardings are at it again. Any minute now we'll be having Clara bursting in.'

Hardly were the words out of her mouth before there was a frantic tapping at the door. 'It's open,' Lizzie called. She got up.

The woman who came in was clutching a bundle and a pair of patent leather boots. In the light from the street lamp she looked distraught. Her fair hair had tumbled to her shoulders and the top part of her dress, ripped from neck to waist, showed a beribboned camisole.

She thrust the bundle and the boots at Lizzie. 'Hide these for me, will you love? They're me best dress and boots. Jack gets into tempers at times but he's gone mad tonight, burning all me clothes. I'll come for these in the morning, he'll be over his temper by then. Thanks, love,' and Clara was away, leaving the door open.

Lizzie went to close it. 'Honestly, doesn't it make you sick. All that yelling and shouting and they'll be walking out in the morning arm in arm.'

Nancy giggled. 'And Clara with a black eye.'

Clara often had a black eye or a bruised face after a weekend but whereas most women would feel ashamed to show themselves after being knocked about Clara flaunted hers with a sort of pride, as though to say her husband did it because he loved her, not because he'd had too much to drink.

She was attractive and a born coquette and with a husband who had flaming red hair and a temper to match it was no wonder they were always rowing.

Lizzie said, 'God, what a place to live in.' She got into bed. 'I wonder if we'll ever get out of the Buildings?'

'You could if you got married,' Nancy said. 'If you married someone rich you could live in Caragan Terrace among the toffs.'

'Get married and have eleven kids like Ma? No thanks.'

'You don't have to have children if you don't want them,' Alice said. She paused. 'Do you?'

'I only know I want to do something with my life – *live* it,' Lizzie retorted, 'before I ever settle down. If I did get married it wouldn't be for years.'

'Lizzie, can I ask you something?' Alice said, a hesitant note in her voice.

Lizzie stifled a yawn. 'Ask it in the morning, I want to get some sleep.'

'I'd rather know now. Is it true that – well, that . . .' she stopped.

'Spit it out for heaven's sake!'

In a rush of words Alice said, 'Is it true that a man puts his thing in your thing to make babies?'

The silence following this was so complete Rose could hear ash from the dying fire pop softly into the pan below.

'It *is* true.' This came with assurance from Nancy. 'I've just told her. Bessie Stacks was telling me all about it this afternoon.'

'Then Bessie Stacks should know, shouldn't she, seeing she's had three kids all with different fathers! But you stay away from her, do you hear, and that goes for you too, our Alice. She's no good.'

'I can't believe people do that.' There was disillusionment in Alice's voice. 'It's – mucky.'

Rose, being a dreamer herself and a romantic understood how Alice felt. She had felt sick when she first knew. It was a shock to discover that the heroes in stories were not knights in shining armour but earthy creatures who planted seed in the girl by a most unsavoury-seeming method.

But as Rose no longer thought of it in the same way, she said gently, 'You'll feel differently when you fall in love, Alice.'

Lizzie hissed. 'You seem to know a heck of a lot about it, our Rose.' To which Rose replied in a whisper, it was what she had read in books.

The neighbourhood seemed to have settled down at last. There was only an odd cry and this in the distance and the gentle rise and fall of her father's snoring coming from the bedroom.

Rose turned on to her side, feeling a quiet pleasure in the thought that Lizzie was not ready for marriage. That meant she was not in love with Charlie. If she had been then she would have wanted to get married. Rose, who had been feeling sleepy became suddenly wide awake. She rolled over on to her back.

This should also apply to *her*. Like Lizzie she was not yet ready for marriage. She had things to do with her life. She wanted to build up a business that would give her scope for all the designs that crowded into her mind. Could one be in love and yet put business first?

Rose tried to imagine Charlie in bed beside her, with her curled up against him, his arm around her. She remembered reading a book where the man and the girl lay naked side by side. At the thought of Charlie's muscular body touching hers a tremor went through Rose. Visualising the act itself had her whole body throbbing. It was the first time she had experienced such a strong emotion and it excited her.

She could understand now how unmarried girls came to have babies. This must *never* happen to her. She must stop thinking about Charlie.

With a small shock Rose realised she had been thinking in terms of being married to Charlie, yet this was impossible. He was already married. His wife could be dead, of course, he had not heard from her for years, but . . .

Rose put Charlie to the back of her mind and began thinking in a determined way of designs for dresses. This would be her main aim in life, at least for the present.

Lizzie stirred, gave a sigh and turned on to her back. Rose, sensing that she too was wide awake, whispered, 'Lizzie, if I can find a shop to rent will you help me to run it?'

'You bet – that is, when the time comes.'

'I want it now.'

'No, it's too soon. We'll talk about it tomorrow.'

'It's not too soon. I want a shop now, I'm going to start looking for one – on Monday.'

'Forget it, you're not ready for it yet. Now stop talking and let me get some sleep.' Lizzie turned back on to her side.

Rose made up her mind she would work doubly hard, save every penny she could and then start looking for a shop to rent. She would show them she could make a business pay.

The following week Charlie brought round some secondhand evening dresses he had purchased, for Rose to see, saying they had come from Paris. Rose studied them with great interest, examining the designs, the stitching, the extra touches, then told Charlie with confidence she could match the work.

He teased her, calling her 'big head', then immediately added, 'No, I believe you could Rosie girl, you have a flair, a dedication. I think whatever you design or make will be special.'

'Oh, Charlie, if only I could get a shop.'

'Be patient, pet,' he said softly. 'Take heed of Edie who said you were trying to run before you could walk. Give yourself six months.'

'But I want to do things *now*.'

'Listen, Rose.' There was a sternness this time in Charlie's voice. 'Many people have rushed into business before they were ready and have failed, gone bankrupt.'

'But how could I fail? If I managed to get a shop with a cheap rent.'

'For the kind of dresses you want to sell it would be no use having a shop with a cheap rent. It has to be in a better class district.'

'All right, I'll look for one. I'll start in a small way and build up.'

Charlie gripped her by the wrists. 'You're not listening, Rose. You *have* to listen. Who's going to guarantee the rent each week or month, who's going to decorate the shop – it will have to be tarted up a little, who's going to pay for the materials for these dresses to stock the shop? Where are you planning to cut them out and make them up? You can't open a shop with half a dozen dresses and promise to supply more in a few days' time. What if you should be ill, who is going to carry on with the work? Now just be sensible and stop and think.'

'I *have* thought about it.'

'But not enough apparently. I was willing to help finance you to get started, Rosie, but I won't carry any debts, not of a size. I can't do it.'

'I wouldn't expect you to, Charlie. I was grateful for what you did. I feel a bit flattened at the moment, but I think you're right.'

'I am right.' Charlie smiled suddenly. 'No hard feelings?'

'No, none.' Rose gave him a wan smile. 'You're good for me. I'm inclined to get carried away. I only wish . . .'

'No wishing, kiddo, from now on it's *doing*. And doing means build up the little business you've started. You have customers ready-made in the market. Keep on with your bread and butter living and put your money aside. You'll soon get a little nest egg, then you can start.'

'There's one thing I would like to do.' Rose spoke tentatively. 'I would like to try my hand at making a good class dress, really good class. Something to my own design. It would be something I could keep and perhaps later make two more, and if I have sufficient money saved I could take them to London to show Mr Rosenberg.'

Charlie looked at her in a half-comical, despairing way. 'By heck, Rosie girl, you've got a stubborn streak in you. You'll get where you want to get all right, no doubt about that, but you'll have a job persuading the family to let you go to London. But I promise you this, I'll help you when the right time comes.'

'Thanks, Charlie,' Rose said softly and kissed him on the cheek.

He stood looking at her for a moment, his expression serious, then he laughed suddenly and gave her a slap on the behind. 'Go on with you, you're a minx. Twist anyone round your little finger you would.'

Rose felt strangely happy.

Charlie too felt happier that night after he had seen Rose home. His feelings for her had been building up recently, and on Saturday evening when he had met her with Lizzie it had taken him all his time to stop himself from drawing her to him and laying his cheek against hers. That was how pleased he had been to see her.

It was her eyes that had haunted his nights recently. They were beautiful, so expressive. There were times when she was daydreaming when they had a dewy, wistful look, as though she could visualise her dreams coming true, yet at the same time wondered if they would ever come to fruition.

When she had been pleading with him that evening, wanting her way over expanding the business, he wished he could have offered her the world. Instead, he had to get angry and scold her. It was the only way to bring her down to earth. And how typical of Rose that she bore him no animosity but gave him her lovely sunny smile. He was big 'brother' to her again and it was best that way. After all, as far as he knew he was still married. Doreen could turn up one day right out of the blue.

Charlie shivered at the thought, yet knew at the same time he would have to see her if he was ever to get a divorce. In the meantime he would go on trying to help Rose, and save all he could for the day he might be able to set divorce proceedings into motion. Nothing must prevent that possibility.

Rose sketched her first 'exclusive' dance dress that evening. She was excited about it. Tomorrow she would try and find time to buy the material.

Unfortunately, she never found the time. They were busy on the stall and there were more demands for the dresses and blouses Rose made, the cheaper ones. She started on some that same night – and was kept at it as the demand increased. Adding to her frustration was the constant complaint from her mother that her life was being disrupted.

The idea of working somewhere away from the Buildings became an obsession with Rose. If she could find a shed she might get an opportunity to make up the special dance dress. She spoke to Charlie about it, to her grandparents and to Lizzie to keep their eyes open, but nothing came of it. The only sheds they knew about were those belonging to people with allotments, and these were in full use. 'One day I'll find something,' Rose said.

It was after this she became determined to look for the material for her special dress. She went to one of the better shops on her own, not wanting Lizzie's opinion to sway her. Rose was not quite sure what she was looking for, but felt she would know it when she saw it.

And she did. It was in a tray of remnants, a sea-green chiffon reduced to half-price because of a flaw in the material. Rose, after being shown the tiny flaw by the assistant, hesitated no longer. The material was just right. She had designed the dress with a long bodice, the skirt to be made up of squares, with the points at the hemline. At the back there was to be a U inset of silver lamé, the U to be surrounded by tiny handmade flowers and leaves. Long flowing ties would be put at the bottom of the U so that when the person danced the material would float. Rose could hardly wait to get back home to start cutting out.

She already had the silver lamé. It was in one of the bags of pieces Charlie had given her, and there was a large assortment of scraps in satins and other materials to make variegated flowers and leaves.

Rose knew the material would be difficult to cut out, and would take time. A wonderful opportunity came two days later when her parents and grandparents were invited to Sam's brother and wife's golden wedding. They would be away for a whole day.

When Edie was shown the material and her rough fingers caught on the threads she said, 'Heavens, girl, you'll never be able to get that cut out in a hundred years.'

Rose gave a confident nod. 'I will, Gran, I'll tack it to newspapers. I've got a stack of them over there.'

Because the material was a challenge and the dress to be a labour of love Rose felt no frustration when her own fingers caught on the material, but she did decide she must rub her hands with fat in future to keep them soft.

Her main problem came in the stitching of the hems of the squares and the flowing ties, all having to be hand-rolled. Seven-year-old Judith, who had nimble fingers for her age, wanted to tackle the making of the flowers, but neither Alice nor Nancy were willing to do so much hand-sewing. It was hard work, they said. Rose had to increase their pocket money.

Because of having to keep the market trade going it was nearly six weeks before the chiffon dress was completed. Lizzie had kept saying that the making of dresses like this was not a viable proposition, they would never be paid for the amount of work, but her praise was as loud as anyone else's when it was completed.

The family oohed and aahed over it, never had they seen anything like it. 'But where will you sell it, Rose?' her mother asked.

'In London, to Mr Rosenberg, I hope. I want to make some more, perhaps another two, then take them.' Then Rose, to stop any protest being made added quickly, 'But that's for the future.'

The dress was wrapped carefully in tissue paper and put away in a chest at Gran's house.

Rose kept on sketching designs for the better dresses but it was weeks before she had a chance of starting to make another one.

One evening when her mother was at a neighbour's, the children were out and Lizzie had gone with a friend to the pictures, Rose's two eldest brothers called. Since they had grown up and slept out there were times when they seemed like strangers to her. Davey, who would be fifteen in a month's time, was quiet like his father. He was apprenticed to a tailor and would be earning his first wage on his birthday.

Frank, who was Alice's twin was a dreamer like her. His headmaster said he showed great promise as a mathematician, but Frank once confided in Rose it was his ambition to go on the stage – as a tap dancer. She had been astonished, and further astonished to find when he gave her an exhibition that he was quite an expert. She wanted to tell the family, wanted them to enjoy his expertise, but he made her promise to keep it secret until he could go for an audition. There was one every Christmas at the Palace Theatre.

Rose, watching her two brothers, thought how little she really knew about their lives. Davey was tall for his age and broad-shouldered. Did he have any secret ambition? Did he think of girls? What would he say if he knew about Frank's ambition to go on to the stage? Rose felt sure he would be against it. Even when they were younger and Rose and Lizzie played with them there was never much fun in Davey. Frank would fool about, but although he was quieter now, no doubt through being with Davey so much, he was always fun to be with at Christmas time.

Rose, looking at him now, knew he was going to be in for a great deal of opposition from the family if he wanted to make dancing a career. She also knew she would be on his side.

A few minutes later Sam came in and he began chatting to the boys, bringing them out about what they had been doing. Then the children came in followed by Sally, and Sam asked Rose to walk round home with him. Charlie had left something for her.

On the way he said, 'What's up, love? You look as if you'd lost a shilling and found a penny.'

She talked about her frustration, not being able to find a shed to work in, and when would she get a shop? Weeks, months, were flying over and she wasn't getting anywhere. When would she start to progress?

'Listen, Rosie,' he said, 'and I'll tell you a story. When I was a lad I played with a boy whose britches were made up of patches. He was quiet, was Josh, never had much to say. They were a big family and when the father was drunk he'd beat the kids, all except Josh. I never knew why. One day when we were fishing Josh said, "When I grow up I'm gonna be a doctor". I laughed and said, "Oh, yes?" Josh drew the cuff of his jersey across his nose and turned his head. "I am gonna be a doctor and neither me father nor anyone is going to stop me". And you know, Rosie, there was something in his eyes then that made me know why his father never belted him. It was a sort of inner light, a superior intelligence, it was the look a man might have who sees into the future. Do you know what I mean? A sort of visionary.'

'And did he become a doctor, Granda?'

Sam nodded. 'He became one of the top operating surgeons in a London hospital.'

'But how could he with his background? It must take a lot of money to become even a medical student.'

'Josh earned it, yes I know it's hard to believe, but he did. While other kids were kicking a ball about Josh was looking for jobs. He would earn a penny or sometimes only a ha'penny carrying luggage from the railway station. He ran errands all over the place, took on many a mucky job, he helped in a slaughter house, and believe me he earned every penny. When he left school he got a job in a hospital, again doing all the mucky jobs. He bought secondhand medical books, asked nurses questions and perhaps because of this look Josh had they gave him the information without hesitation.'

Sam tapped the dottle from his clay pipe, stopped to fill it then went on, 'Then came the day when Josh was there when a child was injured by a runaway horse and cart. He attended to the boy and went to hospital with him. The doctor was impressed with Josh's treatment, said his action had saved the boy's life. And it was this doctor who gave him his chance to study.'

Rose started to speak but Sam held up a hand. 'I know what you're going to say, Rosie – he was lucky to meet that particular doctor, but don't forget, if Josh hadn't been determined to get on, if he hadn't worked and saved every penny –'

Rose smiled wryly. 'In other words I should go on saving and hope one day that *my* "doctor" will come along and give me my chance.'

'He's already come along, Rose,' Sam said quietly. 'Your Mr Rosenberg. He's the one to help you.'

'But Granda, I'm never getting a chance to go and see Mr Rosenberg! You know what the family were like when I wanted to go to London.'

'You'll get there, girl, you'll get there, but all in good time, be patient. When the time comes I'll do all I can to help.'

'Oh, thanks, Granda.' Rose got up and threw her arms around his neck and kissed him. 'I feel better already, you've done me good, I love you.'

Sam sniffed and looked a bit self-conscious. 'Yes, well, a little help is worth a great deal of pity.'

What Charlie had left for her was some rolls of braid, luxury braid, and a note to say he had a treat in store for her and Lizzie. He would be telling her about it the following evening.

Sam declared he knew nothing about any treat, but Rose knew by the twinkle in his eyes it was no secret to him.

The next night Charlie came breezing in and announced he was taking Rose and Lizzie on a charabanc trip to Blackpool on the Saturday to see the illuminations.

'Blackpool!' the two girls echoed awestruck. Then Lizzie said, 'Impossible, who'll look after the kids?'

'Edie's taking over. The charabanc will be leaving on Saturday morning prompt at half-past five and will set off from Blackpool at midnight. Lord knows what time we'll get home.' Charlie was grinning. 'You'll have a good time and you'll be well looked after, Harry Prentice will help me cope with the pair of you.'

'So Harry will be there.' Although Lizzie's tone was casual her eyes showed she was more than a little interested.

Rose glanced at her mother, half-expecting opposition, but Sally was smiling. 'A day out will do both you girls the world of good, and as for *me* I shall have a lovely peaceful Saturday for once without all the clattering of the sewing machine.'

The trip was run by the market traders and Gran had made the tart remark she bet it would be a boozy affair. To this Charlie had replied with a laugh, 'Show me one that isn't.'

'Yes, well, just you see you take care of the girls, Charlie Eagan, do you hear? Remember what your Uncle Adam said, you're not to let them out of your sight for a minute.'

The girls had already promised their father they would behave themselves and Charlie had given his word to look after them. He said now, 'Yes, Ma,' and winked at Lizzie and Rose.

Chapter 7

On the Saturday morning Lizzie was so afraid of oversleeping she had Rose up at four o'clock. By half past, they were washed and dressed and ready to leave, all keyed-up. The waiting was endless. At last they left to walk the two streets to where the charabanc would be standing on a piece of waste ground. Charlie, who was in charge of the list of those travelling, had warned everyone to be there ready to board by twenty minutes past five, or else!

There was as much activity in the streets as there was midday with men on their way to the shipyards and shawled girls and women going to laundry and bakery and factory. The steel-studded boots of the men struck up sparks every now and then as they crossed the cobble-stoned road. When Rose had worked at the laundry she had always found it strange going to work in the dark with the street lamps still lit. She gave a little shiver of excitement. But this time it was for pleasure.

Before they reached the charabanc they heard the sound of beer bottles rattling in crates. Lizzie laughed. 'They're loading up, it's going to be a boozy do all right.'

Although they were early there must have been about twenty people already there of the thirty who would be travelling. There were guffaws of laughter and a few bawdy quips, apparently levelled at Bessie Bracken, a big woman whose whole body wobbled like a jelly when she laughed.

Charlie, a list in his hand hailed Rose and Lizzie as they came up. 'All bright and early and raring to go! And a lovely pair of mashers you look. I've put you in the front seats.'

Bessie called, 'More fun in the back, Charlie boy.'

'That's where I've put *you*, Bessie, so you can get up to all the shenanikins you want.'

She gave a belly laugh, blew him a kiss and told him she loved him.

Some of the men came up and greeted Rose and Lizzie. One said, 'Prettiest lasses on the trip – Cherry Ripe and Alice Blue Gown!'

Lizzie was wearing a red tam o'shanter and red coat. Rose had a knitted woollen cap with a bobble on top that matched the powder blue coat. Charlie had brought both outfits for them, saying they were from one of his best customers, who had worn them once only during a winter holiday in Switzerland. Their mother said the girls looked 'classy'.

Lizzie kept looking around her and at last she said to Charlie in a casual way, 'Did you say Harry Prentice would be coming?'

'I did and here he is now.'

Harry appeared in a pool of light from a street lamp. He had been a gawky boy at school, with bony wrists protruding from jacket sleeves that always seemed too short. Since then he had filled out and was an attractive man with a shy manner and a slow smile. But when he did smile it lighted up his whole face.

Lizzie called to him, 'Hello there, Harry.' He came over and acknowledged both girls with a nod. 'Lizzie – Rose – nice morning, a bit nippy but I think the sun might get out.'

Both girls had brought thick woollen scarves, warned by Charlie that although the cover of the charabanc would be on there would be no side curtains unless it was raining. Rose saw that the charabanc was open to the elements.

All the passengers were in their places by half-past five, much to Charlie's astonishment. 'Not even one straggler,' he said. 'We'll have a thunderstorm, or it'll snow – or something!'

Charlie was seated next to the driver, Rose next to him then Lizzie and Harry and another couple at the end. As soon as the charabanc got under way a group began singing the popular music hall ballads, *All the Nice Girls Love a Sailor*, *Boiled Beef and Carrots* and *Daddy Wouldn't Buy Me a Bow-Wow*.

Charlie, who had been talking to the driver turned to Rose. 'You warm enough, love? Here, tuck your scarf in, don't want you catching cold.' He leaned over her. 'Are you all right, Liz?'

'Yes, fine. Glad I'm sitting next to Harry, he's as warm as an oven.'

Charlie began to sing *Rose of Tralee*. He had a lovely tenor voice and the people let him sing the verse before they joined in the chorus. Lizzie was singing as feelingly as any of the others and when Rose looked at her she gave a nod and a smile. All felt right with the world.

They had left the town and to their right the fires of the blast furnaces of the iron foundry lit up the countryside with a warm red glow, blotting out the starkness of slag heaps. Stars began to appear and as clouds rolled away a crescent moon gave a touch of romance to the night.

The singing soon subsided and many settled for sleep. Charlie put his arm around Rose and drew her head against his shoulder. 'Try and doze, Rosie, you have a long day ahead of you.'

Rose did not want to sleep, she wanted to savour every moment of this new experience. They travelled from North East to North West, over moors where thick-fleeced sheep were the only sign of life, along roads where rock formations could have been figures. She saw the sun come up, the sky at first that lovely delicate apple green, then the burst of flame that changed to gold.

With Charlie's arm around her, his hand covering hers, Rose felt they were the only two people on an island. She wanted the journey to go on for ever.

They arrived at Blackpool just before ten o'clock. All the

passengers had roused when the first glimpse of the sea was announced. It was a glorious morning, the air clear and sharp, the sky a cloudless blue and white horses capping the water. Even before they reached the front there was the pungent smell of seaweed. One woman called they wouldn't need to salt their fish and chips at midday, there was plenty of salt on their lips.

The party decided to split up into groups, but were to meet at a restaurant at half-past twelve where tables were booked. While they were sorting themselves out several men who were touting for boarding houses came up offering accommodation. One man offered bed and breakfast, with a cooked breakfast, for three shillings. Three more offered the same for two and sixpence, a fifth man told them they could have a bed – with clean sheets and a cup of tea for one and sixpence.

Even when they knew the party did not intend staying overnight they insisted on leaving addresses. 'You never know what might happen,' said one. 'You could be stranded if you missed your train. It does happen.'

This prompted Charlie to say to the party, 'Now this is something we must settle here and now, folks. Anyone not at the charabanc by midnight gets left behind, then you *would* have to find somewhere to stay.'

Harry said that once when he came at the height of the season and everywhere was full up a landlady had let him sleep in the bath, on cushions, for a shilling. Charlie grinned and said he had once slept in a bath, without cushions, for sixpence, to which a voice called from the back that he had once slept in a bath – with a blonde – for nothing. There was a burst of laughter and cries of 'You've won, Clarence!'

On this happy note the party split up. Rose wanted to go to the Fun Fair, Lizzie fancied going into the Tower, Harry said he was easy either way. Charlie suggested they walk along the famous Golden Mile, go to the Tower when they came back and leave going to the Fun Fair until the evening. They all agreed.

The Golden Mile was a stretch of promenade where, in front of shops and cafés and restaurants, with a space between, were stalls of every description. Hoarse-voiced traders vied with each other for custom. 'A string of pearls for your ladyfriend for sixpence, a golden slave bracelet for a shilling . . .' 'Come on folks, test your skill and win a prize, three darts for a penny . . .' 'How about a coconut for your lady love, sir? If she drinks the milk she'll have a rose petal complexion, and if *you* drink it it'll put hairs on your chest! . . .' 'Hoop-la, hoop-la, win a silver pocket-watch, three rings for sixpence, step up, step up!'

Harry and Charlie had several tries at winning a coconut but left empty-handed, with Charlie declaring the coconuts were glued to the stands. When Harry announced his determination to win a pocket-watch Charlie warned he was wasting his time, that the wooden hoops would be too small to go right over the display stand. The hoop had to lay flat on the table to win any prize. To the surprise and jubilation of all four, and to the apparent consternation of the stallholder, Harry ringed the watch with the first hoop. The man, quickly recovering from this phenomenon, made use of it, inviting passers-by to come and see the man who had won a silver pocket-watch at the first go! People came crowding around.

Although the watch had never been within a hundred miles of a silver mine it had a loud and lively tick. Harry put it in his waistcoat pocket and patted it. 'That's a start. By the time we go home we'll need a couple of charabancs to hold our prizes.'

'Big head,' Charlie teased.

They rolled pennies on numbers, won a handful each and lost the lot. They licked their way happily round giant cones of icecream, bit delicately at gossamer mounds of pink candyfloss on sticks, gulped down sherbet drinks and ended up with Lizzie at a hot potato stand, declaring she felt famished. Charlie said, 'Your insides, girl, must be made of cast iron.'

Rose was dying to have her fortune told but Lizzie kept steering her away from the various booths, saying it was a load of rubbish. Charlie shooed all three away from the con men with their 'Find The Lady' card game, saying the only one to win was the stooge, put there by the gang to draw the 'suckers'.

Rose was entranced by the noise and colour. Groups of trippers, wearing paper hats bearing slogans of KISS ME QUICK . . . LOVE ME . . . BE MY BABY . . . blew on cardboard trumpets with red and white streamers. One boy blew his trumpet close to Rose's ear, making her jump. Charlie waved a fist at the boy but he was smiling.

Charlie suggested they went to the Tower, where there were 'treats in store', but before they could make for the Tower they came across a crowd circling a piano on a platform, where a young man in a straw boater and blue and white striped jacket played popular tunes. He played with expertise and aplomb, running up and down the keys with all sorts of innovations. The four of them joined in the lusty singing of the crowd.

As each tune ended a man and a girl came round selling the song sheets for sixpence. Harry bought Lizzie, '*Yes We Have No Bananas*' and '*On Mother Kelly's Doorstep*'. Charlie bought Rose, '*Ain't Love Grand*' and '*If You Were the Only Girl in the World*'.

Lizzie seemed to take Harry's choice in good part, saying with a laugh, 'Typical Harry, isn't it? Good job I haven't a pash on him. He hasn't a bit of romance in his soul.' Then she added more soberly, 'Not like Charlie.'

'All men are different,' Rose said. 'Some men can't express themselves. I think Harry's a bit shy.'

Lizzie's head went up. 'Which is just as well, isn't it? I wouldn't want him slobbering over me.'

Rose looked at Charlie – where her sister's gaze had gone, and wondered once more if Lizzie was in love with him.

The pianist was playing again and Rose became absorbed

in the singing. They stayed so long they had to hurry to get to the restaurant in time for the meal.

Afterwards they all decided to go to the beach so it was late afternoon when they visited the Tower. Charlie's promise of a 'treat in store' was justified. There was the aquarium with exotic-looking fishes and marine creatures, a strange mysterious world of waving fronds where fishes would dart from behind small groups of rock formations, striped in blue and green, some spotted with bright red. And there were the seahorses, such tiny things that fascinated Rose.

She watched tumbling clowns and acrobatic midgets, beautiful little people who also seemed to belong to another world. An orchestra played music that had her dreamy-eyed. Then there were the monkeys in the Palm Court that delighted young and old as they clambered up and down the foliage, quaint with their young, old faces.

Rose could have stayed hours, but Charlie urged they must leave. It was getting dusk and they must be outside to see the lights of Blackpool switched on. She was not the only one to give a gasp when the whole promenade became a fantasy world of coloured lights and tableaux of fairy tale characters: Snow White and the Seven Dwarfs . . . Little Bo-Peep . . . Little Jack Horner . . . The Old Woman who lived in a Shoe . . . Cinderella . . .

And a further pleasure for Rose was the lighted gondolas on the outdoor swimming pool. She gazed up at Charlie with a rapturous expression. 'Oh, Charlie, thanks a million for bringing us here. I feel drunk with happiness.'

He laughed. 'We will have a drink later, but first we have the Pleasure Gardens to visit. You want a ride on the Big Dipper, don't you? Come on,' he called to the others, 'let's go.'

Rose loved fairs and was caught up in the atmosphere the moment she heard the music in the distance. It was a cacophony of sound, one tune being played against another from the various organs. She loved the garish colours, the blues, the reds, the yellows of the richly-carved fronts of the organs embellished with gold, the puppet figures playing drums, clashing cymbals – She loved the raucous voices of the men outside the peepshows, and the ones urging people to come and see the 'freaks' – the bearded lady, the lamb with two heads, the chicken with four legs. A man could win two pounds for standing up so many rounds with a mountain of a boxer. Pimply-faced youths took up the challenge.

They all went on the Big Dipper, and although Rose shrieked with the rest when the car seemed about to shoot off the rails as it rounded curves, and her stomach was left behind when they dropped down almost vertical inclines, she nodded happily to Charlie when he suggested staying on for another ride.

They went on the beautiful wooden jumping horses with their flaring nostrils and wide eyes, the girls sitting sideways on the front of the horse, the men straddling the back. There was a brass rail in the middle and Rose clung to it, sure she would fall off when the platform began a mad whirling, but there was Charlie's arm to keep her safe. They went three times on the water chute and were drenched by the spray, but no one cared, it was all part of the fun. They had their insides shook up as they struggled to 'walk' the Cake Walk, with its moving platform and shrieked their way through the journey on the Ghost Train, where weird skeleton figures loomed up in a green light and slimy things touched their faces.

Then Rose climbed a narrow tower with Charlie, shared a fibre mat with him and came racing down a corkscrew slope and landed at the bottom with her skirt over her head. Lizzie and Harry were among the crowd of watchers yelling their delight.

Rose, blushing to her hairline was teased by Lizzie. 'So what did they see, a white, lace-edged petticoat . . .'

'I feel awful, our Lizzie, all those people laughing at me, the men –'

'It gave them a treat. They're probably used to seeing their wives in grey fleecy-lined bloomers.'

'Lizzie! Stop it!'

'All right, where are we going now? We must get some sticks of rock to take back for the kids, we promised.' Lizzie had brought a bag with her for the purpose.

'We'll try and win some,' said Harry. 'I feel my luck's in.'

It was not only Harry's luck that was in but Charlie's too. They won between them both large and small sticks of the red and white striped peppermint rock, with the name Blackpool running through it. Harry presented Lizzie with a large teddy bear and Charlie won for Rose a pert-looking Kewpie doll, which she felt she would treasure for always.

Before they left the fair they had to buy another bag to hold the prizes which they had won on the shooting gallery, the darts, knocking down moving ducks, dropping bombs from miniature aeroplanes on to a certain target and getting a ball on the right spot which would drop a man from a wire ledge into a tank of water. Rose felt sorry for the man who kept dropping into the water. Charlie said he would be used to it, it was a job like any other, but Rose still didn't like it. She urged them away from this game.

Lizzie's cheeks were flushed as she examined the contents of the bags. 'What a haul, I bet the two of you couldn't repeat such luck again.'

There were boxes of sweets, tins of toffee, a red glass vase, tumblers, wine glasses, two tea towels, games of Ludo, of Snakes and Ladders, liquorice-allsorts, half a dozen tea spoons and a music box, which Charlie had presented to Rose. It had not been wound up and when Rose wound it and set it in motion her eyes widened as it began to play, '*If You Were the Only Girl in the World*'.

'Well, would you believe it,' she said. 'What a coincidence.'

Lizzie began putting the things back in the bags. 'Yes, isn't it.' The fact that her voice lacked any animation took away some of Rose's pleasure in the gift. She was going to ask Charlie if he would mind if she gave it to her mother then she saw he was looking at her and there was pleasure – and something else in his eyes, and she decided she must keep it. There were other things her mother could have. There was in fact something to give all the family.

Harry suggested having a drink to celebrate. This brought opposition from Lizzie who pointed out that she and Rose had never been in a pub and had never had anything stronger to drink than ginger wine at Christmas and New Year. To this Charlie said they could have ginger wine in the pub, or lemonade, adding he knew where some members of the party would be, and it would be a grand wind-up to the day.

Rose looked at Lizzie. 'I'm game, if you are?' Lizzie, after some thought, gave in, on condition none of the family knew about this particular spree of theirs.

Harry and Charlie crossed their hearts with great solemnity and swore their secret would be safe forever. Lizzie burst out laughing and stepped out happily.

The pub they went to had a Victorian atmosphere, with red velvet settees, ornate gold mirrors and spittoons. Above the hubbub of chatter and laughter they were hailed from about ten members of the party. 'Over here, come on, we'll make room.'

Lizzie felt an odd excitement as they threaded their way among the tables and knew that lemonade was not the right drink for an atmosphere like this. Nor would anyone countenance such a thing when Lizzie gave their order. 'No one drinks lemonade on a day's outing! You can have port like we have,' said one woman. 'Order it, they're having it,' said another. 'We'll christen them.'

Lizzie's eyes suddenly took on an impish gleam. 'Why not, may as well be hung for a sheep as a lamb.'

'That's the spirit!'

Rose listened fascinated to the good-natured quips around

her as she sipped at the enjoyable port. Big Bessie said to her husband, 'Frankie love, this Guinness still tastes a bit off, I reckon I need another port in it.'

Frankie threw up his hands. 'It's you who's off, Bessie, you've already had three ports in it.'

She gave a belly laugh. 'Yes, well, it's just beginning to taste right isn't it.'

Charlie teased her, saying she'd better watch out – that none of the men in this party were strong enough to carry her to the charabanc, to which Bessie replied, 'That'll be the day, the only one to carry me was me Ma and her back's never been straight since. Come on, Lizzie, come on Rosie, have another port in that. Frankie get them one each.'

When Frankie got up Charlie caught hold of his arm. 'No, Frank, no more for the girls, thanks all the same.'

But Charlie was overridden by some of the others. What was he, a spoilsport? Let the girls have some fun. It was only once a year.

It was perhaps this that made Lizzie feel reckless and agree that she and Rose should have one more each, but only one. She stressed this and she kept to it. Even then her eyes were bright and she laughed a lot, mostly at something Charlie had said.

Rose, to her disappointment, felt stone-cold sober. She wanted to feel merry, like the rest of them, she should feel merry. Why did the port wine not affect *her*? Perhaps she ought to drink Guinness, like Bessie.

The air got more and more hazy, the crowd noisier as some of the people started to sing. Charlie got up, saying he could do with a breath of fresh air. Rose got up too, she would go with him. Harry said they would all go. There were wails from some of the party – why did they have to leave, the night was still young?

'You enjoy yourselves,' Charlie said, 'but remember to be at the chara by midnight. Not a minute later.'

'What happens if I lose me glass slipper?' Bessie called.

'I'll get the prince to get it for you,' Charlie answered with a grin.

'You're my prince, darling.' Bessie blew him a kiss. There was a roar of laughter.

One of the men caught Rose by the hand as she was passing so she was the last to leave. When she was outside Lizzie had her arm linked through Charlie's and was smiling up at him. Harry said suddenly, 'The bags, we've left the bags!'

Rose turned away. 'I'll get them, I know where they are.'

When she went back into the room she was greeted by Bessie. 'Here, love, Frankie brought you and Lizzie a port each. He didn't realise you were leaving.'

Rose picked up one of the glasses. 'I'll have one and you have the other.' She drained the glass. She was urged by Bessie to drink the other one. And Rose did. 'Happy days,' she said, 'see you.'

The fresh air hit her. Her legs all but buckled. She giggled, 'I feel tiddly.'

'Where are the bags?' Lizzie asked.

'I forgot them. Ooops, the drink's gone to my head.'

Harry went to find the bags, came out to say they weren't there and Lizzie said she would go with him to look for them. Charlie said, 'I'll be walking along with Rosie, you can catch us up.' He put his arm around her.

'I want to walk on the sands,' Rose said, 'by the sea. I haven't walked by the sea today.'

'Yes, well, some other time.'

'I want to go now.' She stopped and flung out her arms. 'I want to go *now*, and I want to pledge.' She shouted it. 'I want to pledge.'

'Rose, shut up,' Charlie hissed. 'You can't, there isn't time.'

She went on shouting and a man called, 'Why don't you take her, mate, it's no skin off *your* nose.'

'Come on.' Charlie took her by the hand and dragged her across the road. 'I'll take you on the sands, but for heavens sake shut up, people are staring. They'll think I'm beating you up.'

Rose giggled again. 'I wouldn't mind if *you* beat me, Charlie, but not – not anyone else. Not anyone else, do you under – understand?'

'Oh God,' Charlie said with feeling. He led her down the steps to the beach. At the bottom he said, 'Now wait there, I must go and see if I can catch Lizzie and Harry.'

Rose wandered off, kicking at the sand. She took off her shoes, then her stockings, pushed the stockings inside her shoes, tied her laces together and slung the shoes over her shoulder, as she used to do with her boots when she was a child.

The sand was cold to her skin, but the shiver she gave was one of pure pleasure. It was like being in a dream she had once of dancing along the beach naked. At the time she had felt ashamed of dreaming such a thing, now the thought of dancing by the water's edge without clothes brought a quick surge of delicious tremors. Should she take off her clothes? It would be lovely to feel the cold water on her body. She began to undo the buttons of her blouse.

'Rose!' Her hand was gripped. 'What do you think you're doing?'

'I'm going in the sea.' She giggled. 'All over, right up to here.' She touched her chin.

'Oh, no you're not. Come on, I've lost Lizzie and Harry, I must find them, they'll wonder where the devil we are.'

Rose peered into Charlie's face. 'If I can't go right into the sea can I plodge? Please, Charlie . . .'

Charlie looked into the widely-spaced eyes that were more beautiful than ever with their pleading. His gaze then went to the opening in her blouse where pale flesh showed.

'No, and button up your blouse.'

'Please, Charlie, please.' Rose slipped her arms inside his jacket. 'Oh, how lovely and warm you are, how strong. I love you, I love you better than anyone else in the whole world.'

Oh God – Charlie felt the blood pounding in his head and in his loins at her nearness. He touched the silk of her blouse, then his fingers moved to her skin. He slid his hand inside her blouse, cupped a breast.

'I like you to touch me, Charlie, it's nice,' she murmured. The next moment she had drawn away from him and was running towards the sea, laughing over her shoulder and calling, 'Come on, Charlie, come into the sea with me.'

The unexpectedness of her action caught him offguard, then he was running after her. She was fleet of foot and feeling hampered by his shoes he kicked them off and raced after her. She splashed into the foam-frothed waves before he could reach her. He had been afraid she would rush recklessly into deeper water, and when she stopped and flung out her arms he took time to whip off his socks.

'I love you, sea,' Rose shouted, her head back. 'I love you, world, I love everybody!' She moved forward and Charlie splashed into the icy water and caught hold of her.

'You'll get the hem of your skirt wet, Rose.' He took hold of the hem and lifted it – and touched bare flesh. He drew in a quick breath. 'Here, Rose, catch hold of your skirt.' She bunched it up, taking the lace-edged petticoat with it. 'Come on, Rose, we have to go, there's no more time.'

'Oh, it's so lovely, so fresh, so exhilarating. I want to swim.'

He gripped her arm firmly. 'You're coming out, *right now*.'

She offered no resistance, but when they were on the firm damp sand she eyed him with reproach. 'Why are you angry with me, Charlie? What have I done wrong?'

'I'm not angry with you, I'm mad at myself for losing Lizzie and Harry. Come further up on to the softer sand and I'll dry your feet with my handkerchief.'

When Charlie sat Rose on the sand she lay back and gave a deep sigh. 'I would like to stay here all night, Charlie, can we stay all night?'

'No, we definitely can't.' He began wiping the sand from her feet. They were narrow, delicately-boned. Charlie was surprised that touching them could rouse such carnal thoughts in him. He wanted to feel her body touching his, he wanted to – Rose began to giggle. 'You're tickling me, Charlie.' She curled her foot. 'I've always been tickly on the soles of my feet.' His gaze went to the opening in her blouse. That pale flesh was so tantalising he must touch her, he must.

'Rose,' he said harshly, 'sit up, you must put your stockings on. We have to leave.'

'You put them on, Charlie.' She laughed softly. 'I would like you to put them on, you're so gentle –' She began to sing the song *Charlie is My Darling* – then the words trailed off.

He caught hold of her. 'Rose, come on, here – here are your stockings, now get them on, do you hear?'

But Rose did not hear, she had passed out.

Charlie thought he would always remember trying to get her stockings over still damp feet, pulling them up over pale warm thighs and groping for suspenders to secure them. He was sweating profusely and feeling his emotions had been ravaged by the time he got her to her feet. She was limp, like a rag doll and he had to slap her face to rouse her. All she did was giggle.

He still had his own socks and shoes to put on and he had to prop her against the wall to do so, before taking her up to the promenade. She slithered to the ground and went on giggling.

'Shut up, Rose,' he hissed. 'Or I'll hit you, and I'll hit you harder next time.' Oh, God, he thought, what was he saying.

'Oh, Charlie, you're so funny.' She began to sing again '*If You Were the Only Boy in the World and I Was the Only . . .*'

Charlie picked her up, and partly carrying her got her up the stone steps. She revived a little with all the sounds of activity but kept on saying the lights were smudged. By the time he got her to their place of rendezvous he felt he had gone through a trial of strength. Lizzie met them and demanded, in a rage, to know where they had been.

She looked at Rose. 'What have you done with her? Where

did you take her? I've been nearly out of my mind. What have you done to her, Charlie Eagan?'

'I've done bloody nothing!' he retorted. 'Where were you and Harry? I couldn't find you anywhere and I could certainly have done with your help. Don't blame me for the state Rose is in. She must have had more drink than the two ports I saw her have.'

Lizzie blinked at him. It was the first time she had seen Charlie in a temper. 'I'm sorry, I thought . . .'

'Yes, that's the trouble with a lot of people, isn't it, they think but they don't act. Here, I'll hand her over to you. I have to check the list, and I hope to God they all arrive by midnight because we're certainly not going to hang about for stragglers.'

Harry, who had been standing in the background listening, gave Charlie a worried glance then helped Lizzie to get Rose on to the charabanc.

The last group of the party arrived just after twelve o'clock, singing their heads off. Charlie, who had simmered down by then and was ashamed of his outburst, told them quite amiably to get aboard, and even laughed when Big Bessie said, 'I lost me glass slipper, Charlie, when the clock struck midnight and I had to leave the ball. Will you find it for me?'

'I will that, Bessie, and when I find it we'll drink champagne out of it.'

'With *her* sweaty feet?' her husband said.

Bessie pulled a face. 'You can't take him anywhere, can you? When I was a kid I used to dream of being Cinderella and marrying the handsome prince. And what did I get instead? One of the ugly brothers.' She ruffled her husband's hair and gave him an affectionate grin. 'But you're a bit of all right, Frankie, aren't you. Brings me a cup of tea at five every morning.' She mouthed to the others, eyes raised, '*Five o'clock.* Never misses.'

'All right everyone,' Charlie called. 'We'll get moving.' When he clambered aboard he felt a twinge of jealousy when he saw that Harry had his arm around Rose and her head rested on his shoulder. Charlie wanted to be the one to hold her close. He wanted to apologise for his earlier behaviour. Tomorrow he would tell her he was sorry, try and explain how he had let himself get carried away. That is – if she remembered. At the moment she was lost to the world.

Chapter 8

The next morning was something of an ordeal to Rose. From the moment of waking there had been a dull pounding in her head, which she knew was due to the unaccustomed drinking. What really worried her was not being able to remember what happened after she had drunk the ports. And there had been no opportunity to ask Lizzie, for no sooner were they up than not only the children but their mother had bombarded them with questions about the trip.

Then right after breakfast her grandparents and Charlie arrived, with all the excitement of distributing presents.

It was not until Rose had a feeling that Charlie was purposely avoiding her that the images came to her mind, images of the beach, of splashing barefoot into the water, of . . . Charlie touching her bare flesh.

Hot colour rushed to Rose's face. Surely not, she must have been dreaming. Charlie would never take such a liberty.

When the Sunday morning session broke up Charlie was the last to leave. He had kept giving Rose glances and with a feeling he wanted to say something to her, but did not have the chance, she ran after him, and caught him at the top of the stairs.

'Charlie – can I ask something? Last night, did I do, or say anything to upset you? I must explain that when I went back into the pub for the bags I – well, I drank two ports. Frankie had got them in and –'

'Two? In that short time?'

'Yes, I know I shouldn't have done. They – went to my head.'

'You have nothing to worry about, love.' Charlie spoke gently. He touched her cheek. 'Don't give it another thought.' He lingered a moment, looking into her eyes, then said, 'Be seeing you.'

Charlie had gone down a few stairs when Rose called to him. He came back. 'What is it, Rosie?'

'I want to go to London, Charlie, to see Mr Rosenberg. Will you help me to persuade the family to let me go?'

'Hey, what's brought all this on? I thought you'd given up the idea for the time being.'

'It's months ago since I saw Mr Rosenberg. I *must* go, Charlie, I must start trying to build up a business. If only you and Lizzie would come with me. Please try and help me, Charlie, I don't think you realise how important it is to me.'

'I think I do, Rosie. All right, let me know when you plan to go, but you do realise you'll have to have more than a couple of good dresses to show him – I would say at least four or five.'

'Oh, I will, I will, I'll work like mad now I have the incentive.' Rose flashed him a smile. 'Thanks, Charlie, I knew I could depend on you.'

Depend on him, he thought, as he went down the stairs. Depending on him was the last thing she should do. Thank heavens she hadn't remembered what had happened the night before. If she had, her opinion of him would have dropped pretty low. It had taken all his willpower to stop going any further. An ache came into his groin again as he remembered her pale flesh, the touch of her thigh as he had lifted the hem of her skirt clear of the water. He would certainly have to avoid putting himself in such a position again. Charlie began to wonder if Rose had now remembered what happened, or if she had been ashamed and would not admit to knowing. No, she knew nothing, it was apparent by her manner. Rose could not be devious if she tried. There was such an innocence about her. When he had cupped her breast she had said it was 'nice' having him touch her. Had there been any arousal at all?

Charlie determinedly dismissed all thoughts of the incident, it was doing him no good, no good at all.

When, later in the day, Rose told Lizzie she planned to make some more of the special dresses to take to London Lizzie was all for it, adding it was time they made an effort to get out of the Buildings. 'It's a dump,' she said. 'Sometimes I feel I'm stagnating. What kind of dresses are you planning to make next?'

This was enough to have Rose rushing for pencil and paper. 'These are some of my ideas.' She drew with swift strokes and in seconds there were designs on the paper that Lizzie could see at once had flair. 'This one I'll make in beige crêpe-de-chine. There'll be floating panels at the side, with an intricate pattern of bronze bugle beads and the panels lined with a bronze-coloured contrasting material – perhaps shantung, I don't know yet. I'll know when I see the right material. This one will be in powder blue with white piping, the frills at the neck just touched with white. I'll cut the bodice on the cross so I can get batwing sleeves. I rather like this one – what do you think, Lizzie?'

Lizzie grinned. 'I think you're a genius. Hurry up and get them made. They'll take a few weeks.'

Rose tapped her teeth with the pencil. 'I don't want to wait a few weeks. I wonder if Bessie would help out? She's good at hand sewing and she was saying yesterday she hasn't had any work for some time, with the two dressmakers she usually helps out being ill.'

'Bessie?' Lizzie stared at her sister aghast. 'Have you seen her kitchen? The last time I was in she had an emerald green satin dress hanging on the back of the kitchen door and on the gas stove next to it kippers were frying.'

'Yes, I know, but the amazing thing is she never seems to get a mark on anything. She does some beautiful embroidery, and stitches beads on at an amazing rate. Have you ever noticed her hands, how slender, how beautiful and soft and white they are?' Rose nodded. 'Yes, I shall ask Bessie, I'll buy some material tomorrow.'

Bessie, when asked, agreed at once. 'I'd enjoy sewing for you, Rosie, you have ideas, taste, you just tell me what you want doing.' Bessie laughed. 'Didn't we have a good day at Blackpool. I bet you had a head the next morning! Lizzie was furious because you and Charlie had disappeared and Charlie was mad because he had lost Lizzie and Harry, but anyway, all's well that ends well. You had a right good sleep against Harry's shoulder. Slept all the way you did. What kind of dresses are you planning to make, love?'

Rose, who had gone cold while Bessie was talking, had to pull herself together. 'I'll let you know tomorrow.'

So something *had* happened on the Saturday night. Rose's legs felt weak. Where had Charlie taken her? On the beach? Were the images reality? Had she run along the beach barefoot, splashed into the water, and had Charlie . . .?

Knowing she would never have any peace until she found out Rose went straight to Gran Eagan's house. Fortunately Charlie was in, and alone. Rose told him what Bessie had said then added, 'I want to know what happened, Charlie.' She told him about the images she had had, but not about him lifting her skirt. She felt sure if one thing was right the rest would be.

Charlie, sensing she was groping for the truth decided to lie in part, for Rose's sake as well as his own. After all, she would not be very happy if she knew she had allowed him to take liberties. Yes, he said, she had been barefoot, she had gone into the sea but he had managed to get her out – before her skirt could get soaked. Then she had put on her stockings and shoes and they had gone to where the charabanc was waiting. She had slept all the way home.

Although Rose was relieved at first at Charlie's explanation she began to see herself as behaving in an abandoned way, rushing into the sea. She said, 'I think I must have caused you a lot of trouble, Charlie. I must never drink port again.'

'Drink's all right in moderation, Rosie love,' Charlie's voice was teasing, 'but when you knock two more back as quickly as you did on Saturday night . . .'

'Yes, I know, it was awful, I don't know what made me do it.'

Charlie got up. 'I must show you some dresses and coats a customer dropped in today. Good stuff, you'll like it.'

Afterwards they discussed the London trip and Rose came away feeling happy and excited. If she could get the special dresses made they might be in London by the first week in November. What a day that would be. Charlie said they might need to stay overnight but Rose felt sure her mother would want them back the same day. It would be a bit of a rush because there was so much she wanted to see when they were in London, like Buckingham Palace and the Houses of Parliament, and of course they simply must walk down Bond Street and see all the beautiful shops and the clothes.

Once Rose had bought the materials for the beige and pale blue dresses she knew a feverish excitement to get them made-up. There were tiny buttons to go down the back of the blue dress. Young Judith with her nimble fingers covered the buttons, Nancy stitched them on and Alice hand-stitched slender loops and attached them, all working late at night. There were other garments for the cheaper trade to be finished off. Gran Eagan became furious one morning when she came early and found the younger girls were all but dropping to sleep over their breakfast.

'This sewing business has to ease up, Rose,' she declared. 'Look at them, all with dark smudges under their eyes. What's going to happen if they drop off to sleep at school? They'll get the cane, that's what. They can do a little sewing, but not working overtime. Now that's an order, Rose.'

Rose, despairing, said, 'Yes, Gran, all right.'

Her one bright spot that day was Bessie having finished stitching the bronze bugle beads on to the panels. She must have worked at an unbelievable rate to complete the work, for there were hundreds of beads and an intricate design. Bessie herself was enthusiastic about the dress.

'It's beautiful, Rose. I enjoyed doing the work, you're bloody clever to have worked out such a pattern. You ought to have a shop. I'd work for you if you did.'

'Oh, Bessie, that's what I'm planning to do, I'm taking dresses to London and I'm hoping I can get some orders. I want to make two more dresses, this time for day wear. I saw some lovely material yesterday. It was a very fine flannel in pink, a sort of dusky pink. It would need black accessories.'

Rose's eyes grew dreamy. 'I can see a tall slender woman wearing it. She would have a close-fitting hat with an eye veil and a black fox fur would be tossed over her shoulder.' Rose enacted the tossing of the fur. 'And she would have black patent high-heeled shoes and a patent handbag and there would be a narrow belt on the dress.' She paused and frowned. 'The dress would need something else, something different. Pockets on the bodice?' She shook her head. 'The pockets in themselves would be too ordinary.' Her face suddenly lit up. 'I know. On one pocket could be embroidered in black the word PARIS and on the other ROME. Yes, it would give it a Continental flavour.'

Bessie gave her deep belly laugh. 'You know what would happen don't you? A fella would touch the woman's tits and say "Now where shall I go today, Paris or Rome?".'

'Oh, Bessie, you're awful, and you shouldn't use that word. Anyway, I'm talking about London, the moneyed people.'

'Listen, love, don't think a la-di-da voice and wearing a bowler hat makes a fella any less mucky-minded than one in a cloth cap and a muffler.'

'I'm still going to use my idea, I like it.' Rose grinned suddenly. 'And who knows, someone might say "Now who designed this very attractive dress?".'

Bessie poked her in the stomach. 'You'll do, Rosie. Get

your designs noticed, that's how you'll get to the top. What do you want me to do next?'

To Rose, who had felt so frustrated, Bessie was the spur she needed. Lizzie was enthusiastic about her project but could offer nothing in the way of ideas. The moment Rose mentioned some innovation to Bessie the woman had it at once. Rose wanted to make one more day dress and wanted it in a fine cream serge. She designed it more as a pinafore dress, but with a dropped shoulder line and slit to the waist. Lizzie declared it to be daft – it would look as though the shoulder line had been made too wide. Bessie said, 'I like it, it's different.' The dress, bound with pale chocolate would have a stand-up collar, buttons down the front, and a blouse in pale chocolate to match. There would be a long scarf to loop at the neck. Bessie did most of the making up and stitching of this and the finishing off was perfect.

Rose praised her. 'Bessie, you really are a find. Your work is beautiful.'

'It's a pleasure, Rosie. I enjoy working for you. You're not only generous but so enthusiastic. I've finished with those tightfisted miseries I was working for. I had nothing but grumbles from then – I took too long, I wanted too much for my work. I slaved my fingers to the bone for the buggers.'

Rose put a finger to Bessie's lips. 'Stop swearing, Bessie.'

Bessie grinned. 'I restrain meself when I'm with you because I know your Ma and your Gran won't allow swearing in the house, but it comes as easy as breathing to me. I've stood with me Mam and me Dad in the market since I was a toddler and me vocabulary then, according to me Mam, made the other stallholders' hair curl.'

Rose laughed. 'You should have had Gran behind you. A few clips across the earhole from her and you'd remember that if you wanted to swear you'd do it silently. I do often,' Rose confided. 'I have quite a vocabulary myself.'

'Then you keep it silent,' Bessie said, suddenly serious. 'You have class, Rosie, as well as being beautiful. Oh, yes, you are,' as Rose began to protest. 'You'll have plenty of fellas running after you, but you keep yourself decent, love, you could marry into class.'

Rose was not sure she wanted to marry into 'class'. She was happy with her own kind, happy having Charlie around. She would think no further than that. There was a whole new life to be lived.

When the dresses were completed Rose displayed them on a Sunday morning when all the family were there, and pleaded her case to take them to London to show Mr Rosenberg. There was opposition at once and although Gran Eagan was not so fierce as before the objections to the trip from Sally and Adam were, if anything, stronger. Their objections drowned the pleas of Charlie and Lizzie and Rose. Then Sam spoke up and spoke with such strength they all stopped talking to listen.

'What's the matter with you all!' he exclaimed. 'Look at these dresses, at the work, the designs, and ask yourself if such talent should go to waste. It's over-protective parents like you, Adam and you, Sal, that destroy the chance in life of many a clever lad or lass. Give Rosie her chance, or you'll live to regret it.'

Adam rubbed a finger down the side of his nose, said, 'Well . . .' and Rose knew the battle was won.

A discussion followed in which Charlie stated they would need three days for the trip. There was not only a six-hour train journey each way, but travelling to the East End by tram when they arrived in London. Also, it would be foolish for them to make the trip without the girls having an opportunity of seeing the sights.

This was agreed on after Charlie assured them that Mr Rosenberg would be able to recommend clean and cheap lodgings.

And so three days later they left the Central Station at midnight, with a send-off from the family that must have made other passengers think that Charlie and his two companions were about to emigrate to the other side of the world.

Gran Eagan had the last word as she ran beside the carriage when the train began to move, calling, 'Make sure you've got clean sheets on the bed and watch your money!'

When the train rounded a bend Lizzie and Rose collapsed laughing on to the seat, all set for the big adventure.

Chapter 9

When they arrived in London and began the journey by tram to the East End, where Mr Rosenberg had his premises, Rose became progressively depressed. Where were all the beautiful buildings, the lovely shops? This was no different from home, the tenements, the air of poverty, black-shawled women, men in shabby suits, bare-footed children.

Rose, who was sitting next to Lizzie on the tram, said, 'I don't know quite what I expected, but certainly not this.'

The tram began to slow and Charlie, sitting opposite to them in the gangway, got up. 'Come on, girls, this is where we get off.'

Rose walked slowly, looking about her. Charlie laid an arm across her shoulder. 'Rosie, love, I heard what you said. Every city has its rich and its poor. London's no different. At home you have the Lismond area, where the so-called toffs live and you have the Buildings. Don't be taken in by the look of poverty here, there's plenty of people making money, Mr Rosenberg included. But they wouldn't be making money if they had to pay massive rents. That's why they work here. Later, I'll take you to the West End.' Charlie smiled into Rose's face. 'Then you can feast your eyes on all the things you can't afford to buy.'

Lizzie's head went up. 'But Rose will – in a few years' time, you'll see. I know it.'

'And so do I,' Charlie said softly. 'Now, let us beard the lion in his den.'

After going along a number of back streets where the smell

of garlic from a small café mingled with the stink of rotting vegetables in the gutter, Charlie stopped at a doorway and pointed to the signboard above. 'Here we are.' The signboard was so old and weathered the name Rosenberg was barely decipherable. A narrow passage led them to a flight of rickety stairs, caked with the grime of years. Lizzie sniffed. 'I refuse to believe that any man making money would have an office in a dump like this.'

Charlie stopped and looked down at her. 'Liz, I could take you to Hatton Gardens, where every day thousands of pounds' worth of diamonds change hands, and some of the places are no better than this. Well, perhaps a little cleaner, but certainly there's no air of opulence. Come on.'

A sign on a glass panel of the door at the top invited them to enter. As they went in a middle-aged woman emerged, from what appeared to be a cubby hole under the next flight of stairs, and greeted Charlie, her sallow face alight with pleasure. 'How good to see you again, Charlie.'

'And good to see you again, Hannah. This is my cousin Rose and my cousin Lizzie.'

'You have lovely company.' Her smile welcomed the two girls. 'I'll tell Mr Rosenberg you're here.'

Mr Rosenberg's welcome was just as warm, his handclasp firm. 'Come in, come in.' He pulled up three chairs to his desk. 'Sit down.' To Hannah he added, 'Could you manage tea for all of us, please.' She said yes of course, and left.

'Well . . .' Mr Rosenberg seated himself behind the desk and beamed at them. 'So you managed to get the young ladies here, Charlie. Miss Elizabeth Kimberley, if I remember rightly, and Miss Rose Kimberley.'

'Better call them Rose and –' Charlie paused '– Elizabeth. It's going to make it a lot easier.'

'If I have your permission, ladies?' They both agreed although Lizzie looked a little bit on her high horse. Rose hoped she would relax and not make any trouble when she showed the dresses.

The office was certainly cleaner than the entrance and although it was stacked with files and patterns of material it was orderly. Mr Rosenberg asked about their journey then, perhaps sensing Lizzie's impatience, he said, 'And now, I know you'll be anxious to get on with the business.' He smiled encouragingly at Rose. 'Charlie tells me you have several dresses to show me.'

Charlie lifted the rather battered suitcase they had brought and carried it to the long table under the window. 'Here they are, and I guarantee you'll be impressed. Rose, will you lift them out?'

Rose's heart was beating wildly as she divested the dresses of their many wrappings of tissue paper. What would the verdict be? Lizzie got up to help her, and when she stood back to let Mr Rosenberg inspect them her expression dared him not to be impressed.

Mr Rosenberg's manner became brisk and businesslike. He studied the sea-green chiffon dress first, examining the squares that comprised the skirt. 'Hand-rolled hems . . . you must learn to cut corners, my dear. You could have had these picot-edged, by machine.'

'The flowers couldn't have been made by machine,' Lizzie retorted.

'No.' Mr Rosenberg's reply was softly spoken. 'You are right there, Elizabeth. They're very well done, but the thing is –' he turned to Rose '– in the range of goods I sell it would be impossible to pay you for so much work, the price you *should* get, I mean. I'm being fair with you. You must know these things. I go in for small profits and quick returns. Charlie knows this.'

Charlie nodded. 'Yes, I told Rose, but these dresses are – well, I feel they're exclusive. There must be a market for them.'

'Oh yes, but they're in a different world to mine. Don't get me wrong. I can sell them – but –' He moved to the next dress and examined this one more carefully than the first. He went from that to the others and by then Hannah had come in with the tea.

'Come and sit down,' he said, 'we can talk over our tea.'

He took a long drink then put the cup down carefully and looked at Rose. 'I can see you're disappointed. Don't be. I'm going to repeat to you now, my dear, what I said to you when we first met. You have talent, you have exceptional talent, and I would like it to be channelled into the right source. I feel quite sure I could get you a job in a factory as a designer, but one where they mass produce.'

'No.' Rose shook her head vigorously. 'That is something I quite definitely do *not* want. I've been "mass producing" in a small way with the dresses and blouses we sell in the market. It bores me. My head is full of designs. I want to make clothes that are different, like these,' she indicated the dresses on the table. 'And if you are not interested, Mr Rosenberg, then I shall take them elsewhere.' She was near to tears and wanted to go. She stood up.

Charlie, distressed, took hold of her arm. 'Oh, Rose, love . . .'

Mr Rosenberg said quietly, 'Try not to get upset, Rose. I can buy these dresses from you, but they won't be at a price you expect to get. I'm a businessman. I have to sell to someone else and that person has to make a profit. What you really need is to be working in an exclusive fashion house, to be trained, but you would have to serve an apprenticeship for something like three years.'

Rose's tears stemmed. She looked up eagerly. 'Oh, that would be wonderful. I would like that, I would like that very much. Do you know of any opening, Mr Rosenberg? I wouldn't mind how hard I worked.'

'It would mean leaving home,' Lizzie said shortly, 'and you know that Ma wouldn't allow you to do that, nor Dad. So that's out.'

Rose gave a despairing wail. 'Am I always to be thwarted? Why can't I leave home? Other girls do.'

'Other girls aren't you, so leave it at that, our Rose.'

Mr Rosenberg, his fingers steepled, was looking from one to the other. Rose, catching his glances, appealed to him. 'What can I do, Mr Rosenberg? How can I achieve my ambition?'

Charlie, still looking upset for Rose, leaned towards the other man. 'Let me explain something. Rose fancies having a dress shop. If she cuts corners, as you suggest and speeds the sewing side up a bit, she could sell cheaper dresses, but still be doing the designs for them. Later, when she has the business going she can sell better dresses, and better ones still, going up the ladder.'

Mr Rosenberg regarded him gravely. 'Charlie, people who have a creative side don't often have business acumen.'

'I'd be the business acumen,' Lizzie said. 'I happen to have a flair for figures. There'd be no problem there.'

'But you do have a problem, Elizabeth. If Rose was designing individual dresses you would not be turning out enough to make the business pay. Not if you want to sell them cheaply. You would have overheads, people to pay for the making up. Remember the saying that in the first year of business you make a loss, in the second you hold your own and in the third you start to make a profit.'

Lizzie challenged him about it taking three years to make a profit, but when she tried to prove the fallacy of his words he held up a hand. 'You can talk economics as much as you like, Elizabeth, but this is the basic fact of any business. I still say if Rose wants a dress shop then she must mass produce, at first anyway.'

Rose, her mind made up said, 'At this moment I want some money. What would you be prepared to give me for these dresses, Mr Rosenberg?'

He weighed it up and offered a figure which had the three of them looking at one another, appalled. Lizzie said, 'It's sheer robbery and you know it. You'll get a good price for them, easily. You don't care about Rose's talents, just what you can get out of her.'

'You misjudge me, Elizabeth.' There was a sadness in Mr Rosenberg's eyes. 'I am a businessman, but I'm also human. This situation reminds me of when I was a child and a spinster aunt who earned a living giving music lessons, had a small boy as a pupil who showed exceptional talent. Times were hard and she badly needed the small amount the boy brought every week, but she went to see the parents and suggested they get someone more proficient than herself to teach the boy. I suggested that Rose try and get into an exclusive fashion house, but as this is seemingly impossible I can only offer advice from my own experience. If Rose can make a living designing exclusive dresses *and* selling them cheaply then I wish her all the luck in the world. And if she can find someone to buy these dresses I have here at a higher price then I would be pleased.'

Rose said, 'I'll take your offer, Mr Rosenberg. If I make more of this type would you be prepared to make the same offer?'

'Rose!' Lizzie got up, protesting. 'This is madness.'

'Be quiet, Lizzie, I am doing business. Will you, Mr Rosenberg?'

'Yes, as many as you like. But think carefully before you offer me any more. Will you allow me to offer you further advice? On a dress you had on your market stall there was a pleated jabot. The pleating was hand-pressed. You can get this done by machine, from accordion to knife pleating. Some firms even do box pleating. It gives the dress an expensive look and the cost is not too prohibitive.'

'Thank you, Mr Rosenberg, I'm grateful for any advice. I shall let you have some more special dresses soon, I hope.'

'Not if I have *my* way,' Lizzie retorted.

A twinkle came into Mr Rosenberg's eyes. 'It might be wise to listen to your sister, Rose. I think she is a most capable person.'

Lizzie tossed her head. 'Thanks for nothing.'

Rose felt calm now. She pocketed the pound notes Mr

Rosenberg handed over and smiled at him. 'I think I've learned a lot this morning, Mr Rosenberg, more than you perhaps realise. I'm grateful. And grateful to Charlie that we are here.'

They parted then with Charlie carrying the empty suitcase to go to the house where they were to stay for the night, Charlie looking embarrassed, Lizzie furious, and Rose complacent.

Once they were outside Lizzie's anger erupted. 'Of all the fools, our Rose! How could you sell those dresses at that price? Did you see the roll of notes he had? He's cheated you, that's what, he deserves to be prosecuted. If I had known we would end up like this I would never have come.'

Charlie started to say something but Rose interrupted. 'End up like what, Lizzie? I have money in my hand, I can buy more material, make more dresses, yes, my profit is small, but it *is* profit. I can see now how businesses are run. Plough the money back, build up. I'm happy if I can go on designing and get someone else to do the bulk of the sewing.'

'Oh, yes, that's fine for you, but what about me and the kids doing all the hard work?'

Rose smiled. 'I've made employment for four people, no five counting Bessie. I think that's quite an achievement, what do you say about it, Charlie?'

He thrust his hands into his trouser pockets. 'I'm not going to say anything, because anything I do say will be like a red rag to a bull. Actually, I feel chockered with the whole thing. I was uncomfortable – Mr Rosenberg has always been a good friend to me.'

'A good friend?' Rose stopped. 'Then tell me, Charlie, has he ever tried to cheat you? You once told me you'd always had fair dealings with him.'

'I have, I couldn't say anything else. We've done deals otherwise than the rag trade and I've never once had cause to grumble at his terms.' Charlie shrugged. 'We've done a bit of hard bargaining at times, but . . .'

'I'm not in a position to bargain, not yet, but I might be in the future and I would like to bargain with Mr Rosenberg. He's a man I know I could go to for advice and get it. I suggest we go to our lodgings, freshen up, have a meal then go to the West End and enjoy ourselves. How about it?'

Charlie suddenly grinned. 'Why not? That's what we intended to do and we don't come to London every day. Come on, Liz, cheer up.'

Lizzie remained unrelenting until they reached the house where they were to stay then she relaxed a little. And by the time they were ready to leave she was laughing with Rose and Charlie over their perky Cockney landlady. She had given Charlie a key, just in case they were late back that evening. It was the biggest and weightiest key Rose had ever seen. When Charlie teased Mrs Caley and asked if it was to open the Tower of London she said, 'No, ducks, it's the key to heaven, or will be if you fall in the river. You'd sink like a stone.'

They had a meal then got on a tram that would take them on their first stage to the West End. They could have gone by Underground but Rose and Lizzie wanted to ride on the top of the tram and see everything. The Underground could come later.

The West End opened up another new world for Rose. She was enraptured with Piccadilly, with Regent Street and when she saw the big stores in Oxford Street she kept darting from window to window calling, 'Charlie, Lizzie, come and see this dress – these shoes – this coat – Look! Look at that navy and white costume, fourteen guineas. *Fourteen*! Imagine. I bet I could make it for a pound, or a bit over.'

Lizzie put a restraining hand on her arm. 'Now just you calm down, our Rose. Don't let everything go to your head. Remember this, that costume is tailored, by *experts* – look at the lapels, they're perfect. We'll go and take a look inside.'

Rose was almost drooling over the materials, the braids, the laces. 'Oh, Lizzie, the variety, if only I could come and buy things here. We don't see materials like this back home.'

'I think we have a fairly good selection. You didn't do badly with the pieces you bought and made up.'

Charlie stood watching Rose, enjoying her pleasure at each new thing she saw. He felt deeply moved. There was such an innocence about Rose at that moment, a tender charm that belongs only to the very young. He wished he could take her by the hand and say, 'Buy what you want, I'll pay.' Instead he said, 'Rosie, when you have a bit of money saved I'll take you to one of the big warehouses back home. There you'll have plenty of materials to choose from *and* fancy braids and lace.'

'Oh, Charlie, will you? I can't wait, I love you, love you.'

Lizzie gave her a poke in the back. 'Stop behaving like a love-sick fool, our Rose, people are staring at you.'

Not even the tartness in her sister's voice could take away Rose's joy. They went from Oxford Street to Bond Street and there Rose became subdued. She was awed by so many beautiful clothes, awed by the prices, those that *were* priced, that is. She came to understand what Lizzie meant by things being tailored. It was this look that made a dress or a coat distinctive, more she felt, than by the particular style. The styles of some of the clothes were so simple she marvelled at the fact they had an exclusive look. It was something else Rose learned that day. She was in a dream world for quite a while before Charlie snapped her out of it.

'I'll tell you what we'll do, we'll go to the Strand, book seats for a show tonight, then walk along the Embankment and see the Houses of Parliament. The show will be *my* treat – yes, it will,' he said as Rose and Lizzie began to protest. 'The pair of you can buy me an icecream, how's that? I know a place . . .'

It was midnight when they got back to Mrs Caley's. The house was in darkness but she had left candles and matches on a table in the passage. Charlie put a finger to his lips. 'Shhh.'

They negotiated the stairs without mishap, found their rooms and whispered goodnight. Rose's mind was so full of impressions of all they had done she felt it would burst. She was sure she would never be able to sleep, not with all the wonderful songs from '*Showboat*' teasing her brain. She had seen shows at home, but nothing on such a lavish scale. There was so much to tell the family it would take weeks to get it all told! The moment Rose's head touched the pillow she was asleep, and did not stir until Charlie brought them steaming mugs of tea at half-past eight.

'Come on, wakey, wakey! It's a grand morning, a bit nippy but the sun's shining. We should have been on our way to Buckingham Palace by now.' He made to draw the curtains apart but Lizzie stopped him. 'We're on holiday! This is sheer luxury to me, not having to jump up to clear away a mattress, get all the kids fed. I want to enjoy these few minutes. Go take a walk.'

'I will. Breakfast's in half an hour. I'm ready for it now, I could eat a horse.'

When he had gone Rose rubbed the sleep out of her eyes and drew herself up in the bed to drink the tea. 'It is luxury, isn't it? Oh, Lizzie, what a wonderful day it was yesterday, what a wonderful evening, that marvellous show, the dancers, the exquisite costumes. So much colour, so much life. Those tap dancers. Wouldn't it be exciting if Frankie could get the chance of a part in a show like that!'

'Frankie? He can tap dance, I know, but nothing like these people.'

'Oh, yes, he can, you didn't see him the day he did a routine. He's good, really good, but don't say anything at home, not yet. I think he would like to go on the stage.'

'Don't be daft. You're always exaggerating, our Rose. Just because he can tap dance you're already seeing him in a West End show. Hey, mind your elbow, you've spilled my tea – on the clean sheets!'

Rose put down the cup and stretched luxuriously. 'Another whole day to explore. I wish I could stay here for ever and ever.'

No one could have had a more rapturous welcome when

they arrived home the following day. For a time, with everyone speaking at once demanding to know what they had done, how they had got on, it was impossible to hold a proper conversation.

But eventually they simmered down and the story began with Rose saying, 'I don't think I had really lived until I went to London.'

And two days later she and Lizzie were still remembering small items to relate.

Although Rose had been eager to get down to sewing when she came back from London she found herself unable to settle. She blamed this on not being free to work, always having people around her. Lizzie said, 'Well, you can be on your own tomorrow afternoon. Aunt Maude has to go to the hospital for a check and has persuaded Ma to go with her. Yes, I know, I can hardly believe that she agreed. Anyway, I'll take the kids out so you can have the kitchen to yourself.'

As it happened Rose was left with baby Lilian to look after. The baby had the sniffles and Lizzie thought it unwise to take her out in the cold. It had taken both Lizzie and Rose to persuade their mother to leave her.

The baby, eight months old now, was a contented child, fragile-looking with dark hair and big blue eyes. But she was vigorous and lay on the rag rug in front of the fire, kicking her legs, her hands twisting and turning as Rose, on her knees, talked to her.

'And who's the bestest baby in the whole world?' Rose reached for a silver paper ball on elastic they had brought back from Blackpool, and dangled it in front of her. 'Come on then, catch the pretty ball. Here – catch!'

Lilian cooed and dribbled but made no effort to reach for the ball. Rose swung it so it touched her hands, but although the tiny fingers curled to grasp it, her gaze was not following the movements.

'Come on, you're lazy,' Rose teased her gently. 'Catch!'

She swung the ball slowly in front of the big blue eyes – and felt an icy little worm crawling on her spine when Lilian's gaze did not focus on it at any time. She moved her hand in front of the eyes, but there was not even a blink. Rose sat back on her heels, her heart beating in slow thuds.

The next moment she heard Lizzie's voice outside on the landing, calling to the children to stay where they were. When she came in she said, 'Forgot my flipping purse. I did feel a fool in the grocers. Where did I leave it?' She was on her way to the dresser when she paused and looked at Rose, who had got to her feet. 'What's up, what's wrong? You look as if you've seen a ghost.'

'It's Lilian – look.' Rose swung the ball and Lizzie stood motionless. Then she, like Rose, moved her hand in front of the baby's eyes. She did it twice more then she turned to Rose, a stricken look on her face.

'She can't see. Oh, my God – she's blind!'

'Ma mustn't know,' Rose said, a desperate note in her voice. 'Not yet, the blindness might only be temporary. It must be, it *has* to be, God couldn't be so cruel. Lizzie, could you drop by and leave a message for Doctor Smythe, ask if he could call but make his visit seem casual. I'm sure if you explain to Mrs Smythe they'll think of something between them.'

Lizzie nodded. 'I'll go there now.'

Doctor Smythe, like many doctors who practised in slum areas, was dedicated to his profession and worked long hours for little remuneration. Some families, where the husband drank, found it impossible to pay, but people like the Kimberleys would pay their just dues, even if it meant going without food. Sally, who was lax in many ways, kept money in a jar to pay for medicine for her beloved family. Doctor Smythe, who admired this fierce independence, had been good to the Kimberleys over the years. When he called that afternoon no one would have guessed he had come for any other reason than to bring a seed cake for Sally that his wife had baked.

Sally was delighted. 'Oh, you are both so good to us. Do thank Mrs Smythe. She knows how much I love a caraway cake.'

Rose had put the silver ball handy, so it was the most seemingly natural thing for the doctor to pick it up and swing it in front of the baby. After a few moments he said, 'Lilian doesn't seem to be following the direction of the ball. Have you noticed this before, Mrs Kimberley?'

This was the start of the questioning and to calm Sally, who became distraught he said, 'Now you are not to worry. This defect could have been caused by her attack of measles, and could be a temporary thing. But I think it would be advisable to check this with the infirmary.'

The surgeon eventually confirmed the doctor's diagnosis that the measles could have caused the trouble, but although he too said it could be a temporary condition, he stressed also they must be prepared for the fact that the child might not regain her sight.

A gloom settled over the family. Sally was inconsolable. She called Lilian her 'poor blind darling'. The baby was never out of her arms.

Rose, who had been so happy such a short time ago thought of her grandmother's words when the children had fits of giggling, that they would end up in tears before the day was out. They invariably did.

Could this mean that happiness had to be tempered throughout life by tragedy? Surely not. It would be a terrible world if this were so.

She decided to put this to the back of her mind and get on with her sewing. But as with the rest of the family, the baby's blindness had altered the normal course of their lives. Perhaps after Christmas the situation would be different. She would do what sewing she could manage without upsetting her mother. After all, with Christmas looming they would need the extra money.

Chapter 10

It seemed that nothing would lift the gloom from the family, not even Charlie's cheery greetings or teasing. By the middle of December Rose said, 'Something has to be done. I'm going to use some of my savings and give us all a good Christmas, a different one. I'll buy a turkey, a big one, and we'll go to the auctioning-off of toys at Bower's on Christmas Eve, fill the children's stockings for once.'

'And I'll treat you all to the Pantomime on Boxing Day,' Charlie said, then suggested that the older ones take the youngest children to the matinée and the rest go in the evening. This was applauded by both Rose and Lizzie, but when Charlie said he would book seats for all of them Lizzie protested. It would cost the earth and was unnecessary. At least for those who were going to the evening performance.

'We'll go in the gallery, as we always do, and rough it.'

'Rough it is right,' Charlie said with a grin. 'Sitting among sweating bodies, with folks around you sucking oranges, cracking monkey nuts. But perhaps that's all part of the fun.'

Rose said yes, but secretly would have liked to have had a seat booked in the stalls or the circle where she could have seen the clothes of the better-off people. Still, she ought to be grateful they were going to the Pantomime. Circle and stalls seats would come later, when they had the business going.

When the family were told of the Christmas treats the children, never having tasted turkey, made no fuss about it, but they went wild over the visit to the Pantomime.

The only one to raise any objection was Sally, who said

how could she possibly enjoy herself with her poor darling blind?

Gran rounded on her. 'That's enough, our Sal. It's more than enough. You've done nothing but weep and wail over Lilian since we knew. You've coddled her until the poor wee thing doesn't know what's happening to her. If anyone puts her on the floor to have a good old stretch and a kick you snatch her up and just about suffocate the child.'

Sally stared at her open-mouthed for a few moments then her face crumpled. 'How could you, how could you speak to me like that? You know how much I love my poor baby.'

'We all love her, and stop bawling, do you hear? Pray God Lilian isn't going to be blind for the rest of her life, but if she is then she needs some joy to help her along. You, as well as everyone else have to give it to her. Now we'll have no more weeping. We're going to have a good Christmas, and thank the Lord for what we do have. There'll be plenty of folks who'll have nothing but a crust in their bellies on Christmas Day.'

After that Sally made an effort.

Four days before Christmas Lizzie came in from shopping with a Christmas tree and a battered seaside bucket and soil to put it in. That evening the box of baubles they had had for years was brought carefully down from the top shelf of the cupboard and the children gleefully decorated the tree, adding a few wispy pieces of tinsel.

Then Charlie, who always contributed oranges, apples and nuts, brought round the huge turkey which they had to pluck themselves. The feathers flew and there were yells of delight from the children, with scoldings from Gran Eagan for making such a mess, but excitement grew.

Rose felt she could hardly wait for Christmas Eve when she would go to Bower's auctioning of toys after midnight. Charlie and Lizzie were going with her.

'We must be there early to get a place close to the front,' she said, 'otherwise the auctioneer won't hear our bids.'

They were there by half-past eleven and managed to get in the third row. Ten minutes later the department where the auction was to be held was jam-packed, and it was not only people from the poorer areas who attended. When the auctioneer stepped up on to the small raised platform there was a cheer. 'Now you'll all want to get home to get the kids' stockings filled so make your bids quickly and clearly.'

Half an hour later the three of them emerged sweating profusely but triumphant, with three bags of broken toys. Charlie was carrying a wooden barrow without a wheel, and Lizzie a doll's pram without a handle. Charlie said he had a pram wheel at home he could put on in a jiffy and could fix a wooden handle on the pram. They went to Gran's to sort everything out, laughing all the way. Edie and Sam were as excited as children to see what the bags produced. There were lead soldiers, each with a disability like a leg or arm missing and most of them minus a rifle. 'Twenty-five of them,' Rose exclaimed, 'and you know for how much? Twopence the lot! And this, look –' There was a train set for a shilling, which Charlie had bought, and was already straightening the rails, a baby doll with a chipped nose, a tea set with tiny handleless cups, but the teapot was intact, games with counters missing – but Charlie had some in the house. There was a pistol that could shoot out a cork on a piece of string, when they found a cork to fit it, boxes of crackers with two or three crackers missing in each, and endless small things. The whole lot Rose announced with glee, had cost under eight shillings. By the time all the repairs had been made and the baby doll dressed – Gran had knitted some clothes with one in mind – it was three o'clock in the morning. Rose knew that Alice and Nancy were determined to stay awake until they returned and counted on the fact that exhaustion would take over. It had. In spite of Charlie coming round with them to help fill the stockings, and in spite of stifled giggles, neither girl stirred. Rose and Lizzie flopped into bed at gone half-past three, knowing they would have only three hours' sleep before getting up to have the oven heated to cook the turkey.

At five o'clock Nancy gave a great whooping shout and called, 'Come on, kids, Santa Claus has been!' And after that there was no more sleep for any of the family. But for Rose, the work and lack of sleep had been well worth it, to see the looks of joy and wonder on the children's faces. At seven o'clock Tommy burst in, his dark eyes alight with laughter. 'Heard all the commotion so knew you were up. What's everyone got?' Five minutes later Frank and David arrived, David quiet as always, but Frank's face beaming with the atmosphere, the shouts, the excitement, the showing of gifts. The older boys each had fruit, a new sixpence each, a tie and new shirt – which Gran had made. Tommy had fruit, a new penny, a secondhand school satchel in excellent condition, and a pocket ludo set. The boys shared young Freddie's train set.

No one wanted any breakfast but Gran insisted they had something in their stomachs and were given a hunk of bread spread with margarine and plum jam. Afterwards each girl was given an allotted task, Gran saying she wanted the meal prepared so that when church time came they would all be ready to leave. Gran would be staying to baste the turkey. The smell of it roasting, mingling with that of the sage and onion stuffing had mouths watering. The basin holding the Christmas pudding began to make a clatter in the pan on the fire. Lizzie rushed over to draw it on to the hob and raised the lid in case the water was beginning to get too low. Various children, during the morning, were given the task of replenishing the water.

When the church bells began to ring out the whole family, apart from Gran and Charlie, were ready to leave. Charlie had gone to visit a colleague who was ill. He promised to be back in time for the meal. Sam, who would never go to church normally raised no objection on Christmas Day. It was right and proper, he said. Sally, who carried the baby, looked on the verge of tears all the while, and after the service, when the vicar blessed Lilian the tears did spill over. Adam thanked the vicar for his blessing.

It was a day of such strong impressions for Rose she felt she would remember them for the rest of her life. There was the coming into the warm kitchen from the frosty air to see the table laid with a white damask cloth that her mother had been given by her mistress when she left service to get married. Tiny sprigs of holly were laid down its length – a surprising touch from Gran. There was her father saying Grace, then carving the turkey, the ooh's and aah's of the children at the generous helpings. Gran filled a bowl with meat and vegetables and sent Tommy down with it to a family on the floor below, where the father had recently died.

Crackers were pulled and mottoes read and paper hats perched on freshly-washed hair. Rose thought that Alice and Nancy and Judith all looked lovely and fresh in their white pinafores with red ribbons slotted in the embroidered yokes.

Then there was the afternoon, when the children played quietly at games and the adults talked softly, reminiscing. The room darkened and the only sound was the shifting of the glowing coals and the murmur of voices, and now and again a protesting wheeze from the old rocking chair when Sally shifted her position.

Before the gas was lit they munched mince pies and cake and jam tarts, and the older ones had cups of tea and the children mugs of home-made lemonade. By early evening, chestnuts were popping on the glowing coals. Nuts were cracked and eaten, and the air smelled of tangerine oranges. Gran was outraged when Tommy suggested Frank doing a tap dance.

'It's a Holy day. People don't dance on Holy days!'

Then later there were the carols they sang round the fire. Gran asked for '*Silent Night*' and Adam said, 'Let Charlie sing it on his own.'

Although Charlie had been involved with everything they had done since the midday meal Rose had felt oddly detached from him. Now as Charlie began to sing she felt drawn to him.

His voice, clear yet soft and so full of feeling, stirred emotions that brought her to the brink of tears. When the notes died away there was a poignant moment in the hushed room when Charlie stooped and kissed Gran on the cheek. She did not, as she would have done on a different occasion, push him away and say, 'Oh, go on with you.' She laid her hand gently on his.

Rose suddenly became aware that her brother Frank was trying to attract her attention. He was standing by the door. He beckoned to her then indicated he was going outside. Rose glanced about her then followed him on to the landing. 'What is it, Frank?'

His dark eyes had a feverish look. 'I have to tell someone, Rose, and you're the only one who'll understand. You remember when I had that audition for my dancing and they told me they would let me know later if they wanted me – well, I heard yesterday. I have the chance to go touring with a revue company.'

'Oh, Frank,' Rose hugged him. 'I'm delighted for you. This is wonderful news.' She sobered and drew away. 'But is it? What are the family going to say when they know?'

'I'm not going to tell them, Rose. I can't, don't you see, they would stop me, and I have to go, it's something I've wanted to do since I was a kid.' Some of the feverishness died out of his eyes. 'Yes, I know, my conscience is bothering me. I don't want to leave without saying goodbye, without their blessing, but it has to be this way.'

'When will you be leaving?'

'In two weeks' time. I might tell Dad, but even if he says I can't go, I'll go all the same. I couldn't tell Ma, I couldn't bear to see her hurt look, her tears. For all her faults she loves us all.'

'Yes, I know. I might be in the same position as you one day, Frank. I'm determined to go to London, to try and get some training. It's something *I* have to do.' Rose gave him a bright smile. 'If I do, and you happen to be in London we could meet.'

'Yes, it would be wonderful.' Frank's voice lacked animation and Rose wished they could both get the blessing of the family to follow their respective careers without upset.

'Do tell Dad,' she said. 'He might understand. It's different for a boy trying to make his own way.'

'Yes, I'll do that. And thanks for listening, Rosie. Do you know I feel better already.' Frank gave a sudden grin to prove it then executed a few steps, intricate, featherlight.

'Frank, you're great, you'll get there. Perhaps one day we'll see your name in lights.'

'That'll be the day!' Frank was laughing now, his eyes alight in anticipation of such an event. 'You go on in, Rosie, I'll follow in a few minutes. I'll have a walk round the block, clear my head.'

The main topic the next morning was the Pantomime. It was not Gran who bustled everyone but Sam, who was as excited as the children at going to the matinée, and was determined to be there in good time. And it was he who practically dragged Sally away from the baby. She was still throwing Lizzie and Rose instructions when she was going out of the door.

'Honestly!' Lizzie said. 'You'd think we'd never handled a baby before.' She sank into the armchair and it wheezed and groaned as she rocked on it. 'What heaven! No kids, no Gran bossing us around, no Ma to be crooning over the baby. And no Alice and Nancy squabbling!' Lizzie had ordered them to stay out, for an hour at least. 'I don't know what you are going to do, our Rose,' she said, 'but I'm going to wallow in the luxury of my library book. Would you reach it for me, it's on the top of the dresser.'

Rose looked at the title as she brought it across then stopped. '"*Business Management*"? Do you call that a luxurious read?'

'It is to me, it's another world.' Lizzie's face glowed. 'Just to be able to dabble with figures, to discuss finance. If I wasn't going to look after the office side of your business

I would have liked to be in a stockbroker's office.'

Rose began to giggle. '*My* business. I'm a long way from having an office.'

Lizzie brought the rocking chair to an abrupt halt, and it gave a deep grouch. 'You mustn't talk like that. You must think ahead. You *will* have an office. You'll employ staff.'

'But Lizzie,' Rose had sobered. 'I want to get a shop, so I can design clothes, but eventually I hope to train as a designer, in a big fashion house. All I want to do is to design, I'm not really interested in big business.'

'Listen, our Rosie, you just forget about training in a big fashion house. To begin with you don't stand a chance, what's more you don't need it. You're talented. I knew that before I saw Rosenberg's face. He knows he's got a find in you. He wants you to go on working for him, to supply him with exclusive dresses. Well, you're going to work for yourself, and I'll see you do it. You could supply stores . . .'

'Mass producing, which I'm *not* going to do.'

'You can mass produce and still be designing. Don't you see, you can have bread and butter lines and exclusive ones as well.' Lizzie grinned suddenly. 'I've already got you with a string of shops and factories supplying them.'

'Oh, Liz – you're the end. You're letting yourself get carried away.'

'No, I'm not, I'm too practical for that. You're the dreamer, and the one who's going to get us somewhere. I feel it in my bones. I bought you a sketching pad the other day. I was keeping it for a time like this. Now sharpen yourself a pencil and sit down and sketch designs. The pad is behind the back of the dresser.'

Rose thanked Lizzie, but felt her sister was going to take over her life. No, she would not allow it. She, like Lizzie, knew what she wanted and was equally determined to get it. In the meantime she would go on creating new designs. When Rose sat down with the pad and pencil all sorts of ideas were flooding her mind.

Chapter 11

When the rest of the family set out for the evening performance of 'Aladdin' they were all laughing, including the solemn David. Before they left Sam had related just about every joke in the show and would not be stopped. 'I'll just tell you this one,' he kept saying. Gran consoled them that the jokes sounded better when told by the comedian.

They set out early, wanting to get in the front row of the gallery, but when they arrived there were forty or fifty people already in the queue. Charlie said, 'We still might make it. When we get in I'll get the tickets and you lot dash on ahead. I can sprint up the stairs.'

But they had a long wait before that moment came. Within ten minutes of arriving they were prisoners in a pressing, jovial mass, with Lizzie declaring she would be as flat as a kipper by the time the doors opened. There were plenty of lively quips from the crowd to entertain them, however, as well as the buskers – a man who played the spoons and a couple dressed as gypsies, the man strumming a banjo and the girl singing. The girl had a strange dialect, saying 'foire' for fire and 'tonoight' for tonight. The crowd joined in lustily, imitating the dialect. A few coins clinked into the respective hats. Charlie gave a generous contribution to both, saying they had earned it. Both man and girl were scantily clad and the night was bitterly cold.

When the sound of the bolts being drawn from the gallery doors was heard Rose felt as though the breath was being squeezed out of her. Then, oh blessed relief, they surged forwards. Rose and the others raced up the stone stairs and Charlie, by dint of his easy sprinting managed to get them all in the front row. It was important to Rose, who loved to watch the people coming into the stalls, taking note of details of the women's dresses.

The seating in the gallery was no more than a series of wooden tiers, so if you happened to have someone behind you with big feet you were likely to suffer some bruising. With a bit of shuffling around Charlie arranged it so that Lizzie and Rose were sitting in front of a woman and her small daughter.

Although Rose knew she would enjoy the experience some time of sitting in the stalls or the circle she found something funny and happy about the way the people in pit and gallery read out aloud the advertisements on the safety curtain, some spelling the words syllable by syllable. '*Beech-am Pills. Worth a Guin-ea a Box . . . Mazz-a-wat-tee Tea . . .*'

People started coming into the stalls and Rose leaned forward eagerly and peered down. She kept nudging Lizzie. 'Look, Lizzie, look at that pale green dress. What lovely braid. I wonder where that came from? London most likely. Oh, and see that black velvet. How simple, but so effective.'

A family came into one of the boxes on Rose's left, the children all beautifully dressed. The whole family were in view while they were standing but once they sat down most of them were hidden by the red velvet curtains.

These people were considered to be the élite, but to Rose they were simply a part of the theatre scene, just like those around her, with their sweating bodies, noisy sucking of oranges and crunching of nuts, rattling paperbags of sweets and laughing bawdily.

When the members of the orchestra began to file in cheers rose from pit and gallery, but there was an expectant hush when the men began to tune up their instruments. This tuning up was the thread that linked all classes together. It was the announcement that soon the entertainment was due to begin.

Then the conductor rapped his stand, raised his baton and the next moment feet were tapping to a lively tune. This stopped when the music changed to a more gentle melody. With it the safety curtain began to rise slowly and everyone held their breath. Lights dimmed, the red plush curtains began to part, everyone breathed out again and excitement mounted.

All troubles were forgotten as they were introduced to a world of fantasy. They laughed themselves silly at the comedian and clowns, booed the villain, cheered Prince Charming, encouraged Aladdin to rub the lamp, gave a gasp when the Genie appeared in a cloud of smoke, and oohed and aahed when Aladdin entered the cave and beheld the treasures.

Later when they walked home Lizzie said, 'Actually, it was a load of rubbish.' Then she grinned. 'But I enjoyed every minute of it.'

Rose said softly, 'I wish I had a lamp to bring a Genie who would grant me three wishes.'

The bright-eyed and mischievous Tommy said, in an adult way, 'If you had three you'd want more, our Rose,' then added as she made to protest, 'You would, because you would suddenly think of so many things you'd like for other people in the family.' Tommy grinned. 'But if you do happen to come across a Genie, remember me, I'd like a bike.'

Alice and Nancy began to argue about the chorus girls with Nancy declaring she could kick as high as any of them and Alice saying it was impossible. 'They're trained, they're special, our Nancy.'

'Special or not, I can kick as high and I'll show you when I get home.'

This brought the retort from Lizzie that they would be going straight to bed when they got in, so that was the end of it.

Charlie and the boys saw them as far as the Buildings with Charlie promising to see them the next morning. Lizzie put a finger to her lips and said to her sisters, 'Now, not a sound. Ma was going to bed early, said she had a headache, and I expect Dad would go early too.'

They whispered about the pantomime as they got undressed then, when they were all in their knickers and vests Nancy begged Lizzie to allow her to kick her height, just once, and Lizzie gave in.

In the end they were all high-kicking and stifling giggles when the bedroom door suddenly opened and their father came out, belt in hand. He gave each girl in turn two hard welts across the buttocks then said, 'Now get into bed at once, and be quiet, or else!' He went back into the bedroom.

The girls stood, shocked, not one of them having uttered a word of protest or a cry of pain. Their father, in all their lives, had never raised a hand to them.

'He must be ill,' Lizzie whispered. 'He has to be, to have done a thing like that.'

In silence they unrolled the mattress, made up the bed and got into it. Then Nancy grumbled in a whisper that her bottom was stinging and Lizzie hissed there would be more parts of her stinging if she didn't shut up.

Rose lay wondering if Lizzie was right and her father was ill. But why should he belt them on this particular night? There had been some clowning and giggling on other nights, without complaint. Not that Lizzie would allow them to go on for too long if their parents were likely to be asleep. Perhaps her mother's headache had become worse and her father was concerned that she had been disturbed. He never showed any outward affection towards her, but by the way her mother talked at times Rose felt there was a great love between them.

Rose became aware of her own buttocks burning from the belting and was surprised to feel sensual tremors going through her body. It raised questions in her mind. Although she felt sure her father had not punished them all from any sexual motives it did make her think of Clara Harding who flaunted the bruising inflicted by her husband. Did some women enjoy being beaten? Rose, having experienced tremors could understand that this part of the body might be a means of arousal, but how could any woman get pleasure out of being given a black eye, bruised arms, shoulders or cheeks? This to her was brutality, and she hoped she would never be subjected to such treatment. She spent a restless night.

The following morning her mother apologised to the girls for their father's behaviour, explaining they had roused her from sleep and her headache had flared up in an excruciating way, making her cry out.

'Your father worries so much about me, dears. He's always been such a worrier, wondering sometimes where the next penny is coming from, worrying if any of us are ill. You do understand? He would never have hit any of you had it not been for me crying out.'

Later Lizzie said a little tartly to Rose, 'It didn't seem to worry him bringing so many kids into the world, and wondering how they were all to be fed. It would have done us all a bit of good if he'd used some restraint.'

'Then you and I mightn't have been here, that is if they'd stopped after David was born, and they could have done.' Rose smiled suddenly. 'Think what the world might have missed! Can't you see future headlines – Elizabeth Kimberley, the brains behind the fashion empire of – de-da-de-da, and her sister Rose top designer.'

Both girls laughed, Lizzie declaring if the prophecy came true it would be a reason for having been born.

The next event to look forward to was New Year's Eve. The people in the Buildings had a fling on this night and it was useless anyone going to bed and expecting to sleep. For Rose, seeing the New Year in was a momentous and moving event. A year of her life had slipped away, what would this fresh one bring? As at Christmas the family gathered together at this time. Other years, Charlie had left after greetings had been exchanged to go 'first footing'. This year Rose and Lizzie had been given permission to go with him. David, also, had the chance to go, but refused. Frank and Tommy would have liked to go, but their father said they were too young.

At a quarter to twelve there was as much activity going on in the street and in the Buildings as carnival day, with people shouting outside and running up and down the stairs, borrowing cups or glasses. Gran had cut up some of the cake and there were ham sandwiches and pieces of pork pie, a bottle of ginger wine, one of port, and some bottles of beer.

Charlie was to be their 'first foot'. Being dark-haired, he was in great demand. Their next door neighbour declared the worst year they had ever experienced was when they had had a fair-haired cousin for their 'first foot'. 'Silly superstition,' Lizzie said, then added, with a wry grin, 'but I reckon if I was married and had a home of my own I wouldn't want a fair-haired fellow to cross my threshold after twelve o'clock.'

About five to twelve there was a sudden hush, a waiting, then shortly afterwards there was chatter and laughter on landings, 'first foots' joking with one another as they waited outside doors for the maroons to go off to announce the midnight hour. Rose pictured Charlie outside their door holding a bottle of whisky, a piece of coal – to light the year for them, a loaf of bread so they would never starve, and a bag of sugar to sweeten the year.

Gran said, 'Only a minute to go,' and again there was the hush. Rose gave a little shiver of excitement. Then came the dull boom of the fireworks going off and immediately there was a banging on doors, doors opened and there were cries of Happy New Year! When Charlie came in Rose hung back, leaving the older ones to be greeted first. When her turn came he said softly, 'Hello, kiddo, the best New Year for you there can be.' He kissed and hugged her.

Gran began passing round the cake. Adam poured the drinks. 'Charlie – here you are, a beer with a whisky chaser . . .'

Rose's cheeks were flushed with heat from the fire and excitement, when she set out with Charlie and Lizzie to go first footing. There was a white frost and the pavements were crisp underfoot. Lights spilled from windows, there were parties going on all over, with some rat-tatting on doors from latecomers, and cries of 'Happy New Year!'. The three of them were caught up in a group, which was stretched across the road, arm in arm. They linked up and were carried down the street singing '*Auld lang syne*'. They met up with a policeman who called, 'Go steady on the whisky, you lot, don't want to be running any of you in.' Then he added with a laugh, 'Have one for me.'

'We will,' came a chorus, 'Happy New Year!'

They called at so many houses, and Rose consumed so many glasses of ginger wine and pieces of Christmas cake that she lost count. At every house where they called they were greeted with the same remark. 'Come on in, Charlie, first over the threshold! We need a dark-haired bloke to bring us some luck.'

'Guaranteed,' Charlie would say. 'It'll roll in, jobs all round, you'll have so much dough you won't know what to spend it on.'

The laughter that greeted this was affectionately derisive. The people knew there was no easy way to wealth but it was good to wallow in the illusion for that one night of the year.

It was five o'clock when Charlie brought Rose and Lizzie home. There were groups of people rolling along the street, some standing on corners, arms around one another singing themselves hoarse. Drunken men lay in gutters and sprawled on stairways. Charlie laughed. 'There'll be some thick heads in the morning. Mine included! Come on, I'll see you to your door.'

Rose was aware of a keening sound as they went up the stairs, like an animal in pain. Then, as she realised the sound came from their own kitchen she gave a quick glance of fear at Lizzie and Charlie and ran to the door. When she opened it fingers of ice touched her spine. The keening sound came from her mother who was rocking back and forth in the old chair. Gran Eagan, who was standing with her back to the fireplace, was grim-faced. The three girls were sitting on the mattress in their nighties, their eyes red-rimmed, a look of utter misery on each face. Alice got up and flung her arms around Rose.

'Oh, Rose, it's terrible, it's me Dad, he's dead.'

Dead? Rose repeated the word but no sound came. Lizzie said, 'He can't be,' and there was fear in her voice.

Gran Eagan nodded, and kept on nodding as though she were trying to convince herself it had happened. Rose went to her mother and put her arms around her. The keening sound went on. The look of agony in her eyes was unbearable to watch.

It was Charlie who asked what had happened.

Edie put her fingers under her eyes and wiped away tears that had spilled over. 'Adam complained of pains in his chest not long after you had all left. They were severe. I ran next door and asked Fred if he would go for the doctor. By the time he got here Adam was dead. It was as quick as that. I can't believe it.'

Rose looked at her stricken. 'It's awful, Dad was lying here dead and we were enjoying ourselves.'

'It happens Rosie, love. You know what they say, in the midst of life we are in death. It wouldn't have made any difference if you had been here, so none of you must reproach yourself.'

'I'll make a pot of tea,' Lizzie said, and pushed the kettle on to the dying embers of the fire.

During the next few days Rose's grief was mainly for her mother who was inconsolable. Rose at first had been afraid to look at her father in death, but when she saw the peace on his face she could even understand her mother wanting to sleep in the bedroom where he was laid out in his coffin. Sally said she wanted to be near her dear one as long as possible, adding,

'He was a good, kind man was Adam. He had so much love to give but was unable to show it. Everyone liked him.'

Proof of how well-liked Adam Kimberley had been was shown by the double line of mourners who followed the hearse, stretching right down the street. They were men, mostly out of work, shabby, with holes in their shoes, but willing to walk the mile to the cemetery in bitterly cold weather to pay their respects to a man they liked.

Close friends and relatives came back for a ham tea, provided by Charlie. Even the most poverty-stricken family would provide a ham tea and wear mourning, even if it meant getting into debt for the rest of their lives. Rose and Lizzie spent hours dyeing dresses and coats black to fulfil their needs.

The day after the funeral Gran Eagan said they must make plans for the future and suggested that Lizzie and Rose and the two eldest boys, Frank and David, came round to her house that evening to discuss it. Sally wanted no part in the discussion. She said they could plan what they liked, she was going to bed. When Rose went in to the bedroom before they left to see if her mother was all right, she felt a lump come into her throat. Sally was curled up in the bed, face flushed, her cheek resting on one of her husband's vests. 'Poor Ma,' Rose whispered and crept out.

Rose, who felt she had never been really warm since her father's death, welcomed the blazing fire of her grandmother's after coming out of the icy blast of an East wind. Charlie took their coats, Sam brought up chairs and Edie poured tea for all of them.

Before teas had been stirred and sugared Edie said, 'Well now, I've talked over with Charlie and Sam a plan I have in mind, but of course it will have to be discussed.' She addressed her remarks to Lizzie. 'The money that Frank and David earn, plus what Rose and you bring in from the market stall is not enough to keep the home going.'

'Rose and I intend to increase the trade.'

'Perhaps get a shop,' Rose said.

Edie declared it to be 'pie in the sky'. There was no hope of increasing trade. It was January, a bad month. People had borrowed to be able to spend for Christmas and would be paying off their debts – for evermore. No, they could forget that, especially a shop. What she proposed was looking for a bigger house and all of them moving in together.

Lizzie looked bewildered. 'What benefit would that be?'

'I'll tell you if you'll give me a chance to explain. We need more money coming in, right? So, Nancy's left school, she gets a job. Alice can leave now, they'll allow her to under the circumstances. I can help her to cope with the housework and the cooking. You, Lizzie, can get a job. Rose can keep on with the market stall.'

Lizzie was up in arms. 'I thought this was to be a discussion. You have it all cut and dried, Gran, haven't you? Well, I happen to like working with Rose. And, in spite of what you say I feel sure we can go on building up a business. People find money for the January sales and anyway, I can tell you this, you'll not get Ma to move.'

'She'll have to.' Edie spoke quietly. 'Sal will have to pull her weight. Sacrifices have to be made. Do you think that *I* want to uproot myself from my home, or your grandad, or Charlie?'

Rose, knowing there was nothing any of them could say to this, felt despair, as she saw her dreams of having a dress shop fading. The misery in her brother Frank's eyes told that his dreams too of becoming a dancer were also fading.

Charlie said, 'Things that very often seem black turn out for the best. Take Sal, it's grieved her that the boys have to sleep out. She'll have them at home, if we can get a bigger house.'

'And we'll be saving the money she's been paying to neighbours for sleeping them,' Edie declared.

It was this that finally swayed Sally, who had been adamant at first that she would not move, but although she became reconciled to the ideas she made it clear she was going to be miserable living elsewhere.

Lizzie and Edie went house hunting, but although there were bigger houses to rent they were either too far away from the market, did not have enough rooms to make the change worthwhile, or the rents were too high.

Then one morning Rose met a woman in the market who told her about a house that was to let in Orchard Street. It had a lot of rooms and the owner, who was about 'ninety-nine', wasn't interested in the money, she just wanted a nice family to live in it. The rent was cheap.

They soon found out when they went to look at the house why the rent was cheap. A neighbour had come out to tell them that an old man had been living in it, a recluse who had been there years. The windows were so dirt-grimed it was only possible to glimpse curtains that hung in tatters. Paint had peeled from window frames and doors so that in parts the wood was bleached by the weather.

Charlie and Sam had come with Edie and Lizzie and Rose. Sam said 'It's a big house.' Charlie grinned. 'It is in a better class type of district.'

'Better class!' Edie retorted, 'I wouldn't even bother to look inside.' Charlie took the key from her saying one should never judge a book by its cover.

The neighbour called, 'You'll want hankies over your noses.'

'Gas-masks!' Charlie gasped when he unlocked the door. 'Oh Gawd!' The stink was overpowering. It was a mixture of urine, stale food and the accumulation of grease and dirt over the years. The floor of the passage was covered in layers of tattered newspapers. Edie said she refused to go any further but Charlie reminded her of her saying there was no muck that couldn't be cleared with soap and water and elbow grease, then he added, 'Think of the low rent.'

Rose wanted the house. She had been told by the neighbour there was a shed at the bottom of the garden that had once been used as a small factory. For Rose it was a place where she could do her sewing. Perhaps get one or two treadle machines in it, employ some girls. She had told Lizzie about it and with her sister on her side they began to point the merits of the house. The good size of the rooms on the ground floor, the scullery with a sink and running water. All these were covered at the moment with thick wads of newspapers. Wall-paper hung in strips from the walls. Once, when there was a rustling and a heaving in the newspapers Edie said, 'The place is overrun with mice! And there's bound to be bugs.'

'No bugs,' Sam said, 'you can always smell them, and a cat'll get rid of the mice.'

The upstairs rooms had not been used for years and although the paper had peeled off Charlie declared the walls to be sound. He stamped his feet. *And* the floorboards. With the place cleaned up, a bit of distemper on the walls and the skirting boards and doors painted it would be just the job. He offered to pay for the materials.

Edie was dead against taking the house until Sam called them to take a look out of one of the back windows. 'Look, Edie,' he said. 'A garden – and there's apple trees and plum trees, and pears.'

'And a right old jungle it is,' she snapped.

'I've always wanted an orchard,' Sam said softly. 'Me Dad had one, and so did me grandad. We had some lovely fruit pies. There's a shed too, where we could keep the gardening tools.'

Lizzie and Rose suggested they took a look at the shed. It was in surprisingly good condition. The base of the walls were brick, the top part wood. Rose whispered to Charlie what she had in mind and he said, 'Leave it to me.'

But it was Sam who won the day with Edie. There was an unusual gentleness in her eyes as she said, 'All right, Sam, you shall have your orchard.' Then she added, as though ashamed of her weakness, 'But if you don't look after it we'll chop the trees down.'

'Over my dead body,' he said, with a cheeky grin.

And so began the onslaught on number 14 Orchard Street. Charlie brought some of his friends to help clear the place and they burned the rubbish in the garden. The younger children enjoyed the bonfire. Neighbours offered to help to scrub out. Edie and Lizzie with the help of two more women stripped the walls, put fires on to dry out the rooms and distempered most of them. But they papered the front room and the bedroom that Sally would occupy.

In spite of all the workers it took a month before the house was habitable. Every piece of furniture in it was provided by Charlie, the pieces having been given to him by his wealthier customers. There was even a square of green carpet with roses on it for the front room. There was lino on the kitchen floor and in the first floor bedrooms but the attic rooms, the floorboards well scrubbed, had only rugs.

It was not until the house was ready to be occupied that Rose begged Charlie to give her some advice on the shed. He promised to get a friend to creosote the wood and to see to the roof. The sewing machines he said, would have to come later.

The day after they moved into the house they had a party. It was crowded, there was warmth and laughter and Rose said, 'This is going to be a happy house, Lizzie. Even Ma is smiling. We're going to build the business up and I'm going to try for a better trade. There's some good class shops on the main road. We'll get our shop – in time.'

'In time,' Lizzie said, nodding.

Chapter 12

The greatest novelty of the move, to the younger members of the family, was having water on tap instead of having to carry it upstairs in buckets. To the older ones it meant privacy. For Rose it was luxury to be sharing a room with only Lizzie, and to be sleeping in a bed instead of on a mattress in the kitchen. Even Sally grudgingly admitted the house was an improvement from the Buildings.

It began to wrap itself around them.

Rose and Lizzie's worry began when Gran Eagan's prediction of January being a slack month for trade proved true. The only market traders doing any business were those selling secondhand clothes, and Charlie selling the most, simply because he had slashed his prices. He tried to persuade Rose to do the same but she refused, saying she needed a certain profit to contribute to the support of the family. But on a day of freezing cold when she had not sold one of her dresses or blouses she began to have second thoughts.

'I have no guarantee the garments would sell if I did reduce the prices,' she said. 'Folks can find a few pence for secondhand clothes but . . .'

Charlie slapped his hands around himself to keep the circulation going. 'You might draw the women from the better class districts, but you'd have to advertise. You could put notices in the little shops, twopence a week, put it in twelve shops for a couple of bob.'

Two shillings . . . Rose, thinking of the meal that could be provided for that amount, was about to shake her head when she thought of Charlie and Mr Rosenberg stressing 'small profits and quick returns'.

'All right,' she said, 'I can but try.'

Lizzie, who wrote an excellent copperplate script, made out the notices, which announced the sale of good-class dresses and blouses and children's wear, all prices slashed, to be sold in the market on Saturday morning, from eight-thirty.

To Rose's surprise about twenty women were there before they had set out the stall. They clawed through the garments and by nine o'clock all were sold. In a rash moment she promised more for the following Saturday.

They all worked like trojans the following week, with not only Gran Eagan helping, but Sally offering to sew on some buttons. On the Friday evening Rose, exhausted, declared she had learned a valuable lesson. When you offer goods at slashed prices make sure you have plenty to sell.

Although the profit was enough to help the family budget it allowed nothing to be put aside for when Rose acquired her shop. And, in fact, it was not until the sales in the shops were over and the weather better that Rose was able to return to her 'bread and butter' lines at their regular prices.

Whenever she could spare a few minutes she would sketch designs for the middle-priced dresses she hoped to sell and also an occasional exclusive design for Mr Rosenberg, feeling if she lost touch with him she would somehow miss the chance of ever getting into the world of *haute couture*.

After a talk with Lizzie they decided they would strive to get a shop. Twice during the next few weeks there was one in the main street to let but Rose had been unable to apply, not having money to make stock. On an impulse one day she said to Charlie when they were standing in the market, 'Charlie, I don't know what your finances are, but I wonder if you could lend me some money?' Then quickly she outlined her reason.

Charlie eyed her, his expression unusually serious. 'I do have a little bit of money behind me, chick, but that's put by for a rainy day. I've always been like that. If I earn twopence I put a penny of it, or even a ha'penny into a jar.' He smiled wryly. 'Edie's training.'

'Yes, yes, of course, I understand. Sorry I asked.'

'No, don't be sorry, if you don't ask you don't get anything. I wouldn't mind lending you something but I would have to know it was going to be paid back fairly soon. I know your work, know it would sell, at the right price in the right district, I have that much faith in you, Rosie, but you must have a plan.'

Charlie suggested one. They could do up the shed, buy sewing machines, employ women to work them and – look for a shop to rent. He would lend Rose the money, she would be able to pay him back in time.

Until then Rose had thought of Charlie as happy-go-lucky – if his goods didn't sell, he would clear them out, profit or no profit. Now she saw him as a businessman and began to respect him.

When Rose asked him how many women he thought they would need to employ, he said two to start with, adding that Big Bessie would be glad of the job. And there was Amy Hall, whose husband had just lost his job.

'Both women are dependable,' Charlie said. 'I'll take you to a warehouse where you'll pick up some reasonable lines in materials. You'll have to do some mass producing, Rose, if you want your business to pay.'

Rose wanted to make individually-styled dresses but she thought it unwise to mention it. Get the shop and get started, that was the most important thing.

When Lizzie was told of the plan she began to organise the doing-up of the shed. They would limewash the inner walls, buy some lino and look for secondhand sewing machines.

Within three weeks the shed was ready. Two treadle machines had been bought for a song at the auction rooms and Rose had bought end rolls of materials to get her started cutting out. Bessie, who came first to start the sewing said,

'Thank God for some extra money. The pills our Harry was taking began rattling in his belly. What do you want me to do first, Rosie love?'

When Sam began enthusing over the froth of pink blossom on his apple trees Rose found her shop. It was on the main road of the better class district, small but big enough to get her started. And most important the price was right. 'We must give it a name,' she said. 'What do you suggest?'

They had already decided the dresses should be priced at a pound each, Charlie having remarked that the Fifty Shilling tailors had built up their business on this one-price angle. Lizzie said, 'How about the Pound Shop?' Rose thought it sounded like a pound of apples and they discarded the Twenty Shilling Shop as copying the tailors.

'The Sovereign Shop!' It was Charlie's suggestion and they all agreed.

Rose bought five rolls of wallpaper for sixpence in a design that had a white ground with small gold spots, and they painted the doors and window frames in dull gold. Lizzie had made a big poster announcing the 'Grand Opening' the following Saturday.

They had managed to complete a good selection of dresses. There were plain and patterned rayons, cottons, gabardines, some serge, as there could still be cold days ahead, and a range of styles in crêpe-de-chine, which Rose had bought cheaply at the warehouse. There were no more than three of each design. Rose especially liked the selection of fine flannel dresses, all of them piped with contrasting colours with an embroidered motif on the pockets. Grey piped with white, a soft brown with a darker shade, purple with misty pink, burnt orange with cream. All her dresses she knew would have sold in a bigger shop, for more money.

On the Saturday morning they left for the shop, with Charlie calling out that he would bring the barrow later on to cart home their takings!

The rain, which started when they left the Buildings turned

into a deluge and they arrived at the shop drenched.

Not one person that morning gave even a passing glance at the new shop. At midday when water overflowed spouts and cascaded down gutters Rose eyed Lizzie in consternation, enquiring what they would do if they didn't even sell one dress. Lizzie shrugged. What could they do?

In the afternoon a small boy came in to ask the time then no other person set foot inside the shop until Charlie arrived. He had come straight from the market and not only cheered them up by saying trade had been at a standstill everywhere, but brought them hot pies and a basin of mushy peas.

They mopped them up sitting in the tiny kitchen at the back which held a gas ring and a small sink, with Rose and Lizzie declaring he had saved their lives. 'Delicious, Charlie,' Rose said. 'Just what we needed.'

She was dabbing at her mouth with her handkerchief when the shop bell pinged. They all looked at one another startled then Rose jumped up and went into the shop.

A woman stood dripping water on the lino. She wiped her hand over her face. 'Talk about drowned rats. I want a couple of frocks, love, one for me and one for me daughter. Me uncle Henry's gone and died and we haven't a decent thing to wear.'

Rose's spirits sank. Black! The one colour they didn't have.

'Navy blue'll do,' the woman said, as though guessing her thoughts. 'I've a couple of black scarves we can use.'

Ten minutes later Rose was waving two one pound notes at Lizzie and Charlie. 'My first shop sale! No, *our* first shop sale. We must go into partnership.'

'Partnership!' Lizzie exclaimed. 'Sharing what? A fat lot of profit we'll get out of two pounds in a whole day. It isn't even a fraction of what you've borrowed from Charlie. You know what Gran is always saying, you have to learn to creep before you can walk. Start selling and pay your debts then you can talk about partnerships.'

Charlie came to Rose's defence saying it had been the worst

possible day for starting a new business, adding gently to Rose, 'Your goods and your prices are right, you'll get there, Rosie, I know it and so does Lizzie. She's always been the one to encourage you. She must have faith in you or she wouldn't be wanting to handle the business side.'

'Of course I have faith in her,' Lizzie said. 'It's just that, oh, it's this bloomin' awful day, it's got me down. I can't stand sitting around.'

Charlie laughed. 'Hear that, she can't stand *sitting* around.'

Within seconds they were all laughing and not even the drops of water that came plopping from the damp patch on the ceiling could destroy their exuberance. The ceiling could be attended to tomorrow, Charlie said. Today had marked a milestone in what he was sure would turn out to be a lucrative business. He put a bucket to catch the drops.

People didn't rush to buy the following week but those who did buy said they would tell their friends. The friends came and so did sisters and mothers and aunts and cousins. At the end of a month Charlie said they would need to discuss some reorganisation if they were to keep supplies going, and suggested they had a meeting. Gran Eagan invited herself, implying it needed an older head to keep them all on an even keel. Charlie and Rose and even Lizzie had been excited the night before when discussing the takings of the shop. Edie lit a fire in the front room so they could have peace and quiet.

Charlie began the proceedings by saying they would need to employ extra workers if they were planning to keep up supplies. This, of course, would mean buying extra sewing machines, or farming the work out. Rose said she would prefer to have people working on the spot where she could check everything and added that she would also like to employ a woman to do the cutting out, leaving her free to concentrate on new designs.

Lizzie demanded to know why they needed new designs. They should repeat the ones they already had, as the dresses were selling and that was the whole point of having the shop, wasn't it?

Rose said no, the shop was simply a means to an end. Her ultimate goal was to design model dresses, and what she wanted to do was to create one or two now and again and make them up. It was important to her.

Lizzie sighed. 'I know what you want to do eventually, our Rose, but right now you've got to concentrate on what's selling, have money coming in and build up. Then, when you can afford it work on your model dresses.'

'No, I have to work on them now, I must! You have to understand.'

Lizzie said she didn't understand. Rose wanted to design and that was what she was doing. What was the difference between designing a dress to sell for a pound and one to sell for fifty.

Rose declared there was all the difference in the world. It was impossible to give full rein to her ideas with Lizzie constantly badgering her to keep down costs. Even trimmings had to be pared to the bone.

Lizzie flung out her hands. Prices had to be kept to a minimum, there was no time for carrying out expensive projects, not when they still owed Charlie money. There was still material to be made up – what should they do with it, throw it out?

When the argument seemed likely to continue Edie butted in.

'I would like to say something. You, Lizzie, have a business head, and it's a good job you have, otherwise the accounts would get into a mess. Rose is a dreamer, but she's also the designer and a hard worker. I think she ought to have time to sketch and make up a better class dress – on occasions.'

'So do I,' Charlie said. 'We don't want to knock the soul out of this business. At the same time I agree with Lizzie that the material we still have, and there's a lot of it, will have to be made up. I also suggest that the dresses that don't sell, and one or two lines that haven't gone well, should be put on the market stall. I know Rose hasn't time to attend to the stall now, but I thought Nancy could do it.'

Edie raised a protest at this. 'Nancy has a job,' she snapped. 'We need the money.'

'Listen,' Charlie spoke gently, 'Nancy turns out at four o'clock every morning to get to the bakery. She hates it and you and Sal hate her going out at that time. Yes, I know, she has the company of Maggie Stimpson and her daughters, but it's still an ungodly hour for any kid to turn out to work. I'd pay her to help on the stall and I'd take her with me on a Monday when I do my rounds buying.'

Rose was surprised to feel a sudden twinge of jealousy. It was as though Nancy was usurping her in Charlie's affections. Then he looked at her and there was something in his smokey blue eyes that told her she would always have a special place in his heart.

Although Edie grudgingly gave in to Charlie about Nancy, saying in her opinion a bird in the hand was worth two in a bush, Lizzie objected, pointing out that Alice was going to be disgruntled. 'And who could blame her?' she exlaimed. 'She's stuck here at home, the drudge, the Cinderella, while everyone else is getting out and about.'

'You leave Alice where she is,' Edie said sharply. 'She's turned out to be a good little manager and a good cook. What's more she likes being at home, and Sal likes her there, it keeps her from brooding over Adam. The two of them get together discussing their romantic stories, mill girls marrying princes, a load of rubbish but it keeps them happy.'

And so Alice was left doing the job she liked. Nancy started to go with Charlie on his rounds and to the market and proved to be an asset. Two more sewing machines were bought and widows engaged to manage them. Rose also found an excellent woman to do the cutting out.

In spite of the extra staff they were all working long hours to get a stock of dresses ready for the coming holiday in July. It was a week when offices, factories, mines and shipyards closed down and although the workers drew no pay it was the biggest spending week of the year. Even the poorest family would try and scrape up enough money to enjoy what was known as Oakley week. There was not only horse racing on the moor every day but a huge fair on Becket's Common. It was the biggest to congregate and the fairground people came from all over the country. There would be a half-mile of dartboard stands, another of roll the pennies, coconut shies, any amount of roundabouts, dodgems, high fliers, and to round off the evening one could stroll homewards eating a pennyworth of chips and a twopenny haddock from the newspaper they were wrapped in, to the lively piped music of the big organs. It was a family day out and although there might be little to spend, sometimes nothing, you could draw pleasure from the atmosphere around you.

As it neared the holiday week Rose felt drained. She had not only been sewing at nights but standing in the shop, handing down dresses from the rails. There had been difficulty in keeping up the stock. One evening when she and her mother were alone Sally said, 'Rose dear, you look done in. Why do you do it?'

Rose opened her eyes. 'I want to, Ma, it's a part of my life.'

'But you should be thinking of boyfriends, not working the way you do. You're a lovely girl, Rose. You want to get married, don't you?'

'Oh, yes, I do, and have children, but not yet. I must achieve my goal.'

'And kill yourself doing it! It's not worth it, love.'

'I *have* to do it. I have all these ideas crowding my mind, and sometimes I can't get them down fast enough.'

'But why do you put so much work into those expensive dresses you've been making when the cheaper ones are selling so well?'

Rose's eyes took on a dreaming look. 'Because I love working with the expensive material, the pure silks, the velvets, the brocades, the chiffons. I enjoy doing designs for the beaded work, the embroidery, there's a feeling of luxury about them.' Rose turned her head and smiled at her mother. 'I must have inherited this from you.'

'Oh, no, Rosie, I never wanted to be wealthy.'

'I wasn't meaning wealth, Ma. You enjoyed being a lady's maid, enjoyed handling all the lovely dresses. You were always on to us to speak properly, to learn how to spell, to be able to write well. You told us these things were important.'

'And they are, but there's some nasty people among the nobility. I wouldn't want you mixing in that kind of life. I was lucky with my mistress and the master, they were kind to me, but some girls had terrible lives in service, half-starved, and the masters *and* their sons after them for – well, you know what.'

Rose laughed softly. 'I bet you had a few boys running after you. Gran said what a lovely-looking girl you were and you still are attractive, Ma.'

'I had only one boy, Rosie, and that was your Dad.' Sally's face crumpled.

Rose got up and put her arms around her. 'Now, Ma, Dad wouldn't want you to grieve.'

'No, I know.' Sally dabbed at her eyes. 'But I'll never get over his loss. I have all my family around me, a loving family, but you know, love, I'm lonely inside.' The tears welled, and spilled over. 'There's no one who can take the place of your husband.' The desolation in her mother's eyes and voice brought a lump to Rose's throat. 'That's why I want you to get married, dear, to love and be loved. All the money in the world could never replace that.'

Rose felt sure her mother was right, but it did not make her want to change her plans in any way.

On a Friday evening Charlie always had a drink with his friends at the club and came in well after tea. Rose and Lizzie had taken to waiting up for him, enjoying his chatter about the market, the people, and discussing business. On this night of the week Lizzie did the accounts and Rose would be either sewing or sketching.

On the Friday evening prior to the start of the holiday week Charlie came breezing in, full of a tip he had had for the Oakley stakes, which was the main race of the week and held on the Tuesday. 'Straight from the horse's mouth,' he declared 'I've put five quid on at ten to one, so if it comes up . . .'

'Five pounds?' Lizzie exclaimed. 'Have you gone completely mad, Charlie Eagan? Do you know what you could get for five pounds?'

He grinned. 'Yes, the chance of winning fifty quid. And, if you'll let me finish what I was going to say – if Devil's Hat comes up how about the three of us going to London for a couple of days? You, Rosie, would have the chance of taking some of your special dresses to Mr Rosenberg.'

Rose glowed. 'Oh, Charlie, if only I could. It would be wonderful. Absolutely wonderful.'

'Charlie, just you hang on a minute,' Lizzie demanded. 'You're having our Rose floating on a fleecy pink cloud. You know as well as I do that tips on horses are ten a penny. I've had about eight "sure winners" given to me in the past three days.'

'Lizzie, why don't you dream a little as well?' Charlie's face had taken on a gentle expression. 'It's good to dream.'

'I dream, Charlie.' Lizzie ran a hand over the pages of the ledger she had been working on. 'I want to see this business built into something big, and it can be, I know it now. It'll be hard work for a long time, but I'm prepared for it, and so is Rose.'

'Lizzie.' There was a pleading now in Rose's voice, 'We've been working terribly hard, so if Charlie's horse didn't win do you still think we could afford to spend a couple of days in London? I do so want to see Mr Rosenberg.'

Lizzie slammed shut the ledger. 'No, we can't. I know we've sold a lot of dresses, and the money looks good on paper, but you forget there are wages to be paid, material to be bought, Charlie's repayments and then we're just about getting there. A dip in the purse would put us right back. And don't start giving me the old line about all work and no play!'

Rose gave Charlie a despairing glance and he smiled. 'Keep your pecker up, Rosie love, we'll get to London, this horse is going to win, I know it.'

Later, Rose picked up her sketchpad and sitting down at the table was about to push aside the sporting paper that Charlie had brought in, when her eye caught the name 'Sketchpad'. A tipster said it was a horse with an outside chance of winning the big race. Rose's heart began to race. It was like an omen. Dare she take a chance and back it? An outsider? It would be a good price. Perhaps twenty to one. The only money she had was a few coppers in her purse and a pound that Lizzie had given her to buy some braid. The shop was out of the braid until Friday. If she put the pound on the horse and it lost, what then?

Rose got up and said she was going out for a few minutes. She went out into the street as though some force was propelling her. She knew a bookie's runner, she had taken bets for Charlie to him, but what if he told Charlie what she had done? Rose reasoned she would have to tell Charlie whether the horse won or lost.

She found Dickie Daley coming out of the pub and said she wanted to put a bet on a horse – for herself. 'I don't want anyone to know,' she added. 'If it wins I'll give you a pound. It if doesn't, I'm in hot water.'

Dickie touched his nose and grinned. 'You can depend on me, Rosie love. My lips are sealed. How much are you putting on? Are you after a fifty to one chance?'

Rose told him she wanted a straight pound win on Sketchpad and he stared at her, then tried to dissuade her. 'You're mad, love, it's got four left feet.'

She slipped the pound note into his hand and hurried away. When she got back into the house she felt as though her legs would not hold her. Get into hot water, she had told Dickie! She would be banished from the family if the horse lost.

On Tuesday, Rose was on tenterhooks. She had to force herself to eat some dinner, or Gran Eagan would have thought she was sickening for something and want to dose her. The soonest she would get to know the result of the Oakley Stakes was when the local paper got out on the streets. The result of the race would be in the Stop Press.

As it turned out she got to know from Charlie. Rose was slipping out when she met him. 'Sorry, Rosie love,' he said, 'Devil's Hat was third.'

'What won?' Rose's voice was barely above a whisper.

'An outsider. Sketchpad. Hey! *You* should have backed it.'

'I did,' she said, and gabbled out the story. Charlie laughed his head off. It was typical, he said. He spent weeks weighing up form and she won on a whim. When she asked him if he would collect the money and give Dickie the pound she had promised him Charlie shook his head in despair, saying Dickie would have been pleased if she had given him a shilling.

When Charlie brought her the money Rose pushed it back at him and asked him to keep it for her. It was for their London trip. Then she begged him not to tell Lizzie or any of the family.

'Tell Lizzie,' he said, 'not right now, but sometime. And Rose, don't make a habit of backing horses.'

Rose declared she would never back another horse as long as she lived. The suspense had made her a nervous wreck.

Rose decided her next worry was to get the family to agree to their going to London, but they agreed so readily when the project was mentioned she was sure Charlie must have paved the way. Edie said she thought the girls needed a break, they had worked like slaves for the past weeks and, after all, they were combining business with pleasure by taking Rose's dresses to Mr Rosenberg.

Chapter 13

They boarded the train at the Central station at midnight and after breakfasting in London they were at Mr Rosenberg's office just after nine o'clock.

His welcome was heartwarming to Rose. 'My dear young ladies, how good it is to see you again. And you too, Charlie.' He pumped his hand. 'Coffee?' They said no, they had just had breakfast.

They sat talking for a while discussing the progress Rose and Lizzie had made with the cheaper dresses, then Mr Rosenberg turned and said to Rose, 'And what have you brought for me to see, Rose?'

She and Lizzie undid the layers of tissue paper and Rose reverently laid out the dresses on the long table in front of the window.

The first was a silk velvet in duck-egg blue with a bolero patterned in seed pearls and crystal beads. 'Yes,' Mr Rosenberg said, giving no praise, yet Rose knowing by the look in his eyes he was impressed with the work.

The next was a simply cut dress in cream satin, its feature a floating panel at the back consisting of velvet leaves set between two layers of net, shading from palest gold to russet tones. Mr Rosenberg nodded his approval and with each dress displayed his nodding became more forceful.

'Yes, excellent design and workmanship, Rose. I shall have no difficulty in selling these.'

Lizzie leaned forward. 'But only at the right price, Mr Rosenberg.'

He laughed softly as he raised his eyebrows at Rose. 'How could you fail to succeed, my dear, with your sister as your business manager? But this is good, she is what you need. Shall we discuss terms?'

Rose was fascinated by the haggling and full of praise for Lizzie who refused to accept Mr Rosenberg's first offer, but when he offered a price she thought acceptable and Lizzie still refused, she became worried.

'Look at this dress, Mr Rosenberg.' Lizzie selected a crêpe de chine in pale coffee, which was trimmed at waist and neck and with both sleeves closely patterned in bronze bugle beads. 'Have you any idea of the work involved, Mr Rosenberg? My three sisters and one of the women in our workroom put in hour after hour of work on this.'

Mr Rosenberg dismissed it with a wave of his hand and a shrug of his shoulders. He appreciated the amount of work but alas, there were many women all over the country who were putting in equally long hours for similar work and he had to buy at the right price.

'In other words, slave labour,' Lizzie snapped. 'I've heard about these sweatshops.'

Mr Rosenberg's smile was gentle as he asked Lizzie if she considered that her sisters and her workpeople were sewing under ideal conditions. Lizzie said no, not ideal, but they were better paid than most. Mr Rosenberg said if he raised the price he would be unable to sell the dresses, and added if they took them away they would have them left on their hands. To this Lizzie replied confidently she was quite sure they would have no difficulty in disposing of the dresses elsewhere, at a better price.

Charlie looked from Lizzie to Rose. But would they get more? He had always found Mr Rosenberg most fair. They could tramp around the whole day trying to find a firm to give more and not succeed.

Rose said she respected Charlie's judgment but pointed out that unless they tried elsewhere they would never know what terms they could get. However, she added, as they would not want to carry a suitcase of dresses around, would Mr Rosenberg agree to her selecting one as a sample, and accept the other five at the price he had quoted for each. Without waiting for a reply Rose lifted away a pale lemon chiffon with a delicate tracery of silver motifs scattered over the skirt and on the bodice. They were hand-embroidered.

Mr Rosenberg appealed to Charlie, his expression comical. 'Wouldn't you know she would pick the plum! And I thought Elizabeth to be the shrewd one.'

Rose laughed. 'I'm learning from you, Mr Rosenberg. I noticed you gave more attention to this dress than the others.'

He threw up his hands. 'And I teach my sons not to show too much interest in the goods they desire the most! Well, I must start re-learning. Yes, I shall take the other five dresses and I shall also give you addresses of firms to call on, and those to avoid. I know my competitors, it's a hard, ruthless world you are entering. Be prepared for disappointment, for not getting a higher price than I offered.'

Rose thanked him for offering the addresses and he told her he would be pleased to help them in any way that he could. They had only to ask.

'Then I will ask some advice.' This from Charlie. 'The girls are wanting to expand. I don't want to take up too much of your time, Mr Rosenberg, but if you could suggest the best way to tackle it.'

The only way Rose wanted to expand was to get into a world of making better dresses, but she waited to hear what their mentor had to say. He eyed each of them in turn, as though looking over the top of a pair of spectacles then said, 'Expand?' and pursed his lips.

He moved a few things around on his desk. 'I shall quote you my father's words when one of my uncles asked a similar question. He said, "If you have a small factory you will have small profits. If you enlarge it and employ more staff you will have a little more profit; if you have several factories, or one very large one *then your worries will really begin in earnest*.'"

Charlie laughed. 'You're right there!' Rose asked about the uncle, if he had expanded. Mr Rosenberg nodded.

'Yes, he did and got ulcers and suffered from insomnia. But then I have another uncle who has businesses all over the world. He drinks and eats what he likes, smokes heavily, has no ulcers and sleeps like a babe every night. It's a question of temperament. Uncle Aaron is a born worrier, Uncle Abraham is a philosopher.'

Mr Rosenberg paused then said, 'To expand you need to borrow.'

'No,' Lizzie snapped. 'No borrowing, we pay as we go along.'

Rose reminded her sister they had borrowed from Charlie to get the shop going and Lizzie said that was different, Charlie was family.

'Ah,' said Mr Rosenberg, wagging a forefinger. 'Never borrow from family unless they're in banking, otherwise there'll be trouble. Go to the bank, talk to the manager, that's his job. He will talk money, talk interest. He will guide you, but you must have collateral or be able to show you are able to repay the loan. My bank manager says he has never refused a loan. The people themselves do the refusing – they talk themselves out of it. When they first come in they are full of grandiose schemes, they can get money from here, money from there to repay it, but while they're talking these miracle places vanish into thin air.'

When Lizzie said she felt they could show they would be able to repay a loan Mr Rosenberg advised them to wait a while, and build up the business a bit more. He invited them to come and see him again.

Rose said warmly, 'You're so good to us, Mr Rosenberg. Why? We don't bring much business to you.'

His eyes suddenly twinkled. 'Let me give you another quote. This time something that happened to a friend. He's sometimes has a gamble and told me when he was first enjoying himself in this way he went to a bookie saying he wanted to bet a shilling each way on a certain horse. Unknowingly he had chosen one of the big bookies. The man waved him away, told him to take his money elsewhere, for they bet in hundreds of pounds. My friend told him he was betting in shillings now but in a year's time he might be betting in thousands. The bookie said he was quite right and took his money. Now my friend does bet in thousands and with the same man.'

Charlie gave a chuckle. 'I could do with that kind of luck.'

'Not luck, Charlie. My friend built up a business from nothing. All you three have a driving force and Rose has great potential. I feel sure you must succeed.'

They got up then to leave, knowing they had taken up a great deal of Mr Rosenberg's time. They thanked him and said their goodbyes. When they were at the door Rose turned and saw a great look of sadness in the businessman's eyes. It upset her and she mentioned it to Charlie who told her that Mr Rosenberg's only daughter had run away and married a non-Jewish boy. Her father would not forgive her. The girl, who had been told she would have a brilliant future as a barrister, died in childbirth. Ever since, Mr Rosenberg had lived with his grief and remorse.

'I think he wants to help us,' Charlie said, 'to compensate for what he did. And he especially wants to help you, Rose, because of your flair for designing. I feel he will always be a friend to us.'

'But he won't offer us any more money for the dresses,' Lizzie protested. 'And they're worth a lot more, I know it.'

'Not to him, he's a businessman, as well as a tragic father figure. I feel we can believe him when he said we wouldn't be able to get a higher price for the dresses.'

Rose said she agreed but Lizzie insisted they try other places.

At the end of an hour Rose said, 'That's it. We know now

Mr Rosenberg was right. We're not calling on anyone else.'
Lizzie was forced to agree.

Charlie said they would go to Mrs Caley's where they had
stayed before, leave the cases then go and book for a show.
Perhaps '*No, No, Nanette*'.

The evening performance was fully booked but Charlie
accepted three seats in the stalls for the matineé, and was
scolded by Lizzie for his extravagance. It was then Rose
confessed about her win on the horse and offered to treat them
to a slap-up meal. Lizzie said she despaired of both of them.

Once the business side had been abandoned Rose knew an
exhilaration. There was something so special about London
with its beautiful architecture and its cosmopolitan air with
fragments of conversation in every foreign tongue. She
noticed a lovely Chinese girl with raven hair and slanting eyes
in an emerald green cheongsam dress contrasting with a
young fair leggy girl in forget-me-not blue muslin.

Then there was the orchestra of sounds – the blaring of
motor horns mingling with the clip-clop of shire horses
drawing drays, the coarse shouts of drivers, and the booming
voice of a drum major type of man warning his son what
would happen to him if he didn't behave.

Rose wanted to be a part of this rich tapestry. She wanted
to ride on the big lumbering red buses, go into the bowels of
the earth on the underground trains and when she could
afford it hail a taxi cab to take her to her exotic destination.
Her own fashion house . . . Some day.

Charlie took them again to Bond Street, where Rose
drooled over the fashions and Charlie marvelled that there
were three Rolls Royces within a stone's throw of one
another. 'Three!' he exclaimed, 'and I bet they cost about
two thousand quid apiece.'

'Two thousand pounds for a car,' Lizzie said. 'You could
buy four houses on that new posh housing estate for that.'

Rose looked from one to the other. 'Do you know what? I
feel terribly guilty for even being here in London. At this

moment Gran could be trying to make a nourishing meal from three pennyworth of meat bones and two pennyworth of vegetables. I promised you a slap-up meal. I think we had better settle for a sandwich, or at the most, fish and chips.'

'Oh, no we won't,' Lizzie protested. 'We're not going to sit in the stalls with our clothes stinking of fish.'

They found a decent café in a side street near the theatre and had steak and kidney pie, with apple tart and cream to follow, which all declared to be sumptuous.

And when Rose found herself caught up with the matinée patrons in the vestibule and shown to the luxury of red plush seats in the stalls she no longer thought of homemade broth. This was a whole new world, one to be explored and enjoyed to the full.

They came out of the theatre with Rose in raptures, declaring she felt she was floating on notes of music. 'And the dancing! Oh, I wish our Frankie could have seen it.'

Charlie set his trilby at a rakish angle, linked arms with the girls and executed a few dance steps. 'Do you think I'd qualify for the chorus?' He began to sing, 'You for me and tea for two . . .'

Rose and Lizzie laughed. Rose said, 'You've got it all wrong.'

They were still laughing when Charlie stopped suddenly and stared ahead. Rose, following his gaze saw a man coming towards them, his hat too set at a rakish angle. He reminded her in a way of Charlie with his jaunty way of walking, but this man was small and slightly built. He was also immaculately groomed and had what her mother called 'class'.

When he had almost reached them he too stopped and stared. Then a slow smile spread over his face. 'Charlie Eagan, it has to be!'

'Lecky! What do you know!'

The next moment the two men were slapping one another on the back and both were talking at once.

'How long has it been . . .? What are you doing in London? Charlie, it's good to see you . . . Saw your photograph in the paper, Lecky, you dark horse you . . . Are you living in London or visiting?'

Charlie returned to the girls and introduced them with a flourish. 'You must meet my cousins, Miss Elizabeth Kimberley and Miss Rose Kimberley, the two most beautiful girls I know.'

'I have no quarrel with that,' said Lecky.

'Girls, meet my wartime buddy, Mr Leckworth Malgliesh.'

'Hey, hey, just Lecky. Delighted to know you, Miss Elizabeth Kimberley, and Miss Rose Kimberley.' He shook them both by the hand, his eyes twinkling.

'Do you know something,' Charlie went on, 'Lecky enlisted as a private and turned out to be the son of a lord. Did you ever get married?'

'No,' Lecky laughed. 'Saved at the altar. Now come on, tell me, what are you all doing in London and what are your plans?'

Charlie told him about the matinée but also about the main reason they were there. Lecky said immediately, 'You must meet my sister, she's crazy about clothes.'

He asked if they planned to stay overnight and when Charlie told him they had lodgings booked Lecky said they must come and stay at his home. He was not going to part with them until he had caught up on the news. He would send someone to let their landlady know they would not be in that night and the messenger would collect their luggage.

Lizzie grumbled to Rose when he hailed a taxi cab, 'We'll be like fishes out of water. They're not our kind of people.'

'But they will be, Lizzie, if we achieve our ambition and get on in the world. They'll be our customers, so let's get to know what they're really like. This is a grand opportunity. And for heaven's sake, cheer up, for Charlie's sake, if for no one else's.'

The only better class houses Rose had been in were those in the Lismond area at home where she had gone with Charlie.

She had thought some of these quite imposing, but realised how ordinary they were in comparison to Lecky's home. This was an elegance she associated with royalty.

Soft-footed servants had taken their hats and coats, the butler informing Lecky his parents had phoned to say they would not return from the country for another two days. Lecky said, 'Oh, good, I expect my sister has already arranged a party. Clarissa wastes no time when my parents are not here. When the cat is away, etcetera. But not to worry, we shall have plenty of time for talking. I doubt whether any one will arrive for the party before ten o'clock. Come along, we'll find Clarissa.'

They went up to the first landing, thick-piled carpet muffling their footsteps. From one of the rooms came the sound of a gramophone being played, the tune '*Bye Bye Blackbird*'. Lecky stopped at this door and called, 'Clarissa, where are you?'

From the open doorway could be seen a lovely book-lined room with a massive carved oak desk near the window. The gramophone was perched in the middle of the desk, surrounded by a number of records. A tall fair girl, with fashionably bobbed hair came into view, the ends of the two chiffon scarves wrapped about her throat floating out behind her.

'Clarissa, we have three extra guests, very special ones.'

The introductions were made and any shyness Rose felt at first coming into such surroundings were dispelled by the sincerity and warmth of Clarissa's welcome.

'Elizabeth – Rose, how lovely to meet you. Aren't you both attractive! And Charlie, my goodness, I feel I know you like my own brother, Lecky has talked so much about you. But he didn't tell me how handsome you were. Such eyes!'

'Clarissa,' Lecky protested, 'you're embarrassing the fellow.'

Charlie laughed. 'I can take plenty of that kind of talk.'

'Charlie, I like you. Unhappily I won't get a look in when

the hordes descend this evening. The girls will gobble you up. And you, Lecky, won't stand a chance with Elizabeth and Rose when the men arrive.'

'What men?' Lecky teased.

'Alex de Veer has agreed to come.'

'Oh, great, then we will at least get *some* intelligent conversation. Who else have you invited?'

Clarissa reeled off a list of names then said to Charlie and the girls, 'Oh, I'm so glad you are here for our party tonight, you'll enjoy it.'

Lizzie said stiffly, 'I'm afraid we'll have to miss the party, we – well, we didn't bring any – party dresses.'

Clarissa dismissed it as being no problem. It was an Eastern Night. She explained that her Uncle Wilbur had had a mania for collecting Eastern dress of all kinds, so they had Japanese kimonos, cheongsam dresses, Mandarin robes, the costumes of Japanese warlords and emperors, peasant smocks – everything, and as Uncle Wilbur was dead, who was there to object?

Rose found herself liking both brother and sister.

When later the girls were shown to their large airy room with a four-poster bed, Rose was wildly excited, exclaiming to Lizzie to come and look at that. What about the beautiful chintz bedcover, *hand* quilted and with such tiny stitches. Just wait until she told Ma and Gran about it. And what about the bathroom that led off the room. Had Lizzie ever seen such a big bath? It would hold all the kids at one time. And how about these two Japanese prints on the wall. Weren't they beautiful? Oh, Lizzie would look lovely in a kimono with her dark hair and eyes.

Rose, who had kept on poking around the room, opened a cupboard and brought out two chamber pots with a willow pattern on both. She collapsed with laughter. What was funnier, wearing a kimono or sitting on a chamber pot with a willow-patterned bottom?

Lizzie's lips twitched. 'I don't have a willow-patterned

bottom.' The twitch developed into laughter then Rose joined in and they had one of their giggling fits, tears running down their cheeks.

'Japanese poes!' Rose kept exclaiming, happy now, knowing that her sister would join in the fun that evening.

But before they started to prepare for the party the crêpe de chine dress was shown to Clarissa, at Lecky's insistence. Clarissa went into raptures over it. What talent, Rose's own design! She must come to London to live and open up a shop. Many titled women had opened dress shops and were doing awfully well. Rose said her mother would object to her living in London and, as for opening a dress shop, she had no money for such a venture. Not yet. Clarissa then declared she must get someone to finance her, and appealed to her brother.

'Lecky, don't you think that Alex de Veer would be interested in such a venture? He has oodles of money and has his fingers in all sorts of pies.'

Lecky said there would be no harm in asking him.

Clarissa said they could all help her to unpack the trunks and they went to the 'den'. The word had conjured up for Rose a small, cosy place, and she was surprised to find it huge, with the furnishings beyond anything she had ever seen. The red wallpaper had black tracery on it. There were blown up photographs of Mandarins, warriors, of geisha girls and demure Chinese maidens. There were skin rugs on the floor and piles of cushions. Divans were draped with exotic-looking fabrics. Greenery was intertwined in trellis which circled potted plants and flowers. Small niches had been made holding fat-bellied buddhas, some of which nodded their heads when touched. Joss-sticks were placed ready to be lit when the party started and wind bells hanging from the ceiling tinkled when Lecky opened and closed a door. A bar had been set up and Clarissa said that 'Gerald' had planned some suitable cocktails. She read a list of them: Dragon's Tongue, Mandarin's Talons, Cobra's Poison and Flame Scorchers.

Lecky remarked wryly if anyone was fool enough to drink Gerald's potions there would be no party. They would all be flat out cold on the floor. Clarissa simply gave him an indulgent smile and told him he was exaggerating.

They all helped to unpack the trunks. Rose was in her element with all the lovely brocades and satins and she frantically sketched designs of dragons, swirls of flowers and exotic-looking birds. The two men were like schoolboys wielding hefty swords, fortunately blunted, and trying on metal helmets. Clarissa confided to Lizzie and Rose that the men were seeing themselves dressed up as warlords for the party, but she had other ideas for them. Wait and see!

When it came to the time for dressing Clarissa decided that Lizzie should be a geisha girl, and produced a beautiful deep gold kimono embroidered in jewel colours, with a wig and make up. Rose had always accepted her sister as being attractive but when she saw the completed 'geisha' she was astonished at the change. This was a really beautiful girl she was looking at. How long Lizzie's lashes were. She had not noticed them before, it must be the mascara that was emphasising them. And what a lovely shaped mouth, cherry red at this moment. Lizzie, warming to the part, glanced at them from under her long lashes, her expression demure yet tantalisingly provocative. Clarissa clapped her hands in delight. 'Splendid! Exactly right! Now what shall we make of Rose? Perhaps a Chinese girl. Some Chinese girls do have blue eyes.'

Rose, who would have liked to have been a geisha girl too, was disappointed. Then Clarissa brought out a midnight blue satin cheongsam dress with silver embroidery and a slit at the side from hem to knee. The dress fitted Rose perfectly. With an impish grin she put a hand on her hip, thrust out a curved leg and tossed a come-hither look, which brought a sharp comment from her sister.

'Hey, our Rose, just you watch it, we'll have none of that larking about!'

'Oh, Elizabeth,' Rose teased, 'you've completely spoilt your image. And anyway, who are you to talk with your tempting glances.'

Charlie and Lecky came in. Lizzie put on her demure act. 'Me Morning Sun. This little sister. She Lotus Blossom.'

Charlie looked startled for a moment then he began to laugh. 'Hey, I didn't recognise you for a moment. You look great, both of you.'

Rose tried not to feel jealous that Charlie's gaze had stayed on Lizzie as he said softly, 'You really are two very beautiful girls.'

Clarissa came out from one of the two rooms that had been set aside for guests to change into their costumes.

'Oh, there you are, Lecky. I need you, and you too, Charles. Come with me.' To the girls she added, 'Hand out the costumes if anyone comes before I get back, but I won't be long.'

Clarissa came back on her own as the first of the guests arrived. Then all three were kept busy handing out the costumes. From the two changing rooms came bursts of laughter.

During a slight lull a tall, rather distinguished but austere-looking man came in. Clarissa went up to him and kissed him on the cheek. 'Alex, darling, so glad you could come.'

The two sisters exchanged glances and Lizzie mouthed, 'Alex de Veer?'

Rose nodded and Lizzie whispered, 'A cold fish, if ever I saw one. I don't think we'll get much joy out of him.'

Chapter 14

Clarissa explained to the newcomer about the theme of the evening and pointed out the costumes, but he waved them aside with a dismissive hand. 'Not for me, Clarissa, no dressing up.'

She began coaxing and such was her persuasion he took a robe from her and went to change. Then Alex de Veer was forgotten as a spate of guests arrived and all three girls were kept busy handing out the costumes.

By ten o'clock Chinese and Japanese were rubbing shoulders with one another. The noise was deafening and cigar and cigarette smoke drifted in a thick haze to where windows had been opened at the top. Then a resounding blow on a massive gong brought a silence. A stentorian voice cried, 'Make way for the Emperor!'

A bamboo screen was lifted aside at the end of the room, disclosing a man sitting in a large cane chair. Wooden poles had been attached to the chair and two Chinese coolies, in smocks and flat straw hats complete with pigtails, lifted the chair and came with jog-trotting steps into their midst.

There was a burst of applause and laughter, but the guests, playing their part, bowed low, hands clasped. The man in the chair, sitting stiffly erect, his hands tucked into the sleeves of his magnificent robe, looked imperious enough to be an emperor. Lizzie said, 'Isn't it that Alex de Veer?'

The room was dimly lit, the lights red-shaded. Rose said she could not be sure. Lizzie gave her a nudge. 'Well you can see who the coolies are, can't you? It's Charlie and Lecky.' She laughed. 'They're good, aren't they?'

The man at the front of the chair suddenly stumbled and fell. The 'Emperor' was shot forward and landed on top of him. Both men lay helpless with laughter. Lizzie said, 'I was wrong, it couldn't be Alex de Veer, he seemed a cold, humourless fish.'

During the next half-hour Rose saw Charlie and Lecky trying to get through to them several times, but each time they were grabbed by girls. Rose was not bothered, neither was Lizzie, since they had their own admirers. It was a heady thing, Rose decided, as heady as the Dragon's Tongue cocktail she had drunk. They ate food they had never tasted before, like smoked salmon, game pie, pâté de foie gras, lobster – Lizzie's eyes were sparkling. She had kept up her 'Me Morning Sun' talk and the men loved it. One said he would like nothing better than to have this 'Sun' wake him every morning. Another man, putting his arm around Rose, announced he ate Lotus Blossoms every morning and wanted to nibble this one.

'Over my dead body,' declared Lizzie, bringing a roar of laughter. Clarissa came for them then, wanting them to meet Alex de Veer who, she said, was preparing to leave.

He had changed back into his dark grey suit. After Clarissa had made the introductions she left the three of them to talk.

Alex was standing under an unshaded light and for the first time Rose was able to really take stock of him. His dark hair, with its widow's peak and his winged eyebrows gave him a slightly devilish look, but his eyes were serious. He spoke softly, yet his words had a clarity. Rose thought it a lovely voice. She liked too his courteous manner, and the attentive way he listened to Lizzie as she outlined their plans. He asked questions about finance and Rose was proud of the way Lizzie had all the figures at her fingertips.

'We're in a small way of business at the moment, Mr de Veer, but I feel it could be built up, with help. Rose, as no doubt Clarissa told you, is keen to make better class dresses.

She has a real flair for design. This is the opinion of a man experienced in the trade.'

'I accept that,' he said. 'Unfortunately, I have no time to see the dresses you have with you. Will you still be here tomorrow evening?'

Lizzie told him no, they would have to leave by early afternoon. Alex made an appointment to see them at ten o'clock the following morning. He then left.

'Well,' Rose said, 'he *must* be interested. Deferential treatment! Isn't he attractive?'

'If you like that type. He's a businessman and it's his way to be polite. Don't let that fool you, our Rose, I still think he's a cold fish.'

'And I think he wouldn't have bothered to see the dresses if he hadn't been interested. *And*, I still think he's attractive.'

Charlie and Lecky pushed their way through to them, both apologising for their neglect. Lizzie said, 'Not to worry, we've done all right, kept busy – with men. We've just been talking with Alex de Veer, he's coming to see us in the morning to discuss business.'

'So he *is* interested?' Charlie's tone was eager.

'Oh, he's interested all right, very interested.'

Rose looked at her sister in mild astonishment. Lizzie smiled and there was an impish glint in her eyes as she said to Charlie, 'Actually, I could easily fall for him.'

'Well don't fall for him at this moment, love. The band has just arrived for the dancing. The man with the brass lungs will be announcing it at any moment. Lecky's going to teach us how to do the Charleston.'

As Charlie finished speaking the gong resounded and the man 'with the brass lungs' announced most of what Charlie had told them, but with the addition that those people who had not yet mastered the steps of the Charleston must go into Charleston Alley, to prevent 'injuries' to the experts.

There was laughter at this. Lecky said, 'I got two bruised kneecaps and bruised shins while I was learning. I must be mad to be teaching you lot. Come on, this way.' His cheeky grin took the sting from his remarks.

Rose had heard about the Charleston Alleys in dance halls with a mirror at the end and railings on either side to hold on to while practising. In this case the Alley was a passage with the backs of chairs to act as railings. A gilt antique mirror covered the wall at the end.

To the strains of the band playing the lively '*Yes, Sir, That's My Baby*', Charlie and Lizzie and Rose, with about twenty other people followed the expert instructions of Lecky.

Rose declared she had never laughed so much in her life as they twisted their feet to try and catch the rhythm. She was the first to master the steps and was delighted when Lecky told her she was a born dancer. He found someone else to continue the tuition and took Rose on to the main floor. Within minutes she was doing all sorts of intricate steps. In fact she and Lecky were so good together some couples stopped to watch them and applauded when the dance ended. Rose, flushed and exhilarated looked up to see Charlie and Lizzie smiling at them.

'Hey, Rosie, you're good, where did you learn to dance like that?' Charlie took hold of Lizzie's hand, 'We've got the steps off but we're a couple of old dodderers in comparison to you two.'

Lizzie protested that *she* might be a dodderer but Charlie was good and just watch him when the band started again! The crowd had been demanding an encore. And Charlie was good, very light on his feet, but Lecky was the expert.

It was a night of nights for Rose. Men were lining up for the favour of partnering her. She waltzed and quick-stepped and one-stepped and Charlestoned until four o'clock in the morning when the party started to break up. Clarissa said that some of them would still be there at breakfast time but for once she had to leave them and go to bed, she was exhausted.

It was not only the Charleston that Rose learned that night. Her sexual education advanced by leaps and bounds.

She discovered there could be a sexual relationship between men and also between women, and although intrigued to know how she did not ask Lizzie, who had answered her question as to why Lecky had asked a number of people to leave. To Rose, the fact of one man sitting on another man's knee was just larking about. And the same with two women who were in a corner, one lying on top of the other, the one on top tugging at the other woman's hair and appearing to be having a friendly wrestling match. But according to Lizzie, this sort of action was punishable by law. Lizzie said she had overheard Lecky telling Charlie that although he could understand this kind of behaviour, he could not allow it in their house, his mater and pater would just about go up the wall if they learned of it.

When Rose was in bed she forgot about these strange people. Happy and bemused she found herself thinking about Alex de Veer, imagining him escorting her into a restaurant, going to the theatre – in a box – taking her for a ride in his car. Not that cars meant anything to her, but it must be something special because when Clarissa had said during the evening that Alex owned a three-litre Bentley, Charlie had whistled and said with a note of envy in his voice that some blokes had all the luck.

Lizzie said, 'Are you awake, our Rose?'

'Yes. Hasn't it been lovely and aren't you glad we managed to get these pure silk nighties from Charlie's stall? They wouldn't shame anyone and don't they have a lovely feel, I think I'd like to wear pure silk always.'

Lizzie ran her hands over her body, feeling a sensuousness as she imagined Alex de Veer in bed beside her. She had called him cold, not wanting Rose to suspect how she felt about him, but there was fire under that cool exterior, she was sure of it. She turned her head.

'Rose, listen, don't you ever let Ma and Gran know we didn't come to bed until nearly five o'clock. They'd never let us come to London again.'

'Do you think I would?' Rose laughed softly. 'I could imagine Gran's face if I told her I'd been drinking Mandarin's Tongues. I didn't much like the taste of them but they made me feel good. I wouldn't mind having this kind of life always.'

'You'd get sick of it.' Lizzie spoke sharply. 'If we ever did get money I wouldn't want to mix with these kind of people.'

'But they're lovely, so kind, such fun.' Rose yawned. 'Oh, I'm nearly asleep. See you in the morning.' She giggled. 'It is morning, in less than five hours we'll be seeing Alex de Veer.'

Yes, Lizzie thought, hearing him speak her name. 'Miss Kimberley'. He made it sound as though she were royalty. She would like to hear him say Elizabeth. She must get them at home to call her Elizabeth. After all, she could not enter into the world of haute couture known as *Lizzie* Kimberley.

The world of haute couture? It had a sophistication, aura. She could not accept the behaviour of some of the couples she had seen tonight, sneaking into bedrooms, but then there was no need to mix with their kind. With money one could find a certain seclusion. Lizzie smiled wryly. With money? Like Rose she was thinking too far ahead. Much better to take life and what it had to offer step by step.

Alex de Veer she was sure was going to take them several steps ahead. He had that kind of manner, that kind of mind. She was a fair judge of character and was sure she was right. Tomorrow no, today – she would know.

After only three hours' sleep both Rose and Lizzie were wide awake. When they went downstairs Charlie and Lecky were already in the dining room. They had never been to bed. Lecky said Clarissa talked of getting up for when Alex de Veer came but it was his guess she would not surface until midday. All four said they felt surprisingly bright considering their lack of sleep, and all looked it. Rose, excited at the thought of meeting Alex again was sure she would not be able to eat a bite, but ate as much as the rest. But she was calm when he arrived. He was prompt.

Lecky brought him into the sunshine-filled morning room, where they had congregated after breakfast to talk over all the events of the party.

'Good morning.'

It was not only Alex de Veer's voice that sent a pleasurable thrill down Rose's spine but his appearance. He was wearing brown this morning, a beautifully cut suit, his tie in muted shades of green and brown just the right touch against the pale cream silk shirt. His lean face had given her the impression of being of slender build, now she saw he was quite broad-shouldered. An elegant man about town, but a very masculine one.

Lecky offered him a drink but Alex refused, saying he was just begining to recover from the party. At that moment there was, surprisingly, a twinkle in his dark eyes.

'What a night!' Lecky pressed his palms to his temples. 'I'll never allow that Gerald what's-his-name to make any concoctions again.'

Charlie and Alex began to laugh and Rose and Lizzie exchanged glances. So Alex had been the Emperor after all. Rose felt a sense of relief that Alex did have humour. It was easier dealing with people who could laugh.

But when in the next few moments he turned to the girls, apologising for his neglect of them, his expression was as sombre as though he had arrived for a funeral. They must get down to business. He asked to see the sample dress. Lecky left them then.

Alex examined the dress carefully, complimented Rose on her design and the workmanship then asked if she would sketch him one or two more. Rose did three. They were not styles she had used before, they came to her as soon as the pencil was in her hand. She told Alex this and he said, 'You certainly have flair, Miss Kimberley.'

Rose looked up. 'But it's my sister – Elizabeth – who has the business head.'

'Yes, I realised that last night when we discussed figures. A good combination. I might be interested in financing you, but there is a great deal you need to know.'

Alex talked at great length but when Rose realised he was thinking in terms of a large output of dresses she interrupted.

'Mr de Veer, I'm not interested in mass producing. I want to design and make expensive dresses. I do hope, ultimately, to be a top fashion designer. Oh, I know I'm flying high and I know it will take a long time, but I'm prepared to work for it, and my sister is willing to help me.'

Alex said that hard work was not enough. There were hundreds of talented fashion designers who never found recognition. Luck could play a part in helping to further their career but luck needed to be coupled with finance. Finance was the key word. To make money, big money in this line, meant mass-producing. Rose could go on with her expensive dresses, they would sell. A fashion house could come later, but she must realise the competition she was up against. Alex quoted a list of top designers from which Rose only recognised three. Chanel, Worth and Givenchy. Lizzie had told her about them.

By this time Rose was feeling so flat she felt she had been pressed on to the floor and stamped on.

Charlie said, 'Rose has talent, Alex. You admit it. Is her talent going to be lost in all this mass production? You say she'll get her chance later, but how much later? Let's face it, you are only interested in making money, big money.'

Alex rubbed his fingertips across his chin. 'I'm a financier, Charles, not a philanthropist, but because I have a flair for backing successful business ventures I'm willing to nurse people along who I know have talent and who, I feel, are also capable of running a business. These are the kind of people who build up businesses for the future. Our largest companies in the world started in a small way.'

'But you were just saying,' Charlie began, when Alex held up a hand.

'Let me finish. A combination of hard work and flair are two ingredients for success, but the third and most important is to be able to establish credibility in the world of finance. I am willing to back you in your tender years but you must be willing to be guided by me.'

'In other words,' Lizzie retorted, 'we'd have no say.'

'Oh, you would have plenty of say.' A faint smile touched Alex's lips. 'And I think if it came to a fight, Miss Kimberley, you would make a very worthy opponent.'

'I'd give you a good fight all right.'

'That's good, it's necessary. It's necessary to prove a point, but foolish to be aggressive and unable to listen to reason. When I asked that you be guided by me I meant exactly that. I do have expert knowledge.'

Charlie eyed him thoughtfully. 'But what *exactly* do you expect to get out of it, Alex?'

'I expect a return on my investment. The legal formalities would have to be discussed later.'

Rose looked from Lizzie to Charlie then to Alex. 'I'm afraid I don't know very much about business, but might I ask if you expect to come into partnership with us?'

'No partnership. I would hope to become a shareholder, but that is very much for the future. You would start as a private business, later become a limited company then, when the business is vastly extended you would go public and issue shares.'

It was all double Dutch to Rose but the way Charlie and Lizzie were nodding their heads she presumed they knew what it was all about.

Alex went on talking and although his remarks seemed to be mainly addressed to Charlie and Lizzie he had enough courtesy to ask Rose a question from time to time. Watching him, she found it impossible to associate this dedicated businessman with the one who had laughed helplessly with Charlie over their escapade of the night before.

A phone call for Alex broke up their meeting. He had to leave. He would be in touch with Charles. They would meet again soon, he hoped.

Clarissa came downstairs in time to see him, with Lecky, to the front door. Rose watched with Charlie and Lizzie from the window. A taxi was waiting. Before Alex got into it he raised a hand in farewell to them. When the cab was out of sight Rose said, 'Do you think we've done the right thing in getting involved with Alex de Veer?'

Charlie's assurance that he was positive they had was echoed by Lizzie, but Rose was not convinced, not even after a talk with Lecky and Clarissa, who claimed they were lucky indeed that Alex showed interest in their venture and added it was impossible for them to fail with such a man behind them.

Rose could still not get it out of her mind that the business would be taken over by Alex de Veer, that he would want to employ other designers and oust her. She brought it up when they were in the train and on their way home. Lizzie said rubbish, it was Rose's designs he was interested in, it was the whole point of their business deal. She had confidence in him, although admitting she thought he would be quite ruthless when it came to bargaining.

Charlie declared it was the only way to get on – one had to be ruthless to succeed. After a pause he said, a beatific smile spreading over his face, 'You know that Alex owns a three-litre Bentley – well, he's promised to give me a run in it the next time we're in London. There were only fifteen of them made, imagine! That's what money can give you.'

'Money isn't everything,' Rose said.

Lizzie sniffed. 'Oh, but dear cousin *Charles* would like the life. Did you hear them all, on Christian name terms right away. Oh, there you are, Charles my dear fellow . . .' Lizzie mimicked the exaggerated tones of some of the guests. 'I say old chap . . . Charles, dear boy, who's for champers . . . Well, actually, Charles old fellow . . .'

'And what about *Elizabeth* darling?' Charlie teased, mimicking too. '*Ectually*, I rather adore the name Elizabeth. Suits you, sweetie, much better than Lizzie.'

'I agree,' Rose said. 'I think we should start calling her Elizabeth from now on. Mind you, the family might raise objections, say we're getting too big for our boots.'

Lizzie sat up. 'I'll tell you something. If we're going to enter into this world we've got to be equipped for it. The first thing I'm going to do when we get back home is enrol at night classes for elocution lessons. I suggest you do the same, our Rose. We must get rid of our Northern accent.'

Rose protested strongly. Lizzie could do what she liked but she was proud of being a Northerner.

'So am I,' said Lizzie, 'but I won't be laughed at, not if we're to go into business in a big way. We need all the advantages.'

'I don't think anybody laughed at us,' Rose said.

'Perhaps not, but disparaging remarks were made. Do you remember that girl with the bright red hair whose dress was slit at the back from her neck to her behind? Well, Lecky introduced us to a group of people after we'd been dancing and this girl looked me up and down and asked me where I came from. "Not from Japan" she drawled with a sneer. – Was it by chance that dreadful place Yorkshire? Or could it be that equally awful place Liverpool, or maybe it was Newcastle on the River Tyne, where the people were known as Geordies – or *something*!'

Rose was indignant. 'The cheek! What did you tell her?'

'I told her I probably had a mixture of dialects as I was an interpreter, constantly speaking in seven different languages. Then I called her a "stupid fool" in Greek, in Yiddish, in German and Italian, Russian, Swedish and Norwegian, and asked her which language she would like to converse in.'

'Lizzie, you didn't! What if she had taken you up on it?'

'I knew she wouldn't, the others were laughing at her. She just tossed her head and walked away. But there was an outcome to it. Lecky asked me where I learned to speak seven languages, and there was a respect in his voice. Do you see what I mean?'

Charlie was chuckling. 'I hope you told Lecky that if you're brought up in a tenement with a mixed bag of nationalities you learn a smattering of the language – mainly, of course, all the swear words.'

'Oh, I didn't learn those, sir.' Lizzie looked as demure as she had the night before in her role of geisha girl.

'I bet you didn't,' Charlie said, and they all laughed.

By the time they arrived home they had settled between them how much the family should be told of their visit. Charlie said, enough for them to share in their fun, but not anything that would cause them worry. Rose was the first to go in. 'Hello, hello,' she called, 'we're home.' She made for the kitchen, calling again, but there was no cheery reply and the house was quiet. Where could they all be, she wondered. Her mother at least would never be out at this time of day. Rose opened the kitchen door then, glancing over her shoulder at Charlie and Lizzie she pulled a face and whispered, 'We have a visitor. Guess who? Aunt Maude.'

Charlie groaned. 'Oh, no, of all people!' They went in.

'Hello, Aunt Maude,' Rose said brightly. She looked about her. 'Where is everybody?'

'They're out. I was waiting for you in case you came. Edie thought there ought to be someone here, she didn't want you coming to an empty house – and wondering.'

Maude, in her pudding basin hat, her coat slipping from one shoulder as usual, spoke as though she were reading from a railway timetable.

'But where are they?' Lizzie asked. 'Where've they gone?'

Maude hitched her coat up on to her shoulder. 'The children are with your next door neighbour. Your Gran and your Ma have gone to the hospital. Probably gone to the morgue too.'

The shock was so great Rose felt as though the wall was

coming to hit her. Then it steadied. She tried to say, 'Morgue?' but her mouth seemed to be full of cottonwool. It was Charlie who said it, followed by, 'Maude, what on earth has happened? What's wrong?'

'Your Gran'll tell you, I think that's her now.'

Charlie and Lizzie and Rose all turned to face the open doorway as they heard a key scraping in the front lock. The footsteps coming along the passage were not the short brisk steps of Gran Eagan, but it was Edie who appeared. She looked from one to the other, her face colourless.

'Why didn't you come in answer to the telegram?'

The question was said without reproach, without emotion. It could have been Maude speaking. Charlie said they had not received it and asked again, what was wrong? Edie told them it would be best if they all sat down.

'Tell us now, Gran,' Lizzie urged. 'Aunt Maude was talking about the hospital, about the morgue. Is it Ma? Tell us the truth, we *must* know.'

'The truth is brutal, but you have to know.' Edie looked down at her gloved hands for a moment. When she looked up her eyes were brimming with tears. It was the first time Rose had seen her grandmother cry.

'Frank and Tommy tried to stop a runaway horse. It was heading towards where children were playing, it would have trapped them. The boys stopped the horse but Frank was kicked on the head. Tommy . . .' Edie's lips quivered then she got herself under control. 'Tommy fell under the wheel. They had to amputate his right leg.'

Rose's hand went to her mouth. 'Oh God, oh, no!'

'And Frank?' Charlie asked, his voice taut with strain.

'He was dead when they got him to the hospital.'

Maude said, 'It's a good job he did die. Far better than ending up a looney, I mean to say, a kick from a horse – on the head –'

'Shut up, Maude!' Charlie said savagely. 'And if you can't think of anything better to say then you'd better go.'

Maude got up. 'I have to go in any case, Bert'll want his supper, you know how he is about his food. I'll see you later. Ta-ra, then.' She drifted out.

Charlie made to go after her but Edie laid a restraining hand on his arm. 'Maude is upset, but she can't express her grief. Never could.'

Rose suddenly looked about her in a frantic way. 'Ma, where is she?'

'At the hospital. She collapsed. They put her to bed and gave her something to make her sleep. They told me to leave her there until the morning.'

Lizzie made tea. She and Charlie looked as stricken as Rose felt. Gran Eagan laced their mugs of tea with brandy. There was always a little in the house in case of emergency. They talked of the reason for not receiving the telegram, Rose's voice breaking when she said, 'To think we were enjoying ourselves while all this happened.'

Edie said there must be no regrets. Nothing could be changed. It was the Lord's will, adding that in His infinite mercy He had taken Frank instead of Tommy.

'Mercy?' Rose exclaimed. 'Where is the mercy in taking a boy's life? Frank had such dreams.'

Edie nodded. 'Yes, I know, his dancing. That's why I say it's better for him to have been taken. He would never have been able to cope. Tommy will, he's tough, he's a survivor.'

Rose was dismayed at her grandmother's attitude. Who was she to say that Frank would not have survived because he was a dreamer? Did she know that he had sacrificed a promising career when his father died, to help out with the family expenses? Tommy was tough, she said. Would any boy be tough knowing he had lost a leg? No more shinning up trees, over walls, racing down the street, pounding up the stairs. Rose made up her mind then she could not go and visit Tommy in hospital. She would be unable to bear seeing the laughter, the mischief gone from her brother's eyes. It would be bad enough coping with her mother's grief.

By the following morning Rose saw this as an ordeal. She wanted to run away and hide. Charlie and Lizzie had gone to the hospital to fetch Sally. Rose had refused to go, saying it would be better if she stayed with Gran. People would call, the priest, neighbours, all sorts of people. She saw her grandmother studying her closely then she said, yes, perhaps it would be best.

When her mother did walk in she was surprisingly calm. There were no tears, no signs of grief, and yet Rose found this more frightening than her mother's keening and rocking on New Year's Eve when her father had died. That was a natural thing, this attitude was unnatural. More frightening was the fact that her mother closed them all out except Charlie. It was to him she addressed all her remarks. 'Frankie looked lovely, Charlie. Such a darling boy, so sensitive. Tommy's taking his loss very well. Frankie's loss as well as the loss of his leg. He's quite philosophical about it. Said it could have been worse. Did you enjoy your visit to London?'

Charlie, for once at a loss, looked to Edie for guidance. Edie nodded and mouthed, 'Tell her,' and so Charlie skimmed over the surface of what they had done. Eventually Sally broke in to say she wanted to see the children.

During the next two weeks Sally lived in a world where only Charlie, her younger children and Tommy existed. Rose lived in a world of guilt, having convinced herself she was responsible for all the tragedies with her high flying ambition. A price had to be paid. She was a jinx on the family. The first time they went to London and enjoyed themselves baby Lilian had been struck blind. After their lovely Christmas when she had spent her earnings from the business, her father had died. Now after their wonderful two days there was the dreadful tragedy of Frank and Tommy. She must forget her ambitions, stop designing, close the shop. Lizzie could get a job somewhere and so could she.

'Close the shop?' Lizzie exclaimed. 'You must be mad. Of course we're not going to close it. It's time you pulled yourself together, our Rose. I know you're suffering from shock, we all are, but we can't stop living, eating, and to eat we need money. Stop thinking of yourself. Tomorrow we'll have to start cutting out, the stock at the shop needs replenishing. Bessie and the others are waiting for work. They need the money.'

Rose stared at her for a moment, then without a word she left the kitchen and went upstairs. In the bedroom she put a chairback under the knob. Lizzie came up and began pounding on the door. 'You let me in, our Rose, you've been wet-nursed long enough!'

Rose heard her grandmother say, 'Lizzie, leave her alone. Now do as I say. She needs time.' The voices receded.

Chapter 15

That evening when Charlie came home he said, 'Tomorrow morning you and I, Rosie, are going to get on a tram and go to the coast. We'll walk along the sands, I'll take off my shoes and socks, and you'll take off your shoes and stockings and plodge.'

'I don't want to go to the coast.'

'We're going, even if I have to carry you. We'll leave here early, catch the best of the morning. If you lock your door I'll break it down.' Charlie was smiling but underlying his lightness was a determination. Rose gave in.

The morning was cool when they set out for the tram stop at eight o'clock but the haziness of the pale blue sky at the horizon gave an indication of heat later.

They went up on the open deck of the tram, Rosie making the choice. Charlie said if she felt cold they could go below. She shook her head, and was silent for a long time. Charlie made no attempt to make conversation. This was an experiment and he prayed it would work. He would have liked to have told her about the other time when he was on his way to the coast and Lecky had come into his mind. It seemed impossible to believe they had met up with Lecky right out of the blue, and had had a whale of a time with him since. They must go to London again to talk business with Alex de Veer. He would not let Rose give in to this melancholia without a fight. He would not allow her to waste her talents, nor would he allow her to lose her peace of mind, which was more important still.

The tram rattled its way over the single line track through

the fields where cows and sheep grazed. In two of the fields corn was stooked. Rose took no interest in the surroundings until a frisky foal, head tossing, tail swishing, cantered along by the tram, keeping pace. Then, as it neared a fence it slowed and stopped. Rose looked back. Charlie said, 'A lively filly, isn't she?'

'And a prisoner, like all of us.'

Charlie glanced at her then said, keeping his voice bright, 'I know this, I'd rather be Charlie Eagan than a horse.'

Rose stared straight ahead. 'I'd rather be dead.'

He bit back a retort to tell her to stop talking in that way and said instead, 'Well, don't die until we've seen the sea. It's one of my pleasures and I'll enjoy it more to have someone with me, especially someone I'm fond of.'

Although it brought no visible response Charlie had the feeling it had struck a chord with Rose. They rode the rest of the way in silence.

When they got off the tram Charlie took a deep breath, enjoying the fresh, seaweed-laden air, which always brought childhood memories of seeing the sea for the first time. How awed he had been by its vastness. Over the years he had seen it in all its moods and loved every one.

'Charlie – what do you hope to achieve by bringing me here today?'

Her question, after a long silence, startled him. He sought for the right answer, knowing it was important.

'I can usually find a sense of peace when I come here and walk along the beach. I thought it might help solve your problems as well as helping to solve mine.'

'*You* have problems?' The interest in the gaze Rose turned on Charlie gave him hope.

'Oh, yes, Rosie, I have problems, plenty. Recently one of the skeletons in my cupboard has been poking a bony finger at me, prodding me, warning me not to get too complacent, letting me know it could come right out of the cupboard at any time.'

Rose made no reply but she looked thoughtful, as though weighing up what possible skeleton Charlie could have in his cupboard.

They went down the steps that led to the beach and made for the damp, hard-packed sand near the water's edge. They walked along, dodging the small cream-frothed waves that swirled close to their feet. The only people in sight were two men in a boat fishing, a man throwing a red and green striped ball to a lolloping black mongrel, and a woman tossing a stick into the water for a wire-haired terrier to fetch. The barking of the dogs and their owners' voices were the only sounds.

The sun had come out making the clear air more glaring. Charlie shaded his eyes and gave a sigh of contentment. 'Lovely, isn't it?' Rose was silent. Later when he stopped and asked if she was going to test the water, she shrugged and walked on. He took off his shoes and socks, pushed the socks into the shoes, tied the laces together and slung them over his shoulder. He splashed into the water and yelled, 'Hey, it's great, you're missing a treat.' There was no answer. Charlie turned and watched Rose who was walking at a snail's pace, her hands thrust deep into the short cream jacket she wore over her blue cotton dress. There was something so forlorn-looking about the slight figure, head bowed, tendrils of hair lifting in the breeze, that Charlie felt an ache. Oh, God, how he loved her. If only he could tell her. If only he was free to tell her. But then, what difference would it make, she had never looked at him the way he had seen her look at Alex de Veer. Then there had been a look of wonder in her eyes, almost as if she were discovering love for the first time. Rose stopped and glanced over her shoulder.

'I'll take off my shoes and stockings and come in, Charlie, if you turn your back.' Even her voice had a forlorn sound.

'Righto, don't take all day.' He tried not to think of the night on the beach at Blackpool when he had fastened her suspenders. This was no time for such thoughts.

He heard her splashing towards him. 'I'm ready, you can

turn round now.' Her shoes tied by their laces were slung round her neck. He took them from her, put them over his shoulders and held out a hand. She slid hers into it, almost shyly, like a lover might. He longed to pick her up in his arms, carry her, protect her. He said, 'Right, let's go, we'll walk as far as the rocks and watch the crabs.'

She smiled then. 'You're good to me, Charlie, so kind.'

He was so delighted at getting a smile he stopped and turned her to face him. Then wished he hadn't. The smile held the sadness of loss and in her eyes was the horror of the tragedy.

'Yes, well,' he said gruffly. 'Just you see you behave yourself and do as I tell you, or else . . .' He knuckled her under the chin and took her by the hand again.

The sun was quite warm by the time they reached the rocks. Rose said, 'I think it's going to be a scorcher. I bet these rocks will be red hot by midday.'

It was such a normal remark to make Charlie felt they might have taken a step forward. He picked up a piece of seaweed and trailed it in a rock pool. A shoal of minnows darted about. He looked up. 'Hey, Rosie, just take a look at those little chaps. They're enjoying themselves, aren't they?'

'Yes, and they'd better make the most of it. When the tide sweeps them out to sea again they'll be gobbled up by the bigger fishes.'

Charlie sighed. He was wrong, no step forward, not yet. Should he wait or start probing? He could wait all day. 'Rose, can we talk?'

'If it's about me, no, if it's about you, yes.'

'Leave it,' he said. 'Let's look for crabs.'

With the raising of a small rock two darted out and scuttled with their funny sideways walk, one racing ahead of the other. 'Long legs has won hands down!' Charlie declared. Rose was staring out to sea. An ocean-going liner had appeared on the horizon.

'I would like to be on that ship and sail away to the other

side of the world,' she said. 'Right to the other side.'

Charlie got up and dusted the sand from his fingers. 'And it might be the best thing to do. And for you to stay there!'

She looked up at him, bewilderment in her eyes. 'What?'

'You heard me. Find yourself a ship, clear out, who cares.'

He started to walk away, taking the risk, his heart pounding.

She came running after him, grabbed his arm. 'Charlie!' She looked bereft. 'Don't *you* care?'

'Should I? You don't give a jot for anyone, you only think of yourself, what *you* are suffering. You've never even been to see Tommy.'

'I couldn't, don't you see?' The pleading in her eyes was a pain in him, but he had to remain harsh, he had tried gentleness and patience.

'No, I don't see, Rose. How do you think Tommy feels? What is he saying to himself? Rose won't come to see me because she can't bear to have a brother who's minus a leg.'

'Oh, no, no,' she twisted her hands together in her agitation. 'It isn't that, it isn't that at all. It's because I feel so guilty. I'm a Jonah to the family, every time I've been enjoying myself something terrible happens.' Her words tripped over one another as she poured out her fears and guilt, baby Lilian, her father dying, then Frank and Tommy.

Charlie took her hands in his. 'Oh, Rosie, love, why have you been tormenting yourself? It's not your fault. You might just as easily blame Lizzie, or me, we were enjoying ourselves too. And you can't blame it on your ambition. If that was so, half the successful people in the world would be responsible for a heck of a lot of deaths and tragedies.'

'It's not only that, it's Ma, why has she never cried, why does she talk to you and the children but shut the rest of us out? I don't understand it. When Dad died she said there was no God, now she says it's God's will that Frank had to die and Tommy be maimed. Why? If only I knew.'

'Let's talk it over,' Charlie said. He led her back to the

rocks and when they were seated he continued. 'We'll start with your mother. There's a limit to grief. She told me after your father died she had shed all her tears. She also told me she no longer believed in God. But your mother is a deeply religious woman, Rose. You can't dismiss your beliefs just like that.'

'Do you believe there's a God, Charlie? I don't think I do.'

'Like you I was made to go to church three times on Sunday, my roots were in it, but my belief was shattered when I went to war and was a part of the wholesale slaughter. Then, I saw what could only be described as miracles. One incident I remember vividly was a young boy being impaled on barbed wire, his right arm shattered. He begged for someone to shoot him. Gunfire was heavy, incessant, mortars were exploding all around him, there seemed no hope of rescuing him. Then two soldiers appeared from nowhere and they freed the boy. They carried him back to the trenches and not one of them was hit. The boy recovered. There are times like that when you have to believe, Rosie.'

'Dad told me about people called atheists. They don't believe in a God of any kind.'

'In answer to that I can only say that old Jack Teasdale was an atheist, but when he knew he was dying he called on God to help him. I know that's only one bloke, but don't close the door on your beliefs, Rosie.'

She shook her head with a despairing gesture. 'He's such an unfair God. Bad people live and get rich, the good ones die. Frank had one big chance to go on the stage and he had to turn down that chance when Dad died. Is that fair?'

'Frankie did have a previous chance.' Charlie spoke gently. 'He was twelve then. A family offered to take him into their act. Your parents knew the family, agreed to let Frankie go. But at the last minute he opted out. He was afraid, Rose, afraid to leave the security of his home. Did you know he was physically sick every time he danced in front of anyone who wasn't family, and that he was really ill after he had danced?

Frank was a sensitive soul. He would never have survived the life of the stage, the touring, and he knew it.'

'I didn't realise,' Rose said in a low voice. 'It seems I hardly knew him.'

'Do we ever know ourselves, Rosie? You were asking the reason for your mother's present behaviour in shutting you all out. I would say she's making a world for herself where people are dependent on her. Tommy needs her, the younger children need her. She talks to me because your father and I were very close, we had long talks together when we went out for a drink. Your mother draws me out, wants to know everything he said. It's her comfort. I think it's something that will pass. In time she'll draw you all around her again.'

'It hurts to be shut out,' Rose said. She turned her head and looked at Charlie. 'But that's exactly what I was doing, wasn't it? I must go and see Tommy sometime. Perhaps tomorrow – or the next night.'

'Why not tonight?' Charlie asked gently.

'No, don't rush me. I'll go, when I'm ready.' Rose lifted her face to the sun and closed her eyes. 'It's lovely here, I'm glad you brought me. I know what you mean by a sense of peace, the sun, the breeze, the sound of the water.'

Charlie said on a note of despair, 'Rosie love, you're shelving the issue, you must accept reality.'

'I am, I really am, but just let me enjoy today.'

They clambered over the rocks into the next bay, were in and out of the sea, walked along the pier, came back to the beach. Charlie tried to get Rose to talk about the business, her designing, but she refused to discuss them. They would talk some other time.

They went home with lobsters, already cooked, for tea. Her mother loved lobster. Rose ran into the kitchen calling, 'A special treat, Ma,' then stopped, her hand going to her throat as she saw her mother and her sister Alice standing together, tears rolling down their cheeks.

Oh, God, what now?

Gran Eagan, who came in behind them said, 'Rudolph Valentino is dead.' Then with an expressive shrug added in an undertone, 'Your Ma weeps for a film star and doesn't shed a tear over her sons.'

Rose thought she understood. Valentino had been responsible for transporting thousands of women from their humdrum lives to a world of romance. One could weep openly for a lover who belonged to a fantasy world, but sons were reality. One grieved inwardly for such a tragedy.

That night she went with Charlie to see Tommy. There was a shout of laughter as they neared his bed. Tommy was entertaining the patients on either side of him. 'That lad'll be the death of me,' declared the elderly man on his right, his face screwed up with mirth. Then he said, 'Now you behave yourself, son, you've got visitors.'

Tommy's eyes were full of mischief as he looked to see who was coming, but when he saw who it was his whole face lit up with pleasure.

'Hi, Rosie, I thought you'd gone off me.'

'Oh, Tommy, I've been such a fool.' Rose felt so choked she was unable to say any more. It was Tommy who cheered her.

'I'm going to be all right, you needn't worry about me. I'll be hopping around in no time at all. And do you know something? A chap down the ward is going to give me a Saturday job, helping in his shop. I'll have to wait until I get my wooden leg, of course.' Tommy grinned. 'I've shouted peg-leg so many times after Davie Bootley, I'll not dare complain if anyone shouts peg-leg after me.'

Charlie said, 'We'll see you playing football yet, Tommy.'

'You bet!'

There were so many other patients from across the ward praising Tommy, what a grand lad he was . . . never a whimper from him . . . kept them all in fits of laughter . . . that Rose felt ashamed.

Charlie said when they came out, 'Well, Rosie, that wasn't so bad, was it?'

'No.' She stopped and looked up at him. 'I want to say this now, Charlie. I'll never allow myself again to get into the state I've been in these past few weeks. I'll face up to any troubles or tragedies there might be in the future. If I seem to be forgetting remind me of this moment, will you?'

'Providing I'm there,' he said softly.

'Oh, you'll always be there, Charlie, always a part of my life. I couldn't do without you.'

He drew her arm through his and squeezed her hand. 'Nice of you to say so.'

Charlie had tried to speak lightly, but was aware of a slight catch in his voice. He hoped Rose had not noticed. It would not be fair to let her know just how much he loved her. Not until other things were settled, and that would take time.

Chapter 16

It took Rose several days to settle to designing again, but once she did ideas flowed freely. Lizzie wanted her to get in touch with Alex de Veer to see if he was still interested in financing them, but Rose was reluctant, feeling it was his place to get in touch with her.

There were times when she dreamed about him, and yet, when she would pause in the middle of sketching to try and draw his face she found it impossible.

On a day of high wind and rain when trade had been poor at the shop Lizzie suggested they close early. The wind buffetted them from all sides and it was a job to prevent their umbrellas blowing inside out. Lizzie had put them in the scullery sink to drip when she stood, her head cocked. 'We've got company,' she said. There was a burst of laughter from the kitchen and a slow smile spread over her face. 'It's Lecky, I'd know that laugh anywhere. I bet Alex is with him.'

'They wouldn't come *here*,' Rose exclaimed, panic in her voice.

'They are here. That's Alex's la-di-da voice. Come on, stupid, don't just stand there, get your coat off.'

Rose tried to tidy her hair but Lizzie gave her a push. 'Go on!'

Although the kitchen seemed to be overflowing with adults and children Alex de Veer and Lecky sprang immediately into focus with their immaculate appearance. And yet neither man gave the impression of 'slumming'. Alex de Veer, one elegantly-clad leg crossed over the other was smiling, as absorbed as the rest in listening to Lecky taking off a Cockney barrow boy. The children were big-eyed, and shy.

'Hello,' Lizzie said, pushing Rose ahead of her.

The two men jumped up instantly. Lecky came forward, hands outstretched, welcoming them with a warm smile. 'Elizabeth, Rose, how wonderful to see you again. I hope you'll forgive us for dropping in on you like this.'

Alex, his expression sober, said, 'I told Lecky we should have let you know we were coming North but he wanted to surprise you.'

'Surprise is right,' Lizzie declared. 'You were the last people we expected to see, especially with the weather being so foul.'

They made small talk for a few moments, then Gran Eagan interrupted to say she had lit a fire in the front room, and that it ought to be warm in there by now. She suggested Charlie and the two girls take their friends in there.

The front room was seldom used and although the coals glowed red the fire barely took the chill from the room. Rose, thinking of the richness of Lecky's home tried to see it through his and Alex's eyes. The furniture came from her grandparents' home: the big sideboard, the wood so old it looked black, the shiny black horsehair sofa and chairs, the big oil paintings of Highland scenes in their chipped gilt frames, the whatnot in the corner with the cheap little ornaments which were treasured by Edie. All were familiar to Rose, all a part of her childhood and yet she was seeing them now as though for the first time.

Rose learned then that the two men had been in the North for three days, Alex having business associates to meet. They were staying at the Grand Hotel.

Edie knocked and came in with a tray of tea. There were delicate china cups and saucers, the remains of a set she had been given on her wedding day. Rose was relieved her grandmother had not brought in the enamel mugs they used for every day. Edie put down the tray saying talking was thirsty work and left.

The two men talked briefly of the tragedy, commenting on the bravery of both boys. They said how splendidly Tommy was behaving, a credit to the family and an example to youth. They then spoke of the unemployment situation and Alex, addressing Rose, asked how the dress shop was faring.

She was about to say that business was terrible at the moment with the weather being so bad, but Lizzie forestalled her.

'Oh, we're doing splendidly, we're having a job to keep stocks up. But then we do keep our prices low, with no dress over a pound and our maxim is still small profits and quick returns. I think I told you this the night of the party.'

'Yes, you did.' Alex looked at each girl in turn, was thoughtful for a moment, then asked if they would be willing to meet a Miss Poulteney. He would like her to see Rose's work. Miss Poulteney was experienced in buying for the mass production market. Lizzie immediately tensed, obviously resenting an outsider coming into the business. Rose said yes, of course, they would be pleased to meet her.

Alex then spoke of a property he owned in Beckley Road, saying he thought it would be suitable as a factory. Rose's eyes widened. '*You* own it?'

Lecky grinned. 'Show me some property that Alex doesn't own.'

Lizzie poured the tea.

Charlie said he knew the place, but would it not be a bit too big? Alex shook his head. There had to be plenty of room for expansion.

Rose's greatest pleasure at that moment was in thinking of the work it would bring to the district. As well as jobs for women as machinists they would need men to maintain the machines.

The three men then got into a discussion on the general state of the country and Rose let it wash over her. She sat watching

Alex, noting how his slender hands would stress a point by tapping the backs of his fingers on his left palm. They were expressive hands. His voice charmed her with its beautifully modulated tones, yet the surprising thing was that Alex could give an air of forcefulness without even slightly raising his voice. She felt he was a man who could control an empire. A man she knew she would go on dreaming about, even though his only interest in her might be in her ability to design.

When Alex eventually got up to leave he made arrangements for Miss Poulteney to call at the dress shop at ten o'clock the next morning, and also arranged for them all to meet for lunch afterwards.

The moment they had gone Lizzie flared up, complaining that Alex de Veer was wanting to take them over lock, stock and barrel. Who was this Miss Poulteney, some high-handed upstart from London who would pinch all Rose's ideas then say they were not suitable to mass produce? Charlie, for once, was angry.

'Lizzie, for heaven's sake use your loaf! What do you or Rose know about buying in quantities, materials, threads . . .'

'We've been making in quantities!'

'You've had four machines going. This is *mass* production. I don't know how many machines Alex will install but you'll have to start thinking in terms of producing stuff on a much larger scale. He mentioned the empty premises in Beckley Road, and you know the size of that place. Was it only yesterday, Lizzie, you were talking about learning from the experts? Well, now's your chance, but I'll tell you this, you'll never learn a thing if you're going to constantly get up on your high horse every time someone experienced is introduced.' Charlie ran his fingers through his hair. 'Sorry for blowing my top, but it's now that certain things have to be straightened out.'

Lizzie agreed. She apologised, said she must try and

control her temper in future, and that she would listen and learn from this woman from London, even though she felt she hated her at that moment.

As it turned out there was nothing to hate about Miss Poulteney. She was not the high-handed upstart Lizzie had envisaged, but a quietly dressed and softly-spoken middle-aged women. Her manner, however, covered an efficiency that won Lizzie's admiration. Miss Poulteney approved the style of dresses they had in the shop, and applauded Rose's designs, especially the better class models that Rose had brought along for her inspection. She asked numerous questions – how long had they had the shop, how had they first started, where did they buy their materials, the accessories . . . Miss Poulteney made notes, and Lizzie made notes when the woman started talking about buying – what to look for, what to discard. She stressed the bargaining power one could use, adding that if Alex undertook to go into this line he would want everything cut to the bone. A good man to work for, she said, but ruthless and not suffering fools gladly. By the time they were ready to go to the Grand Hotel to meet the three men, Rose's head was swimming with facts and figures.

When they did arrive at the Grand Hotel only Lecky and Charlie were there to meet them. Alex had had to go at short notice to a business meeting in Leeds. Rose tried to hide her disappointment but Lizzie was not so successful. She demanded of Lecky to know what was the next move. Lecky could only say that Alex, he felt sure, would keep in touch with them. 'Well,' said Charlie brightly, 'I suggest we go and eat.'

The girls had been well-primed by their mother before they left home what knives and cutlery to use for each course. Even with this knowledge Rose felt a little awed by the opulence of the restaurant, with its red flocked wallpaper, gilt, crisp white table linen and array of wine glasses. Lizzie was quiet, looking around her but Charlie took it all in his stride, studying the menu with Miss Poulteney as though he were used to lunching every day in such places.

That the lunch was such a success was due mainly to Charlie and Lecky, who kept everyone laughing with their mimicry.

Miss Poulteney and Lecky were travelling back to London on the four-thirty train. Before they took their leave of Charlie and the girls both said they hoped they would all meet again soon, with Miss Poulteney adding to Rose that her report to Mr de Veer would be *most* favourable.

Gran Eagan and Sam and Sally were all agog to know how they had got on. Sally was interested at first in the décor of the restaurant and she oohed and aahed as they described each course. But afterwards, when Edie began to question more deeply about the business she became agitated. Did this mean the girls might have to go to London to live?

Edie said, 'Let's worry about that when it happens.'

Charlie slapped his knees and got up. 'Well, I must get some jobs done. All we can do now is wait to hear from Alex, it'll probably take a few days.'

When they had not heard anything at all after ten days Lizzie was furious, swearing vengeance on Alex de Veer who had cheated them, sending that Poulteney woman to steal Rose's ideas. There would be a factory, oh, yes, but probably somewhere down South. Charlie kept saying that things like this took time, that their venture was not the only business Alex was interested in, and to exercise patience. Rose tried to be patient but like Lizzie she began to feel let down, especially when another week passed without any word.

Lizzie, venting her temper on everyone in sight declared they would start planning to try and enlarge the business themselves. And was rushing here and there looking for some place larger than their hut when a letter came from Alex. He would be travelling north on the following Tuesday. Would it be convenient to meet him outside the premises at Beckley Road at ten o'clock?

Charlie was jubilant. Things were moving. Rose was quietly pleased, more at seeing Alex than about getting the business under way. Lizzie grumbled, still feeling they had been badly treated by not hearing from him before now.

The greyness and dampness of the morning, combined with the hollow echo of the footsteps in the empty building on the Tuesday, gave Rose a feeling of depression. How big it was! After living in small rooms the walls stretched endlessly. There could be ghosts in it. She shivered.

Charlie said, 'This will take some filling. How many machines are you planning to install?''

'Perhaps fifty – to begin with. One must always think of extending.'

Rose stood looking around her. Fifty – and thinking of extending! Her cosy world of designing and making dresses for Mr Rosenberg and their little shop seemed to be vanishing. Would Alex expect her to be one of a group of designers? Was Lizzie right and was he going to take them over 'lock stock and barrel'?

There was a sudden draught as a door opened. Three men came in. They were neatly dressed but not in Alex's class. Alex told them sharply they were late. The men looked around then they and Alex began discussing the structure. Alex drew Charlie into the discussion, which pleased Rose. She and Lizzie were left standing. Lizzie gave her a nudge. 'Come on,' she said, 'we'll tag along. We may as well learn as much as possible.'

When the men eventually left Alex suggested they go on to his hotel to discuss the rest of the business. A limousine drew up as they left the building. 'A Lagonda,' Charlie said, beaming. Lizzie murmured 'Luxury.' Rose sat watching Alex, guessing he was pleased at having impressed them.

When they went into the lounge of the hotel Miss Poulteney was waiting for them. Rose felt really pleased to see her, she was like an anchor.

And Rose certainly felt the need of an anchor when, after

the waiter had brought and poured the coffee Alex launched into the question of staff. Rose felt bewildered by the number of people that would be involved – maintenance men, electricians, office staff, cutters, embroiderists, bead stitchers, cleaners – the list seemed endless. So did the rest of the business involved. Rose found it impossible to take it all in. One thing did please her and that was Charlie's involvement. He had joked once and said he would be a square peg in a round hole but Alex had given him the job of employing staff, all but the cutters, for Miss Poulteney would engage these. Alex said that Charlie was conversant with the northern people, and would know how to handle them.

Alex had another appointment, or said he had. Rose wondered if it was simply an excuse to get rid of them. They had served their purpose for that morning.

But then Alex gave them one of his rare smiles, a particularly warm one and to Rose the touch of his hand on her arm was something special.

He left, after promising to see them in five days' time.

Miss Poulteney suggested they have another coffee or a drink, as there were one or two things she still needed to discuss, especially Rose's designs. She produced a folio of the designs given her during her visit to the dress shop. Charlie hailed a waiter and drinks were ordered.

Rose was feeling in a happy, mellow mood when the shock came. A breakdown had been done on four of her better class dresses, to simplify and cheapen them for the mass market.

She looked from one to the other with stricken eyes. 'It's a travesty. How could you? My beautiful dresses. I won't allow it, I don't want any part of this cheating.' She snatched up the folio and would have left had not Miss Poulteney restrained her.

'Rose, please sit down. We must talk, you must let me explain, *please*.'

At first, Rose would not let her talk. She blamed Alex de Veer for getting them into the deal under false pretences. It was a terrible thing he had done, and she wanted no part of it. She would be surprised if Lizzie and Charlie would after this.

It was Lizzie who brought her tirade to a halt. 'Will you stop it, our Rose and listen. There's always two sides to everything.'

Miss Poulteney launched into the explanation, speaking briskly.

'The four designs I put before you, Rose, caught my eye at once, when I looked through the selection you gave me. We need something eye-catching. We have to be sure each line has a chance of selling, and selling widely. I broke down your originals only to let you see and ask your permission to use them. You are most creative, Rose, prolific in your designs. I felt these four could be spared to get us started. I give you my word I would not have used them without your permission, and would never at any time if we work together. I have a reputation to uphold. It's important I keep it.'

Rose apologised for her hasty condemnation but said she was not sure she wanted to go in for mass producing. Perhaps they had better find someone else to design.

Lizzie became angry. Alex de Veer had gone to all this trouble and she was behaving like a temperamental film star.

Rose was near to tears. Charlie and Miss Poulteney spoke to her quietly, both pointing out that through mass producing she would have the opportunity of becoming known for her designs and would be able to produce her couture work in the future.

The atmosphere eased and in the end they parted amicably, with Miss Poulteney asking them to call her by her Christian name, Adele.

'Thank heavens we got that lot sorted out,' Lizzie said. 'All we need now is for Alex de Veer to keep his promise and be here in another five days' time. But, after the last time of waiting, it could be a month before we see him again.'

Alex kept his promise to return in five days, bringing with

him his accountant, a thin, stoop-shouldered man whom he introduced as Mr Baston. And on that day a company was formed. Rose felt bewildered by all the legal jargon but it was enough that Charlie and Lizzie seemed to understand it.

It was not until Alex began to talk in terms of hundreds of outlets for their work that Rose began to realise the extent of the world they were entering. She found it a little frightening.

Although the legal aspect had been dealt with Rose did not expect the factory to be operational for some time. She had reckoned, however, without the dynamic force of Alex de Veer. He was constantly on the job, badgering the workmen. At the end of four days a small office was fitted and furnished and a larger one near completion. Adele Poulteney had returned to help Charlie with the recruiting of staff.

There was no need to advertise for workers. Word had flown around about the factory and every day the yard was crowded with men and women. They came from every district, some of them with hardly a sole to their boots. They begged for work, would do anything. At first Charlie and Adele coped with interviewing for the various jobs, but later Lizzie and Rose were roped in to weed out the women who were not experienced. Rose thought it the most heart-breaking task anyone could have. Gaunt-faced women came with hope in their eyes and left, shoulders drooping, defeated, uncomplaining. The genuine ones that is, for there were frauds who would come whining with a host of crying children at their skirts, perhaps a baby at a sagging breast, children who were not theirs. Fortunately they were soon denounced. 'Hi, listen, they're not her kids, kick her out, if you don't, we will. Her old man's working, he's got a good job, the pair of them booze away every penny he earns. Give the likes of us a chance.' Often one woman would push another one forward. '*She* needs a job, her man's dying, she's got six to feed.' Rose was always glad if a woman like this had some experience of sewing.

The people still came even when a notice was put up saying

no more workers were required. They hung about, some of them all day.

During the next few days there was so much going on at the factory, so many people milling around Rose had the impression of chaos, but Charlie assured her everything was under control. Alex had planned for the factory to start in three weeks' time, and it would.

A week before they were due to open Alex said he wanted to take them to a mill on the moors. They would stay overnight and leave after lunch on the Sunday. Alex then mentioned that Lecky would be joining them.

Sally was as excited as if she had been invited too. She had once accompanied her master and mistress when they had stayed at a big house in Yorkshire. They would love the Dales.

The five of them were to travel in Alex's roomy Lagonda, and Lecky would meet them at the inn. They left at seven o'clock on the Saturday morning.

It was a crisp autumn day with the promise of sun later. Once they were past the mining area with the winding gear stark against the skyline, the ugliness of the slag heaps and a scrapyard piled high with rusting machinery, the scene took on a beauty, with the foliage turning to the lovely autumnal tones of gold, brown and russet. The car purred as they began to climb narrow roads that twisted and turned, where hedgerows gave way to drystone walls.

These petered out and they were on open moorland with Rose ecstatic. There was such vastness, such an expanse of sky, and the clarity – she had not seen anything quite like that particular blue before. It was the colour she imagined heaven must be. The heather, a deep purple, blended with the golden lichen clinging to stones, and with the tall ferns in all shades between dark green and brown. There were outcrops of rocks, pinnacles rising majestically in the distance. A glorious desolation. A bird, a hovering black speck one minute, came plummeting to earth in search of prey. 'A hawk,' Charlie said. 'By heck they're quick, aren't they? I remember once talking to a farmer . . .'

While Charlie launched into an account of hawks Rose studied Alex's back. How broad his shoulders were and how arrogantly he sat, back straight, head up. He was wearing a fine dog's tooth tweed suit in black and white, elegantly cut as all his suits were. Was this a Dacre tweed? She noticed how his thick dark hair curled up endearingly at the nape. Rose longed to reach out and touch it. Adele began to talk of clothes and Rose forced herself to concentrate.

When they arrived at the mill and got out of the car Charlie talked about the water wheel and went to take a look at it. Rose's attention was caught by colours through the open doorway of the mill. She went in. There were women of varying ages, men and boys, a few children. It was a hive of activity. Rose watched a man nearest to her working a loom, using both feet and hands, the shuttle flying across, a tug down at a piece of string above his head, the pattern forming, it was all so coordinated, even the clackety-clack of the loom had a rhythm to Rose, a rhythm of music. And the colours, so exquisitely blended – Parma violet with olive green and cyclamen pink; honey with bark brown and cream; delphinium and periwinkle blue with turquoise and a green the colour of holly leaves.

This was not the fine tweed of Alex's suit, it had a ruffled surface to it, yet when Rose saw a girl handling a piece she had the impression it was soft.

'Well, Rose, how do you like our Dacre tweed?'

She glanced up to find Alex smiling at her. 'You had such a rapt expression,' he said, 'I wondered what I was missing. I certainly have no liking for the warm oily smell of the wool, I feel sure the rafters must be impregnated with it.'

'I don't mind it. I'm just fascinated by the colours of the wool, the blending. I want to handle it, feel the texture.'

'So you shall.' Alex turned to a man standing near. 'Oh, Mr Johnstone . . .'

It pleased Rose that Alex had given the man the courtesy of his full name. Mr Johnstone brought a length of tweed over to Rose. She put it to her cheek. It was kitten soft.

'Oh, how lovely. Already ideas are racing through my mind.'

'I hoped they would. Here are Adele and Elizabeth, you can discuss your ideas with them. I want to see Charles.'

Adele questioned Mr Johnstone and they learned that although the tweed was soft it had a strength, and would not 'seat'. He added that the tweed was exported to several countries.

Rose spoke to some of the women. They all looked happy and well-fed. All were wearing spotless white aprons, which Rose thought might have been donned specially for the visit of the 'boss'.

Mr Johnstone spoke glowingly of Alex. They couldn't have a better boss. Paid them half wages when they were sick. Not that malingerers were tolerated. They were quickly out.

Rose watched the wool being combed on a machine, saw it being wound, and had a promise of seeing where it was dyed later. Alex wanted them to go to the inn for lunch.

As they drove away from the mill Rose could still hear the sounds in her ears, the clackety-clack of the looms, the creaking of the water wheel, the heavy splash of water in the pool, the bleating of sheep and the squawking of hens as they scattered in alarm at the approach of the car.

They climbed out of the valley and drove for about ten minutes then Alex pointed out the inn ahead, built right on the edge of the moorland.

They were nearing it when a figure came running out and standing in the middle of the road began signalling with two flags. Charlie roared with laughter. 'It's Lecky! Typical, isn't it.' Alex told them, laughing himself, that Lecky was signalling a welcome.

There was back-slapping between the three men, a hug

and kiss from Lecky for Adele and the two girls, then he said, 'Come on, let's have a drink.'

It seemed to Rose that the pleasures of the morning would never end. The inn, dating back to the seventeenth century was all inglenooks, oak rafters and oak panelling, which reminded her of a film she had seen where part of the panelling opened to reveal a secret room. She gave a shiver of excitement. Dancing flames from a blazing log fire were reflected in brass and copperware, but the most entrancing part to Rose at that moment was the magnificent view from the bow-fronted window. The sun, which had come out, chased shadows across purple shaded hills, sparkled on the water of a stream rushing over small rocks and laid a shimmer of gold on a sheet of water in the distance.

Alex came up. 'Enjoying the view? Do you see that tarn over there.' He pointed over her shoulder. 'It's my favourite spot. We'll walk there this afternoon. I have a painting of it in my apartment in Paris.' As he drew his hand back his fingertips rested momentarily on her shoulder. The warmth through her silk blouse, his closeness, sent an unexpected tremor through Rose. Some force compelled her to turn her head. The gaze of both met and held. There was a depth to Alex's dark eyes. No word was spoken yet Rose felt they were the only people on a tiny island, bound by threads of magic.

Chapter 17

They were brought back to reality by Lecky calling to say drinks were being poured.

'Yes,' Alex said, 'a drink would be welcome.' His voice was cool, steady, but his hand moving up her arm to cup her elbow was to Rose, a caress. 'Shall we go?'

After a five course lunch, which included succulent slices of roast meat cut from the largest joint of beef Rose had ever seen, apple pie with a rich crust pastry served with dollops of whipped cream, no one wanted to go walking on the moors. They spent the afternoon in front of the fire, lazing, drowsing a little, talking in a desultory way about nothing important and groaning when afternoon tea was brought in with homemade cakes and scones to tempt them.

'I must have some exercise this evening,' Charlie complained, patting his stomach. Lecky sat up and said he knew the very thing, there was dance being held in the village hall. Barn dances would give them all the exercise they needed and if they were not already doing the Charleston then they would introduce it. Alex stipulated he wanted to be an onlooker only.

When they arrived at the hall the noisy chatter and laughter died away, no doubt with Alex having the effect of the squire and his entourage putting in an appearance. Before long, however, the tension was eased, not only by Alex exerting his charm and talking freely to the organisers but with Lecky and Charlie chatting and joking with the younger ones.

It was one of the wildest and most enjoyable nights Rose had ever known. She was whirled off her feet in the Scottish reels and the Lancers and was galloped round the floor in a polka. And when Lecky asked for a Charleston tune to be played she and Lecky ended up giving an exhibition, with the applause deafening at the end of it and cries of 'More.'

'Fame!' Charlie teased her. Alex said, 'You really are an excellent dancer, Rose, another accomplishment to those you already have.'

Rose, flushed with exertion and pleasure at the compliment said, 'I've so enjoyed it, thank you for bringing us, Alex.'

They left at one in the morning with pressing invitations from all sides to come again – soon.

A high-riding moon silvered the countryside. A perfect night for romance, Rose thought, but there was no hope of any romantic interlude with the yells of laughter as Charlie and Lecky related various incidents. Charlie said, 'Did you see that fragile-looking lass with the golden hair? I asked her to dance and she said in a voice like pitboots crunching cinders, "Eee, lad, I'm sweatin', will you ask me sister Betty."' Lecky slapped his thighs and roared with laughter, then said he had danced with Betty who was seven feet tall and had flat feet.

On the Sunday morning, to the disappointment of all, a mist shrouded the moors, and although they did go walking an icy drizzle that stung cheeks and seeped through jackets had them quickly back in front of the warmth of the inn fire. Alex went up to his room to look over some papers, Rose sketched and the rest lazed and talked. After an early lunch they said goodbye to Lecky who was going on up into Scotland, then set off for home. Huge raindrops bounced off the windscreen.

It was such an anti-climax after the enjoyment of the Saturday that Rose found herself longing to be home where she could relive it with her mother and grandmother. The younger children would be settled for their afternoon nap and the older ones at Sunday School.

When they did arrive home Charlie said, 'You two girls nip out and get the kettle on, we'll follow.'

Rose and Lizzie raced down the entry to the back door and burst in, calling in unison that they were home. And were in full spate about their weekend when Charlie came in carrying two bulky paper parcels. He dropped them on to the table. 'One for you Rose, and one for you, Lizzie, a memento from Alex of your visit to the mill. He said he'll see you tomorrow.'

Alex had chosen for Rose the Parma violet and cyclamen mixture tweed and the honey browns for her sister.

'My, what lucky girls you are,' declared their mother beaming, then in the next breath added, 'Come on, tell me about the inn where you stayed and what you had to eat.'

Rose had reached the part about the dance when a figure passed the kitchen window. Lizzie groaned, 'Oh, Lord, Aunt Maude, what does *she* want?'

Lizzie was wrapping the string round her finger when Maude came drifting in and said, without looking to right or left, 'I wouldn't have come out on a day like this but I have a message for Charlie. Dorrie's dead.'

The tension in the room was almost tangible. It took Rose seconds before she remembered that Dorrie was Charlie's wife. He was standing motionless, a white pinched look about his nostrils.

'Who told you, Maude?' His voice sounded harsh.

'George Fawcett. He's at our house. You'd better come and see him.'

Maude made for the door and Charlie followed. But before he went out he said, 'When I come back I don't want Dorrie's name mentioned.'

The moment the door closed Lizzie said, 'Well, I don't see why it should be such a secret.'

To which Gran Eagan replied, 'You heard what Charlie said. Let it rest.'

Charlie went away. He was away for three days and when he came back he spent all day and part of the evenings at the factory. Lizzie, who had asked Maude about his wife, learned that Dorrie had been living with a labourer and had died of pneumonia. By then the factory was due to open.

Rose had been prepared for activity at the factory but not on such a large and noisy scale. She could hear the sound of the machines as they walked down Beckley Road. When they went into the factory a man greeted Charlie, but no one else took any notice of them. They were all too absorbed in their various jobs. Every machine was in use, heads were down. Seams were being run up with barely a pause, then the finished garments were whisked away by a youth and dropped into a basket on wheels he pushed down the aisles. Rose was watching, fascinated, when Charlie came up. He gave her a smart salute. 'Charles Eagan, commercial traveller, reporting for duty, Ma'am.'

'Comercial traveller? Oh, Charlie, that's great news.' Rose gave him a big hug.

'Yes, isn't it. Alex wants me to do the Northern area, says I'm good at talking to people.' Charlie grinned. 'What he means is that I have the gift of the gab. And do you know something else? I'm getting a van. I can take the family for a jaunt at weekends.'

'Oh, no you can't.' This came from Lizzie. 'The van's for the job.'

'Nag, nag, nag,' Charlie teased. 'Tell Rosie about *your* job, Liz. No, I'll tell her. Your sister is going on the costing side.'

'And Alex wants me to learn typing.' There was a pride in Lizzie's voice. Rose felt a tiny stab of jealousy. It was as though Lizzie and Alex had become close while she had been organising Bessie and the other three women.

Bessie had asked if there was any chance of getting electrically-powered machines installed, pointing out it would certainly increase production. Rose agreed, but then it was not Alex's province to install machinery to help production for their shop. She could perhaps save for one machine at a time.

Adele came up. 'Hello, Rose – I have some samples for you to see. Come into the office, all of you.'

There were several dresses on hangers. Adele lifted one down. 'Well, Rose, there you are, your designs modified. I hope you approve.'

The basics were certainly recognisable. Rose had designed a walking-out dress in dove grey flannel, buttoned down the left side, the buttonholes to be finely piped in white with a tiny cross-stitch pattern fanning out from each one. The sleeves were buttoned from shoulder to below the elbow, the lower sleeve being of white flannel with a cross-stitched design in grey. A narrow scarf in white with the grey pattern repeated on the ends only, had one end pushed through a tab on the left shoulder. Rose had thought it elegant. There was no elegance, however, in the cheaper version. It was a serviceable dress in gabardine. The buttons were stitched on, the bodice part fastening with hooks and eyes. There was no handwork, no cross-stitching. The lower sleeves and scarf of white material had a pattern of grey. Even then, after studying the dress, Rose felt sure it would sell well at the lower price.

Substitutes had been used in the others, too. Lace instead of intricate beadwork, a shadow-striped material replacing an inset of fine pleating, velvet instead of mink trimmings on neck and pockets and cuffs, and bone buttons instead of buttons covered in the material with a minute motif embroidered on each.

Rose was aware they were all waiting. She turned to face them intending to say it was no use pretending she did not feel hurt at the desecration of her originals, then realising it would serve no purpose said instead, 'It will be interesting to see how they sell.'

'Oh, we already have orders.' This came from Adele.

'So soon?' Rose stared at her in wide-eyed astonishment. 'But the factory has hardly been under way . . .'

Charlie said, 'Sample garments are on the road within hours of being made. You'll get to learn, Rosie love, that our Alex doesn't let the grass grow under his feet. And I won't have to let it grow under mine when I get on the road.'

During the following few months Rose came to learn a lot. She found that to run a successful business one need not be on the job the whole time. It was a question of having the right goods to sell and the right person to manage. Unconsciously Rose and Lizzie had chosen the right person to manage their dress shop by having an older woman. Customers chatted to her, told her their troubles, and bought. The shop had doubled its turnover. Alice, who had now left school was also employed there. To Rose's surprise Alice had turned out to have a flair for design herself, but more important at the moment was the fact that she loved the selling side.

Alex, who was away a great deal had left a highly efficient manager in charge. The factory was working full out with some of the machinists doing overtime. Already there was talk of expansion.

Rose missed Alex, and was always listening for news of him. She missed Charlie, too, who had always been such a part of her life, but she could not begrudge him the time he was away from home. He was doing well and his order book was always full. When he did come home at weekends he kept the family entertained with his 'adventures', and was always full of praise for the way Rose's designs were received. The family also had the added bonus of a ride into the country in the back of the van. Mostly the children went, but the older ones too would take a turn. Sam was always eager to go because Charlie would stop to give the children lemonade while the two of them would have a couple of beers. The rides were a highlight in Sam's life.

Big Bessie and the three women in the shed were working long hours to keep the stocks going for the dress shop and

Rose, frustrated at not being able to get her couture dresses made was now looking around for larger premises, where she hoped to install powered machines, and to employ extra staff. Charlie had offered to help them in this.

Lizzie, who had quickly become an efficient typist was now private secretary to Mr Ward, the manager. She said she was learning all the time. Whenever she had any minutes to spare her head would be buried in business manuals. She had found someone to give her elocution lessons and she had started to learn French. Rose was learning French too but was not so proficient as Lizzie. Her dream recently was to work in Paris. Adele had set her ambition on fire by talking about the fashion houses, the Collections. This was after Rose had sketched some rather way-out designs in clothes and Adele had said quietly, 'You know, Rose, you are wasting your time here, you really ought to be in a fashion house. I would suggest Paris.'

Rose had looked up, her eyes shining and said, 'I shall have my own fashion house one day, Adele. I feel it in my bones.' Then she had added, 'The House of Kimberley. How about it?'

Adele squeezed her shoulder. 'Sounds good. I hope I shall be around to help share in its growth.'

'Oh, you must, I couldn't do without you.'

The day Rose found a bigger workshop to rent Charlie had a letter from Alex with an invitation for all of them to go on a visit to London. When Rose protested it would be impossible for her to go, since she had to see about the renting of the newly-found premises, Charlie told her the visit was a must. Boss's orders. Something special was in the offing. In spite of much coaxing he refused to say what it was, it was to be a surprise. Rose and Lizzie and Adele, after speculating, decided it would be a special party. Although Rose longed to see Alex she felt that sacrifices would have to be made if she was to further her ambition. Someone might have taken the workshop by the time she got back.

'Taken it?' Lizzie exclaimed. 'That workshop has been empty for months. It'll be there when we get back. I plump for London and a party, live it up.' A statement which prompted Rose to think, not for the first time, that one could never really get to know people, especially one's own sister.

With nearly a week to go before their visit to London Rose discussed with Lizzie how they should make up the lengths of the Dacre tweed Alex had given them. Lizzie said she would leave the designing of her outfit to Rose. Something attractive, but not too fancy.

Rose, after draping the tweed around her decided she would make herself a cape. It would be something a little flamboyant, suitable for London. She bought a remnant of shot silk for the lining in the shades of the purple and cyclamen of the tweed, and a piece of soft patent leather for trimming. She cut the patent in strips, punched large holes in it with a borrowed tool and put the strips on the pockets and on the slitted openings for the arms.

For the dress Rose chose black velvet in a simple style and with the pieces left had a hat made to her own design by Bessie, who had a flair for millinery. The result was a perky oval cap which sat on the side of Rose's head with a swinging cord and tassel. Black patent shoes and handbag completed the outfit.

When Adele saw Rose dressed in her ensemble she was silent for so long Rose said in alarm, 'You don't like it?'

'I do, I like it very much. I find myself intrigued. You have such flair – your hat is so different. You could set a fashion, and although capes are not new the tweed is so lovely and with the patent trimming – what are you making for Elizabeth with the honey and brown tweed?'

'I'm not quite sure. I have an idea but I must work it out.'

Rose eventually settled on a suit, the jacket bound in nut brown velvet. To wear under the suit was a honey-coloured silk blouse with a jabot at the neck. A scarf in tweed had appliquéd motifs in velvet on each end and to complete the outfit, a military-styled peaked cap, also in velvet.

Lizzie, who was never lavish with praise, enthused over her reflection in the mirror. 'You really are great, our Rose, you've transformed me. It doesn't look like me at all.'

'But it does, it is you, we all need dressing up. This is what I'm interested in, the right clothes for the individual woman. My cape would not look right on you, I know it. I'll get dressed up too and we'll go down and show the family.'

The girls made an entrance, both flinging out their arms and crying, 'Voila!'

There were gasps of surprise and oohs and aahs. Alice pleaded for Rose to make her a cape too. Sally said, 'You both look so beautiful, oh, my darling girls, I'm proud of you.'

Lizzie laughed. 'Seems we've scored a bull's eye. I only hope we'll make as big an impact on our boss and his London friends.'

Chapter 18

Rose and Lizzie did make an impact on their arrival in London. Lecky and Clarissa who had come with Alex to meet them likened them to film stars.

Clarissa said, 'You can make an entrance at the fashion show. It's Alex's surprise.'

Rose stared at him wide-eyed. 'A fashion show? Do you mean it?'

Alex nodded, smiling. 'A preview of the Spring Collections. I'm sure we shall enjoy *your* pleasure, Rose.'

Rose could hardly contain her excitement. She could not stop talking. 'Adele, you knew all the time, the family knew, I can see that now. Charlie did you know? Of course you did, you're terrible for not telling me.'

Lizzie chided her. 'Will you calm down, our Rose. Look at you now! Can you imagine what you would have been like had you known about it a week ago? You would never have got the tweed made up, or if you had you would have been worrying so much about getting everything perfect all your enjoyment would have been spoilt.'

'Yes, you're right.' Rose clasped her hands tightly together. 'I'll calm down, I will, I will. But, oh, I'm just so excited. I still can't believe it.'

'Don't try and change, Rose,' Alex said softly. 'Your exuberance, your delight, is so refreshing to someone as blasé as I.'

Rose, who had been expecting an ornate entrance was surprised at the unpretentious-looking doorway, and further surprised when they went up well-scrubbed, but uncarpeted wooden stairs. Then she remembered Charlie talking about some of the entrances to diamond merchants at Hatton Gardens, saying that the wealth lay behind locked doors. The door here was wide open, the way leading to a salon, where luxury could be found in the dark green, closely-fitted carpet and gilt chairs and mirrors, and wealth in the clientèle. Women dripped diamonds and furs. There were the beautiful ones, the plain, the weirdly dressed and young excited girls, who Adele informed Rose were the debs. The men accompanying the women were mostly immaculately-groomed, but one or two were in casual clothes. Rose was entranced, tonguetied. Alex seemed to know everyone, but the only person Charlie and the girls were introduced to was a tall elegant Frenchwoman in black. She was especially charming to Rose when Alex informed her that Rose had a flair for design. The woman said she hoped they might meet again. At the moment they must excuse her, there was so much to do.

A background of music, played softly, was the prelude to a woman coming from behind the curtains to announce that the show was about to begin. It was the elegant-looking woman in black. 'Ladies and gentlemen . . .'

Three words that for Rose, opened one of the most exciting and rewarding afternoons of her life.

Slender, long-legged mannequins glided before her eyes, leaving a faint trail of perfume. On show were garden party dresses in chiffon with floating panels, dresses in organdie, in crêpe de chine, the girls twirling parasols; there were beautifully tailored coats, opening to show matching dresses beneath; evening gowns in velvet, satin, silk and brocade; dresses for débutantes with long trains, and head-dresses containing Prince of Wales feathers; cocktail dresses with beads, lace and shimmering sequins.

When the panorama of design and colour had ceased Rose gave a long drawn-out sigh. Alex turned to her, 'Well, Rose, did you enjoy it?'

'Enjoy it? I feel satiated.' She gave a tremulous laugh. 'I've always wanted to use that word but this is the first occasion it fits. Oh, Alex, thanks a million. My mind is crowded at the moment but later I shall sort it all out and be able to assess each garment. I thought I was quite good at designing until now.'

'You *are* good. Do you think I would have financed you otherwise? You will reach the top, Rose, never fear. One day I shall take you to Paris.'

She closed her eyes. 'Don't! I couldn't stand any more excitement. Paris? The ultimate.' She opened her eyes. 'When?'

He laughed with the abandoned laughter she had heard the night of Lecky and Clarissa's party. 'Rose, you really are the most delightful child.'

He sobered. 'No, Rose, you are a young lady, a very attractive one, and I find myself . . .' he stopped abruptly and getting up held out a hand. 'I shall tell you some other time.'

It was the dark, intense look in Alex's eyes that made Rose take his words almost as a declaration of love. Dare she hope? There was no time for further thought, as the other four were crowding round her wanting to know how she felt about her first fashion show. Rose felt suddenly important and touched at their concern, even though she knew that Adele and Lizzie's interest was from a business point of view.

During the visit to London Rose had no time to simmer down. They all went to the National Gallery the following morning and Rose was introduced into the fascinating world of the Great Masters.

She was especially drawn to Rembrandt and his strong contrasts of white ruffles and lace against dark backgrounds and clothes. In one painting Rose felt she could slip her hand under the fine lace collar and drape it over her fingers. Alex said, 'Come with me, I have something to show you.' They went into an adjoining room and stopped at a large painting of a young girl in a crimson velvet dress. The girl was lovely, her expression pensive. 'She's a favourite of mine,' Alex said. 'I met her a year ago. She came alive at once to me. Do you see the resemblance, Rose, to yourself?'

Rose was startled. 'She's fair . . . but . . .'

'And fragile-looking and has a delightful air of naïvety, an innocence.'

She gazed up at him. 'I'm not fragile, Alex, I'm quite tough really, and I'm not – innocent. One learns about life having been brought up in a tenement.'

Alex ran a finger lightly down her cheek. 'Her name is Rosella. She lived in the eighteenth century and was the daughter of a nobleman. I think you are that girl, re-incarnated.'

Rose felt a shiver go through her. 'It's uncanny,' she said. 'My second name is Eleanor. My father, I understand, used to call me Rosella when I was a child. But I don't want to be that girl, I want to be me, living in Orchard Street with my family. Reincarnation, what I know of it, is – witchlike.'

'You are a witch,' Alex said softly. 'You've woven a spell over me.'

'Oh, there you are, we wondered where you were.' It was Charlie. He seemed to have kept apart from them since arriving.

The casual tone of his last few words did not deceive Rose. The hurt was there in Charlie's eyes. He had witnessed, what to Rose, was the most intimate moment yet between Alex and herself. She said, to ease the hurt, 'Alex was studying my features. He seems to think I resemble the girl in the portrait, but I can't see any resemblance.'

The other four who had followed Charlie in caught the last few words. They all agreed there was a resemblance and also agreed, lightheartedly, it must be a reincarnation. Charlie said quietly, 'I don't believe in such stuff, but Rose is certainly as beautiful as this Rosella.' He moved to the next portrait. 'Now there is a fine-looking warrior.'

Charlie was annoyed with himself for not being more

generous towards Rose and Alex. He was behaving like a love-sick youth. It was seeing them together like that, Rose looking up at Alex in such an appealing way and he looking as though he could eat her up. He had known for some time how Rose had felt about him, but he had not thought of Alex feeling the same way about her. Alex was wrong for her, too much of a man about town. What did they know of his love life, he could have dozens of women. Charlie found himself longing to be back on his market stall, joking with the other stallholders, chatting to his customers. He wanted to have Rose selling her dresses and blouses, putting her arms around him and saying, 'Oh, Charlie, I love you.'

Oh, Lord. He was going to bawl. He pulled out his handkerchief and blew his nose. It had a trumpeting sound which made him look around him with an apologetic air. Then Rose came up to him, smiling, whispering, scolding, 'Charlie Eagan, they'll put you out.'

'Probably a cold coming on, or some dust got up my nose.'

'Dust? In this holy of holies.' Rose's mock-horrified look made Charlie smile. She linked her arm through his. 'There's a lovely little picture I want you to see, over here.'

It was a seascape. A young couple, bare-footed, were standing hand in hand looking out to sea. There was something leisurely about the wide, shallow waves rolling shorewards. One had the impression they would end in cream-frothed eddies playing around their ankles. Rose looked up at him. 'Do you remember the day you took me to the coast, Charlie, when I was so upset? You knew, didn't you, that I would find a peace, a healing. I shall always remember it, and be grateful to you.'

'You have nothing to be grateful to me for, Rosie.'

'Oh, yes, I have, for so many things, so many *many* things.'

Charlie realised then the real meaning of love. It was not a demanding, a possessiveness, it was a giving, making sacrifices, understanding.

And so began the healing process for Charlie.

For two days after returning from the London visit Rose lived in a world coloured by dreams of Alex de Veer and of being involved in the glamour and excitement of a fashion house. Then she came back to reality with a jerk. Alex had stayed behind in London to deal with some business and when he did arrive at the factory his manner was so distant Rose had to wonder if the lovely interlude between them had actually happened. When Alex remained cool with her she came to the conclusion she had just been a diversion to him. He probably had a string of girls he dallied with. It hurt, it hurt deeply, but it did one thing for her, it strengthened her ambition to design and produce couture clothes. And with this she viewed her memory of the clothes at the fashion show through different eyes. Until then they had been part of a dream world, but now she saw the work behind them, the perfection, the perfection of fit. This impressed her the most. Sleeves in jackets looking as if they had been moulded in, with not even the tiniest pucker. It was surprising how clearly she could see every dress, every gown, jacket, coat, all the detail. Although there had been elegance and luxury, there was also a simplicity about many of the styles. Rose decided these were the things she would strive for. She would employ the best cutters, the best fitters, seamstresses. Rose smiled to herself. *She* would employ? Still, she did have one perfectionist working for her. Big Bessie. She had seen Bessie once undo every bead in an intricate beadwork design because some of them had been out of alignment. Rose felt a thirst for more and more knowledge. She thought of the Frenchwoman at the fashion house who appeared to be in charge and wished she could have talked with her. She spoke to Adele one day about her and Adele said, 'Blanche Manion? She is a most capable and knowledgeable woman. Tell Alex you would like to meet her and I'm sure he would arrange it.'

'Alex would only arrange it if he thought he was going to get more money out of it,' Rose said, a bitterness in her voice. 'He wouldn't do it simply because I wanted it.'

Adele studied her for a few moments then shook her head. 'You're wrong, Rose. He would do it for that very reason. He's taken with you, I've seen the way he looks at you. I would say he was very fond of you.'

Rose said no more.

It was after this that she managed to rent a workshop. It was big enough to take ten machines altogether. They were all electrically-driven. Rose could only pray they would sell enough dresses to warrant the move. She wondered what Alex would say when he knew. He was abroad at the moment. One morning Nancy came in waving a letter. 'It's for you, our Rose, from America! Imagine!'

Rose took it from her then ran from the room to read it upstairs – with complaints following her up. . . . 'Rotten sport . . . why couldn't we hear what he had to say . . . she should have read it here, we all know him . . . There might be a message in it for us . . .'

Lizzie's voice was the last Rose heard before she closed the bedroom door. The paper was thick, the writing bold, the letters beautifully formed.

Dear Rose,

I've been to New York many times and I've always thought it noisy, brash, car horns hooting, thousands of people milling around, but this time I find a beauty in it. And do you know why? I'm seeing it through your eyes. I see your dear face so full of wonder at each new experience, a radiance, and I find myself wishing you were here with me so I could share your pleasure. Some day I shall bring you. The news from the American agents about your dresses is good, they are selling well. I shall be back in three weeks' time. Give my warmest regards to your family, and of course my best regards to you. Keep sketching.

Yours sincerely, Alex.

Rose hugged the letter to her. It was the nearest to a love letter one could get . . . 'I see your dear face' . . . 'wish you were here with me so I could share your pleasure' . . . Oh, Alex, Alex.

Each time Rose went over the letter she read more and more into it. It was Lizzie shouting up and asking her if she intended to sit there all day that brought her downstairs. All eyes were turned expectantly on her. 'Well?' Nancy exclaimed. 'What did he say?'

'Oh, just chatted about New York, what a busy, noisy place it was.' Rose raised her shoulders. 'And that's more or less all. He'll be back in about three weeks.'

'Waste of a stamp,' Lizzie declared. 'You could have got that information at the factory.'

Her mother said, her eyes dreamy, 'But it wouldn't have been the same to Rose. It's a personal letter. Rose can keep it, put it among her souvenirs, show it to her grandchildren. A letter from America.'

Lizzie said, 'All right, treasure it, do what you like with it!'

On the way to the factory she suggested they open another shop. She had seen one in the Lismond area. In the better class district they could charge thirty shillings for a dress instead of a pound. They could make the same kind of dresses, just make a small alteration in the trimmings. She knew of a competent woman who could take charge of the shop.

Rose felt panic. Lizzie seemed to have everything cut and dried. She had too much to do, there was the workshop to contend with. When Rose pointed this out Lizzie said they had climbed over bigger hurdles, it was no use sitting back and waiting for things to happen. If Rose saw to the making of the dresses Charlie would deliver the stock in the van when he came home on a Friday afternoon, and Lizzie would see to the accounts. As a team working together it would turn out fine. Rose decided she would not undertake any further business until it had been discussed with Alex and although Lizzie demanded, then cajoled, Rose remained firm. Alex had financed them.

When Alex did arrive he greeted Adele and the girls, gave each a brief kiss on the cheek, said it was good to be back and told them he was calling a meeting on the Friday afternoon, when Charlie would have returned. Rose, who had been waiting in a fever of impatience for Alex to come back, felt let down. Alex did not behave towards her like a man in love.

When they were assembled for the meeting on the Friday Alex began by saying that not only had the American agents reported substantial orders for their Rochella dresses, but orders were starting to come in from agents in seven other countries where samples had been sent. Alex then complimented Rose on having made an impact in America with her designs, seeing they did an extensive trade themselves in clothing. He spoke of wanting to promote the Dacre tweed, seeing it as a viable proposition in ready-to-wear garments, capes, coats, suits, and looked to Rose for designs. He talked about bathing suits and bathing wraps, something different, startling, and also mentioned night-dresses and negligées.

Rose looked about her, bewildered. 'Bathing suits, wraps – I've never thought of –'

'Go into it, Rose, talk it over with Adele and Elizabeth. I can see a wide market for these products.' Alex gave a brief smile. 'If you make your name in America I can see you having a trip over there, all of you.' He expounded on a number of other possible ideas and spoke of them becoming a private limited company at some time in the near future – for tax advantages. Rose gave up at this point, her brain refusing to take in any more. Capes, coats, suits in tweed, bathing suits, bathing wraps, nightwear, something different. Different . . . different. . . .

Charlie was enthusiastic about everything, so was Lizzie, her eyes were shining with challenge. Rose felt she was being swept along on a huge tidal wave, and not even Alex's teasing comment later that he was not expecting all the designs by the following morning could get her into calmer waters.

She was racking her brains to think up ideas when her attention was caught by a child's coloured balloon sailing past the window. Immediately Rose saw a design of a bunch of balloons on the back of a white towelling bathing wrap, in bright colours, red, green, blue, orange. How about a man's face? The devil – with horns, a wicked grin on his face. She felt the familiar surge of excitement as her pencil flew over the pad.

'Isn't Alex marvellous,' Lizzie enthused later. 'What a go-getter he is. And so will we be, Rose. I think we'll start looking for a third shop. Rose, you're not listening. I said how about us looking for a third shop to open?'

'I am listening,' Rose said, feeling another rise of panic. 'It's crazy, we haven't opened the second one yet.'

'No, but we will. I know now what it takes to get on – drive and more drive, always seeking new ideas, having many irons in the fire, seeking new openings.'

'Yes,' Rose said, and was aware of a flatness in her voice.

There would be weeks at a time when Rose never saw Alex and then she found she was able to concentrate more on her work. When he went to Paris she thought that at least she might stop longing to feel his arms around her.

Then one day when the trees were in full blossom Charlie arrived at the factory in a state of excitement. Alex had phoned him at the hotel he had been staying at on his sales travels and asked him to collect Adele and the girls and bring them to Paris. They were to join him there.

'Paris?' Rose and Lizzie exclaimed together. 'Why . . . What . . .?'

Charlie said there was no time for explanation, that could come later. They had less than three quarters of an hour to get home, pack and catch the train to London. They had to be on the overnight boat train.

Adele said briskly, 'Well! I never question the boss's orders, come on, girls, move!'

They all piled into Charlie's van and on the way to drop Adele at her hotel he explained the reason for their trip. A man called Charles Lindbergh was attempting a solo flight from New York to France. It was a race with a big prize at the end.

Rose said, on a note of bewilderment. 'But why does Alex want *us* there?'

'Because, Rosie love, this will be an historic occasion, something to tell your grandchildren. It's the most exciting thing that has ever happened. Alex obviously wants us to share in it.'

When this was greeted with silence Charlie went on, speaking in his patient way. 'This man is flying non-stop across the Atlantic ocean. It'll take something like forty hours, he won't be able to sleep. I don't think you realise the importance of it.'

Rose said suddenly, 'It's just beginning to get through to me that we're going to Paris. *This* is the important thing to me. Paris! Imagine!'

She was still saying it when they were home and she was between rushing up and downstairs, collecting clean clothes, and packing her case.

It took some time for her grandparents and her mother to take in the news and when they did they were just as bewildered as Rose had been. Why go all that way to see a flier arrive? Sally began to get worried. They could get lost in Paris. They would be exhausted, with first the train journey to London then overnight on the boat train. They would need sleep.

'And we'll get it,' said Lizzie, coming into the kitchen carrying a small suitcase. 'We'll have a couchette, that's a berth. The back of the carriage comes down to form a bed. Charlie said everything's booked, Alex did it by phone from Paris.'

'By phone from Paris,' Gran Eagan exclaimed. 'What's the world coming to? And I have to think twice about spending twopence on a tram ride to go and see our Will and his wife. Still, enjoy everything while you've got the chance. It only comes once.'

They left in a flurry of goodbyes with Gran Eagan stressing to Charlie, as usual, to take good care of the girls.

Rose had a strong feeling that the relationship between Alex and herself was going to change in some way with this visit, yet there was no reason for her to think so. It was perhaps just a sixth – or a seventh – sense.

Rose wondered if she would ever stop feeling awed at new experiences and new sights, like the luxury of the dining carriages on the boat train, with their shaded lights, sparkling napery and silver cutlery. The carriages were carpeted, with lace-edged linen covers on the backs of the seats. Then there were the people coming to board, so elegantly dressed, with such a mass of luggage – beautiful leather cases. There were women in furs, and some men wore topcoats with fur collars. One man sported a cigarette holder as long as the one she had seen at the fashion show. There were women with poodles in their arms, and one had two beautiful dogs on leads, slender dogs with long narrow heads. Charlie said he thought they were called Russian wolfhounds. Porters abounded. There were officials with masses of gold braid, which gave Rose an idea for a military-styled coat. She noted that the women wore chiffon dresses under their furs, marocain coats, or flimsy-looking capes. It was like seeing a fashion show.

She sketched hastily and Adele laughed, teasing her, saying she was like Alex, always on the job. After a five-course lunch served with wine, Rose swore she would never be able to sleep a wink, but no sooner was she in her berth than she was fast asleep. And she slept nearly all the way on the sea crossing too, much to her annoyance.

They were all, however, suffering from a certain amount of exhaustion by the time they were nearing the end of their journey, and yet all came wide awake when they reached Paris. There was a feeling of suppressed excitement.

Chapter 19

The taxi driver was excited, speaking volubly of 'le capitaine Lindbergh'. Adele translating, said that the city was on its toes waiting for news. When they did arrive at the hotel Alex had them hustled into a limousine, barely waiting to greet them. They were going to the newspaper offices to hear the report of the plane's progress. Rose could hardly believe that anyone could be important enough to cause such excitement. The street outside the newspaper offices was so crowded traffic was being brought to a standstill. When they left the car and reached the offices Alex began questioning the people, and they gave excited replies. The flier was well on his way. Then a great shout of 'Vive Lindbergh!' went up. It seemed he had passed the south west corner of Ireland, which was a signal for many in the crowd to move, including Alex. 'Come along,' he said, 'we must get to Le Bourget airport, which is where he should land.'

They were caught up in a mass exodus of people travelling in vehicles of every kind, and eventually the road became blocked. They had to abandon the car and start walking. Rose had thought they were all mad rushing about like this, but once they had reached the airport she too began to get caught up in the importance of the occasion. There appeared to be thousands of people already there and more were arriving every minute. Special police and soldiers attempted to control the crowd. Word was passed round that Charles Lindbergh had been sighted flying high over Cherbourg and a cheer went up.

The crowd heaved and swayed. People felt elbows in their ribs, but no one complained. The real excitement came when with darkness white fingers of searchlights probed the sky. At nine o'clock rockets were released every two minutes and with each burst of light and stars the people chorused, 'Aaah!' Then at ten o'clock a low drone could be heard. The crowd went wild, yelling, 'Lindbergh! Lindbergh!' – Rose and the rest of them, too. A flare was dropped then the plane began to descend, but the crowds surging forwards, breaking down fences and through cordons caused the flier to rise again and circle before he was able to land.

Although Rose never even caught a glimpse of Lindbergh she shared in the delirium and in spite of bruised ribs made no protest when a number of Frenchmen hugged her, giving her smacking kisses on each cheek. Charlie and Alex laughingly followed suit.

They arrived back at the hotel in the early hours of the morning, with Alex apologising for having rushed them to the airport when they must have been tired after the journey, adding, 'And you didn't even see Lindbergh!'

'But we were there!' Rose exclaimed. 'Just think of the story I can tell my grandchildren.'

Alex said, 'I wonder who the lucky grandfather will be?' He spoke lightly but the gaze he turned on Rose had the intense look that thrilled her.

'Only the Lord knows that,' declared Lizzie, 'and He's not telling. Come on, our Rose, bed. There's no sleeping late in the morning, even though it is Sunday. We want to see as much as we can while we're here.' It was agreed they would all meet for breakfast at eight-thirty.

Although Rose's first day in Paris had been so exciting she thought she must put Sunday as the peak of perfection. In the spring sunshine of the morning they strolled along the Champs Elysées, mingling with Parisian families, lovers arm in arm, priests and nuns and groups of people, obviously tourists like themselves, who spoke in a number of tongues.

There was so much beauty. It was in the dresses, in the variegated greens of the avenue of trees, that stretched far into the distance, crowned with a froth of pink and white blossom. Rose, who wore a simple white linen jacket she had made weeks before over her black velvet dress, with the long tassel of her hat swinging as she walked, was complimented by Alex. 'You look really lovely Rose, intriguing.' He tucked her arm through his, a gesture that had her daydreaming. They were on their honeymoon. Her expression prompted Alex to ask where her thoughts were and Rose, blushing, told him she was thinking how lucky she was to be walking in Paris on this beautiful Sunday morning.

In the afternoon they went to Montmartre and on the way kept catching brief glimpses of the turrets and domes of the Sacré Coeur. Alex said they would be going there later. They climbed numerous steps, and viewed the works of the pavement artists. Alex wanted to buy Adele and the girls a painting each from a stall, but Lizzie pointed out, in her practical way, that paintings were not the easiest things to be carrying around while sightseeing. Alex gave in on this but insisted they had pen portraits of themselves. The likeness to each was amazingly accurate, considering the speed at which they were drawn. Rose said her mother would be absolutely delighted to have them.

It was growing dark when they climbed the steps of the Sacré Coeur. In the dimness and prayer-quiet of the vast, high-vaulted interior Rose experienced a reverence she had never known before. She walked on tiptoe past kneeling women, their heads covered with black shawls, wishing her mother could have been here to draw solace for her griefs; to give thanks for all her blessings.

Rose and Alex became detached from the other three. When they came out Charlie and Lizzie and Adele were below, their backs to them, standing motionless, studying the view. Rose and Alex stopped at the top of the steps. Beyond lay a panorama of Paris, the twinkling lights bringing a romanticism to even the poorer parts of the city. Alex reached for Rose's hand.

'I watched you, Rose, the candlelight on your face, your eyes luminous with tears and I knew then I was in love with you.'

'Oh, Alex, I . . .'

'Are you two coming?' It was Lizzie calling, her tone sharp.

They went down the steps, with Alex saying they would talk later.

But there was no opportunity for them to be alone together that evening. Rose felt she must keep pinching herself to believe that Alex had declared his love for her. Had he been simply carried away by the atmosphere of the evening?

The following morning at breakfast Adele said, 'I don't know what you men are planning to do but I'm taking the girls to the shops. The Galeries Lafayette is a *must*.' Alex said that he and Charles would look at cars, and arranged for them all to meet for lunch.

Back at the hotel they waited for over an hour for the men to return, then had their meal without them. Adele assured them that Alex and Charles would be perfectly all right, time would mean nothing to them if they were looking at cars. Lizzie was annoyed. She could barely keep her eyes open, and said she would like to go to her room and rest but had to see the men safely back first. They were in the foyer watching for them when Alex came out of the lift, alone. He was full of apologies. They had met friends of his, had drinks and Charles was feeling a little 'under the weather'. He was in his room sleeping and they were not to worry.

Adele had talked of having a siesta and Rose wished Lizzie would go too, leaving her alone with Alex. Judging by the glances he kept giving her she was sure this was what he wanted. She felt a stirring of excitement.

And it was Alex who got rid of Adele and Lizzie. Seeing them stifling yawns he said, 'You both look tired, go and have a rest, I'll look after Rose.' Lizzie looked annoyed and seemed about to protest, but she got into the next lift with Adele.

Alex held out a hand, suggesting they get some fresh air, they could talk as they walked. But the only walking they did was to a taxi, which the commissionaire called for them. When Rose asked where they were going, Alex said he had something special he wanted her to see.

The 'something special' turned out to be the painting of the Yorkshire Dales that hung in his apartment. Rose, sure that the painting was not the only reason for Alex bringing her here, felt ashamed that she wanted him to make love to her. A throbbing, which had begun in her limbs the moment she knew where he was taking her, was now an agony and an ecstasy.

'So – what do you think of my painting?' Alex enquired.

It was an exact replica of the scene she had witnessed from the hotel window the evening before they left the Dales – a slanting shaft of sunlight on the still water of the tarn, the mellow tints of autumn in the foliage . . . a peaceful scene.

'It's beautiful.'

'If I've been overworking and come here I find it soothing. What do you think of my apartment?'

It was a bachelor flat, rather sombrely furnished, the furniture mahogany. Rose did not know much about antiques but by the little she did know, guessed it would be expensive. The dark green velvet curtains toned with the square of carpet on the parquet floor. Alex took her by the hand.

'Come and see my kitchen, where I do my cooking. Oh, yes, I can cook, I'm an expert at some dishes. I must have you to dine with me one evening.' The fitments in the kitchen were dark oak, the floor tiled, the only brightness being in the daffodil and white checked curtains at the small window.

He showed her the bathroom upstairs from the opened doorway, a massive bath with equally massive taps, black and white tiled floor, big fluffy white towels, with monograms in black, A de V. Rose had only time to notice the lavatory, *and* the bidet, which she had learned was featured in so many Parisian houses, hotels, before Alex closed the door. He opened a door further along and drew her inside, and there Rose took a quick breath. It was such a contrast to the rest of the apartment. Here there was a woman's touch, in the rich blue carpet and cream silk velvet curtains with looped, fringed pelmets. The furniture was cream with gold touches. There were spindly-legged tables with onyx tops at either side of the bed, and the table lamps had onyx bases. The bed was huge with insets of miniature country scenes on the flat brass rails, the coverlet a quilted chintz with a cream background, patterned with trailing flowers in muted shades of pinks and blues.

It was a lovers' room, Rose thought, and had to restrain herself from asking Alex how many women he had brought here. There was nothing feminine about the groups of pictures on the walls, however. They were hunting scenes or battle scenes and the only items on the dressing table were porcelain candlesticks and a pair of silver-backed men's hairbrushes.

'Well?' Alex said.

Rose, afraid to face him, moved round the room. 'It's lovely. Who furnished it?'

'My grandmother.' Alex laughed softly. 'Surprised? She wanted to stay here when she came to Paris and, being a very feminine woman, hated the plainness of my bachelor apartment. I think deep down she thought if she gave the bedroom a more feminine look it might tempt me to bring a woman here. She was a lovely, wicked lady and disappointed that I was not escorting beautiful women somewhere every evening. And, in case you are wondering how many women I did bring here, you are the first.'

Rose stopped and turned to face him. 'Oh, Alex, do you really expect me to believe that?'

'It's true, whether you believe it or not. Oh, I've had women, but none have come here.'

'Then why did you bring me?'

He took her by the shoulders, drew her towards him and looked deeply into her eyes. 'Because you're different to anyone I've ever known. You haunt my dreams, Rose, I want you. I know it's wrong, wrong to have brought you here, but life would be dull if we had to keep strictly to the proprieties all the time.' Alex ran a forefinger lightly down her cheek then lifted her hair behind her ears, and the throbbing that had eased in Rose surged up again. When Alex toyed with the top button at the back of her dress she drew in a quick breath. She wanted to say 'No, please don't', but the words could not get past the mountains in her throat.

Alex, still holding her gaze, an intense look in his dark eyes, unfastened three buttons. Rose sought frantically in her mind to recall all her grandmother's warnings of what could happen in such a situation.

'It's not only a boy's groping hands and kisses you have to fight against, Rosie, it's nature itself for having given us such strong feelings.'

It did nothing to make Rose try to prevent Alex from undoing another two buttons. When she felt his fingers on her warm flesh she gave a shiver of anticipation. Then she thought of something Bessie had once said . . . 'If you had a baby, Rosie, your ma would bring it up with all the other kids and it would never be able to call you Mam . . .'

Rose drew back. 'No, Alex, please. I'm afraid.'

'You have no need to be, I won't harm you.' His lips, soft and warm came down over hers, moving sensuously, bringing a pounding in her heart. Her dress fell at her feet. He picked her up, carried her to the bed, and lay down beside her. She kept her eyes tightly closed. Alex drew down her shoulder straps and cupped her breasts. Rose moaned. Then, feeling the hardness of him through the silk of her underslip against her thighs she panicked. She began to struggle and he held her tight, soothing her. No harm would come to her, he promised. She was just to relax, she must trust him. Rose let her body go limp, no longer feeling strong emotions, but she tensed and panicked again when she felt Alex's weight on her. Her lids flew open and it was then she caught a glimpse of the ceiling over his shoulder.

'Oh, what a gorgeous blue,' she said.

'Wh-what?' He eased his weight from her.

'The ceiling, that delicate blue and the lovely cupids.' She spoke in a breathless way, relieved she had found something to distract him.

Alex groaned. 'Oh, Rose, for God's sake, I'm trying to make love to you.'

'Yes, I know, but I didn't want you to. It's wrong, I was foolish.'

Alex rolled away from her and got up, tidying himself. 'No, I was the foolish one for bringing you here.' His voice was cold.

'I'm sorry,' Rose said in a small voice. 'Sorry I denied you, but at the same time I'm glad I noticed the ceiling.'

When Alex turned to face her his lips were trembling. 'Rose, Rose, what am I going to do with you? You can say the most ridiculous things, yet be adorable. You haunt my dreams, I'm obsessed by you and I don't want to be. I don't want to be owned by anyone.'

Rose was still. 'And I don't want to own you, or anyone else for that matter.' She paused. 'If I had let you make love to me and I had had a baby what would you have done?'

'You wouldn't have had a baby.'

'I know several girls with babies whose boyfriends told them they had no need to worry, they would take care.'

'Oh, Rose, for heaven's sake! Do you take me for some callow youth who's having his first experience of sex?' He picked up her dress from the floor and laid it on the bed. 'We had better go, you know where the bathroom is.'

Rose fought back tears until she reached the bathroom. It was some time before she felt composed enough to face Alex.

When she went downstairs he was standing at the window, his back to her. 'I'm ready, Alex,' she said.

He spoke without turning. 'I want to get you out of my system, Rose, and can't. I've decided we shall get married.'

Rose stared at the stiff back. If he had suggested such a thing before he started to make love to her she would have been overjoyed. Now she said, clasping her hands tightly together, 'I'm sorry Alex, I don't want to get married.'

He turned slowly and she saw the affront on his face at the rejection. 'Not want to –' He stopped suddenly and his expression changed, softened. He came towards her and took her by the shoulders. 'Oh, Rose, what have I done to you. I've always prided myself on being able to handle any situation, on the factory floor or in a boardroom and here I am loosing the reins because of my stupidity. I was arrogant enough to think you wanted to marry me.'

Rose, not wanting him to suffer the humiliation of her rejection, said earnestly, 'The fault is not yours, Alex, it's circumstances. I want a career. It would be wrong for me to marry you. I hope some day to have my own fashion house and I want to work to that end.'

'So what do I do in the meantime, go on loving you, hoping –'

Rose searched his face. 'Alex, is it me you're in love with or the girl Rosella in the painting?'

'I prefer the flesh and blood Rosella.' He touched her cheek gently. 'You're a darling girl, Rose – perhaps one day.' Alex straightened. 'In the meantime I suggest we get back to the hotel and hope we have not been missed. I would rather not have to think up a story to account for our absence.'

'Nor I,' said Rose. 'I hate lying.'

Her sister Lizzie was fast asleep when she crept into the bedroom. Rose took off her dress and lay on the bed opposite. She felt wide awake. Would there come a time when she would regret refusing to marry Alex? She did want to marry and have children. Was designing dresses more important?

Business was important to Alex, it would always come first with him, she was sure of that. She was young, there had been no chance to prove herself. She must.

Rose found herself wondering what Charlie would have said could he have seen her with Alex in his apartment, and felt ashamed, not only because of that incident but because she had not even bothered to go upstairs and see if he was all right after his drinking session. He was always so caring about her. She would make it up to him tonight, be extra nice to him. No, that was wrong, she was being condescending and Charlie deserved better than that. She loved him. But not in the way she felt about Alex. How did one define love between a man and a woman? She had heard women talking disparagingly of the 'sexual appetites' of men, as though it was something they had never experienced.

Rose's eyelids began to droop. She had a 'sexual appetite'. She giggled a little. It sounded terrible, made her feel like a fallen woman.

A fallen woman? . . . Rose drifted into sleep.

During the following months, Rose had no regrets about her refusal to marry Alex, though there were times when she felt an ache to have him love her. His manner to her was more courteous and polite than affectionate, yet she was sure he still cared for her. It was in the intense way she sometimes found him watching her. Fortunately for her peace of mind, he was away more often than he was in England. The firm was now a private limited company, with sales figures rising each week. Lizzie was like a tycoon herself, here, there and everywhere, organising. They had not only opened the second shop but the third one too and were selling everything they made. Yet, in spite of this, she knew a terrible restlessness.

On a Sunday morning in the middle of November, feeling the need to be on her own for a while, Rose went out into the garden and made for the shed. In the far corner her grandfather, who had fed a pile of dead leaves and twigs to a small bonfire, straightened and stood puffing away at his old clay pipe, the smoke mingling with the pungent clouds that rose and hovered over the smouldering bonfire in the raw dampness of the morning. Sam, gazing around him had the air of a squire surveying his estate.

From the lowering clouds came the mournful 'kwark, kwark' of a crow. Rose shivered and pulling her thick jacket closer to her throat went into the shed. There she stood looking around her. Only a short while ago the shed had been full of life and colour, with dresses being made up, the whirring of the treadle machines and the bright chatter of the women. Now there was only a grey chill, the earthy smell of flowerpots, and creosote.

A creaking sound made Rose look towards the door. Charlie popped his head around it. 'Oh, there you are, Rosie. What are you doing in here, it's arctic.' When Rose made no reply he came up to her. 'What's wrong, love? You've hardly spoken to me since I came home on Friday afternoon.'

'It's nothing you've done, Charlie, it's just that –' Rose shrugged. 'It's probably that I feel I'm not getting anywhere.'

'Not getting anywhere?' He stared at her. 'You must be joking! Your dresses are selling all over the place.'

'Yes, with Alex controlling everything. I would like to handle something that's all my own. We have people managing the three shops, even the making of my couture dresses has had to stop because everyone is mad on mass producing. I know it's necessary if I want to have my fashion house, but when? All Alex can talk about is diversifying – we'll go into cosmetics, into beach sandals, into jewellery. All the while he's building an empire, wanting more and more. Lizzie was telling me that one of his holding companies has bought control of another holding company. Why does he do it?'

'It's simply centralisation of management.'

'But it's crazy, it's like a vast chain that goes on and on. When will Alex be satisfied, when will he stop?'

'Never! That's big business. Look, Rose, I know you don't want to invest in stocks and shares, but it would be a way for you to speed up your fashion house. Liz and I on Alex's advice have done quite well buying and selling. We've both got quite a bit of stock in American companies. If you start you'd get hooked.'

'I don't want to get hooked. I don't want to gamble, and may I remind you, Charlie Eagan, that you were the one to make me promise not to gamble.'

He grinned. 'I know, but this is different from horse racing.'

'I'm still not interested. I would be dependent on Alex for advice, buy this share, buy that. I've told you, I want to do something on my own!'

'But you have, Rose, your designs are your own, they're original.'

'They're a parody of what I want to do,' she said bitterly. 'Lizzie is forever wanting to keep down costs, paring one thing after another. She's like Alex, always thinking of profit, *big* profit.'

Charlie put his arm around her. 'Well, Rosie love, I can only say this, if you get an idea of something you want to carry out, and if there's any way at all I can help, you know you only have to ask.'

'Yes, I know, Charlie,' she said softly, and kissed him on the cheek. 'What would I do without you?'

'It's good to see you smile again, Rosie,' Charlie said quietly. 'I don't like it when you withdraw from the family – from me.'

'Oh, Charlie, you know I would never withdraw from any of you, I love you all too much.' Rose rubbed her hands. 'I can't feel my fingertips. Come on, I'll race you to the fire.'

Charlie followed her slowly, his hand to his cheek. If only she knew what she did to him when she kissed him. But thank goodness it wasn't that she'd been mooning over Alex. He had thought at one time when they were in Paris that there was something between them, but that seemed to have fizzled out. He had a great admiration for Alex, for his business acumen. He was a man of decision, but Alex would not be right for Rose. For all her talk of wanting to have a business completely on her own, she was, deep down, a home girl. She needed a man's love, his care, she needed babies. Charlie sighed, doubting that he would ever get the chance of being a father to them.

By the beginning of July Charlie kept saying he would like to have a talk with Alex. Judging by what he was reading in the newspapers there was a great deal of unrest on the stock-market. He wanted to know if he should sell his shares, for he had a lot of money invested in American companies. In the end he wrote to Alex and back came a reply saying the 'slight slump was only temporary' – people were panicking and unloading their stocks. This was the time to buy. Both Charlie and Lizzie bought. Rose kept her money in the bank.

When the Wall Street Crash came in October the world was stunned. Charlie and Lizzie looked as bereft as though their whole family had been wiped out. Rose said, 'It's not the end. Alex still has the factory. We can start again.'

Charlie looked at her, grey-faced. 'Rose love, if Alex has lost everything there won't *be* a factory.'

'But Alex won't have lost everything.' She said it with confidence. 'He would have sense enough to get out before the crash came. Anyway, if the worst does come to the worst we'll still have money coming in from the shops.'

Lizzie said, on a rising note of near-hysteria, 'You don't know what you're talking about, our Rose! You have no idea to what extent this Crash will affect markets. There'll be nobody to buy your garments. People are bankrupt, some of the biggest businesses in the world. We're finished, finished! All that work for nothing. Oh, God, I wish I was dead.'

It was not until the following days that Rose began to realise that Charlie and her sister had not been over-dramatising. All the terrible details were there in the newspapers – the panic at the Stock Exchange, people fighting to sell their stocks, roads jammed outside. Even banks had failed, so that people who had not owned any stocks and shares were destitute. They lost their homes, furniture, everything they owned. Big businessmen who had lost everything had collapsed with heart attacks, some had committed suicide, one man throwing himself from the top of a building. Rose worried about Alex. Adele had tried to phone him at his apartment and at his office in America but there was no reply.

Then there was news of a rallying. Several tycoons had clubbed together, the figure running into millions, to try and create confidence on the market. They began to buy shares and others followed suit. But this ruse failed. There was another setback, another rallying, and so it went on.

Rose, who had been so sure Alex would have survived the Crash was shocked when he arrived back at the beginning of December a defeated-looking man. He came to the house and Gran Eagan and Sally fussed over him – 'The poor man, what a terrible thing. He must have something to eat, yes he must.' Rose could hardly believe it was the same Alex who had appeared so arrogant at times, yet his very weakness drew her to him. She longed to put her arms around him and hold him close.

Charlie, full of compassion, poured him a stiff whisky, and after Alex had eaten a snack meal he seemed to revive. He thanked them and there was a genuine gratitude in his dark eyes.

'You have no idea what your warmth has done to me,' he said. 'The world has seemed such a bleak place lately, with misery and despair all around me. I had to get away.' He shook his head sadly. 'Not that one can really escape. I dread to think what the unemployment figures will be. I had hoped to save the factory, but it has to go. In any case there would be no buying. Trade is at a standstill.'

'But it will get moving again,' Rose said earnestly.

'Nothing stands still, and I'm going to get prepared for when it does change. I shall make couture dresses, and buy materials now. I should get some bargains.'

Lizzie snapped, 'You're talking out of the top of your head, our Rose. I know I encouraged you to build up a business but this is not the time to talk about luxury clothes.'

Charlie began talking to Rose, trying to explain fully the situation, with Alex adding his contribution, both speaking in a patient way as they might to a child. The Wall Street Crash would make a terrible impact on world trade, but this was just a start. The whole effect would not be felt for some time, it would end in a world recession with millions out of work.

Rose listened and said nothing, but she knew she had to do something. She was not going to let all she had worked for go without a fight.

During the next few days, the thing that most surprised Rose was the defeatist attitude of Alex and Charlie and Lizzie. Even Adele had lost her briskness, her interest, all the people Rose had always thought of as being of strong character. She learned that the factory was to be run down and people laid off. Trade at the Sovereign shops had practically ceased. Then Rose had a letter from Clarissa. The first half was about the Crash and most depressing, her father had lost all his money and her mother was in a state of shock. In the next half Clarissa began to tell of all the fun she was having, with party-going, tea and dinner dances. She raved about a fantastic ball to which all the family had been invited. Lecky, who had sold his shares at the right time, had bought her and her mother the most beautiful evening gowns. – *I wish you could have been with us, Rose, you would have been in your element, the dresses! A thousand guests and every women vying with the other, fashionwise. One found it hard to imagine there had ever been such a thing as the Wall Street Crash . . .'*

Rose said, after reading the letter aloud, 'It doesn't make sense, does it? Clarissa's father loses all his money, her mother is in a state of shock yet all Clarissa talks about is enjoyment.'

Charlie declared it to be a false gaiety.

Rose looked from one to the other. 'What impresses me is the amount of money that must have been spent on dresses for this ball. Multiply this with all the other social occasions and you can see now there *is* room for couture dresses, my dresses . . .'

'Of course there are wealthy people about,' Charlie said, 'but if you're thinking of trying to start a fashion house, Rosie, forget it. You would never even get it under way. It needs money, big money, and a backer like Alex would have been.'

'I have some money in the bank, I didn't speculate. I'm not saying this out of smugness, I just want to let you know I perhaps could get started. With so many businesses failing I might get the chance to find premises in London, and start in a small way.'

'You don't start a fashion house in a *small* way!' Lizzie exclaimed.

'I'd go along with that,' Charlie said, 'but what impresses me about Rosie is her spunk in trying to do something. Here we all are sitting and moaning about our losses, while she is wanting to get up and sock 'em all.' Charlie put his arm around Rose. 'I didn't think you had it in you, love, I've always thought of you as a dreamer. I admire your attitude, even though I think you would be taking on more than you could handle.'

Rose said no more then, but determined to make her couture dresses, decided she would go and see Mr Rosenberg. He would know the situation in London, would advise her, would be honest with her. She planned to leave on the following Monday. She would travel on the early train, leaving a note saying where she was. The family would be upset but she would face the scolding when she returned.

On the Saturday prior to leaving Charlie popped his head round the kitchen door and said, a broad grin on his face, 'Got a surprise for you!' He came in carrying a secondhand gramophone with a big green horn. There was also a pile of old records and ten sixpenny ones from Woolworths of the more popular tunes. It was as though new life had been injected into the family. They played some of the popular ones first and they all sang to them, '*Rose Marie*' . . . '*Show Me the Way to Go Home*' . . . '*I Wonder Where My Baby is Tonight*' . . .'*Always*' . . . This last one was Rose's favourite at the present time.

The jollity remained, and everyone was in a good mood, which made it easier for Rose to leave the next morning. Lizzie was in a deep sleep when she crept out. The morning was dry but the wind icy. Rose had not dressed up.

Chapter 20

Rose tiptoed out of the house at five o'clock. It was bitterly cold, but she felt the excitement of doing something forbidden.

Her one worry was that Mr Rosenberg might be away. But he was in his office and welcomed her warmly. 'Why, Rose, what a pleasant surprise!' He looked beyond her. 'Are you on your own?' She said yes, it was a long story and Mr Rosenberg drew out a chair. His time was hers.

Before Rose had finished outlining her plan he was shaking his head. 'I would like to say go ahead, but it's the wrong time. Things are bad, and likely to get worse. Yes, I know there are the wealthy, and that women will always be buying clothes, but they'll go to the established couturiers. An unknown wouldn't stand a chance. You would have to give credit, and to do that you would need a wealthy backer. I'm sorry to hear about Mr de Veer . . . A terrible thing.'

'Recessions do end,' Rose said.

'Yes, and I like your idea of buying materials now. I've bought two lots of bankrupt stock during the past week and I shall buy more when I get the chance. But I can put mine to use. I have the outlets.'

Rose sat up, her expression eager. 'And I will find one. An idea occurred to me while I was on the train. I thought I could open a small shop, offering accessories, handbags, jewellery, scarves, *exclusive* designs and sell – for cash.'

Mr Rosenberg threw up his hands in horror. 'For cash! You condemn it right away. You may as well put up a notice saying CHEAP. It would scare the wealthy away.'

'Every woman likes a bargain. How about a notice stressing that the exclusive accessories are bankrupt stock, much reduced for quick sale, cash only? I feel sure it will draw a number of women. Inside the shop will be hanging a dress, *one* only. When a customer notices it I, or whoever is attending, will let it be known there are only a few at a special price, perhaps a quarter of the original. Less, even. And, these are for special customers. Don't you think that would appeal?'

A slow smile spread over Mr Rosenberg's face. 'You must surely have Hebrew ancestors, Rose.' Then serious again he added, 'But what do you hope to achieve? This will not get you a fashion house.'

'It will get me money, get me customers, and my dresses will become known. I hope a time will come when I shall be able to say that I'm opening a small fashion house, the House of Kimberley.'

Mr Rosenberg now looked a little sad. 'You're a dreamer, Rose. That is good, you design beautiful clothes, but reality must come into the business side of it. Your shop would have to be in the West End and you'll find that most are rented on a lease. And for that you would need a large amount of money.'

Rose brought her bankbook from her handbag and a list she had made of the expenses she would have to face. So much to be put aside for the family for rent and food, so much for her own expenses living in London, for materials, for work, for wages. It was a long list in which she felt she had covered every exigency. 'I feel I could cope for six months. If I failed then I would have to start again.'

'Start again?' There was warmth and admiration in Mr Rosenberg's eyes. 'I would be proud if you were my daughter, Rose. With such an attitude you *must* succeed. I shall do all in my power to find you the right premises.'

Rose thanked him then they talked about the dresses she had brought. He said to leave them with him for when she found her shop. She would get more for them than what he could pay her. When Rose got up to go she kissed him on the cheek and said softly, 'You've been a good friend, Mr Rosenberg. If I succeed then you must share my success. I hope we shall meet again soon.'

In the train on the way back Rose felt she was more than willing to accept any scolding her family would mete out.

The evening was bitterly cold. When she came out of the station to make her way to Orchard Street, sleet stung her cheeks and ice on a shallow pool cracked under her feet. She longed for warmth and to her joy saw, when she arrived home, the blaze of a roaring fire through the kitchen window. She let herself in, stood a moment and took a quick breath before opening the door.

Rose had been prepared for angry words from her grandmother and from Lizzie, but was unprepared for her mother's outburst.

'How dare you do this to us,' she blazed. 'We've been worried sick all day. I've nearly been out of my mind, imagining you being waylaid, snatched by white slave traders, and don't think it happens only in films. I was reading only the other day in the newspaper . . .'

Charlie said quietly, 'All right, Sal, leave it at that.'

'No, I won't, I haven't finished yet. We've had troubles in the past, tragedies, but the family have always shared. To think that Rose would go off and never breathe a word to us.' Sally burst into tears.

'Ma . . .' Rose went toward her mother but Lizzie grabbed her by the arm and swung her round to face her.

'You're downright selfish, our Rose! You made what money you have because of us, then off you go to London spending it, having a good time. Oh, yes, I know what you're after. You want to live in London, mix with the smart set, go to parties. What about the family, how are they expected to live with no money coming in? *You* are spending *ours*, Charlie's and mine. We made it possible.'

'No, Lizzie, Alex made it possible.'

'But we worked with you, we shared in the shops, I found people to manage them.' Lizzie's face was close up to Rose's. 'Selfish, that's what you are, the most selfish person I know!'

Charlie thrust Lizzie back. 'That's enough. Now, I shall have my say. It's you who should be ashamed of yourself Lizzie Kimberley. You are the selfish one. Rose is the only one who had the guts to try and do something about getting a business going. As for any money she spent, it's hers. You and I gambled our on the stock-market. We were greedy, we wanted more. Rose saved hers. When I realised this morning what she had done I knew what I was going to do. If I can't sell on the road then I shall take a stall on the market and sell anything I can get my hands on. What are *you* planning to do, Lizzie?'

All the fight went out of Lizzie. 'I'm sorry, our Rose. I was envious of you, envious that you did have enough spunk to try and do something. And I'm the one who wants the high life, to go to parties, to dances.' She pulled a face. 'But a fat chance there is of such a thing happening now.'

'It could come.' Rose spoke with confidence. 'But it would need the family to cooperate. We would have to talk about it.'

Alex arrived in the middle of the discussion, when Sally was protesting strongly against Rose, or any other member of the family, living in London. Alex had lost the terrible devastated look he had had after the Crash but his face was still drawn. Rose had the feeling he needed the warmth of family, and longed to put her arms around him and hold him close. Gran Eagan, perhaps sensing his need, said gently, 'Sit you down, Mr de Veer, and get thawed out, you look frozen.'

He looked around him and said he hoped he was not intruding, not interrupting family business. Charlie told him he *was* family and that he had come at just the right time, they needed his expert advice.

'Expert?' A wry smile touched Alex's lips. 'I am definitely the wrong person to ask.'

'The right one,' Charlie insisted. 'You have a world of

business acumen behind you, invaluable to us, and if I know you, Alex, you'll be putting it to good use yourself very soon.'

Charlie had used the right words. Alex began to show interest. 'Well, yes, if I can help in any way . . .'

Rose, at a prompting from Charlie, began to outline her plan, ignoring the look of disapproval on Alex's face when she mentioned trading for cash. Before she had finished he was shaking his head as Mr Rosenberg had done and, like Mr Rosenberg, dismissed the plan as unworkable.

'You might make a success of a small shop, Rose, but a fashion house exists on credit. You would need a vast capital behind you. If the market gets under way, and pray heaven it will, I shall help you, but that is for the future.'

Rose raised her head, a stubborn set to her chin. 'If one shop succeeds I shall open another, and another. I shall have a string of shops.'

Lizzie gave a deep sigh. 'A string of shops and she hasn't even got one yet, nor have we anywhere to live in London.'

Alex looked thoughtfully from one to the other then said he could offer them accommodation. An aunt had left him a house. It was off Park Lane, a Georgian residence.

'Park Lane?' Rose said, wide-eyed. 'Oh, it sounds wonderful.'

Alex went on to say he had never lived in it. It was furnished and although some of the better pieces had been sold, there were still enough furnishings to make the house inhabitable. Lizzie and Charlie were as excited at this offer as Rose, but Sally said it was something that needed discussion, a *great deal* of discussion, and Rose guessed by the expression on her mother's face that the answer would be no.

As it turned out it was Adele who won them the battle. She came the next morning offering to share the house and to help Rose and Lizzie launch a shop. Her capable and authoritative manner had Sally saying, 'Well, with you as chaperon, Miss Poulteney . . .' and Rose and Lizzie exchanged delighted grins.

Alex offered to drive them to London to see the property. The day before they were due to leave a letter came from Mr Rosenberg, saying he had found what he thought was a suitable shop, with a six-month lease. Rose felt sure the fates were with her. She was on the way to fulfilling her dream.

The house was imposing enough but when they went in, the chill air of the untenanted rooms and ghostly look of the furniture shrouded in dust-sheets, made Rose shiver. When Alex pulled aside the partly-closed curtains however, she exclaimed in delight at the curving staircase, balustraded in wrought iron.

'Oh, Lizzie, look, how beautiful, how elegant. Can't you just imagine mannequins coming down the stairs, with draperies floating out behind them.'

'Yes, and probably tripping over their flaming draperies and falling their length on to the marble floor!'

Charlie and Alex laughed, Rose wailed. 'You have no soul, our Lizzie. I shall have a finale with all the mannequins *standing* on the stairs, one below the other.'

'All right, shall we have a dekko at the rest of the house?'

The furniture was dark and heavy but in the rooms that did have floor coverings the carpets were predominantly Turkey red or blue. Adele, caught up in Rose's dreams of the future, began to allocate the rooms – these for bedrooms, these for workrooms, the hall would be excellent as a salon, the small rooms leading off for changing in. Charlie said with a chuckle, 'I'm glad to know where the salon is going to be.'

The salon – Rose tried to visualise it, then gave up. That was very much for the future. They must get the shop under way first.

They were preparing to leave and Rose was standing in the hall looking about her when Alex came up. 'Rose, do you think you will settle away from the North?' There was concern in his voice. 'I know how much your family means to you.'

'I must settle here, though we will take turns at going home from time to time, as there'll be dresses to collect – I'm keeping on the workrooms. Alex, why did you not sell this house? You need money.'

'My aunt Matilda – or I should say, my great-aunt Matilda, would haunt me.' There was a glint of humour in Alex's eyes. 'She always said the house would be mine when she died. She wanted it kept in the family. I was always scared of her when I was young, though – she was quite a formidable lady.'

'I cannot imagine you being afraid of anyone or anything, Alex.'

His expression sobered. 'I'm afraid of a lot of things, Rose, poverty for one and I'm . . .'

'There! Are we all ready?' Adele came in briskly. Charlie and Lizzie followed. Whatever else Alex was afraid of had to be left untold. They went to see Mr Rosenberg.

The shop he had found for Rose was small and in need of decorating, but as soon as Rose saw it she knew it was right. There were glass-fronted display cases on the walls and a room upstairs for stock. At one side was a high-class jewellers and at the other an equally high-class florists. Rose was also pleased to find that Mr Rosenberg and Alex were talking together as freely as though they were old friends.

It was two months before the shop, or the 'boutique' as Adele called it, was ready to be opened. Rose had longed to handle the whole project herself, but had had to turn to Adele and Alex for help. It was they who were responsible for her display of goods of her own designs, hand-painted silk scarves, fine, hand-tooled leather bags, jewellery and sweetmeat boxes.

The idea of the sweetmeat boxes stemmed from seeing young Judith one evening covering a small cardboard box with scraps from the ragbag. It was for her mother's birthday she said, and she was going to put some sweets in it. Rose immediately saw boxes covered in rich materials trimmed with gold and silver braids. Then she imagined them further embellished with insets of beadwork or embroidery, even a hand-painted rural scene. She thought of the chocolates Alex had once bought them during a stay in London – luscious chocolates, madly expensive, and decided if some of the boxes could be filled with these, or other sweetmeats, a man coming into the shop with a woman would surely buy her such a present. Mr Rosenberg, who paid them a quick visit while they were filling their display cases, immediately ordered three for his family. He then declared, as he stood looking around him, that it would be sacrilege to stick a poster on the window announcing bankrupt stock.

Rose smiled and taking a card from a shelf propped it on an easel which stood to the left of the window. It was gilt-edged with tiny posies in each corner and in the centre the announcement, done in a beautiful copperplate hand said, *Advantageous Purchases for Cash Customers.*

Mr Rosenberg clapped his hands to his cheeks. Such genius, such taste! How could Rose possibly fail?

Before the shop was due to open Charlie said they should go home for the weekend to clear everything up. They would have a party there and invite friends and neighbours, and he would stand the cost. Adele said she would stay in London and hold the fort. Alex, who had been invited by Charlie, made the excuse that he was half-expecting a business deal to come to fruition. Rose was glad he had refused. Although Alex fitted well into the home atmosphere of her family, she felt quite sure he would be out of place at the type of party Charlie was planning.

When they did get home, it was arranged they would hold the party in their garden shed. Neighbours had offered the use of a piano. There was baking to be done, sandwiches to be made, but Rose, who was feeling emotional at partly breaking family ties was glad to be busy. Big Bessie, who had come to help said, 'It'll be lovely to have a party and cheer folks up, what with the state the country's in and all that. Not that I'm grumbling, I'm getting in a bit of money from my sewing and Fred's boss has offered to keep him on for another few weeks at least. Mind you, you know what Fred is, the world's biggest spender, money burns a hole in his pocket. I'll have to make him some steel-lined ones!' Rose laughed, she could always get a laugh with Bessie.

On the night of the party so many people turned up they overspilled from the shed into the garden. Tom Simmonds was belting out the latest tunes on the tinny piano, people were singing at the tops of their voices and with the noise of those wanting to talk having to shout above the other sounds Rose felt the party must be heard a mile away.

She had spent most of the time running between the house and the shed getting more jugs of homemade lemonade, sandwiches, sausage rolls, and becoming more and more hot decided to change into a thinner dress. She went into the bedroom and saw Lizzie, who had been missing for some time, standing in front of the mirror above the washstand. Rose stopped and stared. Lizzie, who turned and grinned, was dressed like a flapper, with a short-fringed Charleston-type dress, beaded headband, and chewing gum. She swung a long rope of pearls and, laughing, went into a Charleston routine. 'How am I doing? Been practising. Improved, haven't I?'

Rose closed the door. 'Lizzie, for heaven's sake! if Gran sees you dressed like that she'll stop us from living in London.'

'She won't see me, she's with Ma in the scullery cutting up loaves of bread. I'll sneak out the front way and go round to the back. I just want a few minutes' fling.' Lizzie kicked her height then still dancing went to the door, calling over her shoulder, 'See you, baby!'

Rose stood a few moments finding it difficult to reconcile this image of her sister with the sharp-tongued business girl she had become. Well, as Gran Eagan once said, you could live fifty years with a person and still not know them. Rose changed her dress then went downstairs.

When she arrived at the shed she found the centre of the

floor cleared and Lizzie dancing a Charleston with someone. The next moment Rose was standing motionless, an icy hand clutching at her spine. The man was Alex. Lizzie must have known he was there, known he was coming to the party. The most hurtful thing to Rose was the fact that Alex had always refused to do the Charleston with her in London, saying he was not proficient. He was proficient enough now, they were more or less giving an exhibition. Rose pushed through the crowd, set the jugs of lemonade on the table and turned to leave. She was detained by a friend of Charlie's who wanted her to dance. She told him, later, she was busy, and escaped, and not wanting to have to talk to anyone made her way to a deserted part of the garden.

How could Alex have behaved in this way? He had not even called at the house. Perhaps he had wanted to give her a surprise. Surprise was right! He had looked as if he were really enjoying himself with Lizzie. Perhaps he saw a wildness in her sister, a sensuousness. It was something that Rose was only aware of at that moment. She looked up as someone called her name. It was Charlie. She drew further back into the shadows. Then, realising she could not stay in the garden all evening she started to make her way to the house. And came face to face with Alex.

'I've been looking for you, Rose.'

'I find that hard to believe. Minutes ago you were cavorting with my sister in a Charleston!'

'Oh, that, yes, I thought we danced quite well together.' His tone was distant. 'Why the haughtiness, Rose?'

'Well, considering you told us you were unable to accept our party invitation then turn up . . .'

'Because I'm leaving for America the day after tomorrow. The business deal came off. I had some things to attend to up North and came to say goodbye. I shall be away for a few months.'

'Oh.'

Alex took her by the shoulders. 'I don't want to leave with

you being angry with me, Rose. You know I love you.'

She searched his face. The intense look was back in his dark eyes. For a few seconds, all sounds were cut out and she and Alex were alone on their own island. Then the idyll was broken by Charlie calling, 'Come on, you two, Fred's going to sing! Special treat.'

They went into the hut. Bessie, who was standing near the door said, grinning at them, 'A few beers and Fred thinks he's Caruso.'

'Oh, go on with you,' Charlie teased, 'you know you love to hear him sing.' He left to round up some more people.

Fred sang the older type of songs. He sang with great feeling and there were times when he could move Rose to tears. Now she stood tense, wanting to be anywhere but here.

The pianist played the introduction to the song, '*Because*', and Fred, his eyes closed began, 'Because God made you mine I'll cherish thee . . .'

Bessie said, 'Hark at him, I'll cherish thee! The bugger's been out every night for a week.'

Rose felt a bubble of laughter, then she was laughing and crying. Alex laughed softly with her and put an arm around her shoulders.

It was this and his gentle kiss on her lips later that Rose remembered long after the party ended.

Their first customer at the shop was an austere-faced woman who came in looking as though she were about to attack them. 'Those two necklaces!' she demanded, pointing to a display case. 'I want them for my grand-daughters. Thank goodness someone has the sense to sell goods at a lesser price for cash. I shall tell my friends about it.'

That she had kept her word was proved by the number of women who came in the following week, saying that Mrs Saunders-Bailey had recommended them.

Trade kept on increasing. By the end of two months customers were paying return visits for the second and third time and eventually the profit was covering the rent and other expenses of the shop.

The one thing that disappointed Rose was that although women admired her couture dresses not one was sold. 'It's the cash,' Lizzie said. 'They can find ready money for smaller items but not for dresses.'

Charlie, when he came, brought poor reports of sales. He was only one of many travellers he said who were in the same boat. Trade was picking up at the Sovereign shops, but only slightly.

On Charlie's last visit they had been invited to Lecky's home for dinner. Clarissa and her parents were in the south of France, and had been for some time. Lecky had been in America and brought news of Alex, who was doing quite well in his new venture. Rose suspected that Lecky had backed him. Since Alex had gone to the States Rose had to learn about him in his letters to Adele and that news was brief.

Lecky was much interested in the shop, and assured them that when Clarissa returned they would be getting her custom and that of her friends. Lizzie said sharply, 'It's for cash only,' and Lecky laughed, and told them he applauded the idea.

It was an enjoyable evening in many ways. They had a lot of laughs yet Rose had the feeling of an underlying sobriety, as though the ghost of the Wall Street Crash still lingered. They left with Lecky's promise that the minute Clarissa returned they would have a party.

Rose had been homesick for some time and when Charlie said her mother was fretting for the two girls she and Lizzie decided to go home for a long weekend. They would travel with Charlie in the van and come back by train. For Rose it also meant she could have a talk with the workers. In spite of not selling any of her couture dresses she had a strong feeling she must go on making them. Trade must surely improve soon.

The warmth of the welcome from the family had Rose in

tears. She was kissed and hugged and she kissed and hugged in return. They talked non-stop for an hour with Rose and Lizzie telling them about the shop and they in turn hearing how many babies Gran Eagan had delivered, how many men had beaten their wives, how many pounds of fruit Sam had picked from his 'orchard' and how many people were out of work in the North. The number brought Rose to earth with a bang. So many? What hope was there of trade improving? In spite of this depressing news she went to the workshop and discussed the making of couture dresses with the women. She felt she had to. Bessie said, 'Great! I'm just longing to get sore fingers stitching on beads.' She laughed as she said it, and Rose knew she would always get the best from Bessie.

The cutter who had been employed at the factory had also cut for Rose. She was only too delighted to have work. Rose had told Adele of her plans before she left and Adele had said she was willing to come North and get the women organised. Rose, who had an hour-long discussion with the women did some organising herself, and although some of them were sceptical the dresses would sell all were ready to get started on Rose's designs. Designing was something she had never stopped doing.

On the way back in the train she said to Lizzie, 'Wasn't it lovely to get home, to get all the love and fuss? I have a feeling that things are going to take a turn for the better, that good business is coming our way.'

'You always were the optimist,' Lizzie replied drily. 'But judging from what I heard at home we're in for a tough time. Things are definitely going to get worse.'

Rose dismissed it. People were always saying things like that.

For three weeks there was no change in the trade at the shop, then one morning a pale-faced, rather fragile-looking woman came in. She was fair, pretty, but had a melancholic look. She asked if she could look around, as a friend had recommended the shop to her. There was a slight huskiness in her voice which Rose found attractive. Adele came up and whispered on a note of excitement that their customer was none other than Isobelle Faycott, who was due to open in a play in London soon. Rose became excited too when she saw the actress examining the beaded dress displayed.

'Have you more?' she asked.

'Yes, I'll bring them down.' Rose went tearing up to the stock room with Lizzie following to get the boxes.

Adele was attempting to talk to the woman but Isobelle Faycott did not want to deal with her, nor with Lizzie, only with Rose.

'Heaven knows why,' Isobelle said to Rose. 'You're probably as rotten as everyone else. The whole world is rotten.'

All three stood staring at her, taken aback by such a remark. Then Rose, annoyed, said, 'To quote my grandmother, "you only get out of life what you put into it".'

'And that's a load of crap!' Rose found herself staring again, unable to reconcile this sweet-faced woman with such language. 'And you can tell your *clever* old grandmother what I said!' concluded Isobelle Faycott.

Rose's head went up. 'I wouldn't insult her. I have a great respect for my grandmother. She's hard-working and the most honest woman I know.'

'All right, all right, I don't want a sermon. Are you going to show me some dresses? Even if I buy any it doesn't mean I'll be wearing them. I'll probably throw myself into the river.'

'I hope if you do throw yourself in the river that you won't be wearing one of my dresses,' Rose retorted, no longer caring whether she made a sale or not. 'Every one I design is special to me and a labour of love to the women who work on it.'

'You're full of little platitudes, aren't you,' came the sneering reply. 'I detest your type. I can't imagine why I thought you would be different. Well! Do I get to see these dresses or not?'

She bought three and paid by cheque. Rose, thinking of

cash sales stood looking at it. Isobelle Faycott said drily, 'I promise not to drown myself until the cheque is met. You might hate my guts but I pay my debts. Send the dresses to my suite at the Dorchester.' She swept out.

Rose sank on to a chair. 'I've sold three dresses and I should feel jubilant. Instead I feel like doing murder. If I have any more customers like her *I* shall be the one to be thinking of committing suicide!'

Adele laughed. 'Rose my dear, this is just a taste of what you would have to put up with if you entered the world of haute couture. It's full of difficult women, impossible women.'

'Heaven send some more customers like our Isobelle,' Lizzie declared, taking the cheque from Rose. 'I'll get this into the bank this minute. Let them all come!'

Adele said, 'I feel sure it will bring custom if Isobelle *does* wear the dresses. Let's pray she will.'

But no response came. The play opened and the critics raved over it. Adele said they must get tickets but when they went to book they found that every performance was sold out for weeks ahead.

Trade kept on steadily at the shop and Lizzie talked with almost wild enthusiasm of the London shop keeping all the others in credit balance. Rose became bored, she was ready again for change. One evening when she was doodling, figures began to emerge, Egyptian figures, colourful. Immediately she began to see them as a design on scarves, not handpainted but printed. Adele thought them beautiful. Rose then began experimenting in the evenings with batik, remembering happy days spent dyeing Easter eggs. She was so pleased with the results that she found women who would work on the scarves. Both types were a big success, and in all the excitement of something new Isobelle Faycott was forgotten.

But the actress was to come very forcibly into Rose's mind when one morning she arrived to open the shop to find herself surrounded by reporters and photographers. They fired questions at her, questions that made no sense. 'What is all this?' Rose asked bewildered. 'Yes, I *am* Rose Kimberley.'

Lizzie, who had stopped to buy the morning newspaper came running up waving it. 'Hey, have you seen this, our Rose!'

Large headlines said, 'COUTURE DRESS SAVES ACTRESS' LIFE'.

Inset was a photograph of Isobelle Faycott taken from a hospital bed. She had apparently gone on to London Bridge with the intention of jumping into the river, but remembering Rose's words about the dress had removed it before climbing on to the parapet. In the delay a policeman had arrived and Isobelle, sobbing, had collapsed into his arms.

For the next two days Rose lived in a state of chaos. Women crowded the shop wanting to buy Isobelle Faycott dresses. Rose was furious. 'They're *Rose Kimberley* dresses,' she kept saying, but it made no difference. She was interviewed by journalists from magazines and newspapers, she was on radio, and was photographed handing a bouquet of flowers to Isobelle Faycott in a private room at the hospital, with Isobelle looking beautiful and sad. Rose demanded some time alone with the actress and it was granted.

Once they were alone Isobelle glared at her. 'Don't start thanking me for what I've done for you. You are the one getting all the bloody publicity!'

'I don't want it,' Rose retorted. 'I hate it. I'm being badgered every minute and, worse than that, the women are clamouring for *Isobelle Faycott* dresses!'

'They are? Well, now, that's interesting. I might start a fashion house myself.'

'Not with *my* designs.'

'Why not, I'm giving my name.'

'Let me put it this way. How would you feel if you had worked hard, struggled to get recognised, and just when you thought you were going to get your big chance, someone else, who'd done nothing to deserve it, lands the part?'

'All right, *Miss* Kimberley, you've made your point. I'll probably end up drowning myself sometime anyway, and then my name will be forgotten.'

'Tell me, *Miss* Faycott, why are you so intent on drowning yourself? Why not put your head in a gas oven or slit your throat with a razor?'

A slow smile spread over Isobelle's face then she began to laugh. 'I will say this, Rose Kimberley, you're different from the people I'm used to, fawning over me, but I'm still not sure that I like you. I want to sleep now. Don't come and see me again.' The actress slid down the bed and pulled up the covers. 'On your way out tell that rat-faced nurse I don't want to be disturbed.'

As it happened Rose would have found it difficult to have fitted in any visiting. The shop was a madhouse, with women not only demanding Isobelle Faycott dresses but Isobelle Faycott scarves, handbags, jewellery and sweetmeat boxes! Rose was furious. Clarissa and Lecky turned up to see if they could help. Charlie was there the minute he read the news, and then who should arrive but Alex de Veer, having flown across the Atlantic in a private plane.

'I knew you would need help, Rose,' he said, 'and need backing. I can help.'

Rose, who had not even had one personal line from Alex since the day he had left for America was angry with him, but because they were in his house, and she was grateful for the accommodation, she spoke calmly. 'I don't need any help, Alex. I'm getting all the publicity I want and I've already had offers from three people wanting to back me.' This was true although Rose had turned down the offers.

Alex looked a little exasperated. 'This is the chance of a lifetime, Rose, but it must be handled correctly. I am staying and am helping, so let us get down to business.'

Rose said no more.

Chapter 21

'Now,' Alex began, 'not only are you selling dresses at less than their value, but you have the tag of Isobelle Faycott on them. You can make use of her name until you are established in your own fashion house. The transition must be done as soon as possible. Hot news soon cools. We shall need to revive it, seek publicity in the press, open with a fanfare, let champagne flow. We must plan to open in three weeks' time, less if possible.'

Rose, who had been feeling breathless, laughed. 'Thank goodness for that! I imagined you wanting me to open tomorrow.'

Alex went on to say that once Isobelle Faycott was back in the play he would book seats for '*The Darkening Moon*', and also invite the actress to attend the preview of the fashion house.

Rose in view of what had been said, was not surprised when Alex told her the next day that both objects had been achieved.

The evening they went to the theatre was an unforgettable experience for Rose. The story of the play was of a young woman who has been having an affair with a married man, for three years. The love scenes between them were delicate, heart-wrenching, and the acting of Isobelle Faycott superb. When the man's invalid wife dies the woman naturally expects he will marry her, but he turns to someone else. The bewilderment that Isobelle portrayed, then her grief and isolation, had Rose weeping. At the end of the play the actress took six curtain calls and was showered with bouquets. When they came out Adele and Charlie and Lizzie all said how moved they had been by the acting. Rose said she was sure that Isobelle must have suffered such a situation herself to have played the part so feelingly, and Alex said she had, but few people knew the story. He added that Isobelle's hardness was facade, that underneath she was a warm, loving person. He then changed the subject, leaving Rose wondering how intimately Alex had known the actress.

Rose had not realised what a vast project her fashion house was and knew she would have been helpless without the experience and combined organisation of Adele and Alex. A team of experts moved into Alex's house and it seemed no time at all before it has been decorated, pieces of furniture selected, gilt chairs and mirrors installed. Top cutters, fitters, seamstresses were engaged, and workrooms and changing rooms set up. A Madam Pasquale was brought from Paris to be 'Directrice'. She was a small, blue-eyed redhead, with a brisk manner and a lively sense of humour. Rose liked her on sight. Lizzie declared she looked bossy. Adele assured her that Blanche Pasquale had been well chosen; she had everything – authority, diplomacy and charm. She added, 'You will see what I mean, Elizabeth, when she's dealing with staff, especially temperamental mannequins and, of course, with difficult customers. No, you have no need to worry, you will like and appreciate her.'

Long discussions were held over Rose's designs. She had numerous folios but was asked to design more coats, more hats. Sometimes she clashed with Blanche Pasquale over the choice of materials but most of the time they were in accord. Rose lived at a high pitch of excitement all the time. She worked intensely and at the end of the day fell into bed exhausted.

Rose had wanted to give up the London shop but Lizzie said no, they would keep it on, she could cope for the time being with the help of a girl. Although trade had dropped from the earlier mad rush it was steady enough to keep two people employed.

Adele went North with Rose to pick up the couture dresses that Bessie had written to say were ready. The workmanship was flawless. Adele obtained materials and designs for more to be made while Rose went home. The visit upset Rose, with her mother weeping copiously, saying she wanted her darling girls back, – oh why did the family have to be split?

Gran Eagan was sharp with Sally, and told her she was being selfish. Look at the wonderful chance that had come the way of the girls, she ought to have been delighted for them! Rose soothed her mother and told her that when the business was established she must come to London for a visit. Sally's tears dried. That would be nice, she said, then she could visit Rudolph Valentino's tomb and pay homage to him. But the piteous look in her mother's eyes when Rose left haunted her all the way back to London.

Fortunately, once she was back there was no time to think of anything but work.

Adele, Clarissa, Lecky and Alex between them had compiled a list of notable people to be invited for the preview, with Clarissa saying, 'I know they'll come, they will all want to meet Isobelle Faycott.'

Until then Rose had put her faith in Alex, who had assured her the actress would come, but she began to get worried. Supposing Isobelle stayed away as a form of revenge for her getting more publicity, or at least what she thought of as more?

When Rose voiced her fears Alex said, speaking firmly, 'Isobelle will come. She gave me her word, and I have never at any time had reason to doubt it.' Which settled Rose's mind in one way, but left her thinking that Alex must have been very close indeed to the actress.

As the opening date drew near tension built up. Rose began to feel panic, sure that something was bound to go wrong. The press would not turn up, only a few customers would attend, and one of the mannequins would fall down the stairs, as Lizzie had once laughingly predicted. No, this was impossible, not the way everything had been arranged. The opening was to be the one she had imagined in her mind as a finale, a girl on every step, in pastel shades of flowers. As one girl stepped down into the salon another girl would take her place, and so on.

Blanche Pasquale was not altogether in favour of showing so many dresses at the same time until Rose stressed she was striving for impact, to make an entrance, as it were, and as she was making a feature of the shadings in the dresses and not fresh designs Blanche gave in.

At last the day came and there was such chaos Rose wondered how they would ever get order. Although Adele had warned this was always the case at every fashion show she was unprepared for the tempers of the mannequins, the slanging matches, the snarling at one another, the complaints that they were not going to wear that 'rag' or that shapeless bundle of linen. Blanche seemed to take it all in her stride but at one time Lizzie got mad and yelled at them, 'Will you shut up, the lot of you! This is not a zoo! We have a fashion house to open.'

There was a sullen silence. Blanche said quietly, in an aside to Lizzie, 'This is my domain, Miss Elizabeth. Would you please leave them to me! It will start again, it is inevitable, I would be much alarmed if it didn't.' The wrangling did start again and Lizzie left in a temper.

'A lot of animals,' she declared to Adele. 'And who does Blanche Pasquale think she is, giving *me* orders?'

'The boss, the expert, just as you are the expert in finance, Elizabeth.'

Rose left them, her nerves taut and came into the salon for a few minutes. She must relax, must get rid of this feeling of panic. She examined the curtain that would hide the staircase from view when the people arrived. It had been hung by theatre workmen on pulleys, and looked every bit as large as a stage curtain. What if it stuck when it was to be opened? Alex came along the landing, paused momentarily at the top of the stairs then came running down. Rose caught her breath. He was immaculate in silver grey with a pale yellow rose in his buttonhole. He looked so handsome and the smile he gave her so full of endearing charm she wondered what she was doing here, feeling all panicky over the opening of her fashion house, when she could be married to him, having his love, having his babies. He came to her and said softly, as he took her hands in his, 'Don't look so worried, Rose, everything will be all right, you will see. This evening we shall be celebrating.'

Charlie came in, calling, 'Alex, about this champagne . . .' Alex excused himself.

Charlie had said he would stay in the background, seeing to all the odd jobs that might need doing. Rose was not happy about this as she felt Charlie should be at her side on this important occasion but he was insistent he might be needed and she gave in.

A commissionaire had been employed to open car doors and a page boy called James to usher in the customers. Both were decked out in dark blue uniforms with gold braid. Rose had thought the page boy unnecessary but Adele said that James, who had the angelic look of a choirboy would put the women in a pleasing mood. Rose laughed and Adele did too, saying it was a big con really, but then, that was business!

Rose was summoned to adjust the bodice of a dress and was caught up once more in the mêlée: a hem needed adjusting, a waist to be nipped in, the dresses being whipped away by seamstresses.

The room which had seemed large and cool and empty was now overcrowded and overheated. Rose was glad when she was called away to deal with the press. She and Lizzie had already had good press coverage, for Lizzie was adept at skirting probing questions as to their background, stressing to Rose it was prestige they needed at that moment if their venture was to be a success. 'They're snobs,' she said. 'People want glamour. Look how disparagingly that girl at Lecky's party spoke about us. A millionaire could walk down the street with a flowerpot on his head and they would class him as eccentric, but if Charlie were to do the same thing he would be carted off to the police station for causing a breach of the peace. No, the time to admit to your tenement upbringing is when you're at the top.'

The first question put to Rose now by a young male journalist was, did she not consider herself very lucky that through Isobelle Faycott she had acquired a fashion house? Rose smiled sweetly and said, 'I was pleased, of course, that one of my dresses was responsible for saving Isobelle's life, but actually I was on the brink of opening the House of Kimberley when the Wall Street Crash came. It was simply a question of delaying the moment.' Photographers moved in and light bulbs flashed as Alex entered with Lecky and Clarissa. Alex managed to whisper to Rose that Isobelle would be arriving soon. Rose gave a visible sigh of relief.

Then the first cars arrived and for the next quarter of an hour Rose's impression was of furs and diamonds, of the perfumes of the women mingling with the aroma of expensive cigars, of the clink of champagne glasses, the hubbub of voices, and of a big, coarse-looking man with a beautiful voice nibbling delicately at a smoked salmon savoury. Into the general crush came Isobelle Faycott, looking beautiful and elegant in black, her expression sweet. She came straight up to Rose, kissed her on both cheeks, said, 'Darling, how lovely to see you again,' then added in a low voice, 'You bitch, why didn't you tell me you knew Alex de Veer?'

Rose, smiling, replied in an equally low voice, 'I would have done, had I known how intimate you had been with him.'

'Ha!' Isobelle said, and turned to face the cameras.

No actress could have had more adulation than she had

from the people who had come ostensibly to see a new and young designer launched into the fashion world.

It was Blanche Pasquale who, with great charm, brought this fact to them as they settled down. It was Blanche too who had chosen the records for the background music. They were classical pieces and played quietly enough not to be too obtrusive.

Blanche, in a short speech, paid homage to Isobelle, but made it quite clear that it was due to the genius of Rose that the House of Kimberley had come into being. The applause at this point was polite. There was some chatter.

Then Blanche announced the opening number, Garden Rhapsody, and with a slow but dramatic swish the huge curtain was drawn, revealing the mannequins standing motionless on the beautiful curving staircase.

Rose in the end had decided to dress each girl in the same style, with a full-skirted dress and floppy-brimmed hat. She was depending for effect on the flower shadings, and it was proved to be a success by the concerted gasp from the audience, then the very appreciative applause. Rose released a small sigh and relaxed. Pray heavens the rest of the show would meet with their approval.

Because Rose's dramatic opener had worked so well, Blanche dispensed with each colour fairly quickly. The girls, coming down in a flowing movement, stepped into the salon then, all twisting and turning, their skirts swinging, colours blending, creating a veritable summer garden in a breeze. Rose could only marvel that such wonderful order had come straight out of chaos.

She had spent a great deal of time choosing suitable names for her garments wanting again to make an impact, and had come up with such names as 'Mediterranean Innovation' . . . 'Devil's Kitten' . . . 'Winged Cadenza' . . . 'Hungarian Persuasion'.

'Mediterranean Innovation' was a four-piece beach outfit, in the finest of iced-lemon coloured lawn. It consisted of a backless top, so necessary for women wanting to wear backless evening dresses and display an even tan, a pair of shorts with anchor motifs in white, a button-through skirt and a half circle of the same material fringed in white. This could be draped over one hip and tied at the waist, or used to cover back and shoulders, to protect from over-sunning. The outfit brought a show of interest. But the one that created the biggest stir in the early part of the show was 'Devil's Kitten'. This was a blood-red satin dress with a design of skeletal branches of trees on the front worked in jet bugle beads. On the short train at the back was a beaded black cat, tail up, mouth spitting. To complete the outfit was a swirling black cape lined with blood-red swansdown. This brought enthusiastic applause and a note from Isobelle telling Rose she wanted the outfit. Rose wrote a note back saying she would be pleased if Isobelle would accept it as a gift. Isobelle did.

The words that impressed themselves on Rose's mind at the end of the exhausting day were, 'Rose, you're a success! Congratulations!' She was drunk more with her success than with champagne, sipping it only when she toasted everyone else who had contributed to the success of the day. She had thought she would sleep for a week when she finally got to bed, but her mind was too active. Images kept passing in front of her eyes like a film unfolding – Alex exerting his charm on the customers, Charlie in the background giving her signs of encouragement, then his exuberance at the celebrations, his hug as bearlike as that she had received from dear Mr Rosenberg, who kept saying, tears in his eyes, 'I knew you would reach the top, Rose.' Alex, although showing pleasure, had kissed her lightly on each cheek as he congratulated her. Every garment, every outfit, flitted through Rose's mind and yet, exhausted as she was, she found herself sketching new designs in her mind. It was dawn when she finally found oblivion.

Over the months the House of Kimberley became firmly established as more and more big names were added to the list of clientèle. Alex talked of eventually opening boutiques in London, in Paris, Cannes, Monte Carlo and St Tropez. He had stressed right from the start, however, that the business would not be financially viable unless they also produced ready to wear clothes, which many fashion houses were now forced to do. Rose, assured she would not be too involved in this side of it, had agreed and was pleased when she realised how much employment it would bring to workers in that trade. Not that trade in the lower-priced garments was good – Charlie talked of having to work hard to get orders. Rose only hoped it would improve sufficiently to get a factory going again up North. At the moment their only factory was in the London area.

Rose, happy and absorbed in the business and feeling fulfilled for the first time had kept putting off going home for a visit. Then Charlie came breezing in one Friday morning saying to Rose and Lizzie, 'Get your bags packed, girls, we're going home for a celebration. Young Lilian has got her sight back!'

There was great excitement and when they did arrive they all laughed and cried together and little Lilian, now chatting away, reached for everything in sight. 'A miracle,' Sally declared. 'A blessed miracle.'

It was not until much later that Rose noticed a listless air about her mother, a dullness in her eyes. When she mentioned it to her grandmother Edie said, 'Well, Sal hasn't been too well lately. She still grieves over the loss of your Dad and Frank, and was worrying of course about Lilian. She's had a bit too much excitement, she'll be better tomorrow.'

But Sally was no better. Although she asked questions about the business, about London and all they had been doing, there was not the same enthusiasm. Rose and Lizzie wanted to buy her something and Edie suggested a slave bracelet, saying Rudolph Valentino wore one. It was buried with him and Sally had talked often of how much she would like one.

The girls not only bought a slim gold bracelet but a large flimsy chiffon handkerchief to tuck into it, which was the fashion. Sally's eyes did light up when they presented the gift and although their mother wept too she was brighter afterwards and said the bracelet would be a comfort to her.

But the atmosphere was happy that weekend. Tommy was always good for a laugh. He was coping wonderfully well with his artificial limb and quipped that he wondered how he had ever managed to walk without one! Alice and Nancy and Judith, all so different in temperament, were developing into beautiful girls. There was little trade at the shops and Alice was fidgeting to come to London. Rose said, not yet, in a year or two perhaps. Nancy was the surprising one. She had always been the one to start a fight but although she still flared up she was happy at home looking after the children. A born mother, Gran Eagan said. Sam was still the same, puffing away at his old clay pipe, spitting in the fire and grinning behind Edie's back when she chided him for the habit. He was now a keen gardener and talked knowledge-ably of fruit trees, plants, flowers, vegetables. 'Won a prize for the best leeks,' he boasted proudly.

Until the Monday morning when Rose went out with Lizzie and Charlie she had been happy, but once they got out among the people, around the shops and the market, a depression clamped down on her. In the busy life she had been leading, among beautiful things, and well-dressed people, she had been unaware of the misery in the North. 'It's everywhere,' Charlie said, 'London, other countries. America has millions of unemployed, too.'

Rose had seen poverty before but never on such a scale, with downtrodden men, gaunt women, barefooted underfed children, they were everywhere. The unemployed could claim dole money for just so long, then they were subjected to a system known as the means test. Rose had heard about it but had not realised what degradation decent people suffered to be able to claim money to keep body and soul together.

Charlie explained it. A man would go before a Board which asked probing questions about his possessions, and the man would learn that everything, apart from beds for the family, a table and chairs and household utensils, would have to be sold before any money would be paid him. These items included treasured ornaments like a clock, or a piece of furniture which had been in the family for generations, a Sunday suit, a Sunday coat, a dress – and the money when it was paid was barely enough to keep a family from starvation. Soup kitchens had been set up by the Red Cross and the churches and long lines of people shuffled along with their bowls, like scarecrows.

'It's appalling,' Rose said. 'I feel sick, ashamed that we are living so well. What can we do? Is it possible to get a factory going here, making something that the people who do have money would buy?'

But although they discussed different propositions no conclusion was reached. Charlie said that in time they might think of something.

They went to the workshop to see Bessie and the others and Rose, with Bessie's arms around her, felt as though she had her face in an eiderdown. Bessie was always good for a laugh and they came away feeling less depressed. Lizzie went to visit an old friend and Charlie took Rose's hand. 'Come on, love, let's see if we can find a nice piece of green grass to look at. We'll go to the three-cornered field, I haven't been there since I was a lad. It was a marvellous place, a battleground where we slaughtered hordes of Red Indians, killed all the bad men of the West, swam the "raging torrent" of the gentle little river – yet ran scared from the old farmer's bull if it snorted, even though it was tethered with a rope as thick as an arm!'

Rose laughed. 'I know, we were scared of it too and gave it a wide berth. Lizzie and I used to push the younger children to the field in their prams to picnic. All we had was a bottle of cold tea or water and dry bread with a scraping of jam, but do you know, Charlie, no spread tasted as good as our picnic teas.'

'I know, the simple pleasures. Come on, we'll take the short cut.' They went through mean streets with men hunkered against walls of their houses or standing in silent groups at street corners. Rose was glad when they left that part.

She waited with a feeling of expectancy to see the field again then felt a swift disappointment when she found it was being used as a refuse dump. The river had dried up to a trickle, the bed littered with bottles and tins and old pieces of carpeting.

'Never mind,' Charlie said cheerfully. 'We'll have to find somewhere else. I know, we'll take a penny tram ride to Lismond Park and walk around the bandstand. I know that's still there, I went the other day.'

The park was deserted. Sudden gusts of wind scattered piles of dried leaves, sending them in rustling cartwheels to settle in other piles. Overhead crows kept up a mournful cawing. 'Here we are,' Charlie said as they reached the domed bandstand. 'Shall we take a seat, Madam, and listen to the music?'

Rose shook her head. 'I doubt that I have any imagination today.'

'Right. What other diversion can we find?' Charlie looked around him. 'Somewhere there's a tree where I carved a heart, put an arrow through it and underneath coupled my name with the love of my life at that moment.'

'Oh, and who was that?'

'Well, if you must know . . .' Charlie paused and added with a grin, 'I was about eight years old at the time. I can't even remember her name or what she looked like. But shall I tell you something, Rosie, if I were to carve another name, you know whose it would be? Yours.'

Rose's heartbeats quickened. Although Charlie was smiling there was a seriousness in his eyes, and not wanting him to go on she scolded him. 'You would do no such thing, Charlie

Eagan, mutilating poor trees. I bet trees feel it, I bet it hurts.'

'I hurt all the time,' he said. 'I love you, Rosie.'

Rose, who had drawn her gaze away stared straight ahead at the bandstand. 'What is love, Charlie, how do we define it, between man and woman I mean? I've loved you since I was small. I love you now.'

'Rose, how do you feel about Alex?'

'I'm not sure.' She was astonished to find that her quick response to the question was indeed the truth. And yet for months all her longings had been to have Alex's arms around her. 'I'm not sure,' she repeated. 'It's too big an issue to give an instant decision. I need to think about it.'

Charlie got up. 'In that case I would say that you are not in love with either of us, Rose.' There was a sadness, rather than a bitterness in his tone.

She looked up at him. 'Or perhaps not ready to accept it.'

'Perhaps.' He held out a hand to her. 'I'm always looking for miracles. Who knows, one day!' There was a smile now in the smoky blue eyes. 'Come on, I'll race you to the park gates.'

They arrived breathless and laughing, the old easiness restored between them once more.

They had been back in London two weeks when a telegram came from their grandmother telling them to come home at once. Their mother was in hospital. Both girls were stricken with fear, knowing their grandmother would never send a telegram unless it was of vital importance. They threw clothes into a suitcase, leaving Adele to get in touch with Charlie.

The journey home was a nightmare with each girl seeking assurance from the other, Rose saying in a frantic voice that surely God could not be so cruel as to let her mother die and Lizzie, white-faced, replying that perhaps her mother had to have an operation, it could be appendicitis and not dangerous.

They took a taxi from the station and arrived at the hospital to find that their mother had died two hours before. She had rapidly filled with water, and it had touched the heart.

Rose had experienced grief when her father died and when her brother Frank was so tragically killed but it was nothing to the grief that engulfed her at the loss of her mother. She and Lizzie clung together, sobbing, then Lizzie dried her eyes and said they must go home, they were needed.

Chapter 22

When the hearse arrived that evening Rose was unable to bear seeing her mother brought home in a coffin. Yet wanting to have some contact with her, she went up to Sally's bedroom. She picked up the leather-backed Bible that lay on the chair by the bedside, longing desperately to have her mother's faith that everything the good Lord did had a purpose in it. Rose opened the Book at several places but found no message to comfort her. She opened the wardrobe door, releasing the fragrance of lavender from the tiny muslin bags her mother had always kept hanging in her clothes. She laid her face against a favourite silk dress, her mother's best, and wept silently. Never to see her dear face again . . . How could she bear it?

At the bottom of the wardrobe was a big cardboard dress box, which had been there as long as Rose remembered. It held her mother's papers. She had only once seen the contents when a search was being made for some document.

She brought the box out and laid it on the bed. It was full of newspaper cuttings, some yellowed now, letters, all those that she and Lizzie had sent. There was every item on the story of Isobelle Faycott and the opening of the fashion house. There was a small packet of letters tied with blue ribbon, a piece of heather pushed through the ribbon. Were they love letters? If so, who from? Rose, although feeling she was prying, had to know. She would read one. It was a letter from her father to her mother in their courting days and read,

My dearest dear,
I'm sorry, owing to circumstances, I was unable to meet you on
Sunday. Could you please *be there this coming Sunday. I shall wait* all
evening *by the stile.*
Your devoted Adam.

My dearest dear . . . I will wait all evening . . . your devoted
Adam . . .

To Rose there was a great beauty in the words, a deep love
because they had been penned by her quiet, withdrawn
father. The words blurred. She folded the letter and replaced
it in the envelope, feeling no guilt at having read it. It had
given her a greater understanding of the love there had been
between her parents. Rose replaced the box and went
downstairs.

On the morning after the funeral Rose announced she was
not going back to London, but wanted to stay and help with
the children. The greatest protest came from Lizzie. 'Are you
mad, our Rose? You have a business to deal with! If help is
needed we'll pay for a woman to come in.'

Edie protested at this, saying with a touch of her old
asperity, 'There'll be no paid help here. Nancy and Alice can
cope. Nancy's good with the young ones, they all love her.'

There was a great deal of argument. Charlie, who had
come North as quickly as possible, joined in, reminding Rose
of her responsibilities with the business, especially to Alex
who had financed her. Rose was forced to give in.

Later, she said a little wistfully to Charlie, 'I was even going
to ask you to marry me. I wanted a baby, your baby.'

She watched his expression change from hope to doubt
then to anger. 'No, Rose. I love you, want you, want to marry
you, but not under those circumstances. Definitely not. I
don't want to be a convenient father for your child.'

'It's not like that, Charlie,' she said earnestly. 'Honestly, it
isn't. I love you, really love you. I always have, it's just that
I'm realising now how much I want to be married to you.'

Charlie's anger died. 'Rose love, you're going through an emotional time, certainly the wrong time to discuss anything so important as marriage. You haven't even weighed up what you would be losing.'

He took her in his arms and said softly, 'I'm not turning you down, Pet. Give yourself some time, six months perhaps, then we'll talk about it again.'

The moment Rose was back in London and absorbed in the business she knew she would never have settled at home. This was where her future lay, her work, where everything happened.

Isobelle Faycott's play ended its run and she was now rehearsing for a play on Broadway. Before she left for America the House of Kimberley had given her a full wardrobe. Alex had pressed for it. Although Rose kept telling herself it was not important to her whether Alex, who was in New York at the present time, was seeing Isobelle or not, she knew it was. And when one day Charlie teased her, saying hadn't she mentioned something about a marriage and having a baby she snapped back at him.

'Oh, Charlie, for heaven's sake! When could I find time to get married, much less to have a baby. I'm up to my eyes!'

'Sorry,' he said quietly and was walking away when she ran up to him. 'Charlie, forgive me. I'm just a bad-tempered so and so. Be patient with me.'

'Aren't I always?' The teasing had gone. 'You get on with your job, Rosie, I'll get on with mine. I won't mention marriage again.'

'Charlie . . .' He did not even look back. Oh, heavens, now she had hurt him. But it was foolish to contemplate marriage. It was bad enough finding time to sleep.

At breakfast one morning when Lizzie slit open a letter that had just been delivered Rose presumed it was from home. Then she noticed the American postmark on the envelope, the handwriting, and her heart began a slow thudding. Why should Alex be writing to Lizzie? Rose felt sick. She was the one he was supposed to be in love with. Lizzie finished reading the letter, folded it, replaced it in the envelope and said, 'It's from Alex. He'll be home in three days' time, he just pulled off a big deal, he'll be taking us out for a celebration.'

Rose tried desperately to put the letter to the back of her mind but it kept intruding all day. It was the fact that Alex had taken the trouble to write to Lizzie, knowing he would be home soon. She had written a little note to him a week after he had arrived in America but Alex had not troubled to answer it. Well, he could take Lizzie out celebrating, she would certainly not go.

And she was still in this mood the day Alex was due to return. He phoned her from the airport and when Rose heard his voice all her senses leapt, but she spoke in a cool voice. 'Hello, Alex, congratulations on your big deal.'

'Thanks, we must all celebrate this evening. We'll dine out.'

'I'm afraid I won't be able to go this evening, Alex. I'm exhausted, Adele is away, we've had a madly busy time. You can take Elizabeth.'

There was a pause, 'Yes, I shall do that.' All the warmth had gone from his voice. 'Tell her I shall call for her at seven o'clock.' The line went dead. Rose found herself trembling as she replaced the receiver. What a fool she was, she had wanted to go. She went to deliver the message.

'Oh, good,' Lizzie said. 'I wonder what I shall wear? Perhaps the emerald-green taffeta. Seven o'clock you said?'

At five to seven Lizzie came in ready to leave, pirouetting with a whisper of silk skirts. 'How do I look, Rose dear?'

Rose caught her breath, realising just how much poise her sister had acquired, and how beautiful she was. Lizzie looked radiant. She spoke well and could converse with anyone without giving her background away. Her gift of mimicry had helped her in this. She was the kind of girl who would fit into Alex's life. He already admired her brilliance in finance.

'You look lovely, Elizabeth,' she said quietly. 'Really beautiful.'

The front doorbell clanged. Lizzie snatched up her white fur cape, called, 'Be seeing you, have a good rest,' and was away.

Have a good rest . . . Rose walked over to the window which overlooked Green Park. She had no wish to rest, she wanted to be with Alex, wanted to hear his news. Fool, fool – why could she not behave sensibly, accept that things could not always go the way she wanted. A slight fog made haloes round the street lamps and headlights of traffic. Park Lane, what a magic sound it had seemed when they first heard about the house. Now all the magic had gone.

Rose did not hear her sister come in that night and by next morning she managed a certain degree of calmness when Lizzie talked about the wonderful evening she had spent with Alex. But when she said, 'And guess what? Alex is taking me to a tea dance this afternoon!' Rose could not control a betraying tremor.

Rose kept telling herself that Alex was doing it deliberately to get his own back because she had refused to celebrate with him. But the next day when he called for Lizzie and she saw a genuine pleasure in his eyes as he greeted her sister, she knew she would have to accept that his affections had finally been transferred. When Alex came over and asked if she was feeling better this morning she was able to answer with a smile that she felt fine, ready to tackle anything. Then Lizzie was there, eyes sparkling. 'I'm ready, Alex, ready to tango.'

That evening Rose was alone when Charlie arrived. He gave her a broad grin. 'Ready to marry me yet? Yes, I know I said I wouldn't ask you again but how about it? I'm on my way up North.'

Rose, still hurting from seeing her sister and Alex go out, happily talking, glared at Charlie. 'How about it?' she repeated. 'How very romantic!'

'I love you, Rose. A proposal is a proposal no matter which way you put it. Some fellows would use flowery language. I can't, but I think the words. Please say yes, Rose, marry me next week.'

'Next week? Are you crazy, we're madly busy, we're getting ready for the Collections.'

'You could surely spare half a day.'

'Half a day for a wedding,' Rose said in despair. 'Oh, Charlie Eagan, no other man but you would expect a girl to take half a day off to get married, not unless – well, not unless she *had* to get married.'

'All right, I'll wait. You can have a white wedding, with all the trimmings.'

'I don't want a white wedding, at least I don't want a big wedding with people staring at me. Oh, Charlie, I don't know what I do want. I only know I don't want to get married right now.'

'Okay, love, we'll leave it for the time being.' Minutes later he had gone, leaving Rose's thoughts in a turmoil.

Nor had Rose reached any conclusion as to what she did want to do when, on the following Tuesday who should walk into the salon but her grandmother! At first Rose could not believe her eyes, but there she was, as large as life, dressed in her Sunday best hat and coat with a string bag on her arm, and looking about her in what Rose took to be disapproval. She ran over to her. 'Gran – what brought you here?' Then, in alarm, 'What's wrong, is someone ill?'

'No, no one's ill, I came to see you.'

'But how did you get here?'

'By train, how else? Did you think I'd come on an elephant's back?'

'Oh, Gran, you never change.' Rose laughed and hugged her. 'Lizzie's out but she'll be back soon. Gran, what *did* bring you?'

'I'll tell you when I've had a cup of tea. I'm parched.'

Rose said they would go upstairs and she would make

tea, and as they went up she guessed why her grandmother had come.

And she was right. The moment after Edie had downed her first cup of tea she said, 'All right, Rosie, why won't you marry Charlie? The fun's gone out of him, he's not the same lad. If you don't want to marry him don't keep him dangling on a string.'

Rose felt angry. 'I'm not keeping him dangling on a string, and if Charlie said so I don't think much of him. I haven't said I wouldn't marry him.'

'Oh, for heaven's sake stop getting steamed up,' Edie flapped a hand at her. 'Charlie never said anything. I just put two and two together. He's forever talking about you, singing your praises. You know, Rose,' Edie's voice softened, 'your Grandad and I would be so pleased if you and Charlie married. Charlie's loving, generous, he'd be good to you.'

Rose got up and moved around the room. She felt trapped, and would be pushed into marriage to please her grand-parents if she were not careful. She said, 'I think I realised last night what might be holding me back. Charlie and I are cousins and although with some cousins who marry their children are all right, ours could be . . . well, not quite normal.'

There was a silence during which Edie sat stiffly erect in the high-backed chair staring straight ahead. The hum of traffic in Park Lane and the honking of car horns seemed to get louder and louder.

'I'll have that second cup of tea, Rosie. There's something I have to tell you, something I thought would never need to be told.'

Rose poured the tea and sugared it and her grandmother stirred and stirred it then laid the spoon in the saucer.

'Well, Rosie, this is the story of our eldest daughter.' Edie stared straight ahead. 'There are truths and untruths. It's true that Charlie is Maggie's son and that she died when he was a child, but she never had a husband who died in Africa nor was Maggie . . . our daughter. We adopted her. She ran off with a sailor who deserted her. It wasn't until she died that we knew about Charlie. She left us a precious gift. So although Charlie is not your cousin, Rose, he is illegitimate.'

'Oh, Gran, that doesn't matter and I know it won't to any of us. Does Charlie know?'

'I'm not sure. There was a time when he asked a lot of questions. It was after he had spent the day with Maude and Bert. I didn't ask.' Edie put her hands on Rose's shoulders and searched her face. 'Will you marry him, Rosie?'

Several things ran through Rose's mind at that moment . . . Alex taking her to his apartment in Paris, obviously with the purpose of seduction . . . Charlie caring for her when she passed out on the beach at Blackpool . . . Charlie taking her to the sea when she was distraught over the tragic death of her brother Frank and Tommy's terrible injury – healing her.

Rose looked up and met her grandmother's gaze steadily. 'Yes, Gran, I'll marry Charlie.'

'Oh, Rose, I'm so glad.'

The next moment Edie was all business and briskness, arranging the wedding. The banns would have to be called – Rose would, of course, be married in their church at home. The girls would be bridesmaids, her grandfather would give her away. Rose said, 'Gran, stop! Stop there.' And explained she wanted a quiet wedding, and could certainly not get married until after the Spring Collections.

Lizzie arrived at that moment and the wedding arrangements were shelved while Lizzie greeted her grandmother, astonished at seeing her there and more astonished still when she found that Rose had agreed to marry Charlie.

Their grandmother's visit to London was memorable if for one fact only – she insisted on returning home that same evening, on the milk train of all things. Of course she couldn't stay for a few days, no, not even overnight. Only Sam knew where she was, the rest of the family thought she was visiting an old friend in the country, and heaven help Rose and Lizzie if either should let the truth be known. Charlie would never forgive her if he found out she had come to plead his cause.

The two girls thought they could at least take their grandmother for a tour around London in a taxi before she left but Edie would have none of it. The taxi could break down. She wanted to get to the station in time.

Edie's parting shot to Rose from the carriage window was, 'Don't you accept Charlie right away, Rosie, otherwise he might guess some funny business has been going on. And you, Lizzie,' she added, 'get some suet puddings into you, you're far too skinny.'

Both girls laughed. Carriage doors were slammed, a whistle blew, the big wheels began to turn, they waved, Edie waved, then the tiny ramrod figure was lost in a cloud of steam.

Charlie came to see Rose the following weekend. He came in late afternoon and was unusually quiet. 'Rose, I've asked you to marry me, but this week I've been doing a lot of thinking. There's something you ought to know about me. I didn't tell you because, knowing you, I didn't feel it would make any difference, but now I realise you have a right to know.' And Charlie told Rose what she already knew.

'It doesn't make any difference to me, Charlie,' she said softly. 'And yes, I'll marry you.'

He stared at her. 'What?' Then a slow smile spread over his face. 'Oh, Rose, sweet, sweet Rose.' Charlie drew her to him and hugged her so tight Rose laughed and said he was suffocating her. 'Suffocating you with love,' he whispered and kissed her. It was not the usual gentle kiss of previous times but the passion of a virile man. Rose, feeling a sudden surge of emotion, responded. Charlie drew back and cupped her face between his palms. 'I'll get a special licence. We can be married next week, and no arguing.'

'Charlie, I *must* argue. It's impossible, I have the Spring Collections and I'll be letting a lot of people down if I'm not there.'

Lizzie came in and when Charlie announced the news she made a great pretence of surprise. She rushed away and brought Adele and Blanche.

Charlie said, 'I want Rose to marry me next week. I'm an impatient man, I want her now!' He spread his hands. 'But of course, it's the Collections.'

'Ah, yes, the Collections.' There were nods of understanding and a look of admiration at Charlie from Blanche. Such a man! So impatient for love.

Alex came round an hour later and Rose learned that Lizzie had phoned and told him the news. Alex was smiling as he offered congratulations. He kissed Rose on both cheeks, but when he drew away there was a bleakness in his eyes that tugged at Rose's emotion. She even wondered for a few moments if she were doing the right thing in marrying Charlie, then dismissed it. Of course she was, Charlie was her kind. *Her* man.

The big day of the Collections was upon them, with all its attendant chaos. Mannequins, vendeuses and fitters all behaved like prima donnas, which had Rose wondering for the hundredth time why she had not taken a job as assistant at the corner shop at home when she left school!

But it was another success, with Rose's pièce de résistance, 'Dragon in Mist' bringing loud and prolonged applause. The dress a swirling cloud of flesh-coloured silk, had a dragon embroidered in silver, nestling on its back.

Alex, who had come in late kissed her full on the lips. 'Very beautiful, Rose, I knew you would justify my faith in you.'

Champagne was flowing when Charlie arrived. He had brought the engagement ring. It was heart-shaped, inset with a ruby. 'It's Victorian,' he said. 'I know you like Victorian things.' He gave Rose an anxious look. 'But you can change it if you don't like it.'

She flung her arms around him. 'I love it, it's beautiful. Put it on my finger.'

It fitted perfectly and Rose, between laughing and crying said they must show it to the others. It would be a double celebration. Although Alex congratulated them both he left soon afterwards.

With the Collections launched and Charlie pressing for a date for the wedding, Rose began sketching dresses, her own and those for the bridesmaids. One day she stopped, realising she did not want a big wedding, with the press in attendance, which they would be if it leaked out. She wanted to be married quietly and have a quiet honeymoon. The only thing was, the family would be disappointed, especially her sisters who would have been bridesmaids.

She told Lizzie the way she felt, adding, 'I don't even want to be married in church, for then it would leak out. We could be married at the Register Office.'

'And why not?' Lizzie said. 'It's your wedding, your choice. You can stop worrying about the girls. They can be bridesmaids at my wedding.' Lizzie laughed. 'I think I'll marry Alex.'

Rose's heartbeats quickened. 'It would be nice to have Alex as a brother-in-law.'

'Well, anyway, that's for the future. If Charlie agrees to a Register Office wedding, Alex and I will stand as witnesses.'

The last person Rose wanted to play a role at her wedding was Alex, and she decided there and then if Charlie was agreeable they would keep their wedding date secret. Charlie fell in with all Rose's plans, and said he would fix up for them to have a few days' honeymoon at Brighton.

When Gran Eagan knew what they had planned she said she would ask only one thing, that Rose and Charlie would go to church later and ask God's blessing. They agreed and the wedding was eventually arranged to take place on the second Wednesday in July.

As the day of the wedding drew near Rose began to worry at her own calmness, her lack of emotion. She should feel romantic, excited, but she felt nothing. She felt nothing when she made her own wedding outfit, nor even when her grandmother sent her mother's pearl-backed prayer book to carry. It was unnatural. She made a perfectly plain white silk dress and matching jacket and crocheted a Juliet cap. All was made in secret.

On the morning of the wedding Rose dressed hastily. She put on the pale blue loose coat which she usually wore to go shopping, packed the Juliet cap, veil and shoes in her shopping bag and called to Lizzie, who was in the kitchen, 'I'm going shopping, I might browse around for a while,' and hurried out.

Trade had slackened off, with most of the wealthy spending the summer at Mediterranean resorts so she felt no guilt at having left everyone to deal with what business there might be. She caught a taxi and arrived at the Register Office at twenty minutes to ten. The wedding was to take place at ten. Rose still felt no emotion. The office was part of an old Victorian house. The housekeeper, a plump, rather shy-looking woman, took her into a small room to 'tidy up'. The air was warm outside but as yet there was no sun. The room felt cold. Rose gave a little shiver. 'Nerves,' the woman said. 'It's understandable, but don't worry. Mr Milner is a very nice person, he speaks the service with great warmth and sincerity, not like some who mumble through it. My husband and I will be your witnesses, Miss Kimberley. Our name is Hall.' Rose thanked her. She took off her coat, changed her shoes, pinned a circular piece of veiling to the Juliet cap and put it on.

'You look lovely,' Mrs Hall said softly. 'Very much a bride.'

Then Charlie was there saying, 'Rose, I've brought someone with me. I thought you would like him to give you away.'

Rose tensed, thinking it was Alex – and not wanting him. But it was Mr Rosenberg. She felt a rush of emotion and putting her arms around his ample waist she laid her head against him. He held her close. 'Oh, Mr Rosenberg, how did you know I needed you? I followed the old tradition of wearing something old, new, borrowed and blue, but what I was missing was one of my family. And Charlie and I have always considered you one of our family.'

'I'm honoured to be able to take part,' the old man said, a catch in his voice.

The Registrar came in and Rose drew away, dabbed at her eyes, smiled and held out her hand to Charlie. 'I'm ready.'

Charlie whispered, 'I love you,' and the look in his eyes made Rose wonder how she could ever have had any doubts about marrying him.

They came out of the Register Office to blazing sunshine and after Mr Rosenberg had shared the 'wedding breakfast' Rose went to phone Lizzie to tell her the news. Lizzie pretended to be mad, but was laughing as she said, 'Just wait until the two of you get back! I know it's no use asking where you're spending your honeymoon, but wherever it is have a good time.'

'We will,' Rose said. 'We'll be back after the weekend. All news then.'

Charlie had kept the accommodation where they were to stay a secret and it was not until they arrived at Brighton that he told her he had rented two rooms on the top floor of a big house facing the sea. 'The other people are all away at the moment so we'll be completely on our own. I'll cook the breakfast and we'll have our other meals out.'

'Oh, Charlie, it sounds wonderful. I can't wait to see it.'

And Rose was not disappointed when she stood with Charlie at the window of the living room with the beach across the road and the sea so calm it seemed like a painting.

They went out later and walked along the beach, Charlie's arm encircling her waist, and Rose thought she would always associate the whisper of the water receding among the pebbles with her wedding day.

At ten o'clock when they came back to the house Charlie

opened the door then said softly, 'Go on up, love. I'll be with you soon.'

Rose knew what being married was all about, but she thought now it was a different thing knowing what happened and having it about to happen. She wanted to please Charlie. A girl had once told her that some men liked to undress their brides. In one of the stories her mother used to enjoy, a sheik undressed the girl he had carried off to his tent in the desert. Rose recalled the words, 'He divested her of her last garment and caressed her body that was lily-white in the moonlight.' Rose felt a stirring in her limbs.

Moonlight gave the bedroom a purity. She brought out her nightdress and matching negligée. Both were of soft white satin appliquéd with fine lace. Rose, wanting to look bride-like decided to put them on. If Charlie wanted to remove them, well . . .

A few minutes later she heard movements in the dressing room next door, and shivered with an excited anticipation.

Charlie came in wearing silk pyjamas and dressing gown in a blue that emphasised the blue of his eyes. Rose thought she had never seen him looking more attractive. A wave of love for him swept over her. He came up and said, 'Oh, Rose,' in a strangled voice. 'You're so lovely, so beautiful, I feel I have no right to you.'

She took his hands away and kissed his palms. 'You have every right, I'm you're wife and I love you – and want you.'

Strong arms went around her. Charlie buried his face against her neck. 'And oh, how I want you, sweet Rose, so much, so very much. I've been longing for this moment.' His lips moved over her throat then covered her mouth, moving sensuously, making Rose's body leap in response. A wild throbbing began, astonishing her with its intensity. It was a mingled agony and ecstasy. Charlie slipped the negligée from her shoulders and let it fall to the floor. Then she drew in a quick breath as he began to raise her nightdress, inch by slow inch. Then it too was on the floor. Rose shivered again, this time with an urgency for him to take her. Charlie swept her up and carried her to the bed. Within seconds he was stripped and beside her.

And it was then that the demands of Rose's body died. She was with Alex once more on the bed in his apartment in Paris. Although nothing had happened she felt as guilt-ridden as though it had. Charlie was caressing her body, his lips moving lightly over her skin. He murmured endearments. Rose tried desperately to respond but failed.

'Relax, Rosie, I won't hurt you, I promise. Give yourself to me, don't fight, it will make it easier for both of us.'

'I can't,' she said in a low voice. 'I'm sorry.'

'It's all right, love.' He soothed her, explaining how necessary it was for her to relax and why, but it made no difference. Alex's face was ever there, haunting her. Charlie rolled away from her and slipping his arm around her shoulders drew her to him. 'Don't worry, love, we've got all our lives ahead of us. Perhaps tomorrow night you'll feel differently. You're tired, overtired. You'll feel better after a rest.'

Several times during the night he reached for her in his half-sleep, but she drew away, and felt sick at what she was denying him. Millie Munro had once told her that men suffered terribly if they were denied their rights, that was why so many men came to her and paid their sixpences. Rose told herself that Charlie had a strong will and would control his feelings but it did nothing to ease her conscience.

She fell at last into an exhausted sleep. And when she awoke sunlight flooded the room. She got up and went to the window and all the unhappiness of the night before vanished. There was colour everywhere in the gardens, in the lush green of bushes and trees, the deep red of geraniums, the clusters of tiny white daisies, the blue of lobellia – and the sea . . . She ran over to the bed and shook Charlie.

'Charlie, you must get up, come on, come and look, have

you ever seen a sky or a sea so incredibly blue? And the water, there are golden coins dancing on it.'

Charlie opened one eye, peered over the bedclothes, then a slow smile spread over his face. 'Hey,' he made a grab for her. 'Just the girl I was dreaming about.'

'No, Charlie, no, now stop it.'

'We *are* married.'

Rose managed to get free and ran to the door, saying she was going to make a cup of tea. Charlie called to bring him one but she stopped to say – no, if he wanted it he must come for it, and fled when he made to get out of bed. Her heart was pounding. It was wrong, all wrong, she was behaving badly. Tonight would be different, she told herself.

But it was the same that night and the next night, with Rose freezing into rigidity the moment they were in bed.

On the third evening when Charlie lay beside Rose, awake and silent, not even putting an arm around her or attempting to kiss her she felt a small panic. Had he given up wanting to make love to her? Rose moved a little closer to him. 'Charlie – do you think – I wonder, well, do you think we should perhaps try again?'

'Better leave it, Rose. We don't want to spoil the holiday. There's plenty of time.' He sounded different, strained.

'Well, if you don't want me.' She could hear the piqued note in her voice at his rejection.

'Oh, I want you all right, Rosie, I want you all the time, on the beach, in the car, on the hillside, everywhere we go but I don't want to force something that isn't there. You need to feel crazy for love, feel crazy for me so you won't mind a little pain.'

'I'm not worried about the pain. I *do* want you, Charlie.'

'You don't, Rose, I wish you did. You're lying beside me now and you're rigid, terrified.'

'I'm not terrified, honestly, I'm not. It's just that . . .'

'Just what, Rose? Leave it for tonight, forget it.'

Rose's panic increased. Charlie knew, knew about Alex.

Had she mentioned his name in her sleep? She had to do something. She thought of Millie Munro saying that a woman had to behave like a wanton if she wanted to pleasure a man. But how would a wanton behave?

Rose got out of bed, walked over to the window, took off her nightdress and stretched up her arms. Which brought an immediate response from Charlie who said in a tight voice, 'What do you think you're doing? Are you trying to drive me mad?'

'I was hot.'

'*You* are hot. I have a fire going in me! Get back into this bed.'

A throbbing began in Rose, but she made no move. 'I'm not your slave to be ordered around.'

'You're my woman,' he shouted, and Rose retorted he was being crude.

'I *am* crude. I'm Charlie Eagan, market trader, trying to ape a gentleman, or was. Now get into this bed where you belong, before I drag you in!'

Every pulse was throbbing in Rose. With a feeling of exultancy she turned to face him and ran her hands down the length of her body. And *she* was Rose Eagan, brought up in a slum tenement, with feelings at this moment anything but ladylike, primitive in fact. She got into bed and pressed herself against her husband's bare, muscular chest. 'Yes, Charlie, I'm your woman,' she whispered. 'I don't care what you do to me.'

'Be careful what you say, Rosie love, or you'll be suffering for those words.' The gruffness in Charlie's voice and his shaky laugh told her the extent of his arousal.

'I want to suffer,' she whispered. 'I don't care if you beat me,' and putting her lips to his, parting them, she moved over his mouth in the sensuous way Charlie had done. His fingers dug into her flesh as he gripped her. From then on the 'master' took over.

It was dawn when they finally settled for sleep. A smile

played round Rose's mouth. She was proud of her passionate, virile husband, who had not only brought her to fulfilment but who had taught her that in loving there can be a gentle tenderness as well as a glorious wildness.

Chapter 23

Charlie and Rose returned from honeymoon to a party arranged by Lizzie and Adele, with only one person missing – Alex. Lizzie said he had had to go away. Rose wondered if that was so, or whether he had wanted to stay away.

Champagne corks popped and a wedding cake was brought in, sent down to London by Gran Eagan. Rose then shed tears. But she was not allowed to weep for long – she had to tell them all about Brighton.

Rose described the marvellous Pavilion, built for the Prince Regent and raved about the Lanes, with their beautiful bow-fronted shops. She mentioned in detail the clothes worn by the upper crust there, and said she had masses of ideas and could hardly wait to get started sketching. She might even start that evening. Charlie kissed her cheek and said with a grin he had other ideas about how to spend their evening. Blanche gave a deep sigh and exclaimed, 'What a man!'

Then the wedding presents were brought out. The girls and the workroom staff had clubbed together to buy a full tea service in white bone china with a tiny key pattern in green and gold round the edges. Adele and Blanche and Lizzie had bought a matching dinner service and wine goblets in cut crystal.

'Oh, they're beautiful,' Rose exclaimed. 'Thanks, all of you.'

Lizzie then handed her a parcel saying it had come from Alex, posted from Germany. There were two items, an exquisitely hand-embroidered tablecloth and a small oil painting. 'Well, what do you know!' Charlie exclaimed picking up the painting. 'It's the Yorkshire Dales, the view from the hotel where we stayed that weekend, do you remember Rosie?'

Did she remember? Rose felt a suffocating anger. How could Alex have done this? Just one more thing to remind her of the time they had spent in his apartment. It cost her an effort to say brightly, 'Yes, of course I remember, but I must look at everything again later, I'm dying for a cup of tea.'

When Rose examined the painting later she saw it was not Alex's own but a similar one. Only the edges of the tarn showed on the one he had had done. Even then she was still annoyed, and felt she did not want to see him again. It was a relief when she learned from Adele later that business would be taking Alex from Germany to France.

Five weeks later Rose started with morning sickness. Lizzie said, 'You're mad, our Rose, if you tie yourself down with kids.' Rose said nothing.

When Charlie knew about the baby he was over the moon but was much concerned about the sickness and thought they had best not make love, not for the present. Rose said, 'All right, if you don't want to make love to me, Charlie Eagan, I'll find someone else who will.'

'Oh, you will, will you.' With a chuckle Charlie swept her up into his arms. 'I'll show you who's boss around here.' Rose thrilled to his strength and later to their passionate and joyful union.

As the days went by, Rose went off tea and developed a craze for pickled onions. It was then the staff knew about the pregnancy. The women in the workshop offered cures for the morning sickness. Yvonne and Charmain took up knitting and made matinée jackets and bootees. Blanche and Adele mothered her. Lizzie kept reminding Rose how selfish Charlie had been in getting her pregnant so soon.

Rose had never stopped designing but when after two

months the sickness suddenly stopped she declared she had never felt so well in her life and at times would start work right after breakfast and go on until late afternoon, with only a break for a snack. It was as though conceiving had released a flood of ideas. Some of the designs she did were for maternity wear, glamorous ones which a woman could wear for evening right up to her confinement without being self-conscious of her bulk.

When Rose quickened she shared the joy of the baby's movements with Charlie. 'Here,' she would say, 'put your hand there. Can you feel him?' She had already decided it would be a boy. 'Isn't he vigorous? Just like his Dad?' And Charlie would tease her and say what would happen if it turned out to be a girl, would they want a footballer daughter? They were wonderfully happy and Rose's only regret was that Charlie was away all the week travelling and only home on Saturday and Sunday.

They made a quick journey North when Rose's sickness had stopped and were planning another before she found it too uncomfortable to travel, when Alex returned from his extended trip abroad.

Rose was alone in the sitting room busily sketching when there was a knock on the door. She called 'Come in', then sat motionless, the pencil poised as a familiar voice said quietly, 'Hello, Rose.'

She had planned to be cool with him when he did arrive but her heart was racing and a pulse throbbed in her temple. She got up and turned to face him. 'Why, Alex, what a surprise!'

He kissed her on both cheeks in the continental way. The kisses were light but Rose caught her breath at the emotion they roused in her. She had forgotten how madly attractive he was, immaculately groomed as always, tall, straight-backed, a trenchcoat draped nonchalantly over his shoulders.

'How well you look, Rose.' Alex's voice held a caress. His dark intense gaze held hers. 'Marriage suits you well.'

She raised her head. 'And motherhood?'

He smiled. 'Elizabeth told me. May I offer my congratulations to you and Charlie.'

Rose thanked him for the exquisite tablecloth and Alex asked immediately if she had liked the painting, adding, 'Charles often mentioned the scene from the hotel window and I thought it would be a memento of our visit to the mills.'

'We shall treasure it always,' Rose said, and her voice sounded stilted.

Alex talked about his business trip and she was surprised at how much he had accomplished, how much he had built up, almost a new empire, since the hopeless first days of the Crash. He then talked about opening boutiques in the South of France and asked Rose if she would have lunch with him the next day, so they could go into it further. He was meeting a colleague in fifteen minutes.

Warning signals went in Rose's brain. Why should he want to discuss such a big project with her alone? She heeded the signals. 'I'm sorry, Alex, I couldn't manage tomorrow, nor any time this week. Charlie and I are going home for a quick visit at the weekend.'

His smile was regretful. 'Some other time, perhaps, there's no hurry.' Alex took his leave shortly afterwards.

The moment he had gone Rose felt she had behaved stupidly. Alex was a busy man – why on earth shouldn't he ask her to lunch to talk over his plan? After all, she *was* the designer. She went after him, running down the stairs. She heard Lizzie calling to her but she ran on and out into the street. Alex was about to turn left into Park Lane. She called and raced across the road. She saw him turn, heard him shout something, but it was too late. Rose, who had been only vaguely aware of an approaching dray, felt a sudden fear as she realised the horses were within inches of her. She stumbled and fell. There was a blow to her back, and agonising pain, then she blacked out.

Rose came through a black fog to see faces forming. One

belonged to Alex, the other to her sister. Lizzie was crying. Then the fog was closing in again and she was sinking into mire. Rose tried to fight her way out of it, then strong arms were lifting her and Charlie's voice was saying, 'Rosie, I love you, need you . . .' Rose's eyelids felt weighted. When she opened her eyes again Charlie was above her. His eyes were red-rimmed and there was stubble on his chin. He was so fussy about being shaved she wanted to tease him but her face felt stiff.

A woman came up in a white starched apron. She felt her pulse. A nurse . . . Suddenly it all came flooding back, the dray, the horse, the kick – Rose felt panic. The baby? The nurse said to Charlie, 'Go home and get some rest, your wife is over the worst. Yes, I shall be gentle when I tell her.'

Rose knew then she had lost the baby. Tears were welling somewhere inside but there was no release. She wanted to die. It was the doctor who eventually told her about the baby, but even his gentleness could not relieve her anguish.

'There will be other children, Mrs Eagan. There is some damage, but it will heal. Give yourself time, a year perhaps before you think about it.'

Her body might heal, Rose thought, but not her mind. She would always be conscious of her infidelity, because that was what it really amounted to, this thinking of Alex de Veer, wanting to be with him, having his admiration. And so Rose went on tormenting herself through the days when she refused to talk to those who came to visit her. Not even to Lizzie, who had been surprisingly gentle with her, nor to Charlie, who was always so distressed. Masses of flowers were delivered from well-wishers, letters came from the family, warm loving letters, that normally would have moved her deeply, but which now did nothing to break the ice holding her in its grip.

Then one visiting time, as she lay, as always, on her side away from the door where the visitors would come in she heard a sharp voice say, 'Now, Rose Eagan, what's all this business of refusing to speak to anyone, having folks at their wit's end to know what to do.' Rose turned over on to her back to see her grandmother's tiny black-clothed figure, her expression stern.

Outraged at the tone she said, 'I suppose you *know* I've lost a baby?'

'Other women have lost them, Rose, myself included, a boy first then twin girls.'

Rose stared at her. 'You never said anything, Gran, I didn't know.'

Edie sat down and her expression softened. 'Rose love, don't think I haven't grieved for you, I have, but life has to go on. I had other babies and so will you. One year out of your life is nothing, especially when you're young. Charlie is hurt and bewildered that you reject him. He wants to love you, comfort you, and you won't let him. He's now blaming himself for making you pregnant.'

'No, no.' Rose moved her head from side to side. 'He's not responsible for what happened, I'm the one to blame. If only I hadn't run after Alex de Veer that night. Oh, Gran, I've been such a fool.'

After a short silence Edie said gently, 'Do you want to talk about it, love?'

In a low voice Rose told her about the attraction Alex had for her, about his inviting her out for lunch, and why she had run after him after he had gone, but did not mention having once lain on a bed with him. Edie told her she was torturing herself unnecessarily, she had done no wrong, but Rose corrected her.

'Don't you see, Gran, the wrong is in my mind for having wanted to be with Alex. That is why I didn't talk to Charlie. I didn't want to hurt him, but I realise now I shall have to tell him, in all fairness.'

'What's fair about it?' Edie retorted. 'You get rid of *your* burden and put a double one on Charlie. Take my advice and say nothing about it. Any confession or regret you have won't alter a thing. Oh, Rosie, there are tragedies and joys in the lives of everyone. Accept them as God's will. You and Charlie love each other. If you stop looking for perfection in your marriage *and* in yourself, you'll make a good life together.'

Rose nodded slowly. 'Yes, Gran, I think perhaps you're right.'

When Charlie came that evening and Rose saw the ravages caused by the loss of the baby and her own rejection of him she was filled with remorse. 'Oh, Charlie . . .' She held out her arms to him. 'I'm so sorry.'

They clung together, Charlie whispering endearments. When they drew apart he traced a finger gently round her mouth, a glistening of tears in his eyes. 'When I thought I had lost you, Rosie, I didn't want to live.'

The loss of her baby was still a raw thing but Rose knew she must, if only for Charlie's sake, believe in the maxim that time heals all wounds.

Alex had sent flowers several times but had not come to the hospital. Rose rather dreaded meeting him but when they did meet he made it easy for her. He came with Charlie and Lizzie to bring her home. He kissed her and gave her a quick hug as a brother might have done. 'It's good to see you again, Rose, you've been very brave. We all love you. Come along, you are going to sit by me. Charlie can have you all to himself later.'

Later, when Rose looked back on that day she realised it had been a turning point in her life. She could now look on Alex as a friend, instead of a potential lover.

Three weeks later Alex called a meeting. Opening boutiques was one part of the expansion Alex had in mind.

Charlie said he was aware that couture dresses were selling well but queried the advisability of expanding into mass production when this side of it was selling slowly. Alex sat back, a pencil between his fingers and expounded his views. There was a time for expansion and he was convinced this was it. It was a question of getting established with the right kind of garment at the right price. Holiday resorts abroad were expanding, building new hotels, to cater for growing numbers of travellers from all classes of society. More people would be taking holidays in England and abroad, people who had never taken them before. They would want attractive holiday gear, reasonably priced.

After the meeting Charlie said, 'You've got to hand it to Alex. He almost has the whole thing launched while we're still thinking it over. Dynamic, that's what he is. I wish I had his brains.'

Lizzie said, her tone sharp, 'But then it wouldn't be *you*, would it? Just stay as you are, Charlie Eagan, and it will be good enough for us.' Which made Rose wonder if her sister was getting all the attention she had hoped for from Alex.

Lecky and Clarissa called one evening. They had been abroad with a group of friends, and knew nothing about Rose losing the baby. Fortunately they kept their commiserations brief then spoke of the party they were giving. Everyone must come. Rose asked to be excused – it would be unwise at the moment.

In bed that night Rose nestled into Charlie, wishing the next year would go quickly so they could start thinking about another baby.

Many things happened in that year.

While the wealthy still went on spending, some of the unemployed were starving. Thousands marched to London with a million signatures to get rid of the hated means test. It took a contingent from Glasgow five weeks to get there. The march was well organized, with food kitchens and cobblers set up at certain points on the way, but some of the men's boots were past repairing. When the marchers arrived in London, there were thousands more to meet them in Hyde Park and Trafalgar Square. Unhappily, owing to the stupidity of some misguided body the police charged with batons. The means test stayed but there was a small increase in the dole money. People went on starving.

Lizzie astonished Rose by becoming one of the social crowd, a dedicated party-goer. A different man escorted her every few weeks. She developed her own style in dress and was always on at Rose to design something new for her. Yet, when dealing with business she was brisk, brilliant with figures, and had a fantastic memory for transactions which had taken place a year previously. Rose felt there was a false gaiety in her sister's social life and was sure that Alex had something to do with it. Whenever he was there in any company Lizzie was at her brightest, her wittiest, showing off, flirting with every man in sight. Alex for his part watched her, showing neither approval nor disapproval. At times, Rose and Charlie gave a small dinner party and always invited Alex. He treated Lizzie as he did the other women but Rose felt that Alex was aware every moment of what Lizzie was doing.

A month later Charlie came home in great excitement. Alex had asked him to go to America with him, to get the feel of big business. 'Do you mind, Rose?' he said. 'It would mean my being away for two or three weeks.'

'I don't mind at all, I think this is a wonderful opportunity. But you watch what you're doing, Charlie Eagan, with all those lovely American girls.'

Charlie grinned. 'I wouldn't dare do anything else but behave myself, knowing you were back home waiting to nag me. Oh, Rosie,' he swung her off her feet, 'I can't believe it. America! You should have been coming with us, Alex said you could, but I knew you would be far too busy.'

'Oh, you did, did you?' Rose laughed. 'You're right, of course. I couldn't go. I do have too much to do. But another time. Yes, I'd like to go to New York. And I *shall*, one of these days.'

If Rose had not been kept so busy while Charlie was away the time would have dragged. Lizzie asked her to come to a party but Rose refused then said, 'And don't you think you are over-doing the high living?'

'Oh, for heaven's sake! Don't go all pious on me, that's the last thing I want.' Lizzie snatched up a short fur coat and draped it round her shoulders. 'No one is suffering for what I'm doing.'

'Only you,' Rose said quietly. 'You have the feverish look of the Bright Young Things who are always seeking new adventures. I can't really believe you enjoy coming home at five o'clock in the morning in a car loaded with people shrieking with laughter and with car horns blaring.'

A bleakness came suddenly into Lizzie's eyes. 'Tell me something to replace it?' Without waiting for a reply she left. But that evening she was home and in bed before midnight. And the following week she went out only three nights and was again home early each time.

Rose, convinced by now that her sister was in love with Alex ached for her as she remembered how she had felt when she was so attracted towards him. If only she could have had a heart-to-heart talk with Lizzie, but the closeness of their tenement days had gone. A price, it seemed, had to be paid for their rise in the world.

There was a joyous reunion when Charlie came home. He looked different but Rose could not place what it was. He was the same Charlie who went away, with his familiar laughing blue eyes with their thick dark lashes, the same curly hair and exuberance, then she knew what it was. It was his suit, expensive, beautifully-cut. Before she could remark on it he said, 'Hey, I've got something for you. Hang on a minute –' He produced a small leather-covered box and opened it with a flourish. 'How about that then?' On a bed of green velvet lay a gold necklace, with a heart-shaped chased gold medallion, a glowing ruby in its centre. 'It matches your ring, Rosie. I couldn't believe it when I saw it. Bought it on Fifth Avenue,' Charlie said with pride.

'Oh, it's beautiful, Charlie, but the cost – Fifth Avenue!'

Charlie talked non-stop for a good ten minutes and Rose, smiling, let him talk. If he had his way she was sure they would have emigrated to America the following week.

Charlie told her that Alex had decided to stay on for another two weeks. Then he gathered her to him and said softly, 'But I couldn't bear to stay away from you another day.' He cupped her face between his palms. 'I missed you all the time, missed you at night curled up against me all soft and warm like a cuddlesome kitten. Oh, Rosie, we'll never be parted again.'

Some weeks after this Lizzie came home early one evening in a temper. 'You'll never guess,' she said, 'but Alex de Veer has asked me to marry him. The nerve of the man!' She threw her handbag on to the settee. 'For months he's been so aloof with me you would have thought I was some inferior being. Then this evening, right out of the blue, he asked me to marry him!'

Rose's heart began to beat a little faster. 'What did you tell him?'

'What did you expect me to tell him?' Lizzie picked up her handbag, walked to the door, stood a moment then left without another word, leaving Rose feeling sorry for Alex. What a blow it must have been to his pride.

A short while later the door opened and Lizzie looked in. 'I'm going away for a few days but don't ask me where.' She was about to close the door when Rose called her and asked if she was going home.

'Possibly. I'll write, and for heaven's sake don't look so devastated! I'm not going to throw myself into the river. Be seeing you.' The door closed. Rose started to go after her then stopped. What good would it do? When Lizzie made up her mind that was it. And perhaps it was best that she went away. But why had she turned Alex down when she had made it clear some time ago she was all out to get him? They had gone out together, dined, gone to parties, the theatre. Something had happened. But what?

Charlie was due home on the Friday afternoon. A few minutes after he had arrived a telegram came. Although Rose had come to accept that all telegrams did not contain bad news she felt a qualm. Then she was scanning the words, stunned: *Alex and I married. Stop. Honeymooning in Scotland. Stop. Love Elizabeth.*

'Something wrong, Rosie?' She handed Charlie the telegram. A slow smile spread over his face. 'Well, what do you know! Alex and Liz married! Never did I think when I stood in the market selling secondhand clothes that I would have a big business tycoon as my brother-in-law.'

And Alex is mine too, Rose thought, but did not at that moment feel at all sisterly towards him. All she could see was her sister in Alex's arms, an image that tormented her, even though she hated herself for having created it.

Chapter 24

When the honeymooners returned Lizzie was glowing, Alex looked quietly happy. Lizzie flung her arms around Rose. 'Fooled you, didn't I?'

Alex had arranged a small dinner party and as soon as Rose had a chance to be alone with her sister she said, 'Tell me, are you in love with Alex?'

Lizzie met her gaze squarely. 'With you, Rose, I'll answer honestly. I think Alex and I have a need of one another. Some people might think this an unlikely basis for a good marriage but I feel it will work. There is affection and we respect each other. I shall certainly do my best to be a good wife to Alex. Satisfied?'

Alex and Lizzie moved into a Mews cottage and Lizzie was as excited as any young bride planning furniture and decoration. Money was no object and the result was a small, quietly elegant home, with Lizzie remarking they would, of course, have to buy something larger when they started a family.

Rose tried not to think of her own loss.

Three months after Lizzie and Alex were married Lizzie became pregnant and a month later, to Rose's joy, so did she. Lizzie sailed through the nine months without discomfort, had a short labour and gave birth to a lusty boy. Rose suffered once again with morning sickness and later endured agonies with backache. She was in labour for twelve hours and was also delivered of a son, a quiet, long-limbed baby. Lizzie declared laughing that her son could easily pass for Charlie's child, with his sturdy figure and dark curly hair, while Rose's baby could pass for Alex's boy.

The christening was private, with only Lecky and Clarissa standing as godparents for both children. Lizzie and Rose had decided on the names weeks beforehand and, with their husbands' approval, the de Veer baby was christened Jonathan Alexander, and the Eagan boy, David Charles.

Jonathan's howls filled the church as the Holy Water was sprinkled on his head, while the sleeping David slept blissfully on. Charlie whispered to Rose he was his lad all right, never making a fuss over anything. Rose smiled indulgently at him, but put a finger to her lips.

They went back to the Mews cottage for a christening tea and afterwards Alex said he wanted to make an announcement. Although his expression was serious Rose had the impression of suppressed excitement, like a schoolboy about to play a trick on someone. Rose looked to Charlie for guidance on what the announcement could be but he shook his head.

Then Alex was saying, 'This concerns Rose. As you all know, Rose has been responsible for the success of the House of Kimberley. Without her designs there would have been no fashion house and so, to celebrate the birth of her son I am handing over to her my controlling interest in the company.'

There was a silence so complete Rose heard her sister draw in a quick breath. She sat up. 'But Alex – I couldn't! I mean to say . . .'

'Of course she couldn't.' Lizzie jumped up, with a rustle of her taffeta underskirt. Her face was livid. 'What's got into you, Alex de Veer?'

Alex regarded her coldly. 'Please sit down, Elizabeth, this is no concern of yours.'

'No concern of mine? I would say it most definitely is! I've worked and slaved as hard as Rose.'

'That was before I met you, Elizabeth. Now will you please sit down and let me finish what I have to say?'

Lecky and Clarissa got up saying they had better go, with Lecky trying to treat the matter lightly to save embarrassment. 'It happens,' he said. 'I've been involved in a few family discussions. We'll leave you to sort it out, which I know you will. And don't worry, any of you, it hasn't spoiled our day.'

Alex saw them out. Lizzie sat wooden. Charlie looked helplessly at Rose and again shrugged his shoulders. When Alex came back Rose, distressed, said, 'I think we had better go too, Alex, and discuss this another time.'

'No!' Lizzie spoke firmly. 'We'll settle this once and for all. Alex is not giving you controlling interest in the company, Rose, and that is that.'

'And how do you propose to stop me, Elizabeth?' Alex's voice was now dangerously calm. A pulse beat in his throat. 'May I remind you that although you are my wife you are not my business partner. I financed the project, and I must say, Elizabeth, I'm deeply disappointed in the attitude you've taken.'

Lizzie stood, hands tightly clasped, her knuckles showing white. 'Why are you doing it, Alex? *Why* are you giving so much to my sister? What are you to each other – lovers?'

'Elizabeth!'

Charlie jumped up. 'That will do, Liz! You've said enough, more than enough, and you've no grounds for making such an accusation.'

The tension went from Lizzie. 'I'm sorry,' she said in a low voice. 'It was a terrible thing to say, and you're right, Charlie, I have no grounds for saying it.'

Rose said quietly, 'I appreciate your offer, Alex, but under the circumstances it would be impossible to accept.'

'You must,' Lizzie said, speaking earnestly, 'otherwise I'm going to suffer for it for the rest of my life. I don't easily ask anyone for forgiveness but I'm asking you now to forgive me, Rose. I don't know what got into me. It wasn't because of greed. Try to imagine how you would have felt had the positions been reversed and Charlie had made such an offer to me.'

Rose nodded. 'Yes, I think I might have felt the same.'

'No, Rose, you wouldn't,' Alex said. 'You are not of that nature.'

Rose saw a look of fear come into her sister's eyes and guessed she realised just how much she had antagonised her husband. Judging by Alex's rigid figure and expression it could be some time before he would unbend enough to forgive her. Rose said to Alex, 'Please don't think I'm not appreciative of your offer, but it is something that will have to be thought about and talked over. It's sensible that we leave now.'

Lizzie reached out a hand. 'Rose – we're not going to fall out over this, are we?' There was a bleakness in her eyes.

'Of course not.' Rose put her arms round her. 'We're too close for that. I'm grateful for all your help and I shall still need it. I depend on you.'

Rose and Charlie left soon afterwards. They drove home in an uneasy silence but once they were home Charlie said, 'All right, Rose, now tell me why Alex offered to present you with his controlling shares.'

'I have no idea, Charlie. I can only assure you we have not been lovers as your manner now suggests.'

'I'm not accusing you of being lovers! I only know there's something going on that I'm not aware of.'

'I don't *know* what goes on in Alex's mind! He's a complex character. He admires people who struggle to achieve their ambition. He admires you for the way you've worked. Perhaps its a gesture for both of us. I don't know. But I do know this, Charlie, if you don't trust me in our marriage then as far as I'm concerned it's finished.' Rose stormed towards the door but Charlie caught her and swung her towards him.

'All right, I'm jealous! It nearly drove me crazy this evening imagining you in another man's arms.'

'Jealousy is a mean and hateful thing.'

Charlie swept her up in his arms. 'So I'm mean and hateful. I love you, want you and I'm going to take you.' Rose protested she would not be taken in this way and Charlie said, 'You'll be taken and like it, my girl!'

Rose fought all the more. 'I'll claw your face if you don't put me down.'

'Claw my face and you'll get the biggest hiding of your life.'

He went upstairs with her. He kicked the bedroom door open, set her on her feet and began to tug at the buttons of her dress. Rose still fought him but with less vigour. Every part of her body was throbbing. She knew again the primitive wildness she had experienced on their honeymoon. 'I love you, Charlie,' she whispered, giving in at last. 'Only you, *always*, and I want you too, want you . . .'

'Oh, Rosie.' His mouth covered hers, his emotions as wild as her own.

Rose found herself wondering if Alex and her sister had made up their quarrel, and if there had been a wildness in Alex's anger. Or if they had lain rigidly side by side, with Lizzie suffering for her outburst.

The next morning Lizzie arrived before breakfast, distressed. Alex had left to go to Paris early. He had kissed Jonathan before he left but ignored Lizzie. With her sister looking tearful and woebegone Rose was not sure who she pitied most – Lizzie, or Alex, who was creating a hell for himself. She only hoped when he returned he would appreciate his wife and child waiting for him.

That Lizzie's marital troubles had blown over was apparent when she came in a week later all smiles. 'Guess what, Rosie! Alex is taking me on a Mediterranean cruise. It's a private yachting party. Isn't it marvellous! I shall be able to try out my French in earnest. I must have some new outfits, lots of them. I want to be the best-dressed woman on the cruise. Alex has to be proud of me. And by the way, will you please, *please*, start calling me Elizabeth.'

'*Yes*, Elizabeth, I shall try and remember and I shall pass on your instruction to Charlie.'

Later in the day Alex came to Rose and said, 'I've made my peace with Charles. He understands now why I offered you the shares. And I can understand why you refused, Rose.'

Rose never did find out what had transpired between the two men, she was only glad there was no dissension between them.

The de Veers returned from the cruise deeply suntanned with Lizzie raving over the tropical nights, the exquisite cuisine, the titled people she had mixed with and the interest shown in Rose's designs. Several of the women had promised to visit The House of Kimberley. Five did keep their promise but this was several months later. By then Lizzie was in a panic because she thought she was pregnant again. 'I don't want any more children,' she wailed. 'I have a feeling that Alex finds pregnant women distasteful.'

Alex showed nothing but pleasure when he knew about the baby and Rose, longing for another baby herself, felt envious of her sister. She hoped that another miracle would happen and she would become pregnant a month after Lizzie, as she had done with David. But the months went by, Lizzie was delivered of a lovely baby girl, whom they christened Marianne and Rose lavished love on her sister's child.

A year passed in which the unemployment figures rose to three million in England and nearly thirteen million in America. Alex de Veer, returning from a trip to the States spoke of the big deals he had pulled off. Charlie, who had accompanied him, talked of the ever-lengthening bread queues, of quite well-dressed men searching the garbage cans at the backs of restaurants for scraps of food. He spoke of two decent young men he had met called Henry Fonda and James Stewart who, not having worked since leaving college and thereby not qualifying for Relief were singing for dimes on the sidewalks.

In England from time to time there would be upsurges of

unrest from groups of people but invariably the hunger-weakened men would be forced to retire.

In London, the Bright Young Things were still throwing parties, the noisier the party and the more food and wine there was the better. And while this was going on and expensive restaurants were packed, black-shawled women were existing on a crust of bread a day to give what available food there was to their families.

The House of Kimberley, its trade ever increasing, now numbered among its clientèle a sizeable number of titled women, a foreign princess, two film stars and an opera singer. But although Rose felt a sense of achievement and loved every minute of her work, she went on longing for another child. She adored David, would have fought to the death to protect him, but she never felt, oddly enough, he was wholly hers. Rose had never seen such a serious child. The only one who could draw a smile from him was Charlie, then it was brief. 'He's going to be a professor,' Charlie would say.

There came a time when Rose was in a terribly restless mood. Charlie teased her, and said she was broody. A week later she started with morning sickness and announced with great glee, 'I'm pregnant, I'm pregnant!'

On a bright June morning Rose gave birth to a baby girl, after only four hours' labour. They named her Caroline, which was Charlie's choice. She was a sunny-natured baby who was treated with great solemnity by David, with loving abandon by Jonathan, who would plant smacking kisses on her brow whenever he could get near her, and as a doll by Marianne.

The months sped by, the business went on thriving, yet there was still massive unemployment. When Alex learned that the people in the next house were planning to move he took over the lease. They would expand, enlarge their fur trade. Two weeks later he bought a family house in Kensington. Elizabeth was in her element, buying furniture and furnishings. Rose, who longed to have a home of her own felt a little envious, yet knew at the same time the present arrangement was convenient – she was able to live on the job and could be with her children in moments if needed. When the children were older then perhaps she and Charlie could look for a home of their own.

Sometimes Rose felt a sense of wonder at how far they had progressed since their early market days. They were constantly diversifying and were involved in so many businesses she found it difficult to keep track of them all. They had gone into men's wear, and boutiques in Monte Carlo, St Tropez and Cannes were under way. Alex spoke of opening one in Paris and New York, and also fashion houses in these cities, but this last proposal had been left temporarily on the agenda.

Charlie began to accompany Alex abroad on almost every trip. Alex said he had an astute mind, and an excellent bargaining manner. Rose came to realise that her husband was acquiring a stature, a polish, a more positive approach to business yet fundamentally he was the same Charlie, ready for a joke, ready to make love at any time during the day or night when he was home.

Lecky, who had married a Grecian girl, was living in Greece. Rose was looking forward to seeing the wedding photographs which Anna had promised faithfully to send. They came by the same post as a letter from Gran Eagan to say Alice was getting married. She was pregnant. Charlie sent money to the couple and Rose sent a layette. Alice had the baby but it lived only two days. Edie said Alice was heartbroken, but was young, there was plenty of time. There would be other children. To anyone casually reading the letter it would seem an uncaring attitude but Rose knew her grandmother, knew she was deeply upset.

At the beginning of 1934 Alice and her husband Jimmy came to London, Alice to work with Rose, and Jimmy as warehouseman in a factory owned by Alex. At Jimmy's insistence they moved into furnished rooms until they could rent a house of their own. Jimmy would not accept any further help.

Alice was responsible for opening another side of the business, babywear. She was forever sketching baby clothes and graduated to designs for older children.

But although the Kimberley companies and other big concerns were doing well, unemployment in many places was still rife. In Jarrow, a ship-building town on the river Tyne, with perhaps the highest rate of unemployed, the majority of men had not done a day's work in five years. Then a small red-haired woman, an MP named Ellen Wilkinson, took up their cause and eventually led a contingent of men out of Jarrow on a march to London to plead their cause. Some of the men were pitifully clad in threadbare suits and holed shoes, but they walked with a dignity and a determination that shamed a lot of well-clothed, well-fed people. There were many who were poor themselves who sacrificed a precious overcoat or a pair of shoes and who brought the marchers food. Other groups of unemployed joined up with them on the way.

The men marched in pouring rain, slept at night exhausted in church halls and more often than not left the next morning in damp clothes and shoes. Some through illness were forced to drop out. Unhappily, like the 1932 march, little was achieved. The only thing it did was to bring notice to their plight, through the Press and others witnessing the march, to thousands of people who were not even aware of it.

At the time the march was taking place Alex and Charlie came back from a visit to Germany with talk of imminent war.

People hoped that things would settle down, but instead they worsened. Adolf Hitler, not even bothering to issue his troops with ammunition, reoccupied the Rhineland. Another treaty torn up, said Charlie angrily. Jews were being persecuted, not only in Germany but in Italy by Mussolini. Austria was annexed by Germany and the British Navy was mobilised. There came an underlying panic, a fear. Where would it all end? Hitler, power-drunk, was after ruling the world. There were all sorts of demands, high-level talks.

Rose did not understand all the implications of this, but only knew like the whole of the country, a great relief when Chamberlain, after another visit to Germany, came back waving a piece of paper. There would be Peace in Our Time! Chamberlain was a wonder, a saint. The Mall and Whitehall held thousands of joy-mad people who swarmed up lamp posts, on railings, singing and laughing and crying with relief.

But the peace looked like being short-lived. Hitler was not satisfied with Sudetenland, he wanted the whole of Czechoslovakia . . . and got it.

Larger countries began drawing-up defensive agreement pacts. An Anglo-Polish treaty was signed in London. Conscription was begun in Great Britain. All over were signs of preparation for war and plans were under way to evacuate mothers and children to the country.

One evening Alex and Elizabeth came round looking worried. Alex said they had decided to send their children to stay with friends in America, on a ranch in Texas, then he added, 'The Mathers are more than willing to have David and Caroline too, in fact they said over the phone they would be delighted.' What did Charlie and Rose think?

Chapter 25

Rose felt a mounting panic. 'Why send the children away now?' she asked. 'War hasn't yet been declared.' Charlie ran his fingers through his hair and asked what more proof did she need that it would come. They were digging air raid shelters, sandbagging buildings, removing art treasures, issuing gas masks. Did she want her children to be gassed?

Rose gave in and it was arranged that Elizabeth would travel to America with the children, but would of course, come back.

Jonathan and Marianne and Caroline were full of excitement about travelling on a liner to America and, although David was quiet about it he did show more interest when he knew they would be living on a ranch and would learn to ride. During the next few weeks they 'lassoed' everything that projected both inside and outside of the house.

Rose, full of heartache at losing the children wrote to her grandmother, complaining that she thought it was a terrible thing to uproot children from loving parents and homes. By return of post came a letter from Edie saying it was a sensible decision. She herself was making preparation for the children to be evacuated. Nancy was going with a group of people to try and get the evacuees settled into various homes. But she said she wanted to come back to do hospital work. Edie wrote, '*It's not my wish to send the children away, Rose, but with this being a ship-building area we could be a target for enemy action. We must think of the children and not our own heartaches.*' A postscript said that Davie was going to volunteer for the army and that Tommy was mad that because of his leg he was unable to enlist for any of the services. He was hoping to do ambulance work.

Rose felt ashamed at having complained.

When the time came for Rose to part with the children Caroline, glowing with excitement, kissed Rose, then was away. David, to her surprise, put his arms round her neck and clung to her. But when she said, her voice breaking, 'Oh, David,' he drew away and left without a backward glance. When the car nosed its way into the traffic on Park Lane Rose wept.

When Elizabeth returned a month later she said the children had settled in amazingly well. Already they were riding on the ranch, were friends with the cattlemen and were not allowed to have their own way by Mrs Mather.

A week after this Alex was invited to the offices of the Ministry of Supply. Charlie, speculating about it to Rose, said that with factories going over to war production, of clothing, footwear and so on, Alex with his knowledge would be invaluable to the department.

This not only turned out to be the case but Alex said he had asked for Charlie to work with him, which prompted Elizabeth to say wryly, 'Of course, with the great Alex de Veer recommending him, how could they refuse!'

Alex gave a wintry smile. 'How indeed. We are all, of course, involved, the only difference being that our output will go to the Ministry. The couture trade will continue until we are informed of any change.'

Two weeks later both men turned up in uniform, Alex with the rank of Major and Charlie with that of Captain. Rose thought that each man looked as distinguished as the other, Alex with his air of authority, his arrogance, Charlie with a pride and dignity underlying his present jocularity as he teased Rose, saying she would now have to jump to his command. The following day the two men left to tour the country on a reorganisation plan.

And two months later, after Germany had invaded Poland, Britain and Germany were at war. Britain and France immobilised, and compulsory service was announced for men between the ages of eighteen and forty-one. Rose was thankful that Alex and Charlie had administrative jobs and would not, as far as she knew, be involved in any fighting.

Young men did not wait to be called up, they rushed to volunteer, and as they left their jobs women filled them. And wore trousers. Kneebreeches for the Land Army girls, trousers for the munition workers, for women porters, for riding bicycles, for driving vans. Women everywhere began to knit for the troops, balaclava helmets, mitts, scarves, pullovers to go under their tunics.

Society girls began working in canteens, helping with all kinds of charities to aid the war effort. Many were working in chilly buildings and sloppy sweaters over trousers became the norm. There were also sweaters for evening, adorned with jewellery, some beaded, some embroidered in gold thread. Simple styles came in and with them, the 'little girl' look, tight-waisted, full-skirted with white puritan collar and cuffs.

Although Rose, like other couturiers would be using cottons for evening wear as well as day wear she would also be utilising the rich silks and satins and brocades which Charlie had stock-piled at the threat of war. These expensive materials would eventually come to an end and Rose doubted they would be replaced, but as Elizabeth said – use them now, the time to worry was when there were none left.

Up to now Rose had kept all her staff. When war was declared Blanche had wailed, 'Mon Dieu, I must go home, my country, my family needs me.' Then clapping her hands to her head she said, 'What am I saying? The only family I have is my sister and she is here in London. I will work and fight for this country.'

Blanche was found knitting for the troops at every spare moment she had.

Charlie had brought men in earlier to convert the cellars

under the two houses into air raid shelters. Blanche had made some colourful cushions and Adele had provided a drinks cabinet, saying one never knew what guest might drop in during a raid!

But before any heavy concentration of bombing was to take place on London itself the Germans had invaded Denmark, Norway, Holland, Belgium, the Luxembourg and France. There had been Dunkirk, the Battle of Britain and the consequent raids on South and South-East coasts and other coastal areas.

Many of Rose's clients, who at first ignored the air raid warnings, now thought it sensible to go to the cellar shelters to be fitted. And, in fact, they liked the shelter, said it had a special atmosphere.

Someone jokingly called it the Kimberley Club and the name stuck. Rose never raised any objections to these visits. A social life was important to her sister and Elizabeth not only worked hard in the business but was working part time with the WVS.

Alex and Charlie were away weeks at a time. Charlie would never say where they had been and once Rose teased him and said he was either on secret work or had a mistress on the side. Charlie grinned and told her she was right on both counts.

David wrote stilted letters from time to time and Caroline would add rows of kisses. Snapshots enclosed showed the children with animals or on horseback. They all looked radiant with health, and happy. Even David was laughing.

Rose went through a strange period, when although she knew people were being bombed out of their homes and killed and injured, and sirens went and people ran for shelters, she had a feeling of complete detachment. And yet, she worried about her family up North. The children were with a middle-aged farming couple and liked the life. Nancy had come back and was working in the hospital and Tommy had joined the ambulance service. All seemed well but Rose had a feeling that her grandmother was holding something back when she wrote. Had there been raids and she had not said anything, not wanting her to worry? Rose wrote to Nancy and asked her to phone often, and reverse the charges.

Nancy was anything but forthcoming on the phone. Everything had to be dragged out of her. Yes, they were all right. Yes, there had been raids, but not near them. Yes, she enjoyed working at the hospital. The maternity wing was overflowing and she liked being with the babies. No, she was not going steady with anyone, but she had gone out once or twice to the pictures with an orderly who had come recently to the hospital.

Rose was so used to these responses she was therefore surprised when Nancy phoned one morning after breakfast, sounding excited. 'Big news to report,' she said. 'Three bombs dropped last night, it was a stray raider. One fell on the playing fields, one on the church hall and the other on the shops at the back of us. No one was hurt but we could all have been killed.'

Rose's limbs felt weak as she thought of what could have happened. When she asked if her grandparents were all right Nancy said yes, just a little shocked like all of them. Fortunately the sirens had given them warning and they had gone to the street shelter. Then she added, 'But you could feel the blast. Grandad's fruit trees have gone. There's some cracks in the ceiling and walls of the front room and all Gran's little china ornaments are broken but there isn't even a chip in the big vase on the mantelpiece.'

Rose told her at once she was coming home – she would see about trains. She sought out Elizabeth to tell her what had happened.

Elizabeth warned her there could be delays, for the times of trains were erratic, but Rose said she was prepared for that, she just had to go.

It turned out to be a nightmare journey. There was a raid in progress and the train was shunted into a siding. It was ten o'clock the next morning when Rose walked from the station, needing some fresh air. There was a stillness, as though people had gone to ground. Rose went down the back entry then stopped, her breath catching in her throat. The garden was covered in rubble, white dust covered the roof. All that was left of the fruit trees were stumps. Her grandfather was standing motionless in the midst of the debris, his shoulders slumped. There was a frailty, a defeated stance about him Rose had not seen before. A few wisps of his sandy hair lifted in the breeze. She fought to control her emotions, not wanting to go to him weeping. When she called to him softly and he turned she saw that his faded blue eyes were brimming with tears. 'Oh Grandad,' she said, and went stumbling to him. He put an arm around her and began stroking her hair.

'Well, lovey, what a surprise. Who'd have thought we would see you today? There now, pet, don't take on so. We're fine. It's grand to see you, Rosie, but I'm sorry you had to see the garden in this state. That German bloke certainly played me a dirty trick, didn't he, not even leaving me one tree.'

'Oh, Grandad, we'll plant some more.'

Sam gave a wan smile. 'I doubt I'd live long enough to see them fruit, Rosie. Not unless I live to be a hundred and twenty or something.'

'Heaven forbid!' said Gran Eagan's voice from behind them. 'When did *you* arrive, Rose? I've just got back from delivering another puny baby to Elsie Dunford. I reckon folks shouldn't have babies in wartime.'

Sam said, 'Edie – you'd think you'd seen Rosie yesterday. She's come all the way from London to see us, she was worried about us.'

Edie's expression softened. 'Sorry, Rosie, I was with you in my dreams the night before last and it was just as if we had resumed talking where we left off. You shouldn't have come all this way, but it's good to see you.' Edie kissed her. 'Come on, I've put the kettle on. Let's have a cup of tea and we can hear all your news.'

They were walking towards the house when Edie stopped and pointed to where the deep pink of a geranium flower was peeping above the rubble. 'See that, Sam? I reckon if that flower can survive with all this weight on it, we can survive with only the weight of worry on our shoulders.'

'You're right, Edie.' Sam gave Rose a wink. 'As usual!'

Edie treated the bombing incident in her down-to-earth way as one of the hazards of war. Yes they could have been in the garden when it happened, or at least Sam could, he was in the habit of searching the sky at night. She spoke of the children and said how glad she was they were away and how lucky they were to be with such kind and homely people. She accepted that Davie had joined the army, everyone had to do their bit for their country, but cracks showed in her armour when she mentioned the son of a neighbour who had been taken prisoner of war, and again when she spoke of her little mementoes having been broken.

'I would never sleep at night if I knew that Davie was in enemy hands. He's such a sensitive boy. Tommy has more staying power.'

And later, when they were in the front room Edie, after pointing out the damage done to the ceiling and walls by the blast, turned to the table where there was a small pile of broken pieces of china. She picked one up which showed the beginning of the word Scarborough in gilt and said, pain in her voice, 'It should be a lesson to me, not to attach too much importance to my possessions.'

'I don't agree with you, Gran. It's the small things, our precious little possessions, that make up life. Without them we would have nothing. I'll get some glue and we'll stick all the pieces together.'

Edie shook her head. 'No, I'll leave them in the dustbin. Nancy threw them there. She was always complaining about them being dust traps. She's become hard in many ways, Rosie, yet she's lovely with the children.'

When Rose left her grandparents to return to London she

felt as though she had gone through a deeply emotional experience. For the first time she realised something of what it must be like to be made homeless, to lose one's dearest possessions, possessions that would be considered worthless to some but precious to their owners. She knew a longing to help these people in some way and decided she would join the Women's Voluntary Service when she got home. She could manage part-time, as Elizabeth did.

Elizabeth when told, warned her not to get too sentimental. If the raids really hit the city hard there would be some gruesome sights.

Rose said she would accept that.

She had been with the WVS a month and was helping to man a post in the East End of London when the Luftwaffe decided to switch their activities from the South and South-East coasts to concentrate on London. When the sirens went there was the usual mad barking of dogs, the continual staccato bark of ack-ack guns and the slamming of front doors as people hurried to the shelters. But there was extra activity that night, the clanging of fire and ambulance bells. Rose and one of the other women ran to the door. And there Rose stood, fascinated and fearful. It was bright moonlight, a 'bombers' moon' night, as it had become known. Searchlights criss-crossed the sky, there was an incessant drone of planes. Rose went to the corner then gasped. A line of warehouses was blazing, orange and red flames leaping from windows, from roofs amid billowing clouds of smoke. There was a gruesome beauty about the scene, the incendiary bombs illuminating a darkened street, hissing and sparkling with a greenish light. Silver barrage balloons, which always seemed to float in a fairy-tale way without attachment were turning to flaming scarlet, the fragments drifting earthwards.

'Rose, come on, we have work to do,' called her companion and Rose went hurrying back.

While they worked, preparing for people who had been made homeless, wave after wave of planes went overhead.

There was the crunch of bombs, the *whoof* of explosions. Before long the first batch of bombed-out people were being escorted to the basement shelter, the adults dazed, faces smoke-grimed, children screaming. An old woman came shuffling in carrying a parrot in a cage, the parrot squawking, 'What a bloody carry on!' The woman said, 'Oh, Poll, for pity's sake shut your face,' and she threw a piece of blanket over the cage.

Some people were glad to sink down on to mattresses and have a blanket tucked around them, others wandered around, a hopeless look in their eyes as they sought relatives or neighbours. Rose took milk and biscuits to the children and tea to the adults. Most refused food as this stage. Rose, who had recently felt a little peeved at times that her children seemed not to be missing her at all, was now thankful they were on the other side of the Atlantic.

It was a long night, a long raid, and the overspill of people had to be taken to other centres. With every hand needed Rose had worked a ten-hour stretch and was reluctant to leave when someone came to take her place as dawn was breaking. 'You must get some rest, Rose,' she was told, 'or you'll be no good to anyone.' She was asked if she wanted a lift home but Rose said no, she would find her own way. She felt a need to walk a while.

The devastation appalled her. What had once been streets of houses were now piles of rubble. Men were working like Trojans as they searched for people buried beneath the débris. There was the acrid smell of charred timber, the stink of gas seeping from fractured pipes . . . the smell of death. Two firemen carried the body of a young girl to a waiting ambulance, her fair curls dancing. 'She's gone,' said one of the men and you could hear the emotion in his voice at such a waste of a young life. One house, still standing, was minus the facing wall. To Rose there was something merciless about the exposure of people's lives, a line of grey-looking washing stretched across a room, a slit in a flannelette nightie, a big hole in a vest. A slop bucket stood by the side of a bed. An empty milk bottle stood intact on a table while every other piece of glass and china lay shattered. Groups of men and women stood around, waiting fearfully for their families to be dug out of the rubble, people whose eyes were sunken, faces paper-white. A black cat, its fur streaked with grey dust, picked its way daintily over bricks and mortar. There was the sound of a gruff bark and a man shouted, 'I've got him, Jack, here, lend a hand.' The dog, a mongrel, was lifted out. One paw was injured. It stood on its three legs, tail up, and looked about it in a pugnacious way as though to say, 'Which one of you did this to me?' It brought a laugh from the men, relieving tension.

That night was the beginning of the Blitz on London, when the Luftwaffe having suffered enormous casualties in day raids decided to switch to night bombing. Night after night they came, wave after wave. When the sirens went in the evening thousands of people sought safety in Anderson garden shelters, in street shelters, in the Underground. One evening when the All Clear had gone and there seemed to be a lull Rose decided to visit Mr Rosenberg. His premises had been damaged by a bomb and so had his house, but both were usable. When it had first happened he had taken it all philosophically, saying he was lucky, he could have been killed. But on this evening when Rose called, his aged housekeeper said he wasn't at all well. Delayed shock.

Although he seemed a little frail his interest in what she was doing was just as exuberant. 'Come and sit down, Rose, tell me how you are doing. Oh, it is good to see you.'

They talked for about an hour and she had some supper, which Mr Rosenberg and his housekeeper insisted on and when she got up to leave Mr Rosenberg was showing signs of exhaustion. She put her arms around him, kissed him and said gently, 'Take care of yourself, I'll call again to see you.'

'I will, and you, dear Rose. Get a taxi, there could be a raid.'

When Rose left she had an awful premonition that she might not see him again. Then dismissed it. It was losing people tragically that made for premonitions.

Rose got home safely, but there was a raid later. The next morning Hannah, from Mr Rosenberg's office, phoned to say that he and his housekeeper had been killed going to the shelters.

'Oh, Rose,' she said, 'I feel broken-hearted. He was part of my life, a wonderful man. Everybody loved him.'

Rose felt sick as she thought of her premonition. 'If only I had known,' she said tearfully. 'There was so much I would have said.'

'I think it's just as well we don't know these things, Rose. I'll let you know when the funeral is.'

When Charlie knew he was deeply grieved. 'He was such a good friend to me, Rose, to both of us. We shall always remember him.'

The raids continued, night after night. Guns barked, incendiaries pattered on rooftops and pavements, people were killed, maimed, made homeless, yet life had to go on. In the West End it was difficult to believe at times that there was a war. People danced, went to theatres, cinemas, restaurants and hotels were full. One evening Rose and Blanche and Adele stood in a long queue to see '*Gone with the Wind*'. The sirens went but no one ran for shelter. Adele said there came a time when one had to risk one's life and added she only hoped this film would be worth taking that risk!

The three of them came out enraptured. They hated Scarlett O'Hara, but admired her, suffered with her. And they fell in love with Rhett Butler. Blanche said to Rose, 'Such a man! He reminded me of your Charles, so virile, so masterful.'

That night Rose longed more than ever to be curled up against her husband. She worried constantly about him, never knowing if he was in a danger zone. He phoned from time to time but there were long gaps in between.

The old restlessness was on Rose again, the necessity for change. But what could she do that was different? It was not as if she could start a new line and put it into production. More and more factories were being taken over by the government, some for storing equipment.

It was a new cleaning woman that inadvertently set Rose off on a new upsurge of creativity. The woman conscientiously told Rose she was courting danger by keeping bales of stuff in the attics. An incendiary bomb dropped through the skylight could cause a conflagration. For a moment Rose could not think what could be in the attics then remembered Charlie saying it was rubbish mostly that had been included in bankrupt stocks of material he had bought when war threatened. Rose took Adele up with her to sort through the bales and boxes.

Their first find was a large stock of hanks of string-coloured cotton with a linen thread running through it, which would make for strength. It could be used for knitting and crocheting garments. There was a bale of butter muslin, hundreds of boxes of beads, wools in all colours; braids and fringes of every description, and masses of buttons. With the butter muslin Rose designed shawls with Tyrolean embroidery and coloured fringes, large ones and shoulder ones. There were sashes with embroidered and fringed ends, skirts with bands of braid, Magyar blouses. Once started Rose found it difficult to stop sketching. And in between she manned posts for the WVS, travelled with mobile canteens and the more tragedy she saw the more she wanted to make attractive clothes, especially ones that the average person could afford to buy.

In November there was news of a massive raid on Coventry. The toll of dead and injured was high. Hundreds of people were made homeless, a large proportion of shops were destroyed and so was the beautiful cathedral. Many of the people evacuated went back to see what could be salvaged from their homes, and were involved in further raids.

Rose, depressed, said, 'It's all so crazy. They bomb our cities and we bomb theirs.'

Her depression persisted until a batch of letters came from America, which included news from all the Mather family and letters from Caroline as well as David. Mrs Mather said they were sending food parcels.

The American people had generously sent thousands of food parcels to the people of Great Britain, which were a godsend, with butter and bacon rations being only four ounces a week and an allowance of just over a shilling a week for meat.

Although the children in their letters had not said they wished they could be home for Christmas Rose was moved when David wrote, 'I really miss you, Mum and Dad,' and she shed a few tears at Caroline's higgledy-piggledy printed words, 'I love you, Mummy, I kiss your photograph and Daddy's every night before I go to bed.'

In the middle of December Alex and Charlie arrived back and to the delight of Rose and Elizabeth said they would be home for Christmas. Alex had changed. Like Elizabeth he too seemed to be constantly needing a social life, but Rose and Charlie were willing to join in. They dined out, danced, sang in the taxi home, held parties in the cellar shelter – and made love. At least Rose presumed that Alex and her sister would make love. In quieter moments she was often aware of Alex's gaze on her and she would look quickly away, still finding something disturbing in his manner towards her.

Those few days were the only happy ones of the men's leave. Two days before Christmas Nancy phoned to say they had had word that Davie was missing. 'Gran didn't want you to know until after Christmas,' she said, 'but I knew you would want to know.'

Rose wished that Nancy did not sound as though she relished the drama.

Nancy then went on to ask if Charlie and Rose were coming North. 'I think you should,' she said. 'I'm on duty all over the holidays and the kids are staying at the farm for Christmas. Gran thought they should on account of the bombing.' Rose said they would be travelling that day.

Alex and Elizabeth were out when Rose phoned so she could only leave a message with the housekeeper to say what had happened. Alice made the excuse for not going North that she thought she had picked up a 'flu bug, but Rose suspected that Alice, like their mother, could not bear to be involved with sorrow.

Gran Eagan greeted them dry-eyed but with a haunted look in her eyes that hurt Rose. Sam, who had been the bane of Edie's life in the past with his drinking and losing jobs, was now her comforter. 'Sit you down, Edie love, and I'll make us all a nice cup of tea.'

The decorated Christmas tree and the paper chains stretched from wall to wall seemed somehow incongruous to Rose at such a time. But she and Charlie played along with Edie who was trying so desperately to act as normally as possible. She reminisced about other Christmases and smiled a little at the way the girls had squabbled the year Rose had added the silver thimble, the ring and the shoe to the silver Joeys in the Christmas cake.

Charlie kept trying to boost up the old people's hopes by saying that 'missing' men were turning up all the time. It was chaos at the front and, when he and Rose had to leave, Edie's parting words were, 'We must live in hope that Davie has been taken prisoner and pray that the New Year will see an end to all the horrors.'

But two days before the year ended there was to be further horror. As well as heavy bombing, thousands of incendiary bombs were dropped on London, causing raging infernos, fires it was almost impossible to control because of the extent of the area and the incessant bombardment. The next day fires were still smouldering, some still flaring up. People were stunned by the devastation, shocked that Buckingham Palace had been hit in part by a bomb. Fortunately the Royal

Family had not been in residence at the time, but supposing they had been there?

It did nothing to help that German cities were suffering equal devastation. But what did help was the profoundly stirring speech made by Winston Churchill, as his speeches had done in every crisis.

'People will pick up their lives again and carry on as before,' Rose said on New Year's Eve. Alice had come to see that New Year in with Rose and Blanche and Adele. Jimmy, now in armaments, was on night shift. Elizabeth, who had gone to a party, turned up unexpectedly at ten minutes to midnight. 'I don't know,' she said, 'it just didn't feel right, I wanted to be with the family.'

Rose found something startlingly beautiful about her sister that evening. The white stand-up fur collar on her evening coat framed her dark hair, which was done in a chignon. Her eyes held a luminosity as though with unshed tears – and there was a softness about her mouth that Rose had not seen for some time. She poured her a drink.

There were no church bells ringing to welcome in the New Year. They were only to be rung if the dreaded invasion came, but when the women clinked their glasses and gave the toast, 'Here's to peace in nineteen forty-one,' no one gave it more hope or sang '*Auld Lang Syne*' with more emotion than the five of them who, although different in temperament, were joined together in a common cause, the fight for freedom.

They sang the '*Marseillaise*' for Blanche, went through a whole repertoire of songs and if they were all a little drunk, said Rose, as they prepared to go to bed, who could blame them?

Chapter 26

During the next few months three things happened to affect Rose's approach to her business. Women from the age of sixteen to sixty, apart from mothers with young children, were to be directed to war work. This meant Rose losing quite a number of her staff. Then the 'utility scheme' came into being which meant that fifty per cent of all cloth manufactured was controlled in price and quality. Following this came clothes rationing, on a points system.

'Sixty-six coupons a year!' Elizabeth exclaimed to Rose as they listened to the news on the wireless. 'How on earth do they expect a woman to dress with that amount when it's fourteen for a coat, eleven for a dress and two for a pair of stockings? And that's apart from everything else one needs. I think we may as well close down now.'

'You're a defeatist,' Rose said. 'If Lelong and the other couturiers in Paris could keep the Houses going, then we can. We shall cope.'

Rose was sketching furiously when right out of the blue came a bonus for the fashion houses with the Government persuading all the leading couturiers to design a joint collection to send to South America. It was to be a display of luxury clothes now strictly for export only, and not to be available in England. Hardy Amies, she learned, was to be given leave from the army to help.

Rose was in her element. Although she enjoyed the challenge of producing fashion wear from the cheaper materials she still loved working with the rich materials.

The South American venture was such a success it was decided to found a permanent organisation to give British couture a common voice in dealing with new problems and wartime restrictions.

The Collection was a bright spot to Rose in a world of nightly bombing raids.

When Charlie came next on leave he said to Rose, 'Get your coat on, we're going to look at a house in Surrey. No one wants to live there any more, so I can get it cheap. Not that I want you to live in it now, I thought we could have it ready for when the children come home. There's stabling, they can have . . .'

'Charlie – stop there, you're talking too fast. Why are you trying to sell me this house? What's wrong with it?'

'It's a lovely house, Rosie, but of course there are always planes about, but I don't think it will ever get bombed.'

'Oh, so the enemy are going to say, now listen that house belongs to Charlie and Rose Eagan, don't drop any bombs on it.'

Charlie grinned. 'Something like that. But I think it's worth buying, worth taking the risk. It's partly furnished, so we could spend an odd weekend there. Come and see it.'

She gave in, and in spite of there being a constant movement of planes overhead she appreciated being out in the countryside. It was a lovely September morning with a slight nip in the air. Through the lowered window of the car came the pungent smell of a garden bonfire. There was the plaintive bleating of sheep, the lowing of cattle and birdsong. A peacefulness. It seemed impossible to believe that she and Charlie had been with a group of fire-watchers during the night dousing incendiary bombs with stirrup pumps.

Rose kept looking for road signs then remembered they had all been removed, in case of invasion. After a while she semi-dozed, rousing only when Charlie said, 'Nearly there, now.' They turned right into a tree-lined drive. Rose, alert now, looked about her with interest. There was an air of neglect, with weeds waist-high along the verges, and soon they reached what had once been gardens and lawns but at the moment looked like overgrown fields. Perhaps the house would be more pleasing, she thought.

But the house was a big disappointment to her. It was brick-built, solid-looking and without one feature of beauty. Charlie, standing away from it said, looking pleased with himself, 'Big ugly old thing, isn't it?'

Rose wondered why on earth he had chosen it. She sought for words to describe it. 'It's misshapen, lopsided.'

Four storeys dropped to two storeys, then shot up to three and as an added appendage a piece jutted out at the end that had no windows. Even the porch, set between the four and two storeys seemed out of alignment. Shallow stone steps, two of them broken, led up to a solid front door with a tarnished knocker.

'Come and see the inside.' Charlie took hold of her hand. 'You'll like it.' A reluctant Rose, who was determined she would not like anything about this house, had to change her mind when she stepped inside and saw the wide staircase with its gracious curve and delicately-wrought ironwork. 'I don't believe it,' she said. 'Surely the person who designed the house could not have designed this staircase.'

'He did, and he lived in the house. He was apparently an eccentric old chap.'

'But the outside is so . . .'

'Nothing is ugly to those who love it, Rosie. And do you know something, it has a lovely name. "Larkrise".'

'Oh, Charlie,' she said softly, 'who could resist it with a name like that.' He hugged her, then led her by the hand on a tour of the rooms. Rose felt a little alarmed by the number of them but Charlie kept insisting it was a family house. There might come a time when they wanted to entertain the whole family, including grandchildren, nieces and nephews. One had to think of the future.

Rose was murmuring about the surprises one could get

when Charlie opened the door leading into the conservatory, and then she was standing looking about her in utter astonishment. The conservatory, with a high-domed roof, ran the length of the back of the house and was over half as wide as it was long. Tropical plants grew in wild confusion. The humidity was that of the greenhouses at Kew Gardens. The floor was covered in soil and debris but there was beauty in balconies set at various levels on three of the walls, balconies without doors. There were hanging baskets, the foliage in the containers all but reaching the floor, huge ornamental pots, urns, troughs. The outer wall, the top half of glass, was also weather-grimed.

'What a pity it's been allowed to get in such a state,' Rose said. 'It would be beautiful if it were all cleared.' She rubbed the toe of her shoe over the floor, then paused as a tiny piece of brilliant blue was exposed. She rubbed away some more of the soil then said on a note of rising excitement, 'Charlie, look, mosaic!' They cleared a sizeable part, disclosing exotically-coloured plumaged birds in a woodland scene of bright green leaves and slim-trunked trees. They discovered other bird designs, set in circles, in squares, in ovals . . .

Rose, brimming with ideas, said they must buy the house. She loved it.

Within a month of Charlie and Rose buying Larkrise Alex and Elizabeth had bought a house a mile away. 'We're not trying to compete,' Elizabeth laughed, 'but it's a sensible idea for us to be neighbours.'

Elizabeth liked no part of Larkrise. She thought it the ugliest house she had ever seen, shuddered when she went into what Rose now called the Bamboo Room, and asked who wanted a conservatory the size of St Pancras station?

Alex said quietly he liked every bit of the house and he was sure it would be a lovely, interesting family home. He stressed the word home. Rose felt she could have hugged him.

Elizabeth's main interest during the next few weeks was furnishing their new house. Rose's was mosaic, she lived, breathed, dreamed about it. Using designs that excited her, she spent hours sorting through large bags of scraps, mixing velvets and satins and plain brocades in patchwork-mosaic assemblies.

Weeks later there were headlines, 'ROSE KIMBERLEY STARTS PATCHWORK CRAZE'. According to the report everybody was making patchwork bags, skirts, jackets and hats. One newspaper said, 'The war brought people working together in friendly unity. Rose Kimberley has been responsible for numerous groups of people getting together making quilts, all to be auctioned when completed for charity.' Another article was headed, '*Dig into your ragbags*'.

'Well,' Rose said, 'who would have expected such repercussions? I only wish it had been something to help to end the war.'

But the war was to drag on. There were victories and defeats with heavy casualties on both sides. Fewer and fewer goods were available, and women wore wooden-soled shoes because of a shortage of leather. Food was becoming even more scarce. The butter ration was cut to two ounces a week and people were having to use packets of dried egg. Fish, which was unrationed, was becoming almost non-existent.

The American Forces were prominent in London but Rose had not known one personally until a Lieutenant called Chuck Davis called to see her. He said he was a friend of the Mathers. And he not only brought food parcels and nylons but very welcome news of the children. Elizabeth and Rose bombarded him with questions, which he answered patiently.

The children were fine, they were all excellent riders, the men liked them and if the girls got a bit sassy they felt the weight of Mrs Mather's hand. Rose said she was pleased they were disciplined. Hearing about them in this way made her longing to see them so great it was a physical pain. After that first visit Chuck was a regular visitor. He was invited when Alex and Charlie were on leave and the three men talked war until Elizabeth begged them to change the subject. Alex then suggested they all spend a weekend in Surrey, and show Chuck their respective houses.

But they never got away for their weekend. News came through of the bombing of Pearl Harbour and they all sat stunned. Then Chuck, white-faced, said in a voice charged with emotion, 'It's a big base for the Pacific Fleet. There's one thing certain – it won't be long now before we are in the war.'

Soon afterwards America declared war on the Axis powers.

In spite of the heavy losses at Pearl Harbour there was a feeling with the British people that America with her vast manpower and industrial strength would bring victory, but no one was optimistic enough to believe it would come soon. It seemed to Rose whenever she listened to the news or read the newspapers that there were a hundred different wars going on all over the world. And, in spite of Lease Lend from America and all other aid, shortages of many things were becoming acute. Shelves in many food shops were almost bare. A box of matches from under the counter was a treat. Rose ate out quite a lot and felt she was lucky to be able to afford to do so. There were restrictions on restaurants. Only one main meal could be served and the charge was limited to five shillings a head. Some restaurants made cover charges but the majority seemed to find it a challenge to comply with the ruling. There was talk of reducing the petrol ration and now fuel and paraffin were to be rationed. People were asked to restrict their number of baths and were put on their honour not to use more than five inches of water.

What hit Rose and other couturiers hardest was the Board of Trade introducing the Civilian Clothing Order, with its numerous restrictions. Only a certain amount of material could be used for a garment. There was a suggestion it would be limited to four yards, the number of models to be limited. There were to be no buttons on sleeves or pockets, the number of pleats was to be restricted, and large patch pockets were out. Eighty-five per cent of material manufactured had to go for Utility clothing, whereas before it had been fifty per cent. Stockings were in such short supply it was said that if women did not go stockingless in the summer, then they certainly would in winter. Some women who did already go without put 'seams' down the back of their legs with a pencil. The lucky girls and women were those who knew Americans and had gifts of nylons. Rose came into this category and although at times she felt guilty knowing they were not supposed to have them she wore the nylons just the same, assuaging her guilt by saving her sugar ration to give to any of the staff whose daughters were thinking of getting married. Most brides had to depend on family providing ingredients from their rations for a cake. And as no cake was allowed by law to be iced, brides had to hire fancy cardboard covers representing icing and trimmings. When Rose heard from her grandmother that Nancy had become engaged she started putting aside ingredients to help with a wedding cake.

When the war started, Lecky and Clarissa had gone out of their lives. There had been postcards from places abroad for a time then they had stopped, so that when Rose heard Lecky's name mentioned between two customers in adjoining cubicles in the salon she eavesdropped. 'Yes, I do know Lecky and his sister,' said one woman to the other. 'But I haven't heard about them for some time.'

'And you won't, dear,' replied her companion. 'He and his wife and Clarissa joined the Partisans and my husband told me this morning all three had been killed. Terrible, isn't it? Do you know I'm not a bit sure about the colour of this dress . . .'

Rose was not aware of how tightly she had been gripping the back of a chair until Elizabeth prised her fingers from it and said quietly, 'Sit down, Rose, it may not be true.' But it was true, there was a notice in *The Times* the following morning.

When Charlie phoned that evening Rose wondered how best to break the news of the tragedy, but he already knew.

He said, a bleakness in his voice, 'There are many unsung heroes and heroines. Some day I'll be able to talk about them, but not now.'

Two days later there was a letter from Gran Eagan to say that Nancy and Judith were to have a double wedding, it had all been arranged in a rush. Nancy's fiancé, who had applied for hospital work abroad was now going to Africa and Judith's prospective bridegroom, an air cadet, had been posted to Canada to train as a pilot.

Edie said, 'They're young, Rosie, it's wartime, everything has to happen now. Joe has only two days before he leaves and Nick barely twenty-four hours.'

When Rose phoned Elizabeth to tell her the news Elizabeth said it seemed they were never going to get the chance to make a wedding dress for their sisters. To which Rose replied that if the war kept dragging on they might be making them for Marianne and Caroline!

The thought of grown-up daughters and sons had Rose's throat aching with unshed tears. She was missing their developing years, they could be strangers when they next met. Rose wrote long letters to both Caroline and David, filling them in the tiniest details of life in London, the good and the bad, and begged them to write soon.

Gradually a little hope crept into the war news and when it was announced that the African campaign had ended, followed by the news that British, American and Canadian troops had marched into Sicily, there was great jubilation. The end of war seemed at last to be in sight.

But it was another two, heartbreaking years before it ended and during that time Chuck had been killed and Rose learned that her beloved, quiet brother Davie, missing earlier in the war, was dead. His grave had been found at a remote farm where the elderly couple who owned it had died. Why they had never told the authorities of Davie's death would forever remain a secret. Edie said it was a comfort to know that he had been decently buried.

Rose thought then how lucky they were that their children and Alex and Elizabeth's had not been old enough to go to war.

The last snapshots that had come of them had Elizabeth saying, 'They're grown-up! I can hardly believe it. Especially the boys.' In each one the boys were astride horses, both laughing. The girls were in various poses, on horses, sitting against a fence, lolling against a tree, swinging on a hammock on the porch. They all looked gloriously happy and healthy. Although Rose was delighted to see all the children looking so well she felt a terrible ache that other people had been involved in bringing them up.

When the end of the war came at last one thing was uppermost in Rose's mind. They would have the children home. Charlie kept warning her she would see big changes in them, and there could be some strain.

But all her worry was unnecessary. They came racing towards her, loving, exuberant. When she had been unprepared for was their quick fire talk, their nasal twang and their greetings of, 'Hi, there, Mom, Hi there, Dad!'

Rose was laughing and crying as first Caroline and then David was holding and kissing her. Then she was being lifted off her feet by Jonathan, his voice gruff. 'Auntie Rose, you don't look a day over seventeen.' Elizabeth, also between laughter and tears, complained that he had not said that to her! Last came Marianne who had big tears running down her cheeks as she proclaimed, 'It's great to be home.'

For days all the children talked about was the Mathers, whom they called Aunt Mame and Uncle Edgar and the men of the ranch, Billie, Joey, Hippy, Col . . . And Rose watching them marvelled at the change in them, the maturity they had acquired. Jonathan, who could have been Charlie's son, sturdy, always joking and David, tall and lean with a slightly arrogant air like Alex. Marianne, with her dark hair and deeply-tanned skin had a Spanish look about her, while

Caroline's skin had a golden glow and her fair hair was bleached to ash blonde by the sun.

The boys in particular wanted to see all the damage caused by the bombs and their grumble was that they had missed all the fun of the war. Useless for Alex and Charlie to explain grimly there was no fun about war, they could not be convinced.

They were taken to the theatre and could not see enough films, and it was planned to take them to Larkrise and to Treetops, Alex and Elizabeth's house, where all four children would be able to ride.

This was when the trouble started with David. He looked from his mother to his father in an arrogant way and said, 'Do you mean that Caro and I are going to live at this house in Surrey while you and Mom live in London?'

'For the time being,' Charlie replied. 'For one thing I'm still working for the Ministry of Supplies, my job takes me away from home and your mother has her work. As we've already explained, Aunt Alice and Uncle Jim are going to live at Larkrise. They will look after the four of you. We thought it best you all kept together, rode together.'

'I think you are being utterly selfish.' There was contempt in David's voice. 'Especially Mom. In all her letters she said how much she was missing us, and how she was longing to have us home.'

'And I was, and am,' Rose said earnestly. 'But I can't just throw aside all I've built up at a few days' notice. Aunt Elizabeth and I both have cars now and we shall come out to Larkrise as often as we can. Petrol rationing, of course, limits the visits.'

David's chin took on a mutinous thrust. 'I still say it's selfish, you're putting money above your children's welfare.'

Charlie said sharply, 'Let me remind you that the money you so disparage was responsible for you and Caroline living a carefree life, and in safety.'

'I didn't want to go! But you took no notice of me. You couldn't wait to get rid of me. *And* Caroline.'

'That's not true,' Rose protested. 'It's because we loved you that we made the sacrifice.'

David swung one leg over the arm of the chair and sneered, 'Oh, yeah? Tell that to the Marines.'

Charlie jumped up and Rose got up too and laid a restraining hand on his arm. 'Charlie, please . . .' He shook off her hand and went over to David. Although his eyes were sparking anger he kept his voice under control.

'To begin with, get your leg off the arm of that chair and sit up.' When David started to move leisurely Charlie grabbed his leg and swung it so that David was forced to sit up. 'Now listen to me,' Charlie went on, 'and listen carefully because I am not going to repeat it. You're in England now and *I* am the boss, not the Mathers. The Mathers might have allowed you to speak the way you wanted to but –'

'They didn't.' David looked slightly shame-faced. 'They disciplined us, neither would have allowed any of us to speak the way I did to you and Mom.'

Rose felt grateful that David had always been able to admit his faults. There was a moment's uncomfortable silence then Charlie said quietly, 'I know it must be difficult to adjust to a different way of life, David, but many men had to adjust during the war, including Americans, some of them coming from ranches. Thousands were killed to help give us freedom. And quite frankly, I don't think you will be suffering too much hardship to live at Larkrise, to be with horses and to have occasional visits from the family.'

'I agree, Dad, it's just that –' David shrugged then gave a wintry smile. 'I reckon I'll survive, we'll all survive.'

When Rose and Charlie were in bed that night she said, 'Oh, Charlie, are we doing the right thing? Should I give up the business?'

'Definitely not. We can't run our lives by the demands of our children. It's not as if they're being cast off.'

'But you know, Charlie, when I was young Ma was always there when we came home from school. If she happened to be in a neighbour's house, which was rare at that time of day, we would go searching for her. We felt bereft.'

Charlie gave a cluck of impatience. 'Oh, Rose, for heaven's sake! They're not on the other side of the Atlantic now. If they want to come home all they have to do is use their legs, cross the fields and catch a train, or a bus. And if they haven't the energy to walk a couple of miles then it's their lookout!' Rose said no more.

Chapter 27

As it happened the arrangements turned out satisfactorily. Alice mothered the children, Jim disciplined them, and so did the groom. He was a man who said he would stand no messing about where children were concerned. They took his orders or they didn't ride.

The children had been told soon after they arrived home that they would be going to boarding school after Christmas, and although there was some grumbling from all of them they eventually accepted it and had actually discussed the idea amongst themselves with some enthusiasm.

The children had been at boarding school a month when Caroline, who was allowed a weekly phone call home, spoke to Rose while she was at Larkrise for the weekend. Her tone was aggrieved as she said, 'It's not fair, Mom, all the girls here have two grandmas and two grandpas and David and I haven't got any. I did tell them I had great-grandparents but had to admit I hadn't seen them since I was very small.' There was a pause then she added, her tone now wistful, 'They must be awfully old, Mom. I *would* like to see them before they die.'

Rose felt as though a great hand was clutching at her heart. She told her they would try and arrange a visit soon then changed the subject. When eventually she replaced the receiver she stood a moment, realising how little she had taken in of the last part of Caroline's conversation.

Rose, thoughtful, made her way slowly towards the kitchen, which had become her sister's favourite spot. Alice, who was sitting toasting herself in front of the blazing fire looked up as Rose came in. 'Everything all right? No demands for extra pocket money – Is something wrong? You look as if you've seen a ghost.'

Rose told her of Caroline's comments then said, 'I've always thought of Gran and Grandad as being indestructible, they never seem to look any different, any older, but I've just realised they must be in their seventies.'

'They are. Gran is seventy-seven and Grandad a year older.'

'That old? I can't believe it.' Rose felt a sudden chill. She came over by the fire and sat down. 'I feel I must see them. We could invite them for Christmas. We could invite all the family, how about it?'

Alice was all excitement, all enthusiasm. They could get a big turkey from the farm, have their own Christmas tree from the garden, pick holly and mistletoe. It would be just like old times.

A reply to Rose's letter came by return. Edie said she was not one for being away from home for Christmas but Sam was delighted at the idea, he thought it would be lovely to have all the family together. So yes, they would come. But mind you, no expensive presents, just something simple like a few odd cups and saucers, she was getting short of them.

Rose smiled to herself. Typically Gran. She folded the letter. Now that she knew they were definitely coming she must speak with Elizabeth about it.

When Elizabeth appeared to hesitate Alex said at once it was an excellent idea. It was time Jonathan and Marianne met their great-grandparents. Rose wished that her sister seemed more enthusiastic.

The boys were as excited as Caroline and Marianne about the family Christmas and there were a lot of secret talks going on about presents. Rose bought a tea service for her grandparents with the pot-bellied cups that Edie said kept the tea hot. Charlie came in one day with a big fat eiderdown, saying if the weather got any colder they would need it.

The children, who had been longing for a white Christmas had their wish. It started to snow four days before Christmas and it laid, thick and soft. They raced about, revelling in it, tossing it, making snowballs and snowmen everywhere. They gathered holly, placed it all over the house, brought in mistletoe and fastened it to beams and to an oak chandelier.

Charlie was going to fetch Edie and Sam. Rose wondered what the children's reactions would be to Sam's nicotined moustache and clay pipe, Edie's ramrod-stiff figure and her sharp way of speaking. Rose, guessing this was the reason why Elizabeth had hesitated about a family Christmas wrote to her grandmother, offering to have a dress made for her. Back came a reply from Edie saying she had bought a very good dress in the market for ten shillings, also a coat. She would not disgrace them. Rose then felt shockingly guilty, knowing she had wanted her grandparents to look smart for the children's sake. 'I was being terribly snobbish,' she told Charlie. He laughed and said, 'How like Edie, she could have a couture dress but preferred to buy one secondhand. But then,' he added, 'she'll probably feel more comfortable, and that is the most important thing.'

Edie said in her next letter she did not intend sitting on her bottom and doing nothing over Christmas, she would help with the cooking. Rose decided to let her take charge of most of the Christmas Day meal.

On the afternoon of the day Charlie had gone North Rose stood at the window of the room she had chosen as her private sitting room. It overlooked the garden, the lawns and the countryside beyond, a vast area of whiteness without one visible footstep. The day had been bright, the sun sparkling, the snow and the sky a clear, hard blue, but now the sun was beginning to set and sky and snow were tinged with pink.

To the left, on the slope where the children had tobogganed earlier the snow lay trampled and broken, the slide itself shadowed in dark blues and greys, the shadows echoed in the circle of lake, the water now frozen. There was a starkness

in the black outline of hedges that criss-crossed the countryside like a vast jigsaw, but in nearby bushes the lovely
red of holly berries peeped among the spiky dark green
foliage.

The following afternoon she stood in the hall, looking
around her, trying to see it through her grandparents' eyes,
wanting their first impression to be one of homeliness. Before
the children had gone out tobogganing they had piled the
grate of the big stone fireplace high with logs. The flames,
leaping from them, were reflected in the copper jugs and
bowls Rose had bought specially and in the bright baubles
thick on the massive tree. The pictures were hung with
evergreens and holly, and garlands of paper chains, made by
the children, were draped from wall to wall. The black and
white tiled floor was covered in the centre with a bright red
rug, the red echoed in the velvet cushions on the wooden
settles at either side of the fireplace. Rose, satisfied that
nothing more could be done, went upstairs to change.

She was zipping up her dress when, hearing a car, she ran
to the window. It was Charlie and her grandparents, two
hours earlier than expected. Rose's heart ached with love for
the two elderly figures standing looking up at the house. Sam
was spruce in his Sunday suit, his boots polished to a mirror
shine and a trilby hat replacing his usual cloth cap. Edie was
all in grey.

Rose, who had never seen her grandmother in anything
but black marvelled at the difference it made, it gave her a
youthfulness. Wherever Edie had bought the outfit it was
quality, a stylish coat with a grey fur collar, a narrow-
brimmed felt hat framing her hair, white now, grey suede
shoes, gloves and handbag. A touch of white showed at her
throat. Good for you, Gran, Rose thought.

They were all in the hall when she ran down the stairs.
'Gran, Grandad, you made it!' After hugs and kisses had been
exchanged Rose said brightly, 'Well, what do you think of it?'

Edie peeled off her gloves. 'I must say that when I came in I thought we could have been in Buckingham Palace, but I must admit, it's cosy.' Sam said it was the fire, had anyone ever seen such a big grate, and just look at the Christmas tree, they'd never see a bigger one.

They were suddenly all silent, listening, as the strains of music came from the direction of the kitchen. Rose smiled. Charlie must have brought the old gramophone, and the tune he was playing was 'Tea for Two', from 'No, No, Nanette'.

'Now that's just what I wanted, a cup of tea.' Edie, like a homing pigeon made off in the direction of the kitchen. Rose, knowing that Alice was in there hurried after her, with Sam calling, 'Hey, wait for me.'

Rose was right behind her grandmother when Edie paused in the open doorway of the kitchen. Alice, a broad smile on her face, was rocking in the chair. Edie said softly, 'Oh, now isn't that nice. My goodness, Alice, how like your mother you are, I hadn't realised until this moment.' She turned to Rose. 'Do you know something, I was quite worried coming away from home at Christmas, feeling I was leaving all our loved ones behind, but of course I was being silly, they're with us in spirit wherever we go. Charlie, I thought you would have had the tea made.' Edie took off her coat and hat, rolled up her sleeves and pushed the simmering kettle on to the fire, brushing aside Alice's offer to make it. 'As my grandmother used to say, if you want something done in a hurry, do it yourself. Where's the teapot and the caddy?'

Charlie and Rose exchanged smiling glances. It was going to be all right. The house had been accepted.

There was a sudden shout of 'Grandma – Grandpa –' followed by running footsteps along the passage. Caroline and Marianne came hurtling in, both looking as if they had been rolling in the snow. Caroline's knitted bobble cap was awry and one end of her scarf so long it was all but tripping her up. She flung herself first at Edie then at Sam. 'Oh, Grandma, Grandpa, I'm so glad you came, we're going to have a lovely Christmas.' Edie and Sam were hugged and kissed as enthusiastically by Marianne. Then the boys came in, Jonathan with his usual exuberance, David a little shy. The boys shook hands with the old people, but Edie kissed them and said, 'My, aren't you all grown. I would never have recognised any of you had I met you in the street.'

Rose was delighted at the immediate rapport there was between the old and the young, Edie telling the girls about her girlhood Christmases and Sam talking about the war. This was prompted by David asking about the bomb that had dropped close to Orchard Street. War was David's favourite topic.

Charlie and Alex went to meet the rest of the family at the station, then they were all there – in the kitchen, all talking at once, Judith and Nancy with their respective husbands, Tommy and his wife and Cynthia and Lilian. The two girls were still in the Land Army and Edie said it was a treat to see them looking pretty in silk dresses instead of arriving home in their kneebreeches and sweaters stinking of farmyards.

Elizabeth and Alex were the last to arrive. Rose expected her sister to turn up expensively dressed and make an entrance. Instead she wore a simply-styled tweed coat, a beige dress with brown velvet trimmings and a headscarf over her dark hair. She seemed genuinely pleased to see the family and, after greetings had been exchanged she asked Rose if there was anything she could do to help.

Rose had arranged a small party for the Christmas Eve, making the excuse that as the Mathers and many of their American friends had generously sent some presents for all the members of the family, they should give them out that evening and distribute family presents on Christmas morning. They all agreed.

The Mathers and their friends had also sent food parcels, which were more than welcome. Although the war was over food continued to be rationed and, in fact, there had been some cuts, the butter rationing now being only two ounces a week, sugar eight and tea two ounces. Rose could afford to buy in the black market but deploring this practice, refused to do so.

As well as the parcel containing a tin of butter and sugar and tea there were tins of ham, tongue, beef, some cakes and other goodies.

Rose had once been given her mother's large damask tablecloth by Edie and now on the length of its snowy whiteness lay sprigs of holly with their rich green leaves and bright red berries. The children had made the kitchen festive, blowing up coloured balloons and hanging them on the paper chains, and bringing in a small Christmas tree and draping it with tinsel.

'Just like home,' Edie declared when they were sat down to the meal. She was wearing her ten shilling dress in a pale grey silk which had a pattern of small rosebuds and a tiny white collar. When Rose admired it Edie said she thought it had been a mistake to buy it. The dress would show every mark, it was much too light. Rose could not help laughing.

A wind had sprung up, a door banged somewhere upstairs but no one took any notice. It was cosy in the kitchen, with flames leaping up the chimney and candlelight giving a warm glow.

'Oh, I'm so happy,' Caroline exclaimed. 'Isn't it just wonderful having supper on Christmas Eve with all my aunts and uncles and dear Grandma and Grandad.' Her lovely grey eyes glinted with tears.

Tommy placed an arm across her shoulders. 'It's great for all of us having our nieces and nephews with us. We must meet more often in the future. It's this wretched war that's kept us apart. Where's your party hat, Caro? Come on, get it on.' Tommy placed the pink tissue hat on her head and Caroline grinned up at him.

Rose looked round the table at her family, having an odd feeling that she must register every face, that there might not be another time like this when they would all be together for Christmas.

She was sitting between Charlie and Alex with Elizabeth on Alex's right. Next to Charlie was Marianne. She had asked to sit next to him. She loved her uncle Charlie, took everything he said as gospel. At the moment she was quiet, having been scolded earlier by Alex for making too much noise. Then came Alice, who was so like her mother it hurt, round-faced, comfortably plump, good-natured and lazy. Alice's husband Jim reminded Rose at that moment of her father, and she was surprised she had not noticed it before. He had the same way of listening intently to what was being said, but offering little in the way of conversation. He was listening to Lilian and Cynthia relating between them some amusing incident of their farming life. Both girls had a weather-beaten look, were attractive and had provocative smiles. Nancy had improved with marriage and was less sharp-tongued, but her mouth would still tighten, as Elizabeth's did, if something displeased her. Nancy's husband had changed little during the war years, in spite of having experienced dreadful sights in hospitals in war zones. He was a likeable man, given to getting into long discussions but always seeing the other person's point of view. Judith and Nicky always gave the impression of hating to be separated yet were never embarrassingly demonstrative in public. This evening they kept exchanging glances and Rose, feeling there was some deeper meaning behind them, wondered if by any chance Judith might be pregnant. She hoped so.

At the end of the meal Sam got up to give a toast. He said, 'This is a very special Christmas, a very special Christmas indeed . . .' At this Edie gave him a frantic nudge and shook her head at him. He patted her hand, gave her a reassuring smile and continued, 'It's special because we have all our dear family together under one roof, including our loved ones who have gone, who I know are here with us in spirit. To absent friends.'

There was a scraping of chairs as they got up and a clinking of glasses. 'To absent friends'.

Rose, afraid some morbidity might come into the proceedings, announced brightly they would now distribute the American gifts. There was a great rustling of paper and oohs and aahs as gifts were disclosed, silver-handled riding crops for the children, a pure silk blouse for Edie, a meerschaum pipe for Sam, nylons and lace-edged handkerchiefs for the women, white silk evening scarves for Charlie and Alex, leather wallets and linen handkerchiefs for the other men.

Caroline then said that although she and Marianne and David and Jonathan had gifts for Grandad and Grandma for Christmas morning they had a special gift they wanted to give them now.

It turned out to be a picture, the boys having made the frame and the girls doing the painting of it between them.

Edie, who had undone the wrapping held it up to Sam with tear-filled eyes. 'Do you remember, Sam?'

Sam looked at the painting then held it up for all to see. It was a winter scene on a moonlight night, the sky star-studded, in the background the lighted windows of a church casting a golden glow over the snow.

Sam nodded. 'Oh, yes, Edie, I remember.' He turned to the others. 'It was a scene like this that we saw on our wedding night. We were sleeping at my Aunt Jane's – in the attic. It was freezing, but you know something, we didn't mind, we really didn't.'

'Who would?' Tommy teased, 'with each other to keep you warm.'

'Well, that's a point,' Sam said, smiling indulgently at him. Then his expression changed, became solemn. 'But it was more than that. It was the skylight, see. I'm not a sentimental bloke, but I'll never forget that skylight. There were millions of stars out. It was like having stars on the ceiling.'

He looked at each of the children in turn and said, 'But how did you know about this?'

Caroline answered. 'Grandma told Alice and Alice told us.'

Rose felt a sudden small heartache that Alice had to be the one to make a more intimate contact with the children.

Edie began thanking them, saying they could not have thought of a more beautiful present to give them, she would treasure it always. And it wasn't only Caroline and Marianne's eyes that held tears.

After they had all got up from the table there was a lot of talk and Rose was just about to start to clear the table when Alex came up to her and said in a low voice, 'Do you remember another ceiling. A delicate blue one?'

Paris – colour rushed to Rose's cheeks. The incident had not faded from her mind but she had expected Alex to have forgotten it. She was not sure what his expression now held – amusement or regret?

'A delicate blue?' she said. 'It rings a bell, but I just can't place it. Oh, excuse me, Alex, Tommy wants me.'

Rose made a point of avoiding Alex for the rest of the evening. But when she was in bed she found herself wondering what it would have been like to have Alex make love to her.

'I'm wicked,' she said aloud. Charlie stirred and mumbled something.

'I'm wicked,' Rose repeated, 'and I don't deserve you, Charlie Eagan.'

'I love you when you're wicked,' he said, his voice still slurred by sleep. He chuckled softly and reached for her. But the next moment his arm lay heavy across her stomach.

With a sigh of resignation Rose turned to him, curving her body to the shape of his, knowing now that the only comfort she was going to get for her sinful thoughts was the warmth from her husband's body.

Chapter 28

During the following years Rose was to recall that family Christmas. As she had sensed, it was the last one at which they would all be together. Sam died six months later from pneumonia, and Rose ached for her grandmother who went about stiff-backed, still delivering babies, but with desolate eyes. 'Sam and I had our troubles,' she said, 'but he was a good man who wouldn't have hurt a fly.'

Four months after that Edie was found dead, sitting in the old rocking chair. Rose was bereft. She could not believe she would never see her grandmother again, hear the quick tap-tapping of her shoes, hear the sharp voice, the loving voice.

Charlie was gentle with her, comforting her, but Alex was Rose's salvation. He pushed her into opening a fashion house in Paris and in New York, proving to her that work was the great healer.

All four children, to the surprise and pleasure of their parents, had been absorbed into the business, David and Jonathan on the administrative side, Marianne in charge of cosmetics and Caroline designing for the teenage market, a most lucrative side of the business.

Now all four were married, with Caroline promising to make a Rose a grandmother as soon as possible.

Charlie drew her to him and grinned. 'You'll be the sexiest gran in the world.'

'Now then, Charlie Eagan, you should be past that sort of thing.'

'Past it? Are you joking? I'm just getting into my stride, and

I'll prove it. And you needn't start struggling.' He thumped his chest and emitted jungle cries. 'Me, Tarzan . . .'

'Oh, Charlie, stop fooling.' Rose smiled at him indulgently. 'You'll never grow up.'

Charlie, suddenly serious, cupped her face between his palms. 'Rosie, I love you. When we're alone like this I see you as the girl I fell in love with. You're so young-looking, so beautiful, but when I hear you talking earnestly to Alex about business I feel I've lost you.'

Rose's heartbeats quickened. 'But that's ridiculous, Charlie. I talk business to other men – accountants, lawyers, business colleagues.'

'Yes, but it's different with Alex. I don't quite know what it is. When we were younger we used to talk about people like Alex as being class. It's something *you* have acquired but something that I shall never have.'

'You're wrong, Charlie,' Rose spoke earnestly. 'You *have* acquired it, and you have more than Alex. You are at ease with people, whoever you speak with. It's a great asset. Don't belittle yourself. You're very well-liked. In fact I've had women tell me they've fallen in love with you. How about that?'

Charlie clasped her about the waist and rocked her gently. 'It's only you I want to be in love with me.'

There was a forlorn note in his voice. Rose searched his face. 'But I do love you, Charlie, surely you know that by now. What's brought all this on?'

'I don't know. Forget it. I do know you love me, sweetheart.'

Rose would have pursued the subject had not Elizabeth arrived unexpectedly. Without preamble she said, 'That trumpet playing son-in-law of mine has walked out on Marianne.'

Terry played the trumpet as a hobby. Elizabeth had never liked him.

'And I'll tell you something else,' she went on, 'if Jonathan doesn't pull himself together his marriage will be breaking up too. He came last night asking me to lend him ten thousand pounds. Not for business, but to pay his gambling debts. I refused, I've paid too many of his debts in the past. Alex would be furious if he knew.' She wagged a finger at Charlie and Rose. 'If he comes here don't you *dare* give him any money. Jonathan has to learn to stand on his own two feet.'

Marianne's marriage had been stormy right from the start. She was like her mother, restless, always wanting a social life, and Terry had obviously rebelled. Jonathan, like Caroline, was one of the world's biggest spenders. He was wild, exuberant, and lovable. Strangely enough, Rose felt she understood Jonathan more than her own son. David was still more often aloof towards her than affectionate, yet his wife declared he was wonderful, so loving. When Rose told her sister she was sorry she was having so much trouble Elizabeth turned on her.

'I know you two think you're the perfect parents and have the most perfect children in the world but I can tell you this, your David is no angel. I've seen him twice in the Savoy having lunch with an attractive girl and –'

'Elizabeth, stop torturing yourself,' Rose said. 'We don't think we're perfect parents.'

'Oh, yes, you do, and there's your Caroline, have you ever noticed the way she makes up to men, all big eyes, tempting, teasing.'

Rose gripped her sister's arm. 'Now stop it, Elizabeth, before you say something you'll really be sorry for.'

Elizabeth's body suddenly sagged. She pressed fingertips to her temples. 'I've already said too much. I had a row with Alex and I'm taking it out on you.' She looked up. 'Did I say row? No, Alex never quarrels, never raises his voice.' Her mouth had a bitter line. 'He simply says what he has to say then refuses to listen to anything further.' She got up. 'I suppose I'd better go back and make my peace with *dear* Alex, or he'll sulk for days.'

Rose walked with her to the car, feeling angry at her sister's insinuations about David and Caroline. Charlie found it easy to forgive anyone but Rose was not ready to forgive Elizabeth for trying to damn their children in their eyes. Nor did she like the way she spoke of Alex. Rose could not imagine Alex sulking, and she said as much when they reached the car. Elizabeth turned to face her. 'You think you know Alex, don't you, but you don't. I don't, and never will, neither will anyone else. He's a quantity unto himself. So don't hold any beautiful illusions about him, Rose. Just be thankful you're married to a man like Charlie, he's one in a thousand.' Elizabeth got into the car, slammed the door and switched on the ignition. Then, after a pause she lowered the car window. 'Rose, I'm sorry, I behaved badly. I was upset about Marianne. Charlie once asked me what I had against Terry. I think he was the wrong man for Marianne. He's a cold fish – like Alex.' With that she drove off without a backward glance.

This last remark disturbed Rose greatly. She had felt at times that Alex and her sister were not as contented as they might have been, but she had never thought of Elizabeth as being really unhappy in their marriage. Was Alex wholly to blame? Elizabeth could be acid-tongued and if she was not responsive to her husband's overtures of love – Rose found the thought of Alex being unhappy unbearable. He needed love, he had missed so much in his earlier life. He had always enjoyed the warmth of her family. If he had been there at that moment she would have found it difficult not to put her arms around him and comfort him. Charlie's voice calling her brought Rose from her reverie. To his question of what was wrong she said, 'Oh, Elizabeth and Alex seem to have had several differences and I feel sorry for them.' To which Charlie replied, with a note of asperity, it was their lives, they must sort themselves out.

Rose might have gone on worrying for days had not Caroline called later that afternoon with Clive to give their good news. She was pregnant. 'Oh, Mummy, isn't it lovely, we're so excited. Daddy, how do you feel about being made a granddaddy?'

'Great, darling,' Charlie hugged her. 'And congratulations to the expectant father.' He pumped Clive's hand. 'You'll have a handful with this one *and* a baby.'

Clive laughed. 'Anyone who can keep pace with Caroline could easily handle quintuplets.'

Caroline prattled on about baby clothes. She would design and make them herself. Rose smiled. Her daughter had a talent for designing but she was ham-fisted where sewing was concerned. And as for dress, she looked like an urchin at times, with her short fair curly hair and clothes looking as if she had slept in them. Rose had given up remonstrating with her, for Caroline was happy and she was a friend to all people. Her warm personality made her an easy touch. She had a roomful of paintings she had bought from dubious painters and a stable that housed every homeless animal she came across. Clive accepted all this, but although outwardly an amiable man, he put a firm curb on Caroline's mad shopping sprees and no amount of pleading or tears on her part would get him to give in to her. Rose was glad of this. Charlie had indulged his daughter hopelessly. Still would, if Rose allowed it.

Caroline and Clive left to visit Clive's parents and hardly had they gone before Marianne turned up, a Marianne looking pale, composed and chic as always. Today she was wearing a white linen coat with elbow-length sleeves, long black gloves, and a white pillbox hat perched on her dark hair, which she wore shoulder length with a thick heavy fringe. Marianne was strikingly beautiful, with Elizabeth's flawless skin and eyes that were more green than hazel. The vivacity she had had as a child had gone, but she greeted Charlie and Rose with a hug and a kiss.

No doubt they had heard of her marital troubles, she said, and although she had no wish to make a big drama out of it she had felt the need to talk with someone who would understand. Her mother had been furious with Terry for walking out and her father had refused to discuss it at all.

But when Marianne got up to go her marital problems were left hanging in the air. 'Be seeing you,' she said, 'thanks for listening.'

'Listening to what?' Rose said to Charlie when she had gone. 'She didn't even mention Terry.'

'I don't think she wanted to. I think it was enough that we were here and she could talk about *something*. I should imagine Marianne knows what she wants to do about her marriage. Incidentally, Rose, if Jonathan should call and ask to borrow money don't give it to him. I know you have a soft spot for him, and so have I, but Jonathan is earning good money and should learn to curb his gambling instincts.'

Charlie poured two drinks and handed one to Rose. 'I feel sorry for Elizabeth. It's bad enough having the worry of Marianne on her mind without Jonathan adding to it. And I don't think Elizabeth is well. I had a feeling she was in pain this evening.'

Rose glanced up in surprise. 'She's never said anything, not that Elizabeth would, she's another stoic, like Gran was. I'll keep an eye on her.'

Elizabeth was unusually late in coming into the salon the next morning. She apologised, said she had had a bad night, that she had a stomach upset, then dismissed it and got on with her work. She did a lot of phoning to customers abroad, had a long discussion with the accountant, and at lunchtime said she was going to the cosmetic factory to have a word with Marianne.

Rose, busy herself, did not miss Elizabeth until she phoned at half-past three to say she had had a long talk with Marianne and as it was so late she thought she would go straight home. This was so unlike Elizabeth, who made use of every minute of every day, that Rose became worried. She phoned Marianne. But Marianne was not there, she had not been in at all that day. Rose replaced the receiver. What was going on? Why had Elizabeth thought it necessary to lie? Had she hated to admit she felt ill?

A call to the Kensington house brought the information that Mrs de Veer had left word that morning she was going away for a few days. No, Mr de Veer had not gone with her, he would be home for dinner that evening. Was there any message? Rose said no, and phoned the Surrey house. Elizabeth was not there, nor had she been there even on the Sunday morning when she phoned Rose at Larkrise. With the mystery deepening Rose wished that Charlie had not been away. A discussion might have given some clue as to her sister's actions. She did think of phoning Marianne at her home but if the girl knew nothing about her mother's movements it was going to cause her more worry. So Rose prepared to wait for Alex to come home.

But it was he who phoned her. Did Rose know where Elizabeth had gone? She had left a note to say she had decided to go away for a few days but had not said where. Rose told him all she knew, Alex said he would come over.

Rose, watching for him from her sitting room window, felt a rush of warmth for this tall, distinguished-looking man, who found it difficult to express affection. Alex, immaculate as ever, glanced up and seeing Rose, raised a hand in greeting. His dark hair, she noticed, was showing grey streaks at the temple. She wondered why she had not noticed them before.

Alex came into the room with both hands outstretched. 'Rose, what is going on? I feel utterly bewildered.'

Rose gripped his hands. 'Sit down, Alex, I'll get you a drink. I'm as mystified as you.'

Alex sat, the bowl of the brandy glass cupped between his palms. 'We had words early yesterday morning, and Elizabeth went out in a temper. She took the car. When she came back later we made up our differences. She was quiet after that but gave no hint of wanting to go away for a few days. Where could she have gone and why didn't she tell me?'

Alex swivelled the glass, staring at the moving liquid for a few moments then looked up. 'Rose, I want to ask you something. It's difficult for me to say but I must know. Is there another man in Elizabeth's life?'

'Elizabeth? No, never has been, I'm sure of it. Oh, she enjoys the attention of men, what woman doesn't?'

'But it's something more important to my wife than most women, she thrives on admiration, she admits it. I worried about her during the war, knowing she was going round with a bit of a wild crowd.'

'Alex, I know my sister,' Rose spoke earnestly, 'and I am positive that although she flirted with men at times she never allowed any intimacy.'

'You are very loyal, Rose, but I do believe you. Elizabeth is a difficult person to live with. I suppose she could say the same thing about me. Perhaps we are both too absorbed in the business side of life. And yet,' Alex regarded Rose intently, 'you and Charles are both absorbed in business but have a loving relationship. How do you do it? Is it a question of temperament? You are both such amiable people.'

'Oh, you should hear us when we are quarrelling. There are times when it's difficult for me not to pick up something and throw it at Charlie and I'm quite sure he feels the same towards me.'

Alex laughed softly. 'I simply can't imagine such a situation between the two of you.' His expression sobered again. 'Rose, can you think of any place Elizabeth might have gone? She's not at Treetops and I understand Alice and Jim have gone North. Do you think Elizabeth would go North and be staying with Nancy or Judith or . . .'

'No,' Rose shook her head. 'She won't be with any of the family, not if she didn't want you to know where she is. They would be the first to let you know where she was, to stop you worrying.'

Alex raised his shoulders in a gesture of despair. 'Then where can she be? She's not with Marianne. I phoned her –

she had been out all day, and Jonathan can give no clue.'

'Perhaps we're worrying too much, Alex. There are times when a person feels the need to get away from all responsibility for a time. Elizabeth was worried about Marianne.'

'*And* about Jonathan . . .' Alex nodded slowly. 'You could be right. Elizabeth did say she was going away for a few days, not that she was leaving me. After all, we made up our quarrel. I'm sure you are right, Rose. I feel a load has been taken from my shoulders.' Alex took a drink of his brandy then sat back and closed his eyes. 'I know now why you and Charles have so many friends, Rose. You are both so relaxing to be with, you know the right thing to say.'

The stern lines of his face had relaxed and Rose felt an urge to put her arms around him, draw him close, give him warmth, love. He looked so young, so vulnerable at that moment Rose saw him for the first time as a small boy, his only contact with his parents being the times he was taken to the drawing room by his nurse to say goodnight to them. He had once told Rose this, relating it in a matter-of-fact way, not begging for sympathy. She got up, intending to creep out and prepare a meal, knowing Alex would not have stopped to have dinner, but the movement roused him. He sat up. 'Heavens, I almost fell asleep. See what your soothing presence did for me! I must go. Elizabeth might have phoned, might even have returned.'

Alex's anxiety for his wife was not, Rose decided, the attitude of an uncaring man. He took her hands in his. 'Thanks for everything, Rose.' Then he kissed her, his lips soft and warm on hers. She responded for a moment then drew back, saying, 'You *will* let me know as soon as you hear anything about Elizabeth, anything at all?'

Alex promised and left, leaving Rose trembling and annoyed with herself for getting into such a state. After all, Alex had kissed her many times, when the four of them visited or spent a social evening out. But not in that way, the kiss lingering, sensuous. Or had she imagined it, feeling the way she had towards Alex moments before?

Rose made an effort to dismiss the incident and concentrate on thinking of Elizabeth's whereabouts. But it was Alex's face that intruded, the look in his eyes as he had kissed her, the deep intent look of their earlier days, longgone, when he had asked her to marry him.

It was Charlie phoning that broke Rose's train of thought. She told him about her sister and Charlie confirmed Rose's solution, that Elizabeth had wanted to get away from all the troubles of family. 'A day by the sea used to help me solve mine,' he said. 'Elizabeth will come back when she's ready.'

It was three days before Rose had news of Elizabeth and then it was Marianne who phoned.

'Mother is in hospital,' she said. 'She was pregnant. She had appendix trouble. She had an abortion as the appendix burst and she's very ill. Father thought you would want to be here.' Marianne gave the address of a private nursing home and rang off.

Abortion – Rose stood frozen for a moment, then moved. Abortion – a burst appendix – my God, that meant peritonitis. She phoned for a taxi then ran to get her coat.

Rose sat in the taxi, her hands tightly clasped. Elizabeth pregnant was the last thing she had expected. It was possible. Her sister was not yet at the change of life, but after Marianne had been born Elizabeth and Alex had taken precautions, neither wanting any more children. What had gone wrong?

A sudden thought had Rose ice-cold again. Was the child not Alex's? Had her sister, after all, a lover?

When the taxi arrived at the nursing home Marianne met Rose and told her all she knew. The Matron said that Elizabeth had arrived in a taxi. She had already aborted and the appendix had burst. They had found Alex and got his permission to operate. It was now just a question of waiting.

For two days it was touch and go with Elizabeth. In that time Rose, Alex, Marianne and Jonathan had not left the nursing home. They took turns sitting with the patient.

Once when Alex and Rose and Marianne were together, Alex, who looked drawn and ill said, 'Why? Did Elizabeth think I would not want the child?'

Marianne said, 'We must face the truth. Mother couldn't bear to have another baby. She loved her social life, needed it. She needed admirers.'

Alex looked up quickly at this last remark then looked away. All the comfort Rose could offer to Alex had to be shared by Jonathan or Marianne. Jonathan wore a continual hurt look.

When Elizabeth at last took a turn for the better Alex was as near to tears as he could be. They all went home to have some sleep, having cat-napped at intervals for two days. But before Rose sank into bed she phoned Charlie at his hotel and told him the good news. She had not told him about the abortion, only about the appendicitis. Alex had insisted that Charlie was not brought home and also insisted that none of the family up North were told that Elizabeth was in any danger. Rose had a feeling it was because if they had been brought to the nursing home he was admitting that Elizabeth might die.

Elizabeth's convalescence was slow and it was not until she was enjoying visitors and all the attention and bouquets of flowers and get well cards that Rose learned a part of the truth. And was shocked when she did know.

Sunshine was streaming in at the window the afternoon Rose called at the nursing home. Elizabeth, interestingly pale, her dark hair curling softly around her face, greeted her with a brief nod.

'Well, at least your next visit to me will be at home,' she said. 'I'm to be discharged in the morning but the doctor insists I must have a nurse in attendance. I don't want to be bossed around, I'm fed up with being told what to do. I must get back to business. I'm completely out of touch, apart from what you and Alex have told me and that was little enough.'

'It was just enough for you to cope with. Just concentrate on getting completely well before you start talking about returning to the salon. I don't think you realise just how ill you were.'

'I know all right, and you don't have to tell me it was my own fault. I went to a back street quack for the abortion. Crazy, wasn't it, after all we knew about such people when we were younger. Not that this man was the knitting needle, crochet-hook type of performer. He was a professional man, lost his practice through drink. He was sober enough when I went for the "op". Trouble was, the appendix. It burst while he was busy. He went into a panic. He bundled me into a taxi and gave the man my home address. In time I came to and re-directed the man here.'

'But Elizabeth, why in heaven's name didn't you tell Alex you were pregnant?'

There was a slight pause then Elizabeth said, staring straight ahead, 'Because the baby was not his.'

'Elizabeth.' Rose's voice was little more than a whisper.

'Shocked?' Elizabeth turned her head. 'Of course you are, prim and proper Rosie who believes in God and the sanctity of marriage! I bet you would get an even greater shock if you knew who the father of the aborted child was.'

'Elizabeth,' Rose spoke quietly. 'I don't know the reason for your bitterness and hatred, but if you want to get both out of your system, go ahead, I'm prepared to be your whipping boy.'

'Oh, a martyr now,' Elizabeth sneered.

'No, I'm no martyr, only your sister who loves you, and if that sounds maudlin well that's the way it is. You asked me if I was shocked. I was, but I shouldn't have been. It has crossed my mind that the baby might not belong to Alex. Only I dismissed the thought of you having a lover, I didn't think it worthy of you.'

'He wasn't my lover. It was a one-night stand with an honourable married man who regretted afterwards what he had done. I wanted a man to make love to me who had some warmth in him.' Elizabeth's voice had dropped a key. 'It was nothing that was arranged, it just happened. I doubt it would ever happen again.'

Rose reached for her sister's hand and when she tried to draw it away Rose gripped it. 'Elizabeth, listen to me. You're always on about Alex being a cold fish. There was nothing cold about him while you were so ill. He was deeply concerned, I think it's just that he has difficulty in expressing his love.'

'Then it's time he learned how to.'

'Or is it time that *you* learned how to give of yourself? How many times have you been the one to approach Alex, to tease him, caress him, to play at being a mistress instead of a wife? Perhaps you've made excuses when he wanted to make love to you – you were tired, or you had a headache.'

Elizabeth gave a short laugh. 'Ha, my prim little sister seems to know all about it. But then look who taught you, your lovely Charlie. Lucky you.'

'I learned from his teachings, learned to give, as well as to take.'

'So bloody smug, aren't you! Get out of here, get yourself home, make love to your husband, and stop making love to mine.'

Rose, who had got to her feet stood motionless. For the first time in her life she felt she was going to faint.

Chapter 29

Rose made a pretence of bending to pick up something. The blood rushed back to her head. She said to her sister, 'What did you say?'

'Nothing.' Elizabeth looked suddenly shamefaced. 'It's just that I got sick of hearing Alex singing your praises, what a marvellous person you were, such faith you had that I was going to get well, you inspired them all.'

'I can't take credit for your recovery but if my faith helped Alex and the children to get over that dreadful time of waiting then I'm glad I gave them hope.' Rose picked up her handbag. 'I'll see you when you are home, that is if you want to see me. Let me know if you don't.'

Rose was at the door when Elizabeth called her back. 'Look, I'm sorry, I'm a mean ungrateful wretch, I don't seem able to stop this mean streak in me. I'm glad to be well again and something good did come out of my illness, if only the fact that Terry is with Marianne again and that Jonathan seems to have come to his senses about gambling. I want to see you, Rose, if only to hear news of the salon.' Elizabeth gave a wry grin.

Rose went back and kissed her. 'You're terrible. Now don't go and overdo things. Save your strength. I'll see you tomorrow.'

Although they had parted amicably Rose came away feeling disturbed by her sister's attitude towards the baby, by her actions. A 'one-night stand' she had called it. It sounded so sordid. Charlie was due home that evening and Rose wondered how much she should tell him. When he did come home she told him about the abortion. A white, pinched look came about Charlie's nostrils. 'Elizabeth was on the danger list and you never told me?'

Rose explained it was Alex's wish but Charlie still inclined to blame Rose for keeping him in the dark. 'She could have died,' he said.

'But she didn't,' Rose retorted. 'And a husband has more right than a brother-in-law to make decisions. Why are you so upset when Elizabeth is nearly well again?'

'I'm upset because Elizabeth is almost as close to me as you are. I'm going out for a walk.' He slammed the door as he went out.

Rose sat down abruptly as a terrible suspicion formed in her mind. Elizabeth had told her she would have another shock if she knew who the father of her aborted baby was.

Elizabeth had never made a secret of the fact that she was fond of Charlie. She had flirted outrageously with him at times and Charlie, being Charlie, had played up to her. It had all seemed just good fun. Alex as well as Rose had laughed at their antics.

Now Rose wondered if Charlie and her sister had been alone at some time, if things had gone too far and – she got up and walked round the room. It was so easy for emotions to get out of control. If she had kept on responding to Alex's kiss the night he came round when he was upset about Elizabeth leaving they might have made love. But they didn't, that was the point. Rose buried her face in her hands unable to bear the thought that Charlie had been unfaithful to her. It would have been bad enough had it been a strange woman, but with her sister!

Then Rose wondered if Elizabeth had made the remark out of spite. She was obviously jealous of the success of their marriage. Rose had made up her mind to tackle Charlie head on about it then changed her mind as she remembered her grandmother's words: 'Stir up muddy water and you'll bring the dregs up from the bottom of the pond.'

She would accept that Charlie might have been unfaithful once. If it happened again, she would know. Then would be the time to make a fight.

But even when Charlie apologised later for 'blowing his top', Rose could not be loving towards him, and Charlie, for the first time she could remember, withdrew into a shell.

Then, one evening, Rose, unable to bear it any longer curled up against him in bed and Charlie gave an exultant shout and turned swiftly to her.

It was one of their wild nights of passion, as though all pent-up feelings had to be unleashed to lead to more tender moments. It purged Rose. And over the months the incident of Charlie's unfaithfulness, if unfaithful he had been, became less and less important.

The nineteen-fifties saw a major change in fashion trends. Charlie had forecast this when the big baby boom started after the war with couples feeling it was now safe to start a family. 'These kids when they grow up,' Charlie said, 'will be the ones to dictate fashion. They'll have more freedom than our generation.' And he had been proved right.

But the new young designers were not interested in being involved in fashion houses. They concentrated their talents designing creations for boutiques, and selling straight to buyers from the street.

Some couturiers who had never mass produced found they were losing trade, and unable to keep their fashion houses were forced to close. Rose, who had sold off-the-peg clothes for years and had many boutiques, was not affected, nor was the trade at the House of Kimberley. Possibly because, although she catered for the young people in the extremes of fashion, she persuaded moderation to her private customers. When the square-shouldered look swept the fashion world, making some women look like Amazons, Rose coaxed them into having a little softer line. When skirts kept changing hemlines, going up, then down and up again, Rose, although following the trends for the teenage market, kept the hemlines of her skirts for her couture trade to the length worn by royalty and none of her clients demured.

Rose designed for the British and American mail order business and spent part of the year across the Atlantic, staying at her luxury apartment on Fifth Avenue. Sometimes Charlie accompanied her and at other times Alex and Elizabeth would come, too. There were close ties between the four of them and Rose counted among her many blessings the children of Marianne and Jonathan, as well as her own grandchildren.

Rose also had an apartment in Paris and whenever she went, no matter how busy, she would revisit all the places they had gone to on her first visit. And although at times she would think how unworldly she had been when Alex took her to his apartment she had no regrets. It had all been a part of growing up.

With each year there was some innovation in fashion, like the A and H lines, the chemise dress, the sac, the trapeze. There were the pencil-slim skirts, the full ones, boxy jackets, bulky coats, chunky sweaters, shirts worn two sizes too large with the sleeves pushed up to the elbows. The glistening black PVC raincoats made Rose a small fortune, so did her knickerbockers for ski-ing in every shade of leather imaginable. She captured the market with thigh boots in suede and knee-high ones with turnover tops in the swash-buckling style. She designed frilly skirts and exotic waist-coats and velvet pants and jackets for her men's wear boutiques and set up further boutiques selling nineteen-twenty fashions, keeping a team of people employed scouring cities for stock.

She went through the era of Beatlemania and accepted the pleas of the younger members of the family that playing the Beatles' records in boutiques would boost sales.

People spoke of the Sixties as the 'Revolutionary Sixties', and they certainly were. When the mini-skirts came in, models in thigh-high skirts stopped traffic on Broadway and in Times Square. Some men went tieless to their weddings. A famous film actress smoked a cigarette while she was being married. There were cults, like Flower Power, which might have made for a more gentle world had drugs not been involved among many of the young people who wanted everyone to love one another.

Kaftans became the rage, and shift dresses worn with a mass of coloured beads. Goatskin jackets were everywhere, and those skins which had been untreated stank to high heaven. Caroline, who had kept her youthful, tomboyish looks, came in one evening looking as if she had been pulled through a thick hedge backwards. Her hair was awry and there were slits in her cotton dress, which had gaudy motifs stitched on it. Badly stitched. She was bare-footed. Charlie said, 'Good God, Caroline, what the devil has happened?'

Her eyes became dreamy. 'Oh, Daddy, I went to this open air festival. They were such wonderful people, so kind.'

Rose said, 'Listen to me, Caroline, you're not a teenager any more! You're a married woman with a family and responsibilities.'

Caroline could not understand Rose's attitude. This lovely man, this leader was only interested in bringing peace to the world. What was wrong with that?

Both Rose and Charlie talked to Caroline for a long time and although she agreed to change her style of dressing they were both worried because she was so besotted with the Movement – and its leader.

To Rose's relief Caroline did change her ways, and looked lovely in the latest styles, with her hair well-groomed. And although there were times when she slipped back Rose had only to say, 'Clive won't be very pleased to see you looking like a ragbag,' for her to pull herself together again.

Rose's one grief in her life was her inability to get close to her son. David would kiss her when they met and on parting but there was never warmth behind the gesture, not like Jonathan who would hug her and tease her saying, 'And what wondrous creation has my beautiful aunt developed today?'

The only consolation Rose had in regard to David was his wife saying he was a loving person.

Rose still had fits of restlessness and when she did would branch out into something new, and never fail to find outlets for it.

Towards the end of the Sixties she bought control of other holding companies, which controlled yet other holding companies, and felt a sense of achievement. But Charlie said, 'Enough is enough, Rose. I think it's time you retired.'

'Retired?' She looked at him in astonishment. 'I'm just getting into my stride.'

And so Rose went on working and expanding.

By the end of the decade a headline in a woman's fashion magazine said, 'ANYTHING GOES WITH FASHION.'

A girl could be seen during the day wearing a three-piece tweed trouser suit with her hair tucked under a man's cap and in the evening be sporting a floor-length skirt with sequinned top and puff-ball sleeves and her hair free flowing.

Anything went for hairstyles too – frizzed, urchin-cut, bubble-cut, fringes, chignons, little skinny plaits caught up in a bow on the top of the head.

But in spite of there being so many way-out clothes, there was creeping back a demand for more simple clothes, mostly among the older women but there were young ones interested too. There were fewer fashion houses at the beginning of 1970 but those that still existed were flourishing. Rose's Spring Collection had been a big success and so had the Autumn one.

But with the Autumn Collection had come the shock, the shame of a member of the de Veer or the Eagan family resorting to spying.

And now as Rose stood once more at the window of her sitting room at Larkrise, staring unseeingly across the lawns, she felt an upsurge of grief that all she had worked for, all she had achieved, came to nothing compared with this betrayal within the family.

The morning was bright and sunny but Rose felt jaded and wished that all her worries had been just a dream. Kate brought her morning tea and Rose drank two cups, had a bath and was picking at a piece of toast when Elizabeth arrived. Elizabeth looked jaded, too.

'I've phoned Jonathan and Marianne,' she said, 'and asked them to come here at eleven o'clock. I suggest you tell David and Caroline the same. If the plane is on time the men should be here by ten o'clock. That will give us an hour to discuss the problem.'

Rose pushed her hair back from her brow. 'I feel sick at what we have to face. It isn't only a question of questioning the children, it's having to face Alex and Charlie with the awful news.'

But Rose knew by the faces of the two men when they arrived home from their trip to the States that they already knew. After brief greetings Alex said, 'I'm afraid we have some grave news for you.'

Elizabeth told them they already knew, and they all sat down for a discussion. But no light could be shed at all on which one was responsible. Charlie said, in an impassioned way, 'I can't believe it of any of them. There's no need. David, I know, has had this big house built, with all the luxuries, and Jonathan still gambles occasionally, but neither of them are really hard up. And Marianne and Caroline are not short of money – so why?'

'For the excitement?' Rose suggested.

Charlie's eyebrows went up. 'David excited? Can you imagine it?' Then quickly he apologised to Alex and Elizabeth. 'That is suggesting Jonathan could be responsible – No, I still can't wear it that *either* of them is responsible.'

Jonathan was the first to arrive. If he was guilty he showed no signs of it. He pumped the hands of both men. 'Hello, Dad, hello Uncle Alex, had a good trip? Where is Auntie Rose, oh, there you are, and looking more lovely than ever. Hey, what's all this urgent business we have to discuss? Is there a drink going, I was at a stag party last night and oh boy, am I parched.'

Jonathan chatted away and Rose, feeling there was a slight feverishness in the way he was talking, wondered if it was to cover guilt. David arrived while they were talking and looked such a contrast with his slightly pompous manner. 'Glad you got back safely, Father – Uncle Alex – I must say that whatever business needed to be discussed it could surely have waited until after lunch. It means that Betty and the children . . .'

Charlie said, 'Sit down, David. The reason you were brought here is not a trivial one. I'll leave your Uncle Alex to explain.'

By the time he had finished explaining Jonathan was looking utterly bewildered, David's expression gave nothing away.

'Spying?' Jonathan exclaimed. 'Do you honestly believe that either of us was responsible? Good God, is that all the trust you have in us! David and I are your sons, not some scum who would betray you.'

'One of our children is responsible,' Alex said, his voice cold, 'and I feel perhaps you are protesting too much, Jonathan.'

He jumped up. 'Now look here, Dad!'

David said, 'I am the one responsible.'

In the silence that followed this remark the drone of a low-flying aircraft seemed to be inside Rose's head. It couldn't be David, she wouldn't believe it. He might be withdrawn but he was totally honest. As a child if he sneaked a biscuit from a tin he would confess to her afterwards.

Charlie was looking at his son with a stricken expression. 'You do realise what you are saying, David?'

'Yes, Father, I know what I'm saying.' He stared straight ahead. 'I needed the money.'

'But you had only to come to us. To stoop to spying!'

Charlie shook his head. 'I refuse to believe it, there's more to this, there has to be.'

Elizabeth came over. 'David, if you are protecting Jonathan . . .'

'I'm not, and if you believe that Jonathan was responsible then you know nothing about your own son.' Elizabeth flushed. David got up. 'I'll go now. Nothing can be gained by a further post mortem. I'll arrange to retire from the firm.'

'No,' – this from Alex, who moments before had looked as stricken as Charlie. 'We've weathered many troubles, we can weather this. You *are* a valuable member of the firm, David.'

The phone rang. It was Marianne to say she had been delayed. She would be with them in twenty minutes. Charlie had just replaced the receiver when Caroline burst in.

'Hello, everybody. Sorry I'm late . . .' She stopped suddenly and looked from one to the other. 'Is something wrong?'

'Yes,' David said. 'I have just confessed to industrial spying.' He spoke without emotion.

Caroline stared at him wide-eyed for a moment then turning she ran from the room. Rose went after her. She caught her up at the top of the stairs. Rose opened a bedroom door. 'Come in here, Caroline.'

Caroline flopped on to the bed and with her hands to her face began to rock to and fro. 'Oh, Mummy, you'll never forgive me. David's not responsible for betraying you. I am.' She took her hands away from her face. 'I'm bad, wicked. I fell in love with Willard, and he in love with me. He's the leader of the Movement. We've spent a weekend away together.'

Rose felt as though she had been dealt a vicious blow to the heart. Caroline had never looked more lovely, so elegantly dressed this morning, ash-blonde hair curling softly, lovely big grey eyes luminous with tears.

'Caroline.' Rose sat beside her and put an arm around her. 'I thought that you and Clive were so happy together.'

'We were, we are. I don't expect you to understand how

you can fall in love with someone else. Willard is so different.'

Oh, yes, Rose thought wryly, she understood all right, only too well. She said, 'But why the spying, Caroline?'

'Willard wanted to build a tabernacle. He needed money, a lot of money. He told me how I could get it. I didn't want to do it. Clive wouldn't give me any money. I went to David and David told me to forget the Movement, he had more to do with his money than to throw it away on such a thing. He must have guessed what I had done and taken the blame to help me.' Tears were now pouring down Caroline's cheeks. 'Oh, Mummy, I know that you and Daddy will never forgive me, but I'm sorry, so very sorry.'

Rose held her close. 'We love you, Caroline. We'll help you, only Clive must never know nor the rest of the family. I'll send Dad in to you.'

Rose wondered afterwards how they had ever managed to behave as though nothing untoward had happened when the rest of the family came. They only knew that Caroline had had to go and lie down because of a sudden headache, but the strain of trying to keep up appearances took its toll of Rose. In the early evening when the men were playing games with the grandchildren, Rose put on a coat and went into the garden. Mist was swirling above the lake. The hurt over Caroline had gone deep, but she had never loved her son more than when he had been prepared to take the blame for his sister.

When she thanked him for what he had done he was embarrassed. It was nothing, he knew how she felt about Caroline. He refused to let her continue the conversation and Rose knew, that although David would never ever let her get really close to him he had proved his love for her and Charlie by his actions.

Rose was walking past the spinney when she heard someone call her name softly. It was Alex.

'Rose, dear, I felt I must have a word with you. I was so grieved at your hurt. I know how you feel about Caroline and I can understand you rejecting her when you knew what she had done. If Marianne had been the one responsible I doubt whether I would have been able to forgive her. It's always the same when a very special person lets one down.'

Rejected? No, Rose thought, she had not rejected her daughter.

'Shall we walk?' Alex put a hand under Rose's elbow and they skirted the spinney then made in the direction of the lake. When they reached it they stopped. Then Alex said after a short silence, 'You never did see my tarn in the Yorkshire Dales, Rose, did you? I wanted you to see it.' Rose thought she detected a note of sadness in his voice.

'No, but we do have the painting of the Dales you gave Charlie and me when we were married. We both like it very much.' Rose was aware of her ever-quickening heartbeats. Their visit to the Dales had brought her first real awareness that Alex might be in love with her. 'There's something so melancholy about autumn,' she said, and started to walk away. Alex caught her by the arm and turned her to face him.

In the gathering darkness his face was just a pale blur.

'Rose, I love you, I have to say it. I love Elizabeth but in a different way. I would never hurt her, nor would I want to come between you and Charles, I know how deeply you feel about one another. I just had to tell you how I felt although I don't expect you to understand. I could never imagine you being unfaithful, not even in thought.'

He was wrong. She had been unfaithful in her thoughts many times to Charlie regarding Alex, indulging herself in daydreams, but this was something she could never tell Alex.

Rose said gently, 'I think you were wrong in telling me how you feel. I value your friendship and I wouldn't want to spoil it.'

'No, Rose, please, no, that would be unbearable. I take it all back, I don't love you, never have loved you.'

A flippant Alex de Veer was so unusual Rose laughed. 'Oh, Alex, you're such a complex person. Do you remember the fancy dress party Lecky and Clarissa gave when we were all dressed up in Eastern clothes? You were the Emperor and you were brought into the room in a chair carried by Charlie and Lecky. Charlie tripped and you shot out of the chair and landed on top of him. I can hear you now, laughing helplessly, as helplessly as Charlie. Minutes later you were cold and arrogant.'

'Rose, I've never been arrogant! I have no cause to be.' They were arguing about it when Charlie called from the house, 'Rose – Alex – Coffee coming up.'

Before they went in Alex touched Rose on the arm. 'Rose, you won't let what I've said make any difference to us?'

'None at all! I shall argue with you, fight to get my own way in business deals – and go on valuing our friendship.'

'Thank you,' Alex said softly.

Charlie had made a games room for the children upstairs and Rose could hear them yelling in excitement as they came into the house. The adults were all gathered in the hall and were sitting round a roaring log fire. It had become a favourite place over the years. Charlie came from the kitchen carrying a huge tray with cups and saucers. Alice followed with coffee jug and milk. Charlie, glancing up and seeing Rose and Alex said, 'Oh, there you are, you must be frozen the pair of you.'

Rose felt an ache of love for her husband sweep over her. Charlie so warm, so loving, a family man. 'Now who takes sugar?' he asked. 'Alice, I know you take three. Betty, it's one for you, isn't it? Caroline, one and a half.' Charlie gave his daughter a loving smile. Caroline, pale but composed had a woebegone look. Clive's arm was around her shoulders. David was always quiet so that would raise no comment and Jonathan had done his best to keep them all happy.

A wind had suddenly sprung up and Charlie said, 'There, I told you, that's Boris Karloff trying to get in.' Then he laughed. 'But we're all warm and cosy in here, aren't we?'

Charlie had changed little over the years. He had put on a little weight, but not much. His curly hair was still thick but the fact that it was now streaked with white at the temples made him more distinguished-looking than ever. Rose knew suddenly, at that moment, that Alex's attraction for her over the years was gone. Charlie was her man, a family man, yet a wonderful lover. She could let herself go with him, be responsive to the primitive wildness of his love making, something she felt sure she would not have been able to do with Alex. There was a barrier between them. A barrier? This thought surprised Rose. It was something that had not occurred to her before. Was it class consciousness? Surely not – after all, she had climbed to the top, was a big name in the fashion world.

Then it had to be something else. The arrogance in Alex? A condescension? Why had he waited until now to tell her he loved her, there had been plenty of other opportunities. It would have hurt his ego had either Jonathan or Marianne been responsible for the betrayal. He said he doubted whether he would have been able to forgive Marianne, yet in the same breath said she was someone special.

Had he been so grateful that Caroline was the one responsible he wanted Rose to have some recompense, hence his declaration of love? And what was that but condescension?

Alex had missed so much in life. When Elizabeth had displeased him once, he punished her by leaving her to go to Paris on his own. If only he had been ready to forgive.

When the family had gone and Rose and Charlie were making preparations for bed Charlie said, 'Well, Rosie, it's been quite a day.' He wound the clock and put it back on the bedside table. 'If only I had been able to take the weight of guilt off Caroline's shoulders onto my own. I couldn't bear to see her looking so dejected.'

That was love, Rose thought. She said softly, 'Caroline will bounce up again, she's that kind of person. I was only glad that everything turned out the way it did. It helped for tomorrow. I want everyone to be happy on my birthday.'

Rose took off her negligée and got into bed. 'By the way, Charlie, I've decided to retire.'

'*You* retire, Rosie, never! I must have been mad when I suggested it three years ago. Even if you stop going to the salon you'll be sketching all over the place, saying, "What do you think of this, Charlie, what do you think of that?" You haven't asked me yet what I've bought you for your birthday.'

'I don't want to know until tomorrow.'

'Well, you're going to see one of the presents.' There was a chink of money and keys dropping on to the top of the chest then Charlie went into the bathroom. There was a scrubbing of teeth, the gargling, the grunts as he sluiced his face and Rose smiled to herself. In this Charlie would never change.

When he came out of the bathroom in silk pyjamas he was carrying a cardboard box which he dropped on the bed. 'There you are, open that.'

Rose lifted out a pair of black chiffon baby-doll pyjamas. She began to laugh. 'Charlie Eagan, you don't expect me to wear these?'

He grinned. 'For a couple of minutes then we'll put them in the drawer.'

'You're terrible,' she scolded, 'behaving like a youth at your age.'

'But you love me.'

'No doubt about that,' Rose whispered, and her arms crept up about his neck. 'Forever, and ever –'

'–I'll say Amen to that.' Charlie picked her up, kissed her before laying her on the bed, then got in beside her. And the only sounds after that were the sighing of the wind, the beating of their hearts and the gentle ticking of the bedside clock.